THE UNSPOKEN TRUTHS OF CASEMIRO

CHRISTOPHER CLOUSER

ALSO BY THE AUTHOR:

NON-FICTION:

THE MIDWEST ASSOCIATE
A MONTH OF SATURDAYS
TROPHIES AND TRADITIONS
CRAFT THE DRAFT

FICTION:

THE FORSAKEN PROTECTOR
CURATOR OF THE GODS
ARGENT'S MENAGERIE

THE WORLD OF MARCO FLYNN:
LEGENDS IN ADDINGTON
AS THE CITY BURNS
THE YOUNG & THE WICKED
THE GOLD IN THEIR EYES

For more information, or to book an event, contact :
Christopherclouser1970@gmail.com
https://clouserwritesbooks.wordpress.com

Background image courtesy of PX Fuel Wallpapers
Endor and Immortal fonts courtesy of Apostrophic Labs

D2D ISBN - Paperback: 9798224371679

First Edition: March 2023

Dedication

To my wife for continuing to support me
as I pursue my passion.

1

LILLENHOLD

Casemiro's palm grazed across a knife's twenty-year-old etching, a heart containing two 'C's joined by a plus, cut into the oak rail of the Fierce Siren. One letter for him, the other for the woman he lost five years ago, Chantal Sucre.

Casemiro stared into the dark waters of the secluded port of Lillenhold. "Why did I return here?"

The Fierce Siren bounced and skimmed across the small waves produced by the wake of other vessels. Casemiro's knees absorbed the boat's movement as the ship drifted towards an assigned dock. His body leaned against the rail and his hand clutched the wood, attempting to hold fast to anything from his marriage.

Quinto, the ship's captain and Casemiro's brother, stood alongside in tattered clothes in need of washing, or burning, before the next voyage. "Trying to recapture past glory, of course.

Regardless, the Fierce Siren leaves port tomorrow at dawn. If you settle your issues here, you may pay the fare and board. Otherwise, the ship returns in a week for the next cargo load."

Quinto badgered his brother. "I'm still not sure why you persist in this, but the offer stands. Besides, the men enjoy having a wizard onboard."

Casemiro looked at his twin brother, whose black wavy hair, smooth skin, and handlebar mustache hid his true age. Casemiro's hair carried a little more gray near the temples, his skin a little more rough, and his stubble of a mustache and beard added ten years to the wizard's apparent age.

In truth, they were both older than anyone on the ship by at least a half-century. But both pretended to be roughly forty years of age to not intimidate the humans too much.

"I appreciate the offer. If my plans don't work out, I may show up. Good day, Captain." Casemiro mocked his brother by using the titular reference, aware his brother hated the formality.

Never one to allow his brother a victory, Quinto replied in the same spirit. "Consider buying a new belt in the village because that strap cannot keep your gown closed. The locals do not want a glimpse of a wizard's skivvies."

"Don't mock my cloak. Besides I wear undergarments. I am not a heathen." Casemiro cinched the frayed belt once again, refusing to acknowledge Quinto's correct observation. Embarrassment covered the man's face, knowing the underlying brown pants and a white short-sleeved shirt presented an unglamorous outfit for meeting a new employer, regardless of how remote the village.

The sailors found relief from a wizard being aboard their vessel and delighting in his presence for their perceived good fortune. Sailor's superstitions suggested spellcasters provided luck and a safe voyage. Casemiro entertained their fearful natures for a cheaper fare and free food, even if he knew their deference was foolish.

"Let's find out what fate awaits me here." Casemiro cinched up his gray woolen cloak once more and pulled the hood over his eyes to avoid any unwanted stares, even if it meant limiting his vision to what appeared in front of him.

Casemiro exited the ship via the gangway as a glimmer of the morning sun bounced off the rippling water below the wooden plank. He gripped his trusty gnarled wooden staff with an iron tip, and his free hand brushed some stray sawdust from the cloak. The casual rub caught the hidden pommel of the saber strapped to Casemiro's side beneath the garb in the event of a scuffle.

A rustle from a piece of paper grabbed Casemiro's attention, and he pulled out the reason for the voyage to Lillenhold from his breast pocket. The pocket also contained a pair of knitting needles carved from narwhal bone, a small amount of yarn, and a half-full coin purse. But those random trinkets did not concern the wizard now.

The paper read, "Wizard wanted. Wise, powerful, and fearless. Inquire with Forrest at The Pub." A lone sigil denoted the official nature of the paper. Casemiro perused the paper for any of the typical loopholes, or fine print barristers used to entrap unwitting fools and separate them from any hard-earned money.

Casemiro pondered the words as he walked. Fearless and powerful described young sorcerers, warlocks, and wizards lacking experience, or those having never met real magic. Wise applied to the fortunate, or those accomplished enough at avoiding conflict to now sport gray hair. Wanted: a term unfamiliar to Casemiro unless it involved an unpaid bar tab. Wizard suggested a title Casemiro hoped to reclaim. Though the words may not apply today, perhaps in the future; once he recaptured his past glory, to borrow his brother's phrase.

Casemiro ventured onto the pier of the seaside village of Lillenhold, one of a dozen identical ports along this coast of Southern Gaeleos, the realm overseen by the good King Skaranon. The wizard focused his thoughts and fixated on his mission to find the person who posted the advertisement, the individual named Forrest.

Casemiro hid everything from view except his fingers gripping the gnarled wooden staff. The steady stanchion of the pier allowed him to escape three-day's worth of persistent nausea from the boat ride. After a cleansing breath to calm his nerves, Casemiro strode down the pier, his boots and staff providing a consistent rhythm across the weathered wooden planks.

The old man paid little attention to the usual activities and trappings of a seafaring town of this ilk. Men retracting nets and hooks piercing the skin of enormous sea creatures gained a fraction of his attention, but Casemiro catalogued everything.

Rotten fish and salty brine saturated every waft of air the wizard sucked in as he ambled along the pier. He choked back a cough from the foul stench and scanned the pier for any indication on how to reach his destination, the local establishment called The Pub.

A breeze picked up from the water and caused a loud ripple from pennants atop numerous poles in the area. Blue rectangles with yellow stripes in the form of flags waved atop every other pole and stretched from the pier into the village. The flags alternated with banners depicting the unfortunate village crest.

Is that a turkey bent over a stump with an axe suspended above the animal's exposed neck?

The wizard absorbed the view and noticed the pier rose into the village, which extended further up the hill to the noted fixture of Veritas Keep in the distance. Beyond the village, the highest summit of the southern portion of Gaeleos, Mount Siven, rose above the pine and cypress forests with a snow-packed peak.

The village relied on the snow melt for water each spring, no matter if it overflowed the nearby stream and swelled the Bay of Scars. Squinting towards the mountain for a better view, Casemiro believed he imagined a ruddy gray mass scuttling through the white of the snow. He pushed away the ominous thought that entered his mind, convinced of its improbability.

Casemiro continued walking, hoping his business concluded before any unfortunate incidents unfolded and required his saber, or a feeble attempt at magic. The wizard summarized his impressions of the village. "Looks exactly the same as twenty years ago." A sudden break in the clouds released a stray beam of sunlight and the wizard recited a silent affirmation. But Casemiro still lacked any sign of how to reach The Pub.

On his left flank, the wizard noted a whaling vessel and a young, dark-skinned boy carrying a small leaky barrel marked as whale oil. The child placed the container beneath a blazing torch, a light for the nighttime operations of the port. Aware of the potential disaster, the boy snuffed out the flame and turned, bumping into Casemiro.

"Sorry, I didn't notice you there, sir. No need for the torch right now."

The dark-skinned boy struck the wizard as unmemorable in every way, except one. A half-circle scar on his left cheek grabbed the wizard's attention. The boy's gray shirt, loose pants, and no shoes screamed of poverty, the norm for seaside villages such as Lillenhold.

A pang of guilt punched Casemiro, knowing what his departed wife might say. The man rolled his eyes and grabbed the boy's shoulder. "Hold up." Casemiro extended a piece of silver to the young boy. "Show me to The Pub and you receive this coin upon arrival."

"Fair enough. You must have a good reason to enter that cesspool. Follow me." The boy smiled and dashed ahead of the cloaked old man. The child stopped once and implored Casemiro to keep pace by waving his arms. Though impatient, the boy minded his speed to not lose his client.

Casemiro stalked the child but maintained an adequate distance behind. He created a prideful display to inform the onlookers they were in the company of a wizard. Such a display often resulted in opportunities for a free meal, and perhaps gold from menial work.

The ten-minute walk through the crowd and curious onlookers paid off. Casemiro reached the eager boy, who awaited his payment at his destination. A birch sign with "The Pub" scratched in scarlet paint hung from a rusted hook draped over a cross beam extending from the roof of the dilapidated shack. Upon inspection of the building, if one could call it such a thing, Casemiro surmised the four fieldstone walls stood by leaning against each other for the needed support as much as any solid construction.

Casemiro smiled at the boy and gave away the promised coin to the urchin. "Thank you for guiding me."

"It doesn't pay to lose the man offering the coin."

After paying the boy, Casemiro counted five silver pieces in his coin purse. He tucked the small satchel into his hidden breast pocket to keep it safe from sticky fingers. His hand rubbed the knitting needles, and a flash of memories raced through his mind. The wizard recalled the face of his dead wife, Chantal, and the cloying citrus scent of her favorite Bergamot tea. A second image of him emerging from the depths of the sea entered his mind. Casemiro cursed the unwanted images away from his thoughts.

The boy inquired about the man's interest in something called the Extravaganza as Casemiro's focus returned to the moment.

"The what?" Before Casemiro received an answer, the boy darted away, hoisting his well-earned payment above his head and carrying it as it were a trophy earned in battle.

The wizard looked above him and gleaned an idea. He reached up to pilfer the chain and then hung it around his waist with the hook, latching into a link of the chain.

The staff nudged the door open as the wizard prepared for danger from the other side. The clamor from the hovel suggested an early start to the day's business. With only a glimpse, Casemiro questioned the value of the visit to Lillenhold, or this establishment. The coin purse pressed against his chest and confirmed his need for the job and provided the needed impetus to enter. Casemiro pushed the door open further and entered the home of doubtlessly detestable drinks and equally poor manners.

The atmosphere did not exceed his expectations. Casemiro remembered hog pens containing better conditions and more appetizing tenants. The room stunk of urine and stale beer at the door, but as he approached the patrons, the odor grew to full-blown fresh skunk. The limited light glimmered from a wooden chandelier holding a ring of wax candles on their last legs. Casemiro thanked the heavens the dim light prevented him from seeing what constituted the floor he walked over. He hiked up his cloak and tightened his belt to hold the material above the ground.

Multiple conversations prevented eavesdropping on any single voice. All discussions stopped with the wizard's entrance, but the din returned once the patrons deemed him another harmless customer.

Casemiro strolled towards the bartender manning his post behind a massive wooden tabletop spanning twelve feet in length.

The wizard caught the man's attention and hoped any interaction within the tavern concluded quickly.

"How can I help, stranger? Care for a pint?" A smiling face featured two teeth, crossed eyes, and a chin sporting a boil needing lanced.

Casemiro held up the paper. "Looking for someone named Forrest."

The bartender squinted at the note. "Oh, yes, that be his sigil at the bottom. The rest I cannot read. Wickless candle, most say. Wait here while I retrieve Forrest. Have a drink on the house." A flagon filled with a yellowish watery liquid containing pieces of floating flotsam floated slid along the bar.

Casemiro nodded at the barkeep and pushed away the metal cup with the end of his staff. The wizard vowed to avoid touching or consuming anything in this place. He only hoped to not catch some airborne contagion from standing in the hovel.

The bartender cut through the crowd to reach an enormous figure in the opposite corner, presumably Forrest. Across the room, the barkeep exchanged words with the seated patron. The customer stood, eclipsing half the room, but then hunched over to avoid hitting his head on the chandelier and approached.

Casemiro surmised his contact carried an amount of troll blood within his veins to be that large.

Forrest assessed Casemiro, paid for his drink, and motioned towards the door. All without saying a word to the wizard.

Casemiro followed the colossus out of the dank chamber and breathed fresher air, or a reasonable facsimile. As they cleared the doorway, a numbskull belted out a racial slur toward the behemoth. Forrest glared back into the room and silenced the crowd. The subtle standoff spoke volumes to the wizard about Forrest and The Pub's patrons.

Once outside, Forrest stood to his full height of eight feet. A smiling grin full of healthy teeth, olive skin, over-pronounced muscles, and a block-shaped head sitting upon broad shoulders supported the wizard's guess on Forrest's lineage. A mass of unwrangled, brillowy black hair hid much of the typical troll-shaped head. But something about this individual's movement and attitude told Casemiro this person carried human blood as well.

Casemiro asked the obvious question. "That happen often?"

"After living in this village for twenty years, it still happens more often than one might expect."

Casemiro paused at the mention of twenty years.

The troll-man squinted as they hit the daylight. "You appear overjoyed to exit The Pub."

"That obvious?" Snark filled Casemiro's reply.

"Not highbrow enough, visitor?"

"I prefer accommodations that don't compromise my health upon entry." Casemiro pulled the hood from his head, remembering trolls distrusted those concealing their eyes.

"Did a patron threaten you? If so, I shall remedy the situation easily enough. If not, what offended your fragile sensibilities?"

"The filth disgusted me. I've grown spoiled by nicer environs in other ports of Gaeleos." Casemiro examined the bottom of his woolen cloak for anything escaping from the muck and mire left behind inside the establishment.

A rumble of a chuckle rolled from Forrest and erupted into a full baritone laugh. The behemoth regained his breath. "I grew accustomed to it. You will too if you stay here long enough. Anyway, you read the advertisement?"

Casemiro held the piece of paper for the troll-man's benefit. "Yes, and, based on the barkeep's reaction, you are Forrest."

"I am. And your name?" The bulging fingers pinched the paper from the man's hand.

The wizard paused, aware of three potential outcomes from mentioning his name. Two of which meant trouble. "Casemiro. Most recently of Foxshire in Northern Gaeleos."

Forrest raised part of the unibrow above his chestnut brown eyes. "Casemiro. Interesting."

The wizard gripped his wooden staff a little tighter, preparing for one of the two negative responses he typically received. The chances of this meeting going wrong increased and Casemiro pressed the tip of his staff into the ground, preparing for the worst.

A half-second passed before Forrest smiled, and his white teeth gashed through the consistent olive coloring of his skin. "Your reputation precedes you. This job might be beneath your skill if you are the Casemiro I know of."

The third option, and the preferred response, presented itself. The wizard relaxed his hold on the staff, sensing the danger passed. "Let me judge what falls beneath my skill. What is this job?" Casemiro regretted the sharp tone once the words escaped his mouth.

The troll-man grunted his frustration at the subtle rebuke. "For a wizard, you seem impatient and impertinent. Once you meet the person who took out the advertisement, more will become clear. Follow me, Casemiro of Foxshire."

The old man stood his ground, unsure of what waited for him. "Where do we go? I grow weary of walking."

Forrest's meaty hand and fingers resembling over plump sausages rubbed his chin as the troll-man considered his new acquaintance. "Your tone is unwarranted, wizard. Do you fear being too withered for this task? Or is a lack of coin the reason you inquired about the job?"

Casemiro stood his ground, hoping the firm stance might provoke more information on the opportunity from Forrest.

The troll-man called his bluff and signaled towards the stone structure at the top of the hill. "I suppose you may attempt to hire a ride. Either way, we head to Veritas Keep." Forrest began walking from the public house toward the ominous fortress up the hill.

Forrest, as he walked by, bumped the wizard, almost knocking Casemiro down as payback for his attitude. The old man stabilized himself from Forrest's unsubtle gesture and peered ahead to Veritas Keep.

From this distance, the keep, a classic stone structure resembling others across the vast countryside, stood well over fifty feet tall. A lone soldier manned the top turret above the tallest tower, monitoring for potential raids or attacks by land or sea. At the corners of the extensive building, and the surrounding stone wall, stood four turrets thirty feet in height and manned by a soldier each. The stone walls towered above the heads of the guards on the ground.

Overall, the wizard concurred the keep provided adequate defense for this middle-of-nowhere seaport village. The tan, gray, and white walls appeared to offer a beacon, but the shadows spread across the structure foretold much danger.

The wizard felt admonished for his attitude. "I apologize."

"Think nothing of it, wizard. All of us carry frayed nerves in these times."

"Can you at least tell me who lives in the keep?"

"Prince Arenton paid for the advertisement and will describe the job further. A word of warning, the Prince refuses to suffer hostile and indignant attitudes. So, are we walking? Or can I go buy another round of piss-poor ale?"

Casemiro placed his hand on his breast and cupped the light coin purse, a reminder of his perilous financial situation. "Lead the way." The wizard followed the immense chaperone.

"What happens if I tell the Prince of your disrespect towards a wise wizard?" A sarcastic grin emerged across Casemiro's face.

Forrest smirked in reply. "Only desperate people pursue a job of this caliber, and desperate doesn't scare me. For your benefit, do not threaten a half-troll, even in jest. If you don't follow me, do not expect assistance from these people. The streets of this village provide no solace and outsiders are not welcome. You experienced how they treat one of their own. I suggest you keep pace before I leave you to the citizens. Oh, one last thing, welcome to Lillenhold. Or, as I prefer to call it, the seaport of irrelevancy."

The duo departed from The Pub, leaving the sign on the ground sans the hook and chain. The wizard absconded with a new makeshift belt, keeping the cloak snug around Casemiro's waist as he traipsed up the hill to Veritas Keep.

2

VERITAS KEEP

Casemiro followed Forrest to the hill's crest to view the entire glory of Veritas Keep. The wizard's recollection of the keep sprang from his lone, brief visit twenty years earlier. The bulk of his business occurred outside the village and away from the keep, and his minimal familiarity with the interior of the structure resurfaced. Though impressed, Casemiro's stomach rumbled and reminded him to focus on the next chance to eat a meal.

"When can we eat, Forrest?"

"You will wait until after we meet the Prince. You should have eaten breakfast, wizard."

The duo approached a canvas tent adorned by pennants of blue and yellow that flanked the main gate of Veritas Keep. Two soldiers, sporting blue and yellow paint on the edges of their armor, carried shields exhibiting the laughable crest of Lillenhold and a sword of inferior quality, both marred by dents and rust.

The gear dangling from their bodies amplified each soldier's lack of bulk.

As Casemiro drew closer, the craftsmanship of the walls impressed the wizard much more than the armor. Instead of a rough stone texture, the walls of Veritas Keep reminded him of glass or the surface of an unrippling pond. The masons of the current day lacked the ability to build structures of the same quality as their forefathers. The wizard understood how ancient the thought running through his mind made him sound. He also realized the defenses of Veritas Keep rested much more on the structure than the men tasked with said defense.

A third, and much younger, soldier emerged from the blue tent. The man waved to Casemiro's minder. "Good day, Forrest. Captain Gerard mentioned a delivery from Cassenwary that might interest you. So, who followed you into Veritas Keep?"

"Thanks for the news." Forrest pointed at the wizard. "Sir Geoffrey, I present the wizard Casemiro." The troll-man held up the advertisement for the guard's benefit. "He responded to the request for assistance, and I'm delivering him to Prince Arenton for inspection."

Sir Geoffrey's eyes widened at the mention of a wizard. "Well, your friend must turn over his weapons. Wizard or not."

Forrest stared at the wizard. "What weapons do you carry, old man?"

Casemiro rolled his eyes at Forrest. "Fine, but I expect this returned unblemished. King Skaranon himself offered it as a gift."

The wizard slid open his cloak and flashed a glimpse of the blue interior lining. His right hand emerged and held a scabbard of the finest and softest leather. The housing's curve revealed the blade as a saber, distinguishing the weapon from Sir Geoffrey's shortsword. Casemiro laid the scabbard flat across both of his hands and presented the sheathed blade.

The guard accepted, ineffectively hiding his envy of the weapon.

Forrest cocked an eyebrow and examined the quality of the scabbard. "Does the blade match the packaging?"

"I pray you never find out."

Forrest released a grumbling breath. "Anything else, Sir Geoffrey?"

"What about the staff?"

Casemiro pulled the gnarled wooden stick back. "What if the Prince wishes me to perform a spell for him?"

Geoffrey paused with a concerned look. "Fine. I suggest either waiting in the hallway or lingering at the back of the auditorium to remain unnoticed. You remember the routine."

The troll-man nodded and walked through the gap in the twenty-foot-tall wall.

Casemiro followed his massive escort, but paused to ask the guard a question. "Geoffrey, if I may ask, why the name of Veritas?"

"Because the truth shall always protect us."

Casemiro's eyebrows rose from amusement at the proclamation and then turned to maintain pace with Forrest. Upon clearing the gate, a second wall greeted them a mere twenty feet further inside the premises. This particular wall, an intended secondary line of defense, stood as tall as the first but featured offset gates to prevent a straight-line offensive from any potential raiders.

Above them, the walls appeared littered with flags alternating between blue fields, the seal of Lillenhold, and the yellow crest of Gaeleos. A constant ripple of the wind flapped through the legion of pennants and pummeled their ears with the sounds of a hundred horses galloping. The gap between the two stone walls augmented the noise and created a tunnel for the wind to push through. The resulting breeze rippled through their clothing and required the wizard to cinch his new belt.

Casemiro cleared his throat to provide a witty comment, but Forrest raised his hand to halt the wizard from speaking. "Not until I tell you to talk. Stay quiet and follow."

Casemiro's patience ran short, but he withheld his sarcastic response.

The two walked alongside the second wall for fifty strides and found a gap to proceed beyond the second layer of defense. Casemiro inspected the majesty of the massive three-foot thick walls and their smooth polished surfaces where no liquid clung.

The wizard cleared the opening and found a surprising view of a vast flat garden populated by bustling villagers performing various tasks, including planting the spring crops. The extensive area exuded a practical nature, unpretentious scent, and patches of green grass warming Casemiro in his core. He found a gem amongst the sea of dank gray and brown of Lillenhold. At the center of the sizeable garden sat the massive and bulky fieldstone structure of Veritas Keep. From this distance, the keep carried the sophistication of an engineering marvel down to plumb walls and sharp corners built to repel any unwanted attacks.

Casemiro continued forward, absorbing the surrounding wonders, but stopped when a meaty hand grabbed his shoulder.

"Before entering Veritas Keep, wizard, I must forewarn you."

Casemiro expected certain regulations for interacting with the Prince of Gaeleos. The wizard leaned against the stone wall for relief from the walk and received his instructions.

"Today is the village's hearing day and involves the citizens airing grievances between each other, and Prince Arenton administers justice. So, upon entry, we stand at the rear of the chamber until called. Upon his request, walk forward and bow until he allows us to rise and begin the discussion. Do not talk unless the Prince addresses you. Provide direct and short responses. Clear?"

"Yes, Forrest. You recall my experience with royal protocols, don't you?"

Forrest waved the wizard forward. "Let us begin."

The two walked stride for stride into the stone monolith, attempting to avoid attention. Upon entering the massive foyer, Casemiro noted the cobbled path and floor of the keep merged, as if an artisan cut them from the same stone. Within, a variety of people hustled back and forth in the open entryway which branched in two directions. Ahead stood two hefty wooden doors bearing the grain of strong alders and featured adornment of gold hinges and the finest bronze locks. A foot-thick frame carved from an oak tree outlined the double doors. The aperture stood open, allowing anyone to become part of the festivities inside the much larger hall on the other side.

Forrest pointed towards a display case beside the door. "You might wish to look at that."

Casemiro walked over to view a scarlet piece of dragon heartstone and a plaque commemorating the event which occurred twenty years before. A flash of an image with a dragon popped into the wizard's head. He pushed it back out just as quickly and turned to Forrest without reading the plaque. "I guess the village remembers."

"Difficult to forget such an occasion, wizard. Follow me."

Casemiro and Forrest entered the interior chamber to escape the attention of the people staring in the main foyer. As Forrest described, citizens of the community filled the seating of the chamber, a series of wooden pews, and the Prince held court. Forrest nudged Casemiro and pointed down the wall as an indication to slide to an open spot in the back of the room and wait for the proceedings to finish. Their shuffling distracted the people in the chamber. Forrest attracted the bulk of their attention while Casemiro escaped the judgmental eyes.

Without moving his head, the Prince flashed his eyes to the rear of the room. He returned his interest to the woman crying over a man not paying for the services she provided. The Prince who sat on a humble wooden throne covered with gold inlay across the top portion.

Casemiro shifted his focus to the aesthetics of the massive chamber as a distraction. The wizard pulled up his hood and blended in to discover his surroundings in the twenty-foot-high room. A massive tapestry of the village's unfortunate crest hung on the far wall with a ten-foot-tall turkey stretched across the decoration. The absurd depiction drew a chuckle from Casemiro, who hid his laughter by shifting his focus to a painting depicting two young men at the knee of a king.

Casemiro tapped Forrest on the shoulder and pointed to the artwork. "Who is this?"

Forrest glanced at the painting. "The former king and his two sons, the current King Skaranon and the one with blonde hair is Ian, the former king's adopted son and the current Marquis of Cassen."

The wizard returned his gaze toward the proceedings, but barely heard anything other than the noises of incessant whining from the plaintiff and defendant. The builders of the keep did not concern themselves with the science of traveling sound, hence the lack of ideal acoustics in the cavernous hall.

Everyone stopped when the Prince raised his hand and stood to declare his verdict. "The defendant owes payment, or an equivalent amount of goods, to the plaintiff. This court resolved three disputes in the past year between you, and you wasted enough of my time. I order the two of you to avoid doing business together, regardless of your marriage. Now, everyone must leave. Affairs of the realm require my attention." Prince Arenton shifted his gaze to Forrest and the wizard.

The plaintiff and defendant performed their perfunctory bows. Most of the crowd cleared the keep without issue. Individuals reeking of mead needed assistance from the hall, and the guards removed any stragglers from the vast chamber. Once everyone cleared the room, Prince Arenton moved to the ceremonial throne sitting atop a square platform on the far wall of the hall. Casemiro detected a previously unseen stairway rising behind the throne with an ingenious design to blend into the wall beyond.

The Prince waved for Forrest and his guest to come forward. The troll-man and Casemiro stopped ten feet from the throne and bowed.

"You may rise. What brings you here today, Forrest?"

Casemiro studied the Prince's countenance, thinking him a boy, or a young man amid his teenage years. Arenton owned blue eyes shining from exuberance and a crooked smile portraying a young man of pure naivete or incredible stupidity. Casemiro did not trust the youth and inexperience of Arenton, and questioned how a teenage boy might rule a piece of this massive kingdom.

Forrest cleared his throat. "Prince Arenton, I present the first respondent to the advertisement you requested. The wizard Casemiro of..." Forrest gave a questioning gawk at the wizard. "...of Foxshire."

Prince Arenton and Forrest waited for the wizard to confirm the statement. The wizard joggled his head, signifying the correctness of the information. Foxshire represented the closest thing to a home base for the wizard, unless one counted his brother's boat, the Fierce Siren.

The Prince proceeded, regardless of the answer. "Excellent, Casemiro, no matter where you hail from, I welcome you to Veritas Keep. Can you vouch for this wizard's abilities, Forrest?"

Forrest stood at rigid attention and replied with an emotionless response. "Yes, I witnessed first-hand the skills of Casemiro. He saved a troll family from a dragon attack twenty years ago, and the documentation of his efforts exists just outside the doors to this hall. I forget the number of dragons he slayed, but he drove the beasts away and saved a half-troll family, allowing them to find shelter in Lillenhold." Forrest finished and stared straight ahead at the sovereign, unblinking and stone-faced.

Casemiro and the Prince stared in disbelief at the troll-man's response.

The wizard whispered to Forrest. "That was you?"

A quick nod from the troll-man answered the wizard's inquiry.

The taut pressure of the moment increased and required someone to break the silence.

Casemiro obliged, unconcerned with the formalities of court. "What happened to your mother, Forrest?"

"She died two years ago. But that does not concern you at this moment, wizard."

"Regardless, my condolences for your loss. Every child mourns their mother's passing."

A curt nod from Forrest closed the conversation, and he wiped away a single tear from his cheek.

The Prince entered the conversation. "Apologies for being ignorant of such events, Forrest. And I had nearly forgotten that small display. You walk by something day after day after day and it just blends in. Regardless, Casemiro, I owe you a certain amount of gratitude for saving the life of my best..."

He paused. "State your title, Forrest."

"I don't own one, my Prince."

The awkwardness of the moment extended. "Perhaps that should be the next order of the realm's affairs. Do your people even appreciate titles, Forrest?"

Forrest grunted with angst before offering a reply. "My people appreciate the same things as any villager of Lillenhold or citizen of Gaeleos, my Prince."

Obviously distracted by something in the room, the Prince shifted his eyes towards the back of the chamber, near where Forrest and Casemiro stood previously.

Casemiro glanced and spotted a woman in the shadows. Other than her red dress, the wizard perceived little detail from the darkness. Not knowing the woman, the wizard returned his eyes to the Prince.

Prince Arenton asked, "Wizard, do you remember our fine village? How did you busy yourself over the years?"

Casemiro smiled at the fantastical idea of a royal sharing the ownership of the village with those living in its boundaries. "I remember Lillenhold. To pass the years, I worked menial jobs to earn any needed funds. I don't remember you being born when I visited before, but the King's daughter appeared prominently when I last visited this village. Whatever happened to her?"

A hush overwhelmed the chamber and everyone stopped moving, revealing the level of noise created by the people shuffling through the hall.

After a second, Forrest apologized. "My Prince, I did not inform him of the current affairs of the realm."

Arenton shifted his eyes to the back of the room and Casemiro followed the Prince's gaze, but the woman disappeared from view. "Forrest, don't blame yourself. Perhaps if the wizard revealed himself properly, or stayed connected, our family history would be less difficult to follow. As it stands, a simple breach of decorum. I forgive you both."

Casemiro bowed, not sure he breached any sort of decorum. "I did not intend to offend you, or your father, Lord. It appears many events have transpired since my last visit to the village."

The Prince smiled, but his eyes narrowed to show his agitation. "You did nothing wrong, wizard. Your appearance pricked a long-healed scar on Gaeleos. To answer your query, during your employment, I did not exist. My father's first wife passed after you served him. My mother, the current queen, married King Skaranon shortly after her predecessor's death and produced me within a year of their nuptials. The daughter you remember, my half-sister Princess Laural, will undoubtedly make her presence known later."

After another quick check for the woman, Casemiro found nothing and went back to the Prince. "Thank you for the update. I hope to learn about these changes."

The Prince drew the attention back onto himself. "Your motivation encourages me to dive into our connected and shared histories. This link between our lives portends success for this next venture. Forrest, you and the wizard must attend dinner this evening to discuss this opportunity. And please bring the beautiful lady Oleander, so we may discuss her gorgeous flowers. Other affairs of the realm require my attention this afternoon. Enjoy the rest of your day."

Casemiro caught a change in Forrest's face at the mention of the other woman as they bowed. After a moment, the Prince encouraged them to rise and exit the premises of Veritas Keep. The duo walked out of the chamber in haste before Arenton left the throne.

Once the pair exited the keep, Casemiro stopped his escort. "So many questions. Where to begin?"

Forrest huffed and appeared defeated. "Fine. But can you at least wait until after lunch? Once we sit down and eat, I promise to answer the questions I can."

"Fine, but my saber needs returned. And no more secrets." Casemiro walked away but stopped and turned back to Forrest. "And lunch is on you." Casemiro stormed to the tent holding his prized weapon, with Forrest following at a brisk pace.

3

LAURAL

In most small villages, options for food beyond one's table seldom existed. A surprising number of dining choices existed in Lillenhold, especially when one considered the population of the village. This spoke to the tiny port town's importance and the number of ships coming through its waters. Forrest took the wizard to The Skullery for their luncheon meal.

The entrance required walking up three wooden and uneven steps, an improvement over The Pub. The elevation meant the floor consisted of a substance other than mud, dirt, or something else. Wooden walls, grayed from time, suffered no gaps and a furnace provided heat, as evidenced by a plume of black smoke rising from the roof. The Skullery covered four times the area of The Pub to support a larger crowd but still offered the opportunity for a private conversation. Additionally, the building did not reek of urine.

Casemiro absorbed the scents of fish, stew, and mead. A mixture which still drew his distaste. Though filled with better aromas than The Pub, the Skullery measured up as less than ideal to the wizard. Sunday's menu consisted of fish soup with, or without, hardtack. Stale mead poured from the taps, minus the floating chunks included for free at The Pub, a small plus in the wizard's mind.

Forrest secured a specific table to view the comings and goings of the eatery's patrons. The troll-man did not pause at the bones, noting the crunch offered much-needed texture. "Make the tack chewable by soaking the bread in the stew, wizard. Their stew is the pride of the Skullery, so enjoy. Apologies for the limited menu, but only the barkeep and one server work on Sundays. Tomorrow's offerings improve and the drink becomes fresher for your sophisticated palette. If you stay that long."

Beside his bowl, a pile of fine pins and needles of bone accumulated as Casemiro plucked them from the fish in his stew. "It's fine." Each spoonful decreased the wizard's confidence in the food's quality. The old man snarled and drank the rest of his tankard, allowing the empty vessel to wobble on the uneven wooden table. Though still too watery, the brew contained sufficient bitterness and imparted a biting, pleasant flavor. "You owe me answers."

The troll-man requested another drink and rested against the wall behind their table. "You presume I can provide information of any value. Ask your questions so we can move beyond your childish display."

Casemiro grabbed his staff and contemplated burning Forrest into a smoldering pile of sludge, but held back the spell. The wizard doubted his ability to cast the curse, let alone the advisability of performing such a spell in such tight confines. The wizard spat the first question. "What is up with the crest and the turkey?"

The question drew laughter from Forrest. "That is the first thing you ask? Very well, some farmer brought a few turkeys back on a trading ship and began tending to them. They proved smarter than the farmer and escaped his pens. Since, they have become wild and populated a vast part of this region in large numbers. We even have a specific day where we hunt them and celebrate the bounty of the food they provide."

"That explains how a bird like that came to Gaeleos. Now, what is this Extravaganza?"

Forrest crossed his arms and grinned with his large white teeth. "Another answer I can provide. The Prince coined the term for the upcoming event. But what that entails, no one can guess."

The server delivered two new flagons of mead and took the empty cruets. Forrest swigged his drink and Casemiro pushed the container to the side. The wizard spat out the hardtack after taking a bite and then dipped the dense bread into the stew for his second attempt. He chewed the second bite and gave a slight nod as the saltiness and liquid of the broth increased the edibleness of the bread.

Forrest smiled and tipped his cup in acknowledgment of the appreciation for the advice. "What else do you wish to ask?"

Casemiro swallowed prior to asking the question. "What does the Prince want from me?"

Forrest chuckled and responded. "Hell, if I know. The Prince wanted a wizard but didn't say why and only advertised in a few places."

Casemiro grew irritated at the small amount of information gained from his questions and resigned himself to finding out more about Forrest and Lillenhold, two much less interesting topics. "What do you do for the Prince? And who is Oleander?"

Forrest tensed at the mention of the woman's name and refused to address the inquiry. "When the Prince needs something special, he calls."

"And you come running? Sounds like a gopher. What about the woman?" Casemiro refused to halt questioning the troll-man on the topic.

Forrest pounded the table and scowled. "Are you always this annoying, wizard?"

Casemiro stared back at the troll-man and trod carefully. Experience taught Casemiro that everyone wanted to tell their story, if allowed enough space. The wizard wagered angering the troll-man, though dangerous, presented the best chance to obtain the information he desired. He let silence do the rest of the prodding.

After a quiet minute, Forrest surrendered the information. "As for Oleander, she is a person of mutual interest between me and the Prince."

The old man laughed; the gambit paid off. "She must be a beauty to draw His Majesty's interest. Am I correct? And what interests you about her?"

Forrest slammed his hand on the table a second time, jarring both flagons enough to almost tip them. "No more questions concerning Oleander. Switch topics, wizard."

The old man sneered, but agreed. "Why do you end your sentences in such a mocking tone?"

"No evidence since your arrival in Lillenhold suggests you are the same wizard who saved my life twenty years ago. That man deserves my thanks. This poorly dressed traveler, covered with no self-esteem and less confidence, bears little resemblance to my deliverer. Please express my gratitude if you ever encounter the Casemiro I remember." Forrest glared at the wizard, anticipating an antagonistic comment in return.

They both frowned and stared across the table, each waiting for the other to blink. The tension between them diffused into the thick fishy air of the room over several moments of silence. Their stares parted, each needing to recapture their focus and breathe. Casemiro recognized the truth in what Forrest said and attempted to pull up a piece of the esteemed wizard from within.

"One last question. Who wore the scarlet dress at the keep?" The wizard speculated on the person's identity but wanted verification.

Forrest peered up from his cup as the dining hall went quiet. A dented bell chimed as the door opened, signifying a person entered the vast room. Forrest's eyes pointed towards the door. "Ask her yourself."

The woman from Veritas Keep, dressed in red, stood at the door with an unpleasant glare while searching the dining hall. She found Forrest and stepped toward their table as the mass of bodies between the door and the intended destination parted. The crowd's reaction confirmed the wizard's suspicion, and he identified Laural, the daughter of King Skaranon and the Princess of Gaeleos, as the mystery woman.

She pulled her raven hair back into a braid while the red gown hugged across her chest, and form-fitting sleeves ran the distance of her arms to present a regal picture. The bottom of the gown flowed across the floor like a red cloud, and the click of heeled shoes carried a quick rhythm on the wooden planks as she crossed the gap.

As the woman drew nearer, Casemiro noted the piercing green eyes and the button nose balancing the symmetry of the alluring face. Her jawline blended angularity and typical feminine softness and reflected the woman's self-assurance. The glare across the woman's countenance showed nothing soft concerning her demeanor as she fixed her gaze on Casemiro.

The wizard gulped and shrunk into his chair. This woman entered his life with the sole purpose of disrupting his future. The wizard feared what that future entailed.

Laural stood by their table and Forrest offered the seat next to Casemiro. "Thank you, Forrest."

Laural planted two short daggers into the wood of the table, smirking at the wizard to judge his reaction to the edgy and aggressive display.

Casemiro dipped his head in respect but also realized this woman attempted to intimidate him. "Princess, the barkeep may take offense to your knives cutting into his table."

Laural plucked one dagger from the wood and returned it back into a sheath, leaving the other as a reminder of the dangerous persona she presented. Casemiro wondered how close to the truth the presentation was.

The rest of the dining hall remained standing, waiting for a sign to return to their lives. The woman waved over her shoulder. "Carry on." The woman grabbed the wizard's full flagon and drank. Another act of intimidation.

Casemiro shrank away, wishing to avoid an encounter, and asked his question. "What brings you here, my lady?"

A quick glare silenced the woman's tablemates, and she stared at the old man. "Are you the wizard Casemiro I met twenty years ago? Or a fraudulent misrepresentation?"

Casemiro stopped himself from grabbing his drink, knowing the flagon now belonged to the Princess. "I believe Forrest has the same question. My answer is a bit of both, I'm afraid."

Laural pointed at the hardtack still on the wizard's plate. "Do you mind?"

The wizard shoved the plate her way, and she ripped off a piece of hardened bread. To Casemiro's surprise, the woman appeared comfortable associating with the riffraff of the Skullery.

The bewildered wizard asked another question. "Doesn't the keep provide adequate meals for the Prince and his family?"

"It does, but the atmosphere lacks in personality."

"And you find this preferable?" A snark-filled smile crept across Casemiro's face.

Laural swallowed the bite, and another swig of mead followed. "The food didn't entice me, wizard." She displayed the same deriding tone as Forrest. "I wonder if you can help me. And even though the Prince wishes to hire you, my father, the King, requested a task of me. I cannot divulge the details here." The Princess suggested the unsuitability of the room for discussing the topic by waving her hand toward the crowd behind her.

Laural drank and turned to Forrest. "Make sure Oleander joins us for my brother's extravagant dinner."

Forrest grunted, and a nod answered the demand while his agitation at the thought of Oleander and the Prince being near each other became more obvious.

"Tell Oleander I loved the flowers this morning. My gown for the dinner matches the tulips. If you wish to spend some time chasing Oleander, the crown will cover the food and I will take responsibility for the wizard. Thank you for your service, Forrest."

The troll-man got the hint and stood up, shaking the table as his hip nudged it.

Casemiro extended his arm. "Don't forget the Captain of the Guard wished to see you."

Forrest nearly shook the wizard's arm free of the socket. "I did not forget."

The wizard remained uncertain about his feelings towards the troll-man. But Casemiro's trepidation about being alone in the presence of the Princess exceeded that uncertainty.

Laural took another bite of hardtack and finished her drink. She slapped five gold coins, double the cost of the meal, and stood, sheathing her other knife in a hidden slot. "Wizard, walk with me to learn what I need from you. Then, once we reach the keep, you can grab some proper food if you wish."

Casemiro, accustomed to following angry women from halls, aspired for this to be the lone occurrence this week. Even if this one incident set an alarming trend.

The wizard stared at the woman, who he last saw as a ten-year-old girl. Now fully grown into a pretty, but rugged, woman. He wondered how he allowed twenty years of time to progress with nothing to show for it in his own life, other than an unhappy marriage that ended in his wife's death.

Laural and Casemiro walked through the village, ventured back up the hill, and followed the path leading to Veritas Keep. Three guards accompanied Laural, one behind and two on opposite sides of the Princess. None concerned themselves with Casemiro's safety. The guards stepped back upon command, allowing the Princess and the wizard a chance for a private conversation.

Laural broke the silence during the walk on the cobblestone path. "Why the chain and hook?" The Princess pointed at the wizard's unusual choice in belts.

"Sends a message and forces pinchers to question their choices while discouraging them from attempting a stupid act of larceny." The wizard feared this answer insinuated a specific issue and wished to avoid his limited coins. "Also, my other belt fell apart." Casemiro inhaled a gust of wind carrying the briny scent of the sea and asked his own question to move off the topic. "Why the red?"

Laural glared at the wizard. "We both grasp the answer, so asking a princess is both rude and asinine." The Princess caught Casemiro's gaze at the gown before he averted his wandering eyes. She smiled before adding her subtle reply. "Besides, this dress fits well and flatters me. Don't you agree?"

Casemiro studied the laws of Gaeleos and understood the royal family abided by the rules of the land. A Princess wearing red presented the height of scandal for the crown. Casemiro now regretted the question and established a defensive stance in the conversation. For asking such a stupid question, he risked losing his head. Even though he found the woman stunning while his cheeks turned red from embarrassment.

"Ask your other question, wizard?" Her tone reeked of slyness instead of anger. The wizard preferred the latter.

Casemiro stopped when he realized Laural flirted with him. "How old are you? I remember a much younger princess and much too young to..." Casemiro paused, knowing the wrong word might end his life. "Well, much too young to be acknowledged by a man of my age."

The Princess smiled daintily. "When you served my father, I was ten. You impacted my life as a young woman, not a small child. You paid little attention to me, and rightfully so." She continued walking. "But if I were to guess, you are in the range of forty-five years of age."

Casemiro stopped in shock at the statement. He had let his appearance get away from him, but held back on his actual age and went with the number he and his brother attempted to use as a guide. "Forty, actually."

Casemiro examined Laural and accepted the new royal beauty the Princess became between his visits to Lillenhold. The wizard redefined his perception of time's passage. Casemiro stood straighter and sucked in his gut. He caught himself staring once more and tripped over a loose cobblestone, barely saving himself from the embarrassment of a fall in the middle of the street with his staff.

The wizard attempted to hide the stumble by continuing the conversation. "You grew into a beautiful woman, Princess. Does your father hold you as dearly as he should? And you still only hold the title of Princess of Gaeleos? Did no suitors offer enough wealth or a benefitting alliance to the kingdom?"

Casemiro stepped away from Laural, sensing a separation between them might be wise. Asking pointed questions served as a distraction, while her proximity prompted thoughts he wished to avoid. Part of his mind still viewed her as the ten-year-old girl.

The Princess, turning away, absorbed the brunt of the implied insults from the pointed questions. "I declined all those offers. None proved worthy of me, and my father agreed with my judgment. But thank you for the backhanded compliment. Now, I must ask. Why do you seem older than your professed age of forty? Have the past few years proven so difficult?"

Casemiro grimaced, understanding the Princess dished out verbal punishment equal to what she received. Did his reaction communicate too much about his state of mind? Casemiro's critical eye turned inward, and the guilt haunting the wizard for the last five years resurfaced and he backed down. "I apologize if the tone of my inquiries rankled you."

To distract himself from the moment, Casemiro glared at the peak in the distance as two memories flickered: his saber taking a life and finding his wife dead.

The Princess grabbed the wizard's shoulder, snapping Casemiro back to reality. "Did a terrible occurrence shape you into who you are now? You appear a shadow of your former self, and the Casemiro I remember remains far away from here."

Casemiro withdrew from her hand. "You, of all people, should not judge one by their appearance. My tale takes too long to tell, Princess, and my stomach grows hungrier after such a poor excuse for a meal."

Laural continued walking on the cobblestone path as Casemiro and the guards fell in line. Veritas Keep glowered back at them as they approached the stone structure. A darkened sky foretold the coming afternoon storm. The Princess pulled a strand of wind-blown hair back from her face as a stray beam of light landed on the group from the cloudy sky on the mirk-filled day.

Laural picked up the conversation without turning to Casemiro. "I want to say something before we reach the keep, wizard. Only two men recognized my worth beyond my title. My father, King Skaranon, and the wizard I met twenty years ago. He gave me a token to signify his respect." From the gown's left pocket, Laural produced a stone.

The wizard recalled the rock and the day he gifted it to her. Casemiro believed the stone to be a meaningless gesture, but now understood the offering represented much more to Laural. And seeing the stone reminded him of another promise unfulfilled. Much like those made to his sweet Chantal long ago.

Casemiro held out his hand, an unspoken request to handle the stone. The Princess placed the rock in his palm. He rubbed the rough exterior, sensing the magic retained inside, despite the faded sheen of twenty years' time. The wizard sensed the energy within the stone and recalled what he told the Princess twenty years prior. The rock warmed from the wizard's embrace before the wizard returned the stone to Laural, and he now understood where this discussion headed.

"This rock symbolized a promise from you, Casemiro. A promise of assistance in time of need. I held this stone countless times over the last twenty years, and you never showed. But, today of all days, who arrives in Veritas Keep after the King bestowed an arduous task onto me? The sole man to ever make such a promise. I am cashing in on all the times I prayed for your help. I know not what the Prince desires of you, but I demand you uphold your promise of service to me."

The intensity of the words, and the inundation of guilt, pressed Casemiro's heart into immediate action. The wizard resolved to keep this promise, or die trying. Perhaps the wizard might make amends for how he failed Chantal and discharge his past failings. Casemiro kneeled before the Princess and bowed his head. Despite doubting his ability, he accepted the challenge. "Princess Laural, I pledge to you my service."

The Princess turned, appearing to ignore the gesture, and her scarlet gown flapped in the breeze.

The wizard stood and fell in line, with the three guards following her. Casemiro's mind drifted and he wondered if this may become another case of him failing to uphold yet another promise.

Beyond the group, the gaping entrance of Veritas Keep opened wider to take them into its maw; a stone monster hoping to devour the people walking into its clutches.

Casemiro blocked Laural's path. "What do you wish of me?"

"A bath. You stink. Then, find some food and prepare yourself. Tonight, you help me catch a thief."

4

STRANGE IDEAS

Three hours passed quickly for the wizard after he fed on a bowl of potato soup and a leg of under-seasoned chicken. A warm bath relaxed Casemiro to the point he required a nap in the bed of his provided quarters. The bed offered cooling comfort against the stone wall while a thick duvet covered the straw-filled mattress and feather-filled pillow; both featuring the royal seal of Gaeleos sewn in purple thread, demonstrating the wealth of the crown.

The wizard's coin purse and knitting needles sat beside a lump of gray yarn on a nightstand, alongside a lantern and a half-empty can of fuel. A shelf above the bed held additional candles and matches for additional light. An empty wooden armoire filled one corner, and the other housed a wood-burning stove to provide additional heat if required, along with the chamber pot, both unused by the wizard.

Casemiro woke with a series of deep, cleansing breaths prior to preparing for the extravagant meal. The wizard put on his undergarments, the same raggedy white shirt, and disheveled brown breeches. He then focused on the cloak and flipped the garment inside out to reveal the blue interior lining with shining golden rays of thread spread across the material. The wizard rubbed his hands across the fabric and the magical resonance within the fabric called to be released.

Casemiro closed his eyes. "Please, let me do this minor spell." He asked any spirit, or god, listening to provide him the ability to perform the simple incantation.

The wizard rubbed his hands together and whispered in another language. "Goleuo."

The golden threads shimmered, and light flowed through them enough to please the wizard. He peered skyward with a smile and gave a heartfelt nod of gladness. "Small, but a beginning. Thank you."

The old man pulled the cloak over his body and massaged the fabric into place in certain places to best flatter his figure. Wearing the blue side of the reversible cloak boosted Casemiro's confidence for the evening's festivities.

Casemiro studied the coin purse, a pouch composed of blue fabric and crimped by brown twine tying off the end. Within the fabric, a gold 'C' served as a reminder of who gifted the pouch to him, Chantal. The wizard gazed at the pouch; memories flooded his mind as tears welled in his eyes. He wiped away the tears and sniffled his runny nose, deciding to leave the coin purse and the unneeded knitting needles for the evening.

"I apologize for being such a disappointment." Casemiro intended the apology for the spirit of his dead wife, but a pang of guilt stung his soul.

The wizard grabbed the chain and draped the makeshift belt around his waist; the hook acting as a clasp to hold the belt in place. Casemiro grabbed the staff and searched for the saber, forgetting for an instant the guard confiscated the blade upon his return to Veritas Keep.

A knock at the door grabbed the wizard's attention. Casemiro opened the door and found the Princess fiddling with last-second adjustments to her outfit. The wizard stared blankly at the golden garment draped across the woman's figure.

"Are you ready for dinner?" Laural smirked at the wizard's outfit. "I like the new cloak." She looked closer. "Is light passing through the fabric?"

Once Casemiro registered the compliment, the wizard answered. "I conjured a minor spell to last through the evening. Your presence at my door surprises me, Princess."

Casemiro scrutinized Laural's outfit in greater detail, a one-piece gown of dark yellow running from the bodice to the floor. The blouse featured two-inch thick straps covering the shoulders and fit her corseted form. The bottom of the gown hooped out, flowing in tiers to the floor. Gold-colored sleeves matched the bow holding back much of her hair. The wizard noted the ribbon of red draped over the shoulders of the outfit on both sides, a reminder of her failings.

"I told Forrest I would ensure your arrival for the dinner. I fulfill my promises. Do you like my attire for the evening?" She caught the wizard eyeing her attire.

Casemiro avoided any further embarrassment by complimenting the Princess. "A lovely garment, my lady."

"And your beard's gray lessened in the time we spent apart. Amazing what a bath and sleep can accomplish. Perhaps an illusion of magic makes you appear younger." A brief smile crept across Laural's lips, but she caught herself in mid-act and stopped. The Princess peeked around Casemiro's shoulder to investigate the room. "Nice quarters. I lodge across the hall. You should become accustomed to my presence for your time here."

Casemiro entertained the idea of seeing the Princess regularly but concealed any potential giveaways of his thoughts by walking through the door. "I believe we might be late for the dinner."

Laural waved aside his concerns and regarded the coin purse on the side table next to the bed; alongside an in-process knitting project featuring the gray yarn. "I think you forgot something." The Princess entered the room, grabbed the satchel, and brought it to the wizard. As she handed over the object, the Princess rattled off a series of questions. "What material is this pouch made from? What does the 'C' signify? And you knit?"

Offended and embarrassed, Casemiro snatched the purse and pushed it into his hidden pocket. "We should not keep the Prince waiting, and you wish to catch a thief."

Laural took his meaning and refocused on the bigger concerns. "Correct. Sorry for the rude intrusion." Her projection of a gritty exterior returned.

Casemiro shut the door loud enough to convey the message of no re-entry allowed. The wizard bowed towards the Princess. "After you, Your Highness." In his mind, Casemiro vowed to not let Laural lower his guard again.

The lower chamber of Veritas Keep underwent impressive changes in three hours, leaving the Princess and the wizard awestruck. Workers moved the throne onto a small platform along one wall, accompanied by two notable wooden chairs sitting on either side. Workers also arranged the pews on the room's periphery into a circular pattern. In the center of the chamber, the platform from earlier now contained four wooden posts at each corner and a set of ropes strung between the pillars. A matted surface bulging in certain spots from obvious stuffing covered the platform.

Casemiro entered the auditorium, stood at the platform corner after descending the stairs, and asked the obvious question, "What is this?"

Unnoticed by Casemiro, Forrest and another woman stood on the opposite side of the chamber. The Princess called to the other people. "Forrest and Oleander, how pleasant to see you."

The old man shifted his gaze towards the duo and homed in on the sizable suit draped across the body of Forrest, granting the troll-man a human appearance instead of a hybrid. Wearing a black suit and a white collared-shirt, the troll-man took on the unfortunate image of a manservant.

Casemiro's eyes shifted to Oleander wearing a lovely green dress accented by green heels. Her blonde hair trellised toward her waist, and her indigo eyes shimmered. The woman's smile widened as the wizard introduced himself.

After a quick embrace and the perfunctory curtsey toward the Princess, Oleander extended her hand to Casemiro. "Forrest told me much about you. I never expected to meet a true wizard."

Casemiro blushed at the woman. "Our mutual friend withheld the details of your beauty, Oleander. I am honored to meet you as well. As for wizardry, word is your botanical abilities surpass my skill with a spell."

Oleander smiled back at the old man. "Your comments honor me, as the shop is my work of love. You appear much younger than what Forrest suggested, and I adore the fabric of your cloak."

"The wonders of a bath and rest can do miracles, my lady." Casemiro glanced at Laural, who snickered at the stolen line. "As for the fabric, a simple incantation."

Forrest's burly voice boomed across the room. "Soap and sleep won't erase that many years, wizard."

The wizard turned his attention to Forrest. "You look quite fashionable. Could you fetch me a drink?" A sheepish grin followed the subtle joke.

Forrest's shoulders relaxed at the jab of humor, and his suit also relaxed from the release of tension. "I approve of your new cloak, Casemiro. Much more fitting for your position."

Casemiro turned toward the platform. "Any idea about this monstrosity?" He crossed his arms, allowing the flowing blue sleeves of the cloak to conceal his hands, except for the length of his fingers clutching the wooden staff.

Princess Laural stood beside the wizard. "I hoped you might enlighten us with stories of experiencing something of this nature during one of your backwater excursions."

Casemiro absorbed the sting of the intended barb. "And here we were getting along so well, Princess. No, I am unfamiliar with this contraption."

Another voice from behind interrupted their conversation. "We refer to the contraption as a ring."

Everyone turned and found Prince Arenton alongside a person unfamiliar to Casemiro.

The Prince continued, "More on that later. Most of you recognize my chief counselor, James Jewell Heenan. Heenan, I introduce the enchanting Oleander and our newest guest in Lillenhold, the renowned wizard Casemiro."

Heenan stood shorter than the wizard because of a slouching posture, and his waist expanded to the same diameter as his height. A round head covered by wiry yellow hair sat atop the spherical body, but the most intimidating aspects of the man centered on dark blue eyes and a crooked smile missing a single tooth. Heenan's rough appearance from the neck up fell short of the standard from the neck down. The finest leather fashioned the bodice of his outfit, featuring hooked loops holding the shirt together down the front. Black trousers featured tassels running along the seams down to the black boots, made from the finest leather, which finished the fashionable ensemble.

Counselor Heenan bowed to the Princess and exchanged pleasantries with Forrest before greeting the other two members of the group. "I must declare you the loveliest commoner in Lillenhold, a true flower. How fitting, considering you own the floral shop. And you." He turned to Casemiro. "The King still mentions you to this day and we often speculate whether King Skaranon exaggerates your abilities or if his Majesty suffers from a case of nostalgia." Heenan raised an inquisitive eyebrow and asked a question of the wizard without saying a word.

The counselor's snide comments swayed the wizard's mind against the man in mere seconds. The wizard speculated the flamboyant appearance concealed mischievous intentions and vowed to not trust this brash confidant of the Prince.

Casemiro turned to the Prince. "A ring, but square in design? Can you elaborate, Your Highness?"

Arenton fixed a lustful stare on Oleander, which Casemiro regarded, causing a brief delay in a response before the Prince shifted his focus to the platform as he drifted to the nearby throne. "People in the entertainment business call this a ring and the combatants wrestle within the ropes. According to rumors, the spectacle became a sensation among the aristocracy of Austeria over the last few months. The sport bears a long history, dating back to the gladiators of ancient times. Even the scriptures mention the sport, although I'm not knowledgeable about them."

Forrest ensured the royal finished before asking his question. "So, this augments your exercise regimen, my Lord?"

"No, you misunderstand and lack the necessary context, Forrest. For centuries, we rulers used physical contests between those beneath us to appeal to the masses and provide entertainment. I wish to bring joy to this village and beyond, starting with this festival. Lillenhold needs entertainment other than drinking, planting crops, and raising livestock. Conducting wrestling matches represents my contribution to the culture of Lillenhold, beginning with the much-ballyhooed Extravaganza."

Laural whipped her head toward her brother. "Wait, you spent the money from the reserves preparing for this event?"

The Prince met the inquiry with a broad mischievous grin. "Yes, I understand our father sent you to hover over me, dear sister. And yes, I spent a sizable portion of my allotment to conduct this event. Our father doubts my judgment and believes me a fool by concealing the true purpose of your visit. Dealing with my father's disappointment is second nature to me, but your disbelief in me leaves a deeper scar. Now that I sense your disapproval, I am prompted to reconsider my plan."

An embarrassed frown spread across Laural's face. "My apologies for my doubt, but I expected to find a scoundrel stealing the funds. I never considered you using the funds for something of this nature. Where are these wrestlers you mentioned?"

Casemiro noticed a quick look between Heenan and the Prince before the counselor answered the Princess. "They arrive tomorrow for introduction and training. The Prince and I carefully planned this event for half a year and considered almost every detail."

Casemiro laughed aloud at the hubris on display from the duo. "Your majesty, this idea is either brilliant or terrible, but what explains the correlation to hiring a wizard? In particular, me."

The Prince beamed disarmingly. "Your involvement proves instrumental, my dear Casemiro. Our people remember your name. A wizard with your reputation serving as our master of ceremonies lends credibility to the event. Legitimacy and..." The Prince paused. "...and remind me of the other word, Heenan."

"Verisimilitude, Your Highness."

"Yes, verisimilitude. And what better place than Veritas Keep? Where the truth shall protect you."

The group stood in utter silence as the Prince and Heenan waited for validation of the idea. The audience assumed the entire idea a joke and waited for the punchline. Sensing the need to break the silence, Casemiro asked for his benefit. "How much are you willing to pay me?"

Heenan answered, "One evening of matches, two silver pieces. Upon completion of the event, one gold piece. Plus, if you choose, free room and board in Veritas Keep."

"And this constitutes your requirement of me? No menial labor or enforcing the Prince's edicts?"

Heenan pulled out a piece of parchment. "If you sign the contract, you must oversee the events within the wrestling ring. Oh, and if a dragon attacks, to defend the village, defeat the beast, and kill it. Not a problem for a true wizard." With a questioning stare, the counselor placed the parchment on the platform next to an inked quill.

The wizard flashed a wry smile at the counselor. "How likely is a dragon attack? It's been two decades since such an event occurred. Where do I sign?" Casemiro picked up the quill and marked his signature on the contract where Heenan pointed, jotting an unmistakable 'C' on the line. Casemiro shoved aside the ominous warning signs from Mount Siven as the man considered the possibility of a dragon attacking the village more remote than Lillenhold's location.

"Your Highness, what part do I play in this Extravaganza?" Forrest inquired.

The Prince turned to the troll-man. "You should become part of the in-ring talent. A specimen of your size screams of being a prime attraction."

The comment drew a rebuking glare from Forrest. "Sir, I abhor violence."

The Prince appeared unconcerned with Forrest's resistance. "We'll find a position for you once we finalize the details." Arenton addressed the other attendees. "The funds cover the cost of experienced wrestlers, but people don't just want to endure men fighting. These men play certain roles with personalities. They face off against other personalities, fueling audience passions and creating a dramatic environment. I doubt even the famous Globe features theatrics to this level."

The Prince turned towards the florist. "Oleander, we assigned you to serving refreshments and snacks to the crowd at a merchandise stand. We will offer a menu of foreign treats to the attendees, along with drinks. Those supplies arrive tomorrow, and your retail experience fits into our plans."

The Princess broke in. "You hired these men and bought food? How much did this entire event cost?" Laural's hands went to her head as if warding off a migraine. "Never mind. Do these men only perform? Or do they compete for a prize? And, so help me God, if you say the Princess's hand..." Laural clenched her fists to prepare for violence if Arenton suggested the prize included her.

"Fear not for your life of singularity, or your red wardrobe, my dear sister." The Prince tapped Heenan's shoulder and pointed to a box sitting on the throne as the insults to Laural's past hit home.

Heenan ran and retrieved the wooden container. The counselor reached in and pulled out a wide piece of leather with an unmistakable metal on the front.

The Princess approached and examined the belt before admonishing the Prince for his previous comments. "Is that the King's gold?"

The belt featured an impressive flat swath of the metal, accompanied by red gemstones.

"No, the kingdom's gold. And some jeweled dragon heartstones for a touch of color. The entire bauble cost less than you might imagine because the local cobbler pieced it together for a pittance. The tournament, sorry, the Extravaganza will crown a champion to wear this belt when they compete within Veritas Keep. They may not wear the strap outside, for obvious reasons. But consider, for a moment, the high honor of declaring yourself the Golden Dragon Champion of Gaeleos." The Prince shook with excitement while saying the words. "The idea of watching sweaty men wrestle for this title and belt excites me greatly."

Everyone turned with awkward stares toward the Prince.

He recanted, "Well, I overstated my case. So, what do you think? And I demand honesty."

Laural answered. "And I demand you replenish the reserves."

Heenan swelled with pride. "We now reach the genius of the Prince's plan. We allow the people free entry into the first session of the Extravaganza, and we charge an entry fee for the remaining sessions. Once the people understand what to expect and are hooked on the product, their payments refill the reserves." An eerie grin crossed Heenan's face until he caught Casemiro's glare and amended his comments. "After we pay the talent, of course."

The Prince smiled at the group, anticipating praise for the entire concept.

Laural began to reply with a bristled face. "This sounds —"

Casemiro beat her to the punch. "AMAZING! I cannot imagine anything better, Your Highness." He glanced back at the Princess, who nodded her recognition of the wizard, perhaps saving her from vocalizing a regretful criticism.

The Prince released a quick breath of relief and reclaimed his broad smile. "I anticipated your agreement. Now, let's eat heartily while we discuss the details of the event. I only need word from my cupbearer that everything meets my requirements."

A door opened, and a guard entered. Casemiro recognized Geoffrey from manning the post outside Veritas Keep earlier in the day. The guard, slowed by the armor, clanked across the floor, and staggered, an immediate concern to the wizard.

The Prince acknowledged the man entering the massive hall. "Here comes the second most important person in Lillenhold. What say you fine, young man?"

Geoffrey wobbled, and his face turned a greenish hue. "My Lord, I think someone poisoned the food." Geoffrey's eyes rolled back, closed, and he fell lifeless to the floor.

Everyone except Heenan ran to Geoffrey's side. The counselor commented, "Oh, he fell oddly."

5

A MYSTERY AFOOT

Casemiro rushed to Geoffrey's fallen body. Princess Laural yelled for the guards. The wizard checked and found no pulse while holding his hand over Geoffrey's mouth and nose, praying for a shallow breath. Casemiro's shoulders slumped when no breath came after a minute, and he pounded once on the armored chest of the young man. Hoping the compressions to the chest cut through the turkey-adorned metal and might restart the lad's heart. Only the old man's hand throbbed.

Dread enveloped the wizard, and the specter of death pushed through the stone floor as Casemiro grew aware of Geoffrey's spirit passing beyond the physical plane. The wizard let loose a moan of despair as the memory of Chantal entered Casemiro's mind. He pushed back against the chill, neutralizing the blackness encroaching on his soul with focused magical energy. Seconds passed before the wizard's eyes opened and Casemiro found everyone except Forrest backing away from his glowing form.

The troll-man kneeled beside the wizard. "Can you do anything for him?"

An exasperated breath left Casemiro's body as his head tilted toward Forrest. "Even with my powers at their height, I cannot cheat death. Perhaps if a necromancer lived in Lillenhold." The glow faded.

The Prince glanced around the crowd. "Does one practice those dark arts in Lillenhold?"

Laural, Forrest, and Heenan gawked at the Prince with agitation. The counselor reminded Arenton of the fact obvious to everyone in the room. "No, the crown outlawed such awful practices centuries ago."

Arenton shrugged. "Lack of foresight, if you ask me."

The guards arrived and encircled the group huddled around the fallen body of Geoffrey. The Captain of the Guard walked forward and asked, "How did the lad die?"

Casemiro raised his head to the captain. "Call the constable? We believe poison caused the death."

The Captain crouched down and examined the body. "No constabulary exists in Lillenhold; the keep's guard investigates and adjudicates crime in the village."

"Then investigating the murder of Geoffrey falls on your shoulders."

Casemiro noted the Captain of the Guard wore the same armor as the victim, with a few notable differences. The Captain's appearance included a thick blonde mustache, a red bulge for a nose, and two light blue eyes visible through the helm.

"Are you an agitator, wizard?" asked the Captain.

The scent of alcohol on the man's breath drew the recognition of the wizard's nose. "Not if you do your job,

Captain." The wizard grabbed the man and pulled the Captain close. "Can you perform in your condition?" Casemiro released the man.

The Captain's face turned crimson and bulged through the armor with anger. "How dare you insinuate—"

Before the Captain completed any reply to the wizard, Prince Arenton grabbed the man by the shoulder. "Someone poisoned poor Geoffrey; therefore, the villain must be fixing the food for tonight's dinner. To the kitchen!"

In a chaotic scene, guards stumbled over each other while chasing the Prince through the massive hall.

Before the crowd departed, Casemiro boomed a command as he stood. "Stop, you fools!"

Everyone halted, expecting a poignant proclamation or sage advice from the old man. The wizard breathed to clear his mind and focused his actions, knowing a rush towards the kitchen might not flush out the culprit. The guilty party most likely departed the building already, so the situation required a measured response.

Casemiro determined a strategy and pointed to the Captain. "Secure the Prince and Princess and ensure the guards allow no visitors until we give leave. Forrest, accompany Oleander to the safety of her home. Heenan, follow me and the Captain to the kitchen. The rest of the guards can ensure no one else leaves the keep before we complete this investigation."

The Captain begrudgingly agreed. "The man spoke clearly. Now, do he ordered." A sneer found its way directed to Casemiro.

The wizard understood the Captain wanted to convey anger at a stranger overstepping his authority. But Casemiro cared more about an innocent person's death than a grown man's bruised ego.

Laural reached out and hugged Arenton, fear etched across her face for her brother's fate. "Your protection became our priority the moment that body hit the floor, Arenton."

"Yes, but I request food at the earliest convenience." A trio of guards pushed the Prince and Princess towards their quarters on the upper levels of the keep, with no concern for Arenton's appetite.

The Princess scrunched her face in disbelief at Arenton's oblivious comment. "I doubt Geoffrey's family sympathizes with your hunger pangs, dear Prince." After an indignant whip of her skirt, Laural stomped up the stairs.

The Prince stopped to reply, but the guards nudged him up the stairs, keeping Arenton from sounding even more obtuse. The remaining troops shuffled through the hall and into the connecting hallways. Three people hovered over Geoffrey's body as it arched and became rigid; only the metal skin of the armor impeded the body's action.

The Captain broke the silence with his analysis. "A reaction often associated with the use of poison. Now, if you don't mind, allow me to lead this investigation." He pointed his words towards Casemiro and then charged two of the remaining guards to follow him.

Casemiro and Heenan also followed while the wizard recalled any accessible toxins and formed a hypothesis around the killer's choice in his own mind.

The poison must not have tainted the taste in the hopes it might get past the cupbearer. So, a powder mixed into the food at some point. Perhaps a plantlike material ground for ease of use. There are so many but we possess no evidence at this point as to which one.

Casemiro turned to Heenan for context surrounding the dinner. "Who planned the menu for the evening? And what did Geoffrey eat?"

Heenan hesitated before replying. "I believe the chef determined the menu. From what I recall, potatoes with rabbit."

"What about a drink?"

"I do not know." The response failed to inspire Casemiro's faith in the counselor's ability to assist with this investigation and raised suspicion in the wizard's mind.

The group proceeded down a hallway, wrapping around the central hall of Veritas Keep towards the rear of the structure. The lighting flickered as flames sat atop oil-soaked torches attached to the wall via iron sconces. A haunting rhythm echoed through the hallway as the steps of the Captain's steel boots forebodingly scraped and tapped across the stone floor much like a death march. After a minute, the telltale noises of the kitchen welcomed the group of investigators.

Upon entering the room, Casemiro yelled, "Stop working!"

The kitchen crew responded with oblivious stares, a state which Casemiro decided to use to his advantage. Other than those attending the pots steaming and bubbling on the stove in the corner, the entire staff turned their attention to the wizard. Then a lone person took exception to the interruption.

A tall man, whose torso appeared stretched from head to waist, wore a white outfit complimented by a stained apron and a puffy toque atop his head. The man's chest matched the puffiness of his hat, while his chin and nose jutted out like bayonets extending forward from the small black dots of his eyes.

A high, shrill shriek erupted from the man's mouth. "As the head chef here, only I make demands in this kitchen. We need to complete this meal for the Prince, and his guests."

The Captain of the Guard fixed a fierce gaze on the head chef. "I order you to stop, Richard. Do you still object?"

Chef Richard backed away, recognizing the Captain's standing. "No, if you demanded this, I acquiesce to your authority." The head chef whistled, and any remaining movement by the staff stopped. "Order my staff as you wish, Captain." The head chef leaned against a nearby wall to avoid further admonishment and cast a glare toward the wizard.

As the Captain of the Guard talked, Casemiro noted two exits from the space, and he directed a guard toward each to prevent anyone from leaving. The wizard turned his attention to the staff and interrupted the Captain, believing the man wasted precious time. "Bring forward the food the cupbearer ate, now."

The noises of utensils, tools, and plates clicking and clacking filled the room. A member of the crew carried a metal tray full of half-eaten food and presented the plate to the wizard.

Casemiro stepped forward and Heenan backed away, as if the food's vicinity might kill him. The wizard raised everyone's awareness to the movement. "Heenan disappearing only raises suspicion about your possible involvement."

Heenan stopped and the crowd turned their gaze on the counselor.

The wizard asked the crew member, "What's on this tray?"

The sweating boy replied. "A roasted leg of rabbit and boiled potatoes covered in a brown gravy and asparagus."

"Give me a knife." The snarled order evoked a squeak from the youngster.

As the boy gathered a knife, Casemiro asked, "What about a drink?"

The sweating boy shuffled in the background, retrieving Geoffrey's drink. A scar on the boy's cheek drew the wizard's focus, the same scar from the port. Casemiro grabbed the boy and whispered, "We met on the pier earlier today. Meet me tomorrow morning outside the keep for a paying job."

The boy nodded and backed away from the wizard. Fear filled his countenance as he turned over what he retrieved.

Casemiro eviscerated the rabbit and found the meat underdone, but not to the degree of poisoning someone. Overcooked potatoes compensated for the rare rabbit. The asparagus, though stringy, stunk of burned oil. "How was this asparagus destroyed?"

A cook yelled a reply. "Poached in oil, sir!"

Casemiro sniffed the food and found nothing indicating poison and then inspected the flagon.

"Is this the drink and cup for the cupbearer's test?"

With the question, the staff's brains uncovered the implied meaning, and the airborne virus of horror spread around the kitchen. The crew silently questioned if the Prince lived, and a stifled whimper rose from a corner.

The boy who brought the cup answered and vocalized the crew's fear. "Yes, the same tankard and drink. Sir, what happened?"

"You can rest easy if you fear for the Prince's safety. But Geoffrey..." Casemiro left the sentence unfinished for dramatic reasons and scanned the crowd, hoping a random movement might unmask the murderer, but he found nothing.

Casemiro sniffed the drink and turned his head aside, finding the typical bitter odor of a poison, well beyond any beer he ever encountered. The wizard placed a hand over the flagon, gripped his staff, and turned to everyone. "Step back in case this spell doesn't work. Cover your mouths and noses if the fumes prove too strong."

The kitchen staff and others in attendance stepped away from the wizard while Heenan hid behind a cabinet.

The old man murmured a strange word. "Anweddu."

The wizard's staff glowed and the drink within the flagon bubbled and steamed. Casemiro withdrew his hand and stepped away, allowing the drink to bubble over the rim of the container and send a yellow cloud of mist skyward. The flagon fell over, empty except for an oozy golden residue.

"Impressive trick, wizard." The Captain whispered from Casemiro's side. "What did you do?"

"I heated the liquid until the primary ingredient of the brew, water, in this case, evaporated. Thus, leaving the residue of any other ingredients inside the cup: the hops, yeast, and hopefully, the poison."

Casemiro grabbed a towel, picked up the still-steaming flagon, and examined the remaining contents. Using the same knife, the wizard swiped along the inside of the container, and the utensil emerged with a dollop of yellow sludge accented by black dots. Casemiro sniffed the material and grimaced in disgust. "The drink created the color, but this residue is mostly cyanide."

Casemiro gathered a great deal of information from the gloppy material. The wizard recognized the mashed black specks as apple seeds, and, in his excitement, almost announced the findings to the crowd. The wizard held his tongue before declaring what he found, knowing broadcasting the results allowed others to jump to incorrect conclusions and assumptions. Casemiro needed to ensure his correctness prior to exclaiming what the grotesque paste included.

Casemiro turned to Chef Richard. "Show us the barrel containing this liquid."

The wizard understood the head chef comprehended the implications for him and his crew. Richard escorted the wizard without saying a word that might sour the investigator's disposition towards his staff. Casemiro followed the head chef, as the Captain and Heenan chased right behind. The wizard grabbed an empty flagon and a couple of knives while walking through the kitchen.

Once the group cleared the fundamental portion of the kitchen, Heenan levied an accusation. "I bet the boy laced the drink with poison."

Casemiro stopped and grabbed the counselor by the hooks of his leather shirt and pushed Heenan against the wall. "Keep quiet unless I request your opinion." Spittle flew from Casemiro's mouth as he pressed the man against the stone wall. "We hold people's lives in our hands at this moment and saying such drivel only serves to harm the innocents. Do you understand?" Unsure of Heenan's agreement, Casemiro asked once more. "Do you understand, Counselor?"

Heenan shook his head to affirm his understanding.

The wizard marked the Captain's small smile when Casemiro released the man.

The entourage entered an alcove lined by wooden barrels along both sides. Richard explained the layout of the stonewalled room. "Wine on the left, mead, beer, and ale on the right. The last one down the row provided the drink in question."

The room provided an excessively humid and damp atmosphere compared to the rest of the keep. The culprit for the moisture: a clogged corner drain emitting an odor of mildew and sewage from what the wizard refused to guess. The hole accommodated potential barrel leaks and notable spills in the small space.

Beyond the barrels stood a latched wooden door that opened to the outside and ruled out an intruder acting alone in this matter. The wizard stepped toward the barrel; the floor's molded residue grabbed hold of Casemiro's feet and released a resounding squish when he lifted the boot.

The Captain also approached the barrel and questioned Chef Richard. "How do we determine if someone tampered with this barrel?"

Richard came alongside the container and identified points of interest as he spoke. "Each brewer seals the beverage in the container with a cork. This brewer provides additional assurances by sealing the cork in red wax, which remains undisturbed on this one." The head chef directed their attention to a raised bit of scarlet paraffin. "We tap the keg with a spigot here and then pour the beverage. If someone tampered with this barrel, they drilled another hole and covered it before arrival in my kitchen. You can confirm my crew did not tamper with this barrel." Richard emphasized the last point and his crew's innocence.

Casemiro, unconcerned with the head chef's emotions, pushed an empty cup into Richard's hand. "Pour another drink."

Richard pulled the spigot and poured the drink into the clean flagon. Casemiro sniffed the liquid and handed the cup to the Captain, who reacted to the odor. The wizard poured the drink down the drain.

The Captain of the Guard beat Casemiro to the next question. "Who received this barrel and when?"

Richard stood tall, exhibited confidence, and defended his crew's innocence once more. "I inspect every item delivered to my kitchen. We received this barrel from the Marquis of Cassen's brewery this morning."

Heenan gasped and added a sarcastic comment. "How interesting."

Casemiro sneered at the counselor. "Please, Heenan. The Marquis owns every commercial brewery in this region of the kingdom, a well-known fact. Anyone else providing the barrel would be the shock. Stop creating unneeded drama, counselor."

Heenan bristled at the wizard's reproach.

The wizard continued, dismissive of the counselor's feelings, and turned his attention towards the door. "Are all entry points, including that door, always locked or latched?"

"We only open this door, which I possess the lone key, to remove barrels and to accept others for delivery. We accepted an order from the brewers this morning. I inventoried and inspected each barrel as it arrived. My crew constantly man's the kitchen, the only other entry or exit point for this room."

The Captain looked back to the kitchen. "Which means witnesses I must question."

Casemiro interrupted. "Chef Richard, thank you for your help. If the Captain agrees, prepare another meal for the Prince and Princess. I wish to speak with the Captain alone."

The Captain of the Guard shook his head in disagreement with the wizard's orders. "Hold on those commands, Richard. I wish to speak with each member of the kitchen crew tonight before dismissal. But after I talk alone with the wizard."

Once the others departed, the wizard started, "I apologize for overstepping, but immediacy took priority over protocol. Besides, your obvious inebriation affects your mind."

The angry captain controlled himself enough to not attack the wizard. "I agree with your summation of my status, and I welcome your insight and help, but you do occupy a spot on the suspect list. You show up and a murder occurs in Veritas Keep."

Casemiro raised his eyebrows but realized the wisdom of the Captain. "Fair point. How do you wish to proceed?"

The Captain let loose his frustration with the wizard. "Do not hinder my investigation. I preside over the delivery of justice in Lillenhold. Am I understood?"

Casemiro gathered the intended message from the Captain. "Yes, sir."

"But I welcome any help you may provide, within reason." The Captain relaxed his guard in front of Casemiro.

"I follow your lead, Captain."

The Captain recited the next steps of the investigation. "We confiscate this barrel and ensure the contents kill no one else. You may examine the cask after we drain the liquid in the morning. And to address your concern about me, this evening's events sobered me up. Now, before I dismiss you, your name?"

"Casemiro. And yours?"

"Gerard." They shook hands before the Captain dismissed Casemiro. "Good night, wizard. You have done enough, and I have a long evening still ahead of me. Sleep well, but do not leave Veritas Keep without my consent."

The Captain walked to the kitchen to conduct the requested interviews with the kitchen staff and left Casemiro standing in the middle of the alcove. The wizard analyzed the room once more for future reference and then walked away. His first day in Lillenhold proved a complete disaster, but Casemiro found a purpose, if only for a fleeting period. He also knew he wouldn't be on the Fierce Siren at dawn.

6

RELATIONSHIPS

Laural followed Arenton up the stairs, regretting the idea of entering her brother's quarters and hoping for a speedy release. The Princess fretted Arenton held a secret compulsion and feared what awaited her in the Prince's personal space. Laural jokingly asked, "You didn't strap a girl to the bed, did you?" In jest or not, she believed anything would be waiting for them in that room.

Arenton stopped on the stairs. "Do you think me a savage? Of course not. Besides, on Sunday, I allow her to visit with her family for the day." The Prince directed a thin smirk toward Laural while communicating the comedic comment.

A hesitant giggle escaped Laural's mouth, though she still feared the comment contained a semblance of truth. "Sorry, the events of this evening muddled my emotions." The Princess directed Arenton up the stairs. Her pride still stinging from the realization that Arenton spent a large amount of funds under the nose of her and King Skaranon.

The siblings reached the top and entered the princely quarters while the guards assumed their posts outside. The sparseness of the room elicited shock from Laural. A picture window of leaded glass on the western wall allowed a view of the distant sunset. The dusky oranges and purples etched into Laural's mind as one of the loveliest views in her memory. The room contained a four-poster white oak bed covered in purple linens with gold-threaded royal crests. Along the southern wall sat a wooden desk accompanied by a lone chair, while a single lantern hung above the piece of furniture for reading. Next to the chair stood an easel holding an in-process painting of the view outside the window. In one corner resided the wood furnace to provide additional heat, and the opposite corner contained an oddly shaped basin covered by a wooden seat.

Laural wandered around the room, taking in the surroundings. "I imagined this room to be full of meaningless junk. I wish to ask so many questions."

"You and Father always underestimate me." The Prince flopped into the upholstered chair with a huff of anger but welcomed the questions. "Anyway, we must wait, so ask your questions." Arenton peered out the window at the remains of the sunset, paying little attention to Laural.

"You paint?" The Princess picked up the paintbrush and studied the image on the canvas.

"I do not. I hired someone to paint the landscape. The piece adds a needed splash of color and symmetry to the room if hung opposite the window." Arenton pointed to the far wall from where he sat to communicate the envisioned design of the room.

Laural pointed to the chair the Prince occupied. "Do you get much use out of this chair and desk?"

"Royal paperwork consumes much of my time. Most of my waking hours involve reading reports on pertinent matters. People do not understand the details I oversee and assume hired staff address those functions. For instance, our father divides the collections from Lillenhold's port between him and Veritas Keep. That situation forced me to reduce the staff and to bring in these carnival acts. We must generate revenue to maintain this old structure."

Laural faced The Prince. For the first time, the Princess viewed Arenton as an adult. "I apologize for still thinking of you as a naïve young man, brother."

"Well, now you realize. Father comprehends my abilities better than most, but still treats me as a child. The King then sends my sister to nursemaid me and monitor my comings and goings. If word reached other kingdoms over our father's reservations, that scandal might tarnish the standing of Gaeleos. Perhaps knaves from within our own kingdom might challenge our father, especially if the potential scandal impacted their financial investment and public stature."

The Princess sensed a scorned child but lacked knowledge for how to best help Arenton. "What can I do?"

"Tell me your impressions of this Casemiro. You fixated on that wizard over the years. Did the old man meet your expectations?" The Prince approached Laural.

"I expected nothing, honestly. His age disappointed me because I assumed wizards never grew old." Laural laughed at the comment and the underlying infatuation revealed to Arenton.

"Wait, did you expect him to arrive pining for you? Oh, sister." The Prince's laugh came across as a mocking tone, another attempt by Arenton to belittle Laural's past failings.

Laural opened her mouth, ready to reply, but snapped it shut, knowing any response revealed the unfulfilled fantasies of a ten-year-old girl. The Prince filled the awkward moment, pushing aside her embarrassment.

"What about his abilities? Casemiro did not defeat a dragon by himself with those limited powers. Do you believe Father fabricated the entire story?"

Laural cast a sideways glance at Arenton for doubting the word of their father. The Princess answered the question and recalled meeting the wizard twenty years before. "I never observed Casemiro do anything but enchant the stone he gave me. Casemiro presented the dragon's corpse and crystallized dragonheart as proof of defeating the beast. Regardless, how did you find him?"

Arenton pulled back with a defensive tone. "I did not find him. In an amazing coincidence, the wizard arrived on a ship and claimed the position we advertised for in certain locales. Imagine my amazement when Forrest introduced us."

Laural caught her brother in a lie. His voice revealed something about how Casemiro found his way to Lillenhold. Calling out the Prince posed a significant risk. Even in these comfortable confines, the Princess refused to confront Arenton's untruthfulness. Besides, the responsibility of defending the wizard did not lie with her.

She asked a more personal question of the Prince. "Why do you still hold my past over me?" Laural's eyes opened to their full circumference as she fully exposed her weakness. The pain to her soul from the constant reminders and diminishment of her importance ached grievously, and that being done to her by her own brother hurt even more.

Arenton, rifling through papers on his desk, stopped and

turned. "I will not forgive this error of judgment. You created a scandal for our family, the crown, and our kingdom by your rash actions. Luckily, wearing red became your only penance. I tire of these topics. Either ask a more curious question or sit in silence until they release us."

The Princess turned her back, ignoring the comment, and composed herself in front of the Prince. Her love for her brother mounted a vigorous defense against the other thoughts and fears taking over her mind. Laural feared something occurred within the young man, but Arenton kept the Princess at a distance and prevented her from knowing the genuine problem or how to help him resolve the issue.

With her spirit squashed by the boorish behavior of Arenton, Laural relented and remained quiet. Moments passed until the Princess asked another question to crack through the icy wall between the siblings. "What is the basin in the corner?"

Arenton laughed. "The fancy chamber pot? I relieve myself and, when finished, pull on the cord above to dispel the waste through a pipe and into... Well, I fail to understand where the evidence goes from that point, but I assume the waste runs into the other drains departing Veritas Keep and towards the port. I doubt such a device will gain popularity. Although isolating the device from the rest of the room might work."

Laural chuckled at the device while enjoying the Prince acting as he did when they were children, if only briefly. "Arenton, why don't we ever chat as we did in our childhood?"

The Prince turned back toward Laural. "Because we are not children, Laural. I must apologize for my flippant comment regarding Geoffrey earlier this evening. I acknowledge my error, and I will give his family the same funding as others who lost their lives serving the crown. He saved me from being poisoned and deserves the kingdom's respect."

Laural shook her head in agreement. "Very honorable of you, Arenton."

"Thank you, sister. But to be honest, I am famished. Do you think food might arrive soon?"

Forrest and Oleander walked from the hall and continued walking toward the main gate of Veritas Keep. He took in the downhill view of the village and the bay further in the background reflecting the purples and oranges of the dusk-laden sunset. The troll-man forgot the woman until she called to him.

Oleander remained under the lentil of the keep's entrance. "What are you doing?"

"Escorting you back to the village. Why stop here?"

Oleander sprouted a smile. "Wait and find out."

The sounds of clopping hooves announced their arrival before the horses became visible. Around the corner of the keep appeared a carriage pulled by two Ardennais stallions decorated with tasseled coverings. A single guardsman guided the horses from the front row of seats. The carriage stopped at the entrance to Veritas Keep and the guardsman stepped down to help Oleander board.

The wooden carriage featured painted filagree in gold on the white body. The spoked six-foot wide wheels supported the heavy frame of the three rows of seating. A small canopy covered the third row to protect the seats from rain or sun, neither of which presented a problem now. A lone lantern hung from a shepherd's crook next to the driver's spot on the carriage.

Forrest planted himself in the seat beside Oleander. "Did you request a ride?"

The woman giggled in response to the question. "Of course not. A carriage always returns me to the village, an act of kindness from the Prince towards me. And why refuse?"

"This happens often?"

Oleander's toothy smile preceded her reply. "Yes, we enjoy each other's company." She turned her attention to the driver. "Take me home."

Forrest's aspirations pertaining to Oleander deflated with the one sentence. The troll-man accepted his position beneath the Prince in every way possible within Oleander's mind. Part of Forrest wished to jump from the vehicle, but to create a scene might draw too much attention to his secret desires. Instead, he withdrew from the conversation and sat quietly, allowing the cooler night air to wash over him.

With little room to spare, the buggy exited through the narrow gates of the keep. After a moment, Forrest attempted to begin a conversation. Oleander silenced Forrest at each point when he dared to talk, driving the troll-man's spirit even further into submission. The ride remained silent until the twosome reached the flower shop and the guardsman helped Oleander from the vehicle.

Forrest escaped the wagon by hopping over the other side and then joined Oleander in front of the shop as the carriage left them behind.

Oleander opened the door to the flower shop and Forrest attempted to walk in first. He brushed beside her. "What are you doing?" asked the woman.

"I wish to ensure no one hides inside. The events of this evening raised my precautionary nature to a sense of paranoia. Excuse me if I overreacted." Forrest wondered why Oleander rejected his protection.

Oleander flashed a smirk. "Forrest, though appreciated, your effort proves unnecessary. No one concerns themselves with a lonely florist in a small seaside village."

"I concern myself greatly with your well-being. Did the incident at Veritas Keep not upset you? Witnessing Geoffrey's death must be troubling unless God made your soul from heartier material than mine."

Oleander opened the door entirely and stepped halfway inside. "Yes, the young man's death disheartened me, but after a nice blend of Bergamot tea and a night's worth of sleep the event will be forgotten. My mind will allow the events of this evening to drift away as I wake with a rested spirit. Thank you for accompanying me home. I appreciate your misplaced concern. Good night."

The troll-man asked another question before Oleander closed the door. "I thought you wished for me to remove a compost barrel."

The woman paused; a flash of apprehension crossed her face before a ready smile grew over it. Oleander gripped Forrest's forearm and gave a gentle squeeze. "I hired someone to take care of the barrel a couple of days ago. No worries, your assistance may be required in the future. Good night, Forrest." She shut the door and left the troll-man alone at the entrance to the store.

Forrest fixated on the caress of her hand on his arm, trying to understand any message Oleander attempted to convey to him through the motion. The touch provided enough provocation to his heart to wash away the remainder of the evening. His infatuation with Oleander clung to the physical connection and colored the rest of Forrest's thoughts to a near state of worship of the woman.

Forrest returned to the moment and scanned the porch to find where the barrel stood. A ruddy brown ring polluted the wooden landing, remains from the moisture leaking out the barrel.

The troll-man turned and headed further into the village, toward his home. But the jubilance of Oleander's hand upon his skin clouded his judgement, and Forrest diverted his path to The Pub for a late evening drink.

7

THE DAY AFTER

The sunlight blazed across the rippling waters of the sea, producing white shards of light beyond the village of Lillenhold. Casemiro leaned against the fieldstone structure of Veritas Keep, watching the breeze whip the countless number of blue flags and yellow pennants in a natural rhythm, with his staff lying on the ground beside him. The sea air, more salty and less fishy this morning, filled the wizard's lungs. Casemiro witnessed the Fierce Siren pull away from port and the wizard waved goodbye to Quinto.

Fare thee well, brother.

The wizard's fingers worked away at a knitting project, occupying the time until the scarred boy arrived. The wizard wore the traditional gray cloak, including the chain belt, to mark the return to duty and eliminating the pomp of the prior evening. Once he absorbed the view, Casemiro spotted the boy and returned the needles and yarn to his hidden breast pocket. The wizard cinched the frayed and holey coat tighter around his torso to fend off the morning chill.

With a smile, the boy approached. "Good morning, sir."

From another pocket, Casemiro produced an apple and a clean knife he nicked from the kitchen the previous night. "You are polite for an urchin. Before starting, name and age because I no longer trust unfamiliar people." The wizard peeled the fruit while waiting for the boy's response.

"Roman, sir, and I am fourteen. Did you wish to hire me for wizard's work? Or to be your apprentice?"

A robust laugh boomed from the old man's core. "I have no clue what you mean by wizard's work, and I sure as shit don't want an apprentice." Casemiro leaned down to be the boy's height. "You are aware of the murder?"

The boy nodded his head. "Captain Gerard cleared up the situation last night in our interview."

"I need a pair of ears and eyes in the keep. Can you supply what I require, Roman?" Casemiro stood to his full height and peeled the apple; watching the boy contemplate the question.

"Assuming you pay a denomination worth more than a wizard's blessing, I can." A quick smirk of confidence shifted across the face of the child. "Those skills do not come for free, sir."

Casemiro appreciated the sardonic wit, reached into his pocket, and pulled out two items. "I offer you a gold piece every week. A silver piece serving as a down payment, along with this other apple." The wizard offered both components with his free hand.

Roman's eyes bulged as he reached for the food and the coin. Before grabbing the items, Casemiro pulled them away.

The wizard smiled, knowing he now owned the boy's devotion. "One additional directive, because you may need to divulge information when I may not be near. Do you wish to witness some magic?"

The boy nodded and projected an eager smile at the wizard.

Casemiro kneeled. "Take the apple." The wizard tossed the fruit, and the boy caught it, then bit into the flesh to mark his property. "Now feast your eyes on this." The wizard pulled out another silver coin and held the two coins together between the thumb and forefinger of his right hand. "Once I use this spell, the coins will be eternally connected. To relay any information, speak into your coin. As a result, mine will pulse with energy and grow warm. If I ever need you, the process works both ways. Understand?"

The idea of a magical coin transfixed the boy, and Roman nodded his acceptance of the concept.

The wizard held the coins near his mouth and whispered one word. "Cyfun."

Heat pulsed through the wizard's finger and thumb and caused the coins to whiten and then cool within seconds. "The conjoining requires a bit of elemental magic and a sacrifice of flesh." Casemiro showed the burn marks on his thumb and finger. "Do not fret, because I heal faster than most. Here you go." The wizard plunked one coin into the boy's bony hand. "Let's test the coins later today. Pay attention in the kitchen and tell me anything you find regarding the murder. Clear?"

Roman smiled and pocketed the coin as the boy chomped another bite from the apple. "Thank you, sir. I will contact you after the lunch shift, or tomorrow, if the coin doesn't work."

Casemiro nodded and leaned back against the stony structure of the keep. "I like the plan. Now report to your shift before the head chef ends your employment and you become worthless to me."

The wizard finished peeling the remaining apple and ate to the sounds of the distant seagulls. The sun disappeared behind the clouds and projected another ugly day. Casemiro gazed at the distant summit beyond Veritas Keep. The snowcap glistened in the early morning light and the flash from a reflection blinded the wizard for a second. Trees leading east from the mountain rolled in oceanlike waves from a breeze. Casemiro recognized the signs of a hunt, knowing the prey wouldn't like the outcome.

"Hungry after a long night's sleep?" The wizard speculated on what lived on the mountain. A portion of Casemiro feared his guess might be correct, and a wrong from his past needed rectified.

The wizard turned back towards the village, and Casemiro spotted Forrest walking up the hill. The troll-man's arrival reminded the wizard of Geoffrey's death and the inept idea of the Prince to entertain the masses of Lillenhold.

Forrest almost passed the wizard without saying a word. The troll-man's black pants covered the tops of his black leather boots. The thick wool shirt resembled a horse's blanket and loosely hung over the body of the troll-man. Forrest's hair suffered through a night of fitful sleep and jolted from his head in multiple directions.

Casemiro picked up the staff and walked to meet Forrest. "Did the dead body traumatize Oleander? If so, I hope the lady recovered."

Forrest halted as chagrin riddled his face. "Oleander informed me a stiff drink of tea would aid her sleep as she bid me goodnight. This morning, she refused to answer her door when I checked on her. Anything else you wish to ask about the lady Oleander, wizard?"

Casemiro chose grace instead of agitation for this early in the day, sensing a deeper cause drove Forrest's cantankerous nature. "I wish to apologize for my defensiveness yesterday and chalk the nervousness up to being an old wizard in unfamiliar terrain. I do not wish to be on your bad side."

Forrest faced the wizard with shock. "My opinions interest you? Considering that, I apologize for my gruffness."

The comment elicited laughter from the wizard, and Casemiro disposed of the apple core. "Very well, let's enter the keep and confront the idiocy of the Prince's plan together."

Casemiro and Forrest walked into the cavernous auditorium and found others waiting. Captain Gerard, Princess Laural, Heenan, and the Prince stood in a semi-circle near where Geoffrey's body rested the prior night. The group glared at the duo as if the newcomers represented the deceased soldier's ghost returning to haunt them. The wizard's eye gravitated toward the outrageous purple robe and bulbous hat the Prince wore.

Then Casemiro evaluated Laural's outfit featuring flowing blue sleeves and a red band to form a conservative neckline. A matching blue skirt ran straight to the ground, instead of bulging like the fashionable hoop skirts worn by so many of the royal sect.

The Prince shifted a smile across his face and welcomed the twosome. The absurdity of the Prince's outfit kept the wizard's attention as he talked. "About time, you two. We have much to do today. Unfortunately, we must confront the aftermath of last night's wretched affair. Captain Gerard shall speak before we move to the events planned for the day."

Casemiro took note of Gerard wearing freshly polished armor, turkey and all. *Does the man live in that gear?*

The Captain began his rundown. "Thank you, Your Highness. One of our guards already walks the grounds, searching for clues. Also, we drained the barrel from last evening. If the wizard wishes to inspect the container at the meeting's completion..." Gerard stared at Casemiro, hoping the open-ended comment drew a response from the wizard.

Casemiro indicated his cooperation on the task by a nod of his head.

Gerard turned to the Princess. "I may need to reach the brewer in Cassenwary, which may require a personal visit and help to avoid certain obstacles. So, I wondered if you may assist?"

Princess Laural replied, "Do not worry about me performing my duty to the crown if called upon, Captain. I will secure such a visit if required."

Gerard bowed in acknowledgment of Laural's acceptance. "Last evening, I conducted the interviews with the kitchen staff. This morning, I plan to interview those who worked during the day and communicate any findings to the Prince later." The Captain shot a glance at Casemiro to declare his intent to share the findings with the wizard as well.

Casemiro seemed impressed by the Captain recovering from his drunken display of the prior evening in solid fashion. *Perhaps he sustained a one-time lapse in judgement.*

Casemiro sensed a chance to ask about his primary concern. "Where did the body go? Are we pretending the murder did not happen for the Extravaganza?"

The Captain answered in a manner indicating the inquiry offended his honor. "As per our protocol, a healer examines the corpse to verify Geoffrey didn't fall prey to some other malicious event. We wish to rule out any other theories. Does that suffice, wizard?"

"I defer to your process, Captain. Please inform me of the healer's determination when you receive the results." Casemiro absorbed the chastisement for his out-of-line question and shifted behind the others in the group.

The Captain nodded and allowed the Prince to take center stage. A distracted Arenton motioned for his counselor, Heenan, to speak on his behalf.

Eager to express himself, Heenan accepted and addressed the group. "We wish today began on a brighter note, but the Extravaganza proceeds as planned. We wish to dedicate the event to honor the fallen soldier and rename the event the Sir Geoffrey Memorial Extravaganza and plan to allocate a portion of the first night's earnings to the family. We hope this news drives the people from the village to supply donations, since the admission price is free for the first evening. Our Lord's kindness awes me." Heenan allowed the people time to applaud and convey their appreciation of the gesture.

After the customary pause, Heenan wasted no time continuing and prevented anyone else from taking the stage. "Once the contestants for the Extravaganza arrive, we wish to set up the facility and determine the tournament's first-round draw. We will clarify the roles of the wizard Casemiro, Forrest, and Lady Oleander at that meeting as well. Any questions?"

"Any suggestions on how I collaborate with the Captain and take part in the Extravaganza?" Casemiro asked.

The Prince replied. "Just accomplish both, wizard. How you accomplish those tasks falls on you, but I suggest you work through those details today. The Captain of the Guard requested your help, and you will receive a counselor's wage on top of the money from the Extravaganza, a silver coin every other day on top of what we compensate you for the event."

Casemiro bowed with faked sincerity. "Thank you for your generosity, Prince Arenton."

Heenan continued without further questions. "You may do as you wish for the rest of the morning. We meet at dinner to discuss the Extravaganza and the Prince dismisses you until then."

The group dispersed, and a hand grabbed Casemiro's shoulder. The wizard found the Princess behind him, and he stopped a comely smile from creeping across his countenance.

"A minute, Casemiro?"

The wizard guessed at what Laural wished to discuss. "Did you suggest the Prince hire me as a counselor to the Captain?"

The Princess stood upright and defended herself. "When I grabbed your coin purse, it seemed a little..." Laural contemplated the correct word and finished the sentence. "...light. Could this provide a needed source of funds for you?"

Casemiro became defensive at the insinuation of his poverty. "Princess, I assure you, my coin purse is anything but light. Do I appear to require your help or anyone else's?" The wizard crossed his arms the way wizards do to intimidate others and pounded the staff on the stone floor.

Laural's royal training became evident as the Princess stood to her full height to counter the wizard's attempt at shutting her down. "Excuse me, but your tone may require a whipping."

Casemiro smiled in a coy manner. "Would you like that, Princess?" The wizard regretted the words once he said them. Fortunately, a warm tingle in his breast pocket from the conjured silver piece grabbed Casemiro's attention. This provided the perfect escape from this unfortunate contest of trading barbs.

Laural tensed her shoulders as anger flashed across her face and her countenance turned to fuchsia. "Well, I never—" The woman's temperature approached the point of combustion.

CHRISTOPHER CLOUSER

Leaving the Princess fuming, Casemiro stepped aside and pulled the coin out of the purse. The wizard spoke in a soft voice. "What news do you bring, Roman?"

"Sir, I found something odd near the trash barrels behind the keep. I can show you if you wish to meet me."

"I understand and will arrive soon." After returning the coin, Casemiro found the Captain in the auditorium and yelled in Gerard's direction. "Captain, I think a clue worth investigating requires your attention."

The Captain nodded and walked toward the wizard, intercepting Laural's approach to continue the prior conversation.

The wizard grimaced, knowing he stepped over an imaginary line in the previous discourse. "Princess, a pressing matter pertaining to the investigation requires the attention of me and Captain Gerard. I will meet you here upon completing the task, if you do not mind."

The Princess allowed a level head to prevail and waved, as if to push them along. "If this distraction concerns the investigation, then proceed. I can wait for an apology."

Captain Gerard and Casemiro walked from the keep. "What's the quickest route to the trash barrels behind the building?" inquired the wizard. "And away from the Princess?"

Gerard grabbed the wizard's arm. "Follow me. Circling the building requires less time than navigating through the hallways and unlocking doors. And the Princess will not follow us outside in her outfit." The duo raced outside Veritas Keep in search of what may prove to be the next clue in their investigation.

8

BARRELS

Casemiro and Gerard, the Captain of the Guard, traipsed around the exterior of Veritas Keep avoiding the chaos inside. The duo found the trash barrels behind the primary structure of the keep. Seagulls filled the sky as they scavenged for their first meal of the day and squawked warnings for potential rivals to stay away. Casemiro and Gerard avoided the birds and found Roman, the scarred boy, shifting from one foot to the other near the two metal drums.

The foul odor from the barrels intensified as the two men approached, and the rats appeared. Casemiro shivered at the sight of the first one and he stopped walking when the second showed its face. The aroma and vermin signaled that someone needed to burn the waste inside the drums to prevent a bout of disease rising from the refuse.

Casemiro asked from a distance, "What did you find?"

Roman fidgeted as he replied. "Chef Richard will fire me if I don't return to my station soon."

Captain Gerard ambled up and placed an armored hand on the lad's shoulder. "Let me deal with Richard. Show us what you found."

Roman strode behind the two drums to reveal an undisturbed wooden barrel. "I uncovered this when I brought out the trash from the morning's prep work and relayed the situation to the wizard. I attempted to move the wooden cask, but the weight proved too much for me."

The boy received a soft pat on the shoulder and a grin from the wizard. "Good job, son. The Captain and I will oversee the job from this point. Join me tomorrow for your compensation."

Roman smiled enough to almost hide the scar in the folds of his cheek. "Thank you, sir."

Casemiro waited for the boy to run through the keep's unguarded back door, a different entrance from the one shown to the investigators by Chef Richard the prior evening. The wizard and captain examined the barrel and discovered the Cassenwary brewery's brand on one end and a red wax seal covering the cork protruding from the bilge.

"Captain, did the barrel from last night carry a brand on either end?" The wizard waited for his contemporary's answer, despite already knowing the response.

Captain Gerard rubbed his chin as he contemplated the question. "I don't recall seeing one in my inhibited state or when we drained the barrel this morning. I will check that later."

Seeking fresh air, the wizard turned away and inhaled. "Also, verify the brand on the other barrels received from the brewer. This barrel provided both a clue and an answer."

"An answer to what?"

Casemiro smirked and peered towards the wooden door. "Our investigation into how the poisoned barrel ended up in Veritas Keep."

The wizard led the captain away from the stench-filled trash drums to a more suitable location for their conversation. The wizard stopped fifty yards away from the investigation site. "The stench proved too strong for my weak constitution."

"No apologies necessary, as my belly almost turned sour."

Casemiro pointed to the unguarded door Roman used. "Is this entrance to the keep always unguarded?"

The Captain peered at the wooden door. "Oh, this door remains unguarded because the staff use it to run their trash and scraps to these drums. The risk seems insignificant due to personnel always manning the kitchen." Upon saying the words, Gerard realized the problem.

The Captain asked another question with the twitch of his thick mustache. "How did the culprit switch the poisoned barrel with the Cassenwary one and then smuggle the genuine barrel out of the keep with no one seeing?"

"I suppose your interviews this morning can center on that part of the investigation."

Gerard nodded his agreement to the proclamation from Casemiro, now following the wizard's thought process.

Casemiro peered across the grounds and down the hill toward Lillenhold, pondering the morning's clues. The wizard decided where to take his portion of the investigation. "I think that little mystery is enough to occupy us for the day, Captain."

The Captain raised a question. "Do you wish to conduct a test on this barrel for poison as well?"

"I wager no contaminants exist in the ones branded and sealed. Knowing the Cassenwary brewer brands their barrels leads me to believe someone substituted a single poisoned vessel for this one."

Gerard nodded in agreement. "Yes, which means…" The Captain paused, unsure of what to say to complete the open-ended comment.

"We may remove the Marquis of Cassen from the suspect list." The wizard smiled and motioned a hand to lead the Captain of the Guard to the next conclusion.

Gerard took the hint. "Oh yes, now my job becomes simpler once more, and the news may relieve the Prince to learn his uncle did not attempt to assassinate him."

Casemiro delayed, expecting the Captain to reach the subsequent link in the chain of logical thought. After receiving no response, the wizard provided the next logical conclusion. "A person from Lillenhold switched the barrels and someone in the village attempted to kill Prince Arenton. Captain, we must locate an individual with the necessary access to Veritas Keep who can exchange barrels with no second guessing from the kitchen staff."

Gerard jumped to the next conclusion without additional aid. "Then we must ensure everyone stays in the village. We must post guards on the roads to prevent anyone from traveling out of the village. All this while questioning the kitchen staff and evaluating the various barrels. A busy day indeed." The Captain's excitement brimmed to the edge of his proverbial tankard.

"Do not let me stop you. Keep me abreast of your findings from the questioning of the staff. We can connect later and compare notes prior to meeting the Prince. I shall inspect any suspect barrels later today."

The Captain of the Guard acknowledged the wizard with a smile and a nod. "Thank you for the assistance. Let's meet mid-afternoon." The armored man departed to begin his day's work.

Casemiro remembered the promise to resume a discussion with Princess Laural in the keep's hall and begrudgingly upheld his word. The old man walked around the stone structure, processing events until he reached the front of the building and found the Princess waiting.

Laural leaned against the entrance to Veritas Keep. "I wondered if you forgot."

"No, but I must ask you to either walk with me, or we meet for lunch to continue our discussion. An unexpected errand requires my attention."

The Princess raised an eyebrow. "What sort of errand?"

"I need to visit the village's cooper."

Casemiro and the Princess set out from the safe confines of Veritas Keep and ventured down the hill toward Lillenhold. The wizard summarized the morning's events to Laural, including the cask by the refuse drums and his losing any appetite from the stench. Once the discussion bored the wizard, Casemiro changed the subject to one concerning him.

The peculiarity of Laural's fascination piqued the wizard's curiosity. Casemiro considered the reasons and potential explanations throughout the night and morning but failed to forge them into a logical explanation; leaving him no other way to proceed except asking the Princess directly. "Laural, what is your interest in me? You appear preoccupied with my comings and goings since my arrival."

The Princess continued her moderate pace toward the village to keep in step with Casemiro. Laural, not in a hurry to reply, swiped a strand of wind-blown hair from her face before breaking the serenity of the seaside noises. "Why did you, a renowned wizard, disappear for two decades and return now? What happened to you, Casemiro? What aren't you telling me? And why did you fail to honor your word from twenty years ago?"

The wizard guffawed before realizing the seriousness of the Princess. "Renowned, hardly. But did you follow my journeys for the last two decades? What if I bound myself to another, more consequential oath? And, if I may be so bold, why does my past concern you so?"

The Princess simpered back at Casemiro. "What if I classified withholding information as lies of omission? Also, your presence coincides with the first attempt on my brother's life, which warrants my concern."

The wizard bristled at the subtle besmirching of his honor but gave the Princess grace because of the attempt on Prince Arenton's life; believing an unstated motivation drove Laural's comments. "What you consider lies, I deem unspoken truths. If you can provide adequate reason for me to divulge the information, then I will reveal what you must know. I extend an olive branch because of my guilt for not returning in twenty years. Not because you wish for my openness, Princess."

I pledged my service to you. I atoned for not responding to your pleas. What more do you desire?

The Princess stopped on the path. "Casemiro, does my concern surprise you? You remain the second most significant man in my life, even after twenty years. Such influence places a substantial burden on you and an even greater one on my heart."

Casemiro, aware of the implied insult to Laural if he continued walking, succumbed to her aim of discussing these unspoken truths here and now. Against his better judgment, the wizard faced the Princess, squinting in the mid-morning sun.

In the distance, a shadow moved across the peak of Mount Siven and vanished. Casemiro turned towards Mount Siven again, drawn to the uneasiness the peak generated in his gut and expecting the unfinished business to rear its ugly head and force itself into his life once more.

Casemiro returned his gaze to Laural. "My lady, I will share what is necessary, but more pressing priorities require my presence at the cooper's shop. We need to find out who tried to kill Prince Arenton."

Laural focused on where their priorities rested and gave up the pretense of using her royal standing as ammunition against the wizard. "Fair enough, for now." She saved face by handling the situation discreetly in front of the growing number of faces in the streets of Lillenhold.

Laural moved away from the topic. "I caught you staring at Mount Siven just now, as if it holds a story to be revealed."

Casemiro avoided telling Laural another truth. "Recalling old tales of settlers watching from the cave atop the mountain for enemies. We need to keep moving."

Upon entering the village proper, the duo turned left at the major crossroad. On one corner, Oleander attended to the flowers outside her shop and waved towards the Princess and wizard as they passed. Other villagers bustled through the streets conducting the day's business. The pair continued down the street, passing two other shops before ending their journey at the barn-like building marked by a simple sign reading "COOPER" for everyone to read.

Casemiro breathed deeply and released the tension from the prior exchange. The wizard drew attention to something other than himself. "The village carries a better aroma today, and I catch the hints of charred meat and baked bread in the air."

"The fishermen have not returned to unload their haul yet. Once they bring in their nets, the entire village reeks of fish for hours. I believe the aromas you smell emanate from the

Cornelius Inn. Perhaps we will eat lunch at their restaurant."

"If the food matches the scent, lead the way."

"Then we shall eat at the Cornelius for lunch today, my treat. You might find the story of the restaurant's history interesting."

"I salivate at the idea of a fine meal after we chase down this first clue. Let's focus on the reason for our visit."

Casemiro and Laural walked into a spacious barn and encountered a cacophony of assaults on their senses. The scent of burned wood flowed through their nostrils upon entry. On one side of the building sat woodworking tools and ample workbenches, shining metal blades, and wood shavings across the floor. Along the other wall, metalworking tools sat near a small forge that generated enough heat to warm the entire barn. Steam filled the air as a long piece of metal sat in a water bucket to cool. The dirt floor, littered with piles of scrap wood and shards of discarded metal, appeared to be unkept.

The new arrivals caught the attention of a man hunched over a barrel. The cooper's face greeted them with a smile, though blackened across the forehead while beads of sweat dripped down his cheeks from an arduous morning.

Unaware of the identity of his guests from poor lighting, the man abandoned his work on the wooden cask and greeted them. "How can I help you folks?" Upon reaching the duo, the man realized he stood in the presence of Princess Laural. "Sorry, my lady. I did not recognize you from the lack of light."

"I take no offense. Your name?"

"Oh, Angus, my lady. Angus, the cooper. The cloaked person must be the wizard everyone in town keeps discussing."

Casemiro nodded, trying to hide his embarrassment at being the subject of public gossip. "Yes, nice to meet you. Sorry to bother you, Angus, but we have questions regarding barrels. Did we interrupt something of import?"

The cooper turned and pointed. "Only my attempt at a *mise en rose*, me trying to put a barrel together. I can do that job later. What do you desire to learn about my craft? If you are buying, I sell four sizes: the tun, a puncheon, a barrel, and a rundlet. Tell me the purpose of the cask and I can narrow the possibilities down."

The Princess waved her hand to disarm any concerns of the man. "We are not interested in buying but conducting research. Of those sizes, which is most useful to transport mead?"

The cooper ambled over to a wall towards the excess barrel scraps. "Well, the tun is best for grain, so ignore it. Brewers in the area use puncheon or barrel-sized casks." Angus smiled back at the Princess, eager for the next reason to talk in Laural's presence.

The Princess glanced at Casemiro, wanting his approval to proceed with the questioning. "Do you know the size used by the brewery in Cassenwary?"

Angus banged his hand on the top of the puncheon. "They use this size over in Cassenwary. Though a splendid fellow, the cooper in Cassen does something odd by sealing the bung with wax."

Casemiro asked with a raised eyebrow, "The bung?"

The cooper laughed at the wizard's ignorance. "Trade jargon; a bung is a cork stopper pressed into the barrel's widest part, the bilge. If they build the barrel right, the wax is unneeded, but they seal their barrels with wax to appear flashy. So, do you wish to purchase a puncheon?"

Casemiro reached into his coin purse and plunked a gold piece on the counter. "No, we desire a list of the customers you sold this size of barrel to in the last six months, if possible."

Angus regarded the coin and shot a glance towards the Princess to ensure the money belonged to the wizard. Laural nodded, and the cooper picked up the coin, admiring the gold for a second before pocketing the piece and turning to a desk hidden in the corner. "Lucky for you, I keep the best records of any business in the village, apart from Oleander's flower shop. I obey village laws as a precaution against audits." Angus winked at the Princess.

The wizard understood what the cooper intended by his action but grew unsure as to why the flirtation bothered him. "Then I suppose you can provide a copy for us?"

"You only needed to ask because having the privilege of the Princess visiting my shop pays for the deed. But I thank you for the contribution." The man grinned as if he outsmarted Casemiro by obtaining the gold piece. Angus completed a client list for the past six months in a matter of minutes.

The wizard received the paper from Angus and nodded his appreciation. "You require any other help today?"

Laural smiled at the cooper. "Thank you for your kindness, and I will pass along your name to the Prince for the off-chance Veritas Keep requires a barrel to be produced."

Angus blushed, knowing a kind word from the royal family guaranteed a period of prosperity. The cooper kneeled and bowed his head to the Princess. "Thank you, my lady."

The duo left the establishment and Casemiro placed the list in his pocket.

The Princess asked, "Did you get what you needed? Anything interesting on the list?"

"We'll check out the information over lunch." Casemiro turned to the Princess. "By the way, add that coin to my bill for the Prince. My appetite returned, and you promised a visit to the

Cornelius Inn at the expense of the crown." The wizard extended his arm in a gentlemanly manner.

The Princess placed her arm through the opening at the bend in Casemiro's elbow. Arm in arm, they strolled through Lillenhold's streets, catching the eyes of every resident of the village.

9

THE CIRCUS ARRIVES

The Cornelius Inn marked the eastern end of the village and the furthest point from the port. The Inn overlooked the rugged coastline leading out to the Bay of Scars. A panoramic vista of the shoreline continued along a sandy bar until the water wrapped around a peninsula marking the edge of Lillenhold's reach. A grove of trees bordered the pristine view that extended into the sea to the point and obscured everything beyond from the village's curious eyes.

The Cornelius Inn became renowned for three things in the village. The building's beauty spanned up three floors of the immaculately maintained structure. A white façade adorned the three floors, befitting the pure intentions of the building's original owner. The first floor housed the local healer's office. The second floor claimed the village's best restaurant and reason number two for the Cornelius Inn's fame. But what occurred on the third floor provided the wealth for the Cornelius Inn's current owner and sustained the building's auspicious reputation. No one dared to state, or question, the supposed illegal activities which created wide-reaching ripples across the community.

Without a care towards any of this, Casemiro shoveled the last bite of food into his mouth, followed by a contented smile. A meal of a breaded chicken cutlet accompanied by mashed potatoes covered in white gravy and a side of apple cobbler warmed the wizard's gut. A sensation not familiar to him since… The wizard banished the memory and returned his focus to Princess Laural sitting across the table. "As advertised. Thank you for the excellent meal."

Laural wiped her lips with the serviette, a novelty the wizard became familiar with during the meal. "Glad you approved. Nothing beats their food, not even Chef Richard at Veritas Keep."

Casemiro gave a cheeky smile towards the Princess. "You avoid the other renowned delicacies of the Cornelius?" The inappropriateness of the question hit the wizard once the words left his mouth, and he blushed pink. *Why did I say that?*

"We'll avoid the third floor. At least today." The Princess winked at Casemiro but contorted her face to indicate Laural regretted the flirtatious comment.

Egad! Now she's doing it as well.

A moment of awkwardness filled the space between them until the wizard allowed for a hesitant smile at the shared joke, hoping to eliminate the newfound tension. Casemiro noted the four other couples eating quietly in the dining room. Each duo appeared beyond middle-aged and shared a sense of propriety in their attire and manners; oblivious to the activities taking place ten feet above their heads.

The atmosphere of the restaurant presented a pristine and charming ambiance. The flawless wooden floor and ten small round tables, each flanked by four white chairs, occupied the room. Oak panels lined the interior wall to cover holes and prevent unwanted drafts in the winter. The corner fireplace heated the room and emitted a campfire scent to complete the presentation of a temporary respite from the realities of Lillenhold. The view enraptured Casemiro at one time during the meal as the heaving waves beyond the picture window pelted the sand, as if the moans of the ocean beckoned the wizard home.

Laural returned their focus to the events of the morning. "Let's discuss the list." The Princess moved to sit beside Casemiro, drawing attention from the other diners with a loud scrape from her chair sliding across the wooden floor. Also, sitting next to a man not at least engaged to the woman, especially a wizard in a worn gray cloak, appeared too bold, even for a member of the royal family.

Casemiro paused as he absorbed the reactions: one woman held her hand to her mouth aghast at the scene and a man grumbled a low-toned "Well, I never" at the couple.

Laural patted the wizard's shoulder and pushed for the conversation through the public judgment. "Ignore those people and show me the paper. Just a bunch of legalistic old-timers."

The wizard put the list on the table, moving his plate aside to clear the space. The couple perused the list of people and businesses Angus supplied for his transactions over the last six months.

Laural provided commentary and the proper context on each name for the wizard to understand their involvement with the cooper. "Not surprised at Veritas Keep being the top client. Chef Richard uses barrels for various activities, including storing drinks in the basement. The first four names are farmers on the outskirts of the village and they more than likely store grain. Forrest and Oleander being on the client list surprises me."

Casemiro sat back in his sturdy wooden chair. "Do Forrest and Oleander need barrels?"

"Oleander may use one to store soil for her plants, but there could be other uses unfamiliar to me. On Forrest, no clue. Let's ask them the next time we meet."

The wizard grabbed the list and put it in his hidden pocket, grazing the knitting needles as he did so. "We? I collaborate with the Captain of the Guard. You're a tagalong. Besides, your involvement may not be the best idea, considering the number of suspects at this point." Casemiro fixed his glare on the Princess.

Laural understood the hidden meaning of the wizard's comment. "You cannot think I attempted to kill my brother." Her face flushed a bright color of magenta and contorted to reveal her anger.

"Technically, half-brother. Many times, throughout history, a royal family member attempted to eliminate relatives to wear the crown. As strong a motive as anything else."

The Princess slapped the old man. "How dare you?"

The strike's noise caught the diners' attention, eliciting a gasp from a woman.

Casemiro rose from the table, cinched his chain belt, and walked toward the exit. Only the loud thump of his staff broke the reticent hush in the room. The wizard refused to be embarrassed but refrained from revealing any disgust to avoid committing an unsettling act in public. Casemiro continued walking until he reached the outside of the building and waited for the Princess as his anger seethed.

The Princess emerged from the building mere seconds after the wizard. She appeared breathless from the chase and pleaded with him. "I apologize, Casemiro. I overreacted." Laural grabbed his arm as she seemed to beg for his forgiveness.

The wizard turned, a blaze in his eyes, and flailed his arm to remove Laural's hand as she nearly groveled in front of him. Casemiro's pity for the woman's mistake allowed his rage to pass away. "Do not touch me again. At one time, you would have been a puddle of melted flesh. Be thankful, Princess, those days passed me by long ago."

Laural pulled herself upright, refusing to raise her gaze from the ground and crossed her arms in front of her chest, hiding her humiliation. The Princess reached into a pocket and pulled out a gold piece. "Here, this is what I owe you for the cooper's shop."

The wizard grabbed the coin and put it away before he expelled a deep breath and calmed himself.

The Princess stood in the street, on the verge of tears.

Casemiro weighed the proper response in his mind. Part of the wizard still believed humiliation presented the best option for the Princess. Another part desired to reach out and console Laural, accept her apology, and move on, if for no other reason than to save her public embarrassment. The practical side of Casemiro prevailed in a compromise.

"Apology accepted, Princess."

Laural raised her head. "Thank you. I shall return to Veritas Keep now and leave you to your investigation. I wish not to hamper you any longer, Casemiro."

Laural walked away and Casemiro's emotions overwhelmed his practical nature. The wizard reexamined his motivations for the morning's activities and became remorseful. He understood another inclination prompted him to accept the woman's company this morning. An irritation inside his heart beckoned the old man to call for her to stop. "Princess, wait for me."

A smile etched itself across Laural's face inch by inch to create a sculpted masterpiece. "I appreciate the gesture and you not making this worse for me."

The wizard remembered his dead wife, Chantal, always said the right words to others. Life presented Casemiro an opportunity to comfort Laural. "If held to an impossible standard, then none of us succeed, Princess. Even me." Casemiro doubted those words helped, but they represented his best effort to empathize, and he hoped Laural understood that fact. The two walked side-by-side for several paces while Casemiro added a comment to create idle conversation to pass the time. "Well-cooked meals rarely find my stomach since my wife passed."

"How long?" Laural returned a glance, expressing her sympathy.

"Five years." A tear emerged from the corner of the wizard's eye. Casemiro let it roll over his cheek as the wizard pulled the hood of his cloak over his head. The wizard concealed his tears from the onlookers and refused to accept their sympathy or pity.

"I'm sorry."

"Not your fault. Our marriage explains why I never returned to visit you or your father. I met my wife, Chantal, and we married a brief time after I completed my duties in Lillenhold. My oath to her became more important than the one to your father, or you."

Laural nodded her head at the explanation. "I understand, and thank you for sharing. You flatter me by providing the information freely."

"You deserved to hear that unspoken truth."

Laural paused before asking the next question. "Is her death too painful to discuss?"

"Quite the opposite, to be truthful." The wizard pulled the hood of his cloak back, revealing a smiling face.

"Perhaps you'll share more with me, eventually?"

The request lingered, and the wizard hesitated, knowing that opening the wound only led to a deluge of memories from his previous life and a torrent of words about each precious moment. "Unlikely, but you never know." Casemiro extended his arm, an unspoken offer for the Princess to use him for support on the walk. Laural accepted and intertwined their arms for the rest of the trek to the keep. Their conversation ceased as the sea's sounds and scents took over.

Casemiro and Laural reached Veritas Keep and found two massive wagons parked in the sizeable garden. A couple of guards carried enormous trunks from the wagons as another guard tended to the horses, two Ardennais stallions hooked to the drays. The wizard pondered the source of the heavy load.

"It must be for the Extravaganza," said Laural. "Let's check out who arrived." The Princess pulled the wizard by his arm into the auditorium portion of the keep.

Once inside, the two inspected the newly arrived equipment, boxes, and trunks. A group of men sat in the pews surrounding the central platform, laughing and sharing humorous anecdotes. Casemiro pieced together the puzzle and deduced the answer. "This must be the entertainment."

Laural beamed as she stared towards the multitude of muscular men. "I should think so. I may need a cold bath." Her words captured the attention of the men, and each of them turned to the Princess with a smile and look of conquest in their eyes.

Casemiro rolled his eyes before being interrupted by a question. "As I live and breathe, is that the renowned wizard, Casemiro?"

The voice triggered anger as memories flooded the wizard's mind. Casemiro stared at the approaching man and whispered a word, "Tawdd." The metal end of the staff flared to a bright molten orange and waves of heat radiated from the wooden shaft. The wizard's emotions on full display.

This man stood taller than the wizard and bore a much sturdier build with chiseled arms and shoulders. Dark hair cut close to the man's scalp created a façade of youth. His gait featured a slight limp from an unknown injury. The person in front of Casemiro might not be recognized without the unique accent to his voice. A voice the wizard never forgot.

The man continued towards the wizard. "Oh, come on. Surely, you do not still hold a grudge?" The man stopped out of reach of the wooden staff with a cautionary eye. "Please extinguish that thing."

"Explain to me why I should, Horace Ferryman. The last time we met, you fled carrying two armloads of stolen merchandise. My merchandise. My wife suggested mercy and that remains the solitary reason I did not kill you. Chantal believed fate might repay us later." The wizard stepped forward and leaned the staff closer towards the man. "Perhaps today is when fate repays you." Casemiro stamped his staff on the ground and the glow grew more intense.

Horace reached to his hip and tossed a small bag toward the wizard's feet. The coin purse landed on the floor and clattered with the unmistakable sound of gold and silver coins. "Perhaps I can make amends and cover the damages. Also, my condolences for your wife, a lovelier woman I never met. We performed in Foxshire a few weeks ago, and I received word of Chantal's unfortunate death."

Aware of the response Chantal expected, if she stood at his side, Casemiro released the spell, and the glow died away from the staff. After a moment, the wizard kicked the bag of coins back at Horace. "It does not matter now. Keep your money, thief."

The Princess approached Horace as he bent over and picked up his coins, and the man transitioned into a clumsy bow. "Your Highness, my honor."

"You can rise and elaborate on this story."

Horace put the purse back on his belt. "I apologize, my lady, but that tale is not mine to tell. The responsibility lies on the wizard's shoulders. Excuse me, as preparations for the show require my attention."

Laural waved the man away and glared at Casemiro, who grunted and walked to a distant part of the auditorium. The wizard spotted the Captain of the Guard and decided to bring each other up to speed on their morning adventures presented the best course of action and an adequate distraction from the Princess. The wizard sidled up to Gerard and tapped him on the shoulder.

"Oh, Casemiro. The morning turned fruitful, and I gathered some valuable information. How did you fare?"

Casemiro pulled out the sheet he received from Angus, the cooper. "Tell me what you learned and then we can go over what I discovered."

The two investigators sat in the nearest pew. The clang of Gerard's armor on the wooden bench drew eyes and ears from those around them.

"I interviewed Chef Richard and his morning crew. Chef Richard remembers seeing the Cassenwary brand on the casks received."

Casemiro corrected Gerard for his error. "Those casks are puncheons. Sorry, learned that fact this morning from the cooper in the village."

Gerard nodded his head. "Noted for future reference. Regardless, Richard swears the *puncheons* sported a brand. He found it odd the poisoned barrel did not and showed a modicum of distress regarding the situation."

"I suppose we cannot expect the man to confess to allowing in the poisoned barrel. But I guess we must take Richard at his word without further evidence to incriminate him."

The Captain of the Guard smiled. "Well, the case now becomes interesting. In talking with the crew, Richard owes a gambling debt to the Prince. Richard remains in the kitchen due to this indebtedness. He attempted to leave multiple times but remains indentured until he pays the debt in full."

"Men kill for less. Anything else of note from the crew?"

"Nothing from the kitchen. And no one saw the transfer of the barrels. Sorry, puncheons."

Gerard attempted to cross his legs, but his armor refused to cooperate. The Captain resigned himself to leaning forward and placing his forearms across his knees. "None of the other barrels contained poison. We evaporated several samples over intense heat, but we found nothing like the poisoned barrel. We suspected that outcome, but that information reassures me we are only dealing with an isolated source of the poison."

The wizard mentioned another topic. "Any news on the examination of Geoffrey's body?"

"The healer confirmed Geoffrey died from poison, with no other contributing factors. Tell me the details of your morning."

Casemiro summarized the morning's pursuits and the visit to the cooper, raising the curiosity of the Captain before turning the focus on the events surrounding them. "Care to explain this?"

The Captain of the Guard scanned the surrounds. "The wrestlers and their belongings. Having these men here in the middle of this investigation creates additional and unneeded difficulty. I will struggle to find time for the case with their arrival."

"Between us, keep your eye out for a rash of robberies. One man among this crew I know to be a confirmed thief. Good luck, Captain."

The men parted ways and Casemiro backed himself into a shadowy corner, providing an unencumbered view of the cavernous room. The wizard absorbed everything regarding the visitors to Veritas Keep. The reputation of traveling entertainers lacked trustworthiness, and the added specter of a villain increased his trepidation. As Gerard noted, the timing of their arrival created an unwanted complication for the investigation.

As the wizard scowled from the darker confines of the hall, the Prince entered and stood in front of the wooden throne. Heenan stood at Arenton's side and called everyone to order. Everyone in the room kneeled or bowed, except Casemiro, who remained hidden.

Arenton acknowledged their fealty and allowed the men the grace to stand. "You may rise, and I wish to welcome our feature act for the Extravaganza. Lillenhold's world revolves around this Extravaganza for three days and nothing surpasses this event's importance."

Exactly what Casemiro feared.

10⊕

SHOWMANSHIP

With the wrestling troop's arrival, a new attitude of frivolity took over the keep, and Casemiro feared the worst. After the wizard's initial count, the crew consisted of less than fifteen men. The wrestlers huddled near the Prince, jostling and joking over a variety of topics. Casemiro hid near the exit and as far away as possible from the rigamarole but remained within earshot of the Prince, listening for the newest ridiculousness his Highness cooked up. His hand grazed the outline of his saber, which he nicked from the guard station the prior evening.

Across the way from the wizard, Forrest and Oleander entered the hall and meandered towards Casemiro. Forrest asked, "Did we miss anything?"

The troll-man wore his typical brownish attire, and the florist a yellow gown featuring veins of green from top to bottom, evoking the image of a vines growing over Oleander's body. The clothing attracted most men's attention, especially the crew.

The wizard acknowledged the troll-man's presence. "No, but I will not remain unnoticed if you stand next to me. Why didn't you take part in the wrestling?"

Forrest chuckled. "I am a pacifist, wizard."

Casemiro smirked at the reply. "And I'm protesting baked goods." The wizard rubbed his stomach and laughed at the idea of anyone carrying troll blood being a pacifist.

The Prince caught sight of the wizard and his friends. "Gentlemen, let me introduce you to Casemiro, Forrest, and the lovely Oleander. Our volunteers for the undertaking." Arenton waved over the trio and encouraged the threesome to interact with the newcomers. "Come meet our visitors before we break into our respective groups to learn about your specific roles for a successful Extravaganza."

The wizard turned to Forrest. "I told you, *friend*. Nice to meet you again, Oleander."

"The same to you, Casemiro."

As the group joined the larger throng, Casemiro registered Laural's smile from afar. The Princess continued to stare at the wrestlers, unaware the wizard watched. The wizard seamlessly joined the crowd, standing beside a young man who appeared to be from another country. From behind, Casemiro admired a detailed dragon tattoo on the young man's arm. Red scales and the fiery breath attracted the wizard's gaze. The old man complimented the work, and the young wrestler accepted the kind words. Casemiro stepped a stride away to give the larger man more room.

The Prince requested silence from the crowd. "Everyone, your attention. Thank you to the wrestlers and crew who arrived today. I want to recognize the individual responsible for this opportunity, Harley Sweet."

A man carrying a sturdy frame and short neck stepped forward. His ears stuck straight out and appeared malformed as blonde hair flowed straight down the back of his head, partially concealing a patterned bald spot atop his cranium. His crooked nose, obviously from multiple breaks, sat off-center on his face while two flint-colored eyes focused on his surrounds. A slight limp became prominent as he emerged from the group to stand next to the Prince. The enormous smile of the man offset his physical misalignments and balanced out his face.

Sweet cleared his throat and a deep, raspy voice echoed through the hall. "Thank you, Prince Arenton. Our troop is proud to appear in front of your village this week, and we desire nothing more than to deliver an excellent performance. As per usual, I coordinate each aspect of this event inside the ring while the Captain of the Guard administers the security for Veritas Keep." Sweet pointed in the direction of Gerard, who nodded in response. "My unofficial role for the event is labeled as the ring announcer. Lawrence and Philip serve as the referees and alternate between the matches." He gestured at two men and pointed to another man across the room. "Hartwell oversees the merchandise station. For the volunteers, you will work beside one of the four of us and begin your instruction today."

The Prince held up his hands to catch the crowd's attention once more. "Also, for the wrestlers, I want everyone to understand what you compete for. The winner of this tournament receives the title of the Golden Dragon Champion. The ceremonial title means you help protect the village should a dragon attack or another silly event occurs. And I now present the championship belt."

The Prince stepped aside to reveal a cloth-covered item on the throne. Arenton pulled the cloth off and produced the leather, gold, and dragon heartstone belt. Arenton turned to the crowd, sporting a grin the length of his forearm.

A whistle from one wrestler escaped the crowd as others whispered amongst themselves. Amidst the noise, someone asked, "What's the belt's value?"

Casemiro surveyed the grins of interest rolling across the audience. The wizard also spotted the men counting the guards in the keep as if they calculated their chances of a successful heist.

Arenton provided restrictions on the usage of the belt. "The winner may wear the strap in Veritas Keep, or under the strictest security in the village. The value of the belt prohibits removal from this building without my approval and anyone attempting to steal the belt loses their head. Am I understood?" Any comedic undertones existing in Arenton's voice disappeared as a sharp, crisp warning exuded from the words and his expression.

The Prince then assigned the volunteers to specific groups per the direction of Harley Sweet. "Oleander move to the merchandise area. Forrest, please collaborate with the wrestlers and the referees. Casemiro, you work beside Mr. Sweet. Let's create an enjoyable event for the people of Lillenhold." The Prince waved to the guards to follow him upstairs as he returned the belt to a secure location.

As the people disbursed throughout the massive hall, Casemiro walked towards Harley Sweet. The wizard crossed his arms inside the sleeves of his cloak, showing the fingers of his left hand needed to hold the staff and nothing else. Sweet, undeterred by the imposing stance, extended his hand, and the wizard reached out and accepted the greeting.

Casemiro edged closer and examined the promoter in depth. Sweet wore a wool shirt held together by buttons and covered by a leather jerkin with keys and sharp objects hanging from the piece of clothing. He wore coarse pants spotted by tiny holes and well-worn work boots. The man gave the impression of a dangerous nature with the knotted muscles, several scars, and other telltale signs of many scraps. The wizard made a mental note to not challenge Sweet to a fight anytime soon.

"So, you're the wizard the Prince is so proud of?"

"You should be aware, my motivation for doing this is for the money. What do you require of me for the Extravaganza?"

Sweet chortled, leaving the wizard wondering what amused the man more: Casemiro's honesty, or his motivation. "That is the Prince's term for the event? I guess that title beats other names used at other locations. You are the master of ceremonies and will start each session of the event with a flashy display. So, impress me, wizard."

"Now?"

Sweet nodded.

The wizard considered his options. "Where should I perform this flashy display?"

Sweet pointed at the platform. "Preferably in the center of the ring."

Casemiro gave the man a questioning gaze. "You mean the square?"

"Yes, but people in our business call that a ring. The story behind the term is not worth the effort to explain."

The men climbed onto the platform and entered the ring. Casemiro inspected the mat and cast an inquisitive glare at Sweet. "Could someone place a stone in the center?"

Sweet rubbed his chin and contemplated the idea. "No problem, as long as we remove it before the first match starts."

The two men returned to the stone floor and Casemiro prepared himself. For a moment, the grief and guilt left the wizard's mind and the magical energy resided in his body, ready for use. "Does this work?" The wizard tapped the stone floor of the keep with the staff and yelled a phrase. "Tan Gwyllt!"

The metal end of the staff emitted a bright yellow glow, and beams of sparkling light rocketed skyward. Before the blasts of energy crashed into the room's ceiling, they exploded to create a prismatic display accompanied by detonations within the hall. People covered their ears because of the loud bangs, while others covered their eyes for protection from the radiance and the fluttering sparks. The scent of burned paper completed the impressive exhibition, and black vapors floated throughout the room. Gasps and applause from everyone in the keep, even the guards, signaled their approval of the display.

Casemiro leaned against the staff for support as he wavered, smiling at the audience for their appreciation and concealing his weakness. The wizard caught his breath and claimed a seat in the nearby pew, while Sweet allowed the wizard to recover.

Sweet patted the wizard's shoulder. "That suffices. Also, please include a short rhyme or limerick to make it sound official, as if you are prohibiting magical interference within the ring. Help the locals believe the events inside the ring appear legitimate. I give you a free license to exercise your creativity."

"Why the need for subterfuge?"

Sweet smiled in a way that indicated he wanted to bite the wizard's head from his shoulders. "Old man, showmanship is the term you need. Showmanship."

Casemiro grinned at Sweet, understanding he would never trust the man. "Anything else?"

"We need someone to cover my role on the off chance I must manage something else during the event. You will serve as my backup ring announcer."

Casemiro squinted as the idea of serving as an announcer

confused him. "What does the task entail?"

Sweet pulled several loose pieces of paper from a breast pocket, along with pristine spectacles, a prized possession. "The eyes ain't what they used to be. I found these at a shop on the continent, in a city called Pretoria. A beautiful place filled with amazing craftspeople who perform minor miracles. The craftsmen polish these lenses from heated sand to a specific thickness depending on how bad your eyesight is, and the results surpass the spectacles I owned before." Sweet handed the lenses to Casemiro to scrutinize.

The wizard inspected the lenses and returned the cherished contraption to Sweet. "I came across comparable items in my travels. Perhaps my failing eyes might find a pair useful. Anyway, as you were saying?"

Sweet put the spectacles across the bridge of his nose. "Each of our wrestlers receives a brief introduction as they enter the ring and I deliver the words with a touch of gusto."

"Gusto?" The wizard expressed his unsureness.

Sweet held up his hand to stall any questions. "It sounds odd, but listen to an example I wrote earlier today." The promoter cleared his throat and a voice two octaves lower erupted from the man's lungs. "Ladies and Gentlemen! I now give you a man linked to the Titans of old and hailing from Athens, Greece. The man mastered four hundred moves and weighs in at fourteen stone. The Greek grappler, Niiikoooos Aaaaanteeeussss!"

All the wrestlers cheered and applauded, and Sweet grinned at Casemiro. "I believe that works."

The wizard acknowledged his enchantment through the words. "If required, I can do something similar, but I must remember the showmanship."

Sweet put the pieces of paper and spectacles back into his pocket. "From my experience, wizards understand showmanship better than most. Hiding behind your cloak and chain belt presents a specific image to other people. Not to mention the outline of a sword bleeding through the fabric sends an additional message. All of which adds to the showmanship to sell everyone else a particular narrative."

Casemiro cocked one eyebrow toward Sweet and noted to not underestimate the perceptiveness of the man again. "It's a saber, not a sword." The wizard wondered how the man discerned the weapon underneath the bulky cloak.

Sweet smiled more broadly. "Shorter and curved to do more damage. All of this because you are another actor hiding beneath your meager garb."

Casemiro's thoughts drifted back to the days when people feared him, and he carried genuine power. Back when... The wizard almost slipped but focused on Harley Sweet instead of his memories.

"To be fair, I never attended one of these events in my travels. From what I glean, the action is less than genuine."

Sweet chuckled and stood to his full height, but his eyes became narrow and less jolly. "Wizard, I grant you a pass this once. 'Coordinated' is the proper term, but don't question what you witness in the ring. These men manage injuries devastating enough to keep you bedridden for a month. Sure, they may embellish the moves, but these men hurt, and those maneuvers are anything but fake."

The wizard's eyes revealed his curiosity. "How do they accomplish this?"

"These men practice executing these maneuvers to convince the audience the move is painful while inflicting the least amount of damage as possible. For example, we master falling to spread the impact across the widest area of the body. These men perfect these moves to protect their opponent's necks and heads and absorb the impact of hitting the mat. Even though their maneuvers appear more painful than the reality, it still hurts and none of it is a lie."

Casemiro sat in the pew, embarrassed for his rash reaction. "I apologize if I insinuated anything distasteful about your profession."

Sweet sat beside him and slapped the wizard's knee hard enough to serve as a warning. "We often receive that reaction, but you understand better than many others. You're fully aware that in most places, people dislike wizards and accuse them of trickery. It is no different for us. Now, do you wish to help me setup this little tournament?"

"As repayment for the education, I offer my help in any way I can. Do we arrange these matches by drawing the names at random?"

Sweet laughed in a way that sounded like a pot of water boiling over. "You already dismissed the word, showmanship. As part of the show, these men provide a personality geared toward evoking love or hate from the audience. Some are crowd-pleasers, referred to as faces, while others take the role of antagonist, or heels. We seldom want faces to fight each other, or heels. One of those matches may work in this type of event, but we often lose the audience's interest. Opposing forces generate the more vocal reactions from the crowd, what we call the bang, or pop. The job requires a balanced approach. Here's an example."

Sweet pointed to a man standing in the middle of the wrestlers. "See the dark-haired, average-sized gentleman? Eldon Haversmith personifies the term true professional and fights everyone, heel or face. His wrestling name is The Elemental Hammer; flames in one fist, earthquakes in the other, and all the other hyperbole. Though a talented collaborator, Eldon lacks the star power to be the feature act."

Casemiro nodded to communicate his understanding. "So, we want matchups featuring the more extreme personalities?"

Sweet patted the wizard on the knee again, much gentler this time. "The decision for the finals needs to factor in the desired matches. Usually, the final involves the two biggest attractions. For us, that would be Paul Perriman and Otto Schwartz. They go by the names of the Natural Wonder and the Buckland Brawler, respectively. Occasionally, we push a hard worker that deserves additional recognition to generate new interest and create some unpredictability."

"So, you orchestrate the outcomes?"

Sweet wobbled his head and hand in uncertainty. "A tad bit, but we design in flexibility, depending on the audience reactions. Typically, we choose a tournament winner after the first night, but maintain backup options if needed. For our first match, let's use Nikos Antaeus, a crowd favorite. His technical skill might not generate the biggest reaction from the crowd because his moves are less dramatic, but fast-paced. So, we need to extract his personality with a heel featuring a distinctive style. See the hulking guy with the large muscles and the long blond hair? That is Schwartz, a wrestler who lacks finesse and beats people up. Those two create an interesting contrast and can help assess the audience's reactions in our opening bout of the tournament."

Casemiro backed away. "Given your understanding of this process, it's best if you handle it. With a copy of those sheets of paper, I shall practice the introductions and develop my rhyme."

"An excellent plan. Before you go, I wish to show you something else." Sweet whistled over to the wrestlers and drew their attention. "Nikos, to the ring." Sweet walked into the ring with Casemiro trailing close behind.

Nikos Antaeus approached and sported a head of cropped curly hair and a well-groomed combination of a mustache and beard. Nikos carried less muscle than the others but still dwarfed the wizard. "Yeah, what's up Harley?"

"We're demonstrating the deathdrop trap to our friend here, but don't put me on my head."

Nikos smiled at Casemiro. "You will love this. First, I apply a facelock on him. Then I bring him down and pull his head to the mat. On a stone floor, this move hurts something awful and might inflict permanent damage. If I do my job right, he might get a mat burn on his forehead in the ring."

Harley raised his hand to attract Casemiro's attention. "Let me illustrate a real-life use for such a hold. You do not strike me as defenseless and that staff can hurt someone, but you can never predict when an idiot, bigger than you, needs dropped a notch. You pound your staff onto the top of his foot to create a significant amount of pain. They react and lean their head forward to grab their foot. Next, you apply this hold. Go ahead, Nikos."

The wrestler grabbed the promoter, applying a quick jerk with amazing speed. "Check out how I wrap my arm around the skull with my elbow under his chin. When they lean forward, use their own momentum to defeat them, no matter how big they stand. From this point, fall back on your rear end and let gravity do the rest. Chances are you knock the guy out and he leaves you alone for the rest of his life. You might walk away with a bruised hip, but it beats the alternative. I give you the deathdoor trap, or the DDT."

Nikos released Sweet, leaving the promoter red-faced. The blood flow normalized in his face as Sweet turned to the wizard.

Harley sent Nikos on his way, and he winked at Casemiro. "A tip if you ever need to defend yourself. I need to seed the tournament and then I will join you for dinner tonight."

"Thank you for the wisdom, Harley. It enlightened me and increased my appreciation for what you and your men do. I eagerly await the event."

The wizard stepped away to analyze the other people milling around the hall as they prepared for the event, but also noted Oleander standing alone. Casemiro followed her gaze toward Harley Sweet and broke the woman's concentration upon his approach.

"Oleander, pardon me for disturbing you."

A gracious smile crawled across Oleander's face as she pointed toward a pew. "No offense taken, Casemiro. Do you care to sit?"

The woman took her seat, and the wizard sat a comfortable distance from her to avoid any unwanted speculation.

"How did your training go?" The question Casemiro wished to ask would come, but this broke the ice.

The ferocity of her giggle shocked the wizard. "It went fine, but Mr. Hartwell did not think a woman could manage the merchandise table and my success with the shop surprised him. Once we got beyond his trivial problem, things progressed well. And yours?"

The irony of the woman outsmarting the burly man intrigued Casemiro. "I received an illuminating lesson in the mechanics of showmanship and the wrestling business. They're more detailed than I expected, and I'm curious about how this Extravaganza will unfold." The wizard dropped the question he planned to ask the woman. "Oleander, if I may ask, do you ever need a barrel in your business?"

She replied without hesitation. "Of course, I use two barrels to contain the two types of soil I employ in my shop. I also use a couple barrels for waste; one holds the trimmings of my plants I use for other purposes, creating perfume or cooking for example, and the other holds the more difficult to manage and poisonous items, many of which kill people."

The wizard's eyes grew to orbs at the surprising honesty of the comment. "Excuse me, but did you say poisonous? I am aware of the dangers certain plants present, but I never imagined you sold those in your shop."

"A garden can have many beautiful yet poisonous plants. Several varieties of houseplants are dangerous, if not deadly, to humans. I dispose of the unsold items to prevent any unwanted tragedies and Forrest often discards the full barrels for me."

Casemiro moved the focus from Oleander before she became wise to the wizard's tactic. "Speaking of Forrest, he seems quite introverted. He might not answer if I ask him the same question. Does Forrest ever use barrels?"

Oleander smiled in a knowing manner. "You talked with the cooper, correct?"

Casemiro nodded with a sly grin and showed the wizard's surprise at the woman's perceptiveness. "Yes, I am sorry if I come across as not respecting your acuity. I am helping the Captain of the Guard with the investigation and..."

"Say no more. I understand the need for elusiveness in your questions. And we are both clients of Angus. Forrest requires barrels to store a batch of cider when ready for consumption. Ask Forrest for details on his cidery and allow him to gush over it for hours if you wish. Despite it being a hobby, he sells barrels to The Pub and Skullery."

"Cider, as in apples?"

"To my knowledge, he uses other fruits as well, but apples

present the primary element. But ask Forrest for more details."

Casemiro cataloged the information and now understood how he found Oleander and Forrest on the cooper's client list. Even with legitimate reasons for owning barrels, they both remained suspects in Geoffrey's death. Oleander possessed the means with her ample supply of poisonous material. However, the wizard internally questioned her motives.

If the Prince holds a romantic interest in her, as it appears, she lacks a reason to kill the man. But it immediately opens up a reason for Forrest to become a primary suspect.

Casemiro needed time to ponder this information. The troll-man possessed adequate motive, means, and a method to exact the crime. Geoffrey's prior comment about an arrival that would intrigue Forrest stuck with the wizard, who now needed to investigate further. *What was delivered?*

The wizard composed himself before continuing the conversation. "I may dive into the topic of ciders the next time we speak. I have troubled you long enough. Good day." Casemiro smiled at her as he rose from the pew.

Oleander stood as the wizard walked away. "Goodbye."

The old man searched for the Captain of the Guard, but Gerard left the keep during the training session. Casemiro decided to not dwell on this information pertaining to Forrest and Oleander until informing Gerard. Having no other obligations, the wizard retreated to his quarters for rest and recovery from his impressive display of magic.

As he ascended the stairs, the wizard made note of Forrest collaborating with the wrestlers. Despite evidence linking the troll-man to the murder of Geoffrey and the attempted assassination of the Prince, Forrest seemed harmless to Casemiro. The idea of the gentle giant being the culprit troubled the wizard as he continued up the stairs to his quarters. Either Casemiro misjudged the character of his new acquaintance or Forrest belonged on the stage with the finest acting troops.

Casemiro's focus shifted when he reached the landing and found his door ajar. The thump of the staff on the door announced his presence to whoever waited inside the room, and he grabbed the grip of the saber inside his cloak, anticipating the potential need for the weapon, but left the blade sheathed. The wizard pounced through the doorway to scare whoever waited inside his quarters.

Dismay crept across Casemiro's face when he found Laural standing in the room. "Princess?" Yarn fell from her hands to the wooden floor.

"I'm sorry. I wished to talk to you." She looked around and tried to form an explanation. Without another word, Laural skittered to the door and grabbed the wizard's face, pulling it toward her own. She planted her lips on his and kissed the wizard for a magical moment. Laural released Casemiro and placed her forehead against his chin and let out a shallow breath before she whispered to him. "I waited for you to arrive."

Memories of the bliss with his wife, Chantal, flooded Casemiro's brain. The wizard opened his eyes to instead find Laural, reminding him that she provided the source for this moment of contentment. Casemiro's mind shifted, and he pushed away from the Princess as guilt filled his soul. "Woman! Control yourself! Get out of my quarters and never do this again!"

Laural pulled back and tears erupted from her face. The Princess darted out the door and dashed across the hall, slamming her door, and audibly wailing within.

Casemiro, shocked by the entire event, slammed his door shut. The wizard surveyed the room, convinced the woman's embrace and kiss represented a cover for her true intent. Laural searched his quarters for something, but for what went beyond his guess. As the wizard checked, he found nothing amiss and wondered for a second if the kiss stood for her genuine feelings. The wizard banished the concept of Laural's affection from his mind once again, chalking the behavior up to a cover for her misdeed.

Casemiro reserved his greatest discontent for the other emotions stirred up by the Princess that tumbled through his mind. The wizard relished the kiss, her attention, and the moments spent with her throughout the day. He grew more ashamed of his reaction and enjoyment of the moment with every passing second. Casemiro prayed to Chantal for her forgiveness as he broke down in tears.

11

DINNER AND A STORY

The wizard struggled in bed for two hours, fighting against the emotions stemming from Laural's earlier actions. Flashbacks of Casemiro's life with Chantal haunted his mind as the wizard attempted to justify the ghosts. The wizard's mind moved from Chantal to Laural as he reconciled whether the itch within his heart fell into the good or bad column of a make-believe philosophical ledger. He continued to ask one question. *What possessed the Princess to break into this room?*

Casemiro's stomach rumbled and provided a distraction. With ten hours passing since the wizard's last meal at the Cornelius Inn with Laural, the wizard needed some food. Unsure of the time, Casemiro questioned if the Extravaganza festivities finished, but his stomach would wait no more. He knew the kitchen served meals late at night for the guards on duty and would have something prepared.

The wizard strapped on the gray cloak, cinching the chain and hook around his waist. He placed his coin purse in the breast pocket, leaving the ornate knitting needles behind on the nightstand. The money: a backup plan for buying food and drinks if the kitchen proved closed, or a stiff drink might be required.

The wizard opened the door and listened for activity. Across the hall, noises of the Princess rummaging around in her quarters escaped beneath the door. Another stray image of Laural's smiling face bounced into and out of his brain. Casemiro dreaded bumping into Laural at this point and tiptoed towards the stairs. Hoping to avoid people, the wizard paused, listening for a warning of foolishness from the hall, but no noises rose through the stairwell.

The wizard descended the stairs and, upon reaching the base, scanned the wide auditorium. A single man, one of Sweet's top aides whom Casemiro did not recall the name of, sat in the pews. The man acknowledged the wizard's presence with a grunt and nod. The wizard waved and headed to the kitchen.

The nighttime atmosphere at Veritas Keep reminded one of a tomb. Oil lanterns hung in the halls and lit the way through the stone structure, providing enough light to prevent a dangerous collision. A man brushed Casemiro's shoulder as he passed by. The wizard recognized Heenan.

Heenan paused upon recognizing the wizard. "Late run to the kitchen, eh, Casemiro?"

Casemiro noticed the counselor holding a pheasant leg. The pepper and rosemary flooded the air and hit the wizard's nose; his mouth drooled. "I guess I'm not alone."

Heenan laughed. "Yes, I noticed you skipped the meal."

"Wasn't hungry at the time."

The counselor's eyes flickered. "Oh, this belongs to you." He reached into a pocket with the free hand and produced a coin. "The day's wages. The Skullery remains open if you fancy a drink. Oh, to receive your stipend over the next couple of days, collect the coins from the tax collector named Ben. I leave tomorrow for the crown's business."

"Business for the Extravaganza?"

"No, a bothersome bit of toil for the crown in Cassenwary. Anyway, off to bed. Good night, wizard."

Casemiro clutched the coin. "You too, counselor." The wizard wondered if he judged Heenan too harshly after their moment of direct interaction. Without the Prince and others to impress, Heenan seemed almost normal.

The wizard returned to the quest to fill his belly and entered the kitchen. Casemiro's disturbance at this hour surprised the small staff. The crew returned to their duties and ignored the cloaked man. The aromas of roasted bird drew Casemiro further into the kitchen.

Casemiro asked the closest person the pressing question on the wizard's mind. "Any leftovers from the meal?"

The man directed Casemiro's attention to a tub of mashed potatoes and a whole squab at the end of the table.

"How long since you took it off the heat?" The wizard wished to avoid food poisoning at all costs.

"Thirty minutes. The bird is dry as sin, though."

Casemiro thanked the man and took both. While wandering back through the keep, an idea occurred to the wizard. He placed the bird and potatoes on a side table and grabbed the enchanted coin from his pocket.

"Roman?"

A few seconds passed and then the boy replied. "Yes, sir."

"Where exactly do you live?"

The wizard tapped on the loosely hung door to avoid disturbing other residents in the neighboring hovels. As few nails as possible held the wooden shack together. Dried mud covered several holes to prevent drafts, but the little light emanating from the inside exposed the gaps in the structure. The canvas on top shielded those inside from the wet night. The wizard realized Roman's home did not differ from many others in Lillenhold.

Suddenly, a dark man pulled Casemiro inside. The wizard spied a lone lantern on the wall before finding the familiar and scarred face of Roman. A woman and two small children sat in a corner of the small home.

Ignorant of their names, the wizard extended his filled arms and offered the food from the keep's kitchen. "Anyone hungry?"

For the next twenty minutes, all six ate sizable portions of the food. The pepper brought a zing of spice to the dry bird and the potatoes, flavored with salt and a pat of butter, proved filling.

As the family ate, Roman introduced everyone. His father, Russell, worked in the port, pulling in and unloading the nets and fishing hooks brought to the pier. Melody, the mother, stayed home to care for the two younger children and knitted to earn a small pittance as time allowed. Melody and Casemiro discussed knitting techniques for a significant portion of the meal. Laverne and Luther, four-year-old twins, exhibited keen aptitudes and amiable manners but remained quiet for the meal.

The family resemblance to Roman proved uncanny. Dark skin accented by closely cut wiry hair, broad white smiles, and nervous childish energy craving to burst into a flurry of activity. Casemiro wondered how their fortunes might change if not for certain social constructs outside their control. They, like others in this village, fell victim to the circumstances of their time.

Russell pulled aside the wizard. "I appreciate the meal, but what prompted the generosity, sir?"

"Well, I owed Roman a coin for some labor." Casemiro pulled out the silver piece and gave the coin to the boy.

"Thank you, Casemiro, sir." Roman gave the coin to Russell, a gesture revealing the boy's character. "The twins need warmer clothes for the nights, and you can buy a couple of sweaters."

The father nodded and pocketed the coin, while the family prepared the younger children for bed and Roman moved to the other side of the room.

Laverne squealed. "What 'bout a story?"

Melody shushed the child. "Not tonight. It's too late for stories. Besides, our guest must be on his way."

Casemiro walked over and leaned down to the child. "If you don't mind, I can tell one."

Melody's voice and eyes showed uncertainty, but she replied, "Such a kind offer, sir. But wizard tales might be too intense for young children to handle."

Casemiro chuckled. "I promise this story is fine."

Melody glanced towards Russell and the father nodded his consent for the visitor to tell the bedtime story.

Casemiro sat on the floor and the two smallest children sat at the wizard's knees.

"The story begins with two men, brothers in fact, who worked for an almighty sorcerer and wore blue cloaks. None dared challenge this sorcerer's strength or authority. But, in a distant land, the sorcerer heard rumors of someone else attempting to influence the world through ill means. The sorcerer tasked the brothers with finding and defeating this evil wizard. He sent them on a great journey.

"The brothers in blue cloaks battled the evil wizard and defeated this enemy. Afterwards, the brothers discovered additional evils in the wilderness and beyond. Evils much more difficult to fight and control. They battle other wizards, monsters, and other masters of evil. But something changed.

"Evils began to spring up from innocent and simple existence, like wanting nice things for your family or wishing to protect your village. Instead of wizards, evil appeared in the form of men. This bothered the two brothers and they wished to squash these other evils influencing this world. But this was a fight they could not win alone."

Luther's tiny voice softly asked, "Did the brothers ever return to their master?"

"Excellent question. The brothers aided who they could in overcoming these daily evils. And the brothers seemed content for a while. But they felt guilty for not returning to their master for feared he needed them in another larger battle. They could not return to their master, and he never reached out to them.

"So, the brothers continued to fight evils, growing more uncertain of their rightful place in this world. After a particularly lengthy battle, one brother grew tired of the constant fights and stopped caring about the mission the sorcerer sent him to fulfill. This brother believed helping people without being bound to magic presented a better option. This brother desired to create a positive impact in people's lives as a man, not as a wizard. So, this brother bought a ship and sailed across the world searching for ways to help defeat those everyday evils without magic. And he found extraordinary joy in doing so."

"What happened to the other brother?" asked Laverne.

"The remaining brother believed his sibling wrong. So, the second brother pursued his life but retained his magic. This brother achieved wonderful things and received great acclaim for his deeds. This second brother battled monsters, dragons, and evil men and defeated them, all at a price. Then, he fell in love with a beautiful woman. Over time, the second brother drifted further and further from his mission and lost his way. As a result, his marriage suffered until the day his wife passed. This brother carried the burden of guilt for not appreciating his grand life.

"Since the day the second brother's wife died, he struggled to find his purpose. Returning to the life of a sorcerer proved impossible for him by this time. The man lost his magic, and his traveling sibling couldn't help. This second brother searched for any hope, or purpose, to make his life full."

Casemiro struggled to conclude the story. The wizard's eyes begged for help in the lamplight.

Russel squatted down next to the children. "This story sounds familiar." He smiled at Casemiro and talked to his little boy and girl. "The second brother sought to rediscover his values in a small village. He figured out why he didn't go back to the sorcerer and found people who genuinely cared about him. Soon, his magic returned, and this brother found companionship once more. He found a new purpose, one of even more importance than his original goal. The second brother remained happy for the remainder of his life."

Laverne giggled at the ending. "I bet he found a wife. Love always makes people happy."

Luther contradicted her. "Nope. He battled monsters and saved the village and did not need a wife for his happiness."

Melody grabbed the two children. "That is enough for tonight. Tell Casemiro thank you for the story."

The children yelled, "Thank you!" and Laverne hugged the wizard's leg.

Melody thanked the wizard and led the children to the other room to rest.

Russell and Roman walked to the door and Casemiro followed them outside the home.

After leaving the light, Russell extended his hand. "Thank you for the food and the story."

"Thank you for finishing the story. I talked myself into a corner." Casemiro avoided revealing too much about his life. The wizard wished to keep the ideas he found uncomfortable hidden. Those details stood at the edge of Casemiro's mind, waiting for him to reveal them to anyone. But he refused to do so on this night.

Russell asked, "Did you intend for that story to come across as biographical?"

Before Casemiro answered, Roman stepped in. "The story does not matter, Dad. The better question is how the story ends."

Roman walked back into the hovel, leaving the adults aghast at the boy's wisdom.

Casemiro asked, "Is he always so philosophical?" And close to the mark?"

"More than you would believe. But is he wrong?"

Casemiro laughed at the realization the boy might be a philosophical savant and nodded his agreement with the comment. "Goodnight, Russell. Your family is beautiful, insightful, and a treasure to be cherished."

After the men parted, Casemiro walked back to Veritas Keep in the dark, accompanied by his thoughts. Over the quarter hour it took to conquer the hill, the wizard relived a lifetime of memories and regrets. He replayed them in his mind while questioning what he wanted in life. Guilt entered Casemiro's heart and soul once more and he reached a conclusion.

Why should I find joy and happiness?

Casemiro denied himself joy and happiness because of his guilt for the life the wizard wasted in his marriage, and by default, denied Chantal from living. Casemiro believed himself unworthy of living a joyful life. The wizard justified fate denying him the choice of a simple, or enjoyable, life because of his sins.

The fatigued wizard found himself outside of Veritas Keep when he stopped questioning his choices. He entered the keep and struggled up the steps, leaning on the staff for support. Upon reaching the landing, Casemiro paused at what waited for him.

Laural peered through a gap between her door and the frame. In the limited candlelight, her dried tears provided the obvious evidence of her crying. The Princess stepped halfway out of her quarters and nearly said something.

Casemiro interrupted the Princess. "Laural, I apologize for my unwarranted reaction and anger. You deserved better from me."

A slight smile creeped across Laural's face as her lip quivered.

"My emotions cannot handle this situation with you or me. The problem and the reason you need to stay away centers around me. You understand I created this problem, right?"

Laural's nod conveyed both understanding and uncertainty regarding the wizard's words.

"I apologize for that as well. Goodnight, Princess." Without a backwards glance, the wizard walked into his quarters and shut the door.

Casemiro wanted to not only distance himself from Laural but also from the emotions rising within that he considered an affront to the life spent with Chantal. Rather than pursue something Casemiro may find joy in, the wizard allowed the guilt to overtake him and enjoyed no sleep that night. The cries of Laural across the hall polluted his thoughts every time his eyes shut. Casemiro allowed himself no joy until he found forgiveness from Chantal; something the wizard pursued every day for the last five years without finding a sign of its existence. Casemiro feared the trail he followed for that treasure went cold with no foreseeable end. Or worse yet, never truly existed at all.

12

THE EXTRAVAGANZA

The first day of the Extravaganza arrived. Casemiro welcomed the distraction as he focused on fulfilling his contractual obligation. The volunteers filled the morning walking through the administrative aspects of the event and understood their role without fail. The group ended the session with a lunch of roast boar and carrots accompanied by a baked treat someone referred to as a pie. Once the food disappeared, Harley Sweet dismissed everyone for a few hours to relax.

At the appointed time in the afternoon, Casemiro emerged from his second-story quarters to perform. This day's events featured the entire first round of the tournament within two sessions as eight wrestlers received the opportunity to fight for the Golden Dragon Championship.

The wizard turned his cloak inside out to reveal the blue lining and cast the simple spell to provide the illusion of gold strands flowing with light. Though Sweet suggested shaving the beard, Casemiro kept the facial hair. Before descending the stairs, the wizard pulled the hood over his head to embrace the ominous tone of the event.

Prince Arenton and Sweet expected a modest crowd for the first session, and the turnout exceeded their estimates. Casemiro entered the hall of the keep and found a massive number of villagers filling the pews, and countless folks standing around the perimeter of the cavernous room. Their noise bounced off the walls as the crowd sang songs and chattered while the scent of the morning's work permeated the room. Heenan's marketing and the free admittance for this portion of the event worked as the Prince planned. The wizard owed Arenton an apology.

As practiced earlier in the day, a bass drum thrummed out a note to mark the beginning of the event. The wizard began his descent down the steps to the reverberating beat. Casemiro continued walking through the silenced crowd until he positioned himself at the center of the ring and found the stone. The wizard prayed to Chantal for power, fearing failure. That fear allowed him enough magic to perform his task. Casemiro thumped the stone with the wooden staff in time with the last drumbeat. The crowd went silent as the wizard yelled his lines.

Let those who wish ill
Fear this wizard's might.
For none shall obstruct
The course of this fight!

Casemiro pounded the staff on the stone once more and yelled the magic word. "Tan Gwyllt!" Sparks flew from the staff, shot to the top of the hall, and provided one solitary boom. The crowd, ignorant of what happened the previous day in rehearsal, erupted with applause. Casemiro bowed toward the Prince and exclaimed, "Let the Extravaganza begin!"

The wizard stumbled across the floor, lightheaded from the use of his power, and sat next to the Prince once he found his seat.

Arenton chided Casemiro, unaware of the price the wizard paid to accomplish the less entertaining feat. "A tad disappointing after the display yesterday, wizard."

"My apologies, Your Highness. Magic can be finicky at my age."

The Prince returned his glare to the wizard. "You appear fatigued. Is a healer required?"

The wizard waved away the offer for help. "No, the weakness will pass."

"The toll appears unworthy of the price."

"Think nothing of it, Your Highness." Casemiro closed his eyes and breathed for a few seconds, waiting for normalcy to return.

The wizard opened his eyes to find Princess Laural glaring from the other side of the Prince. She wore a red blouse with a black velvet skirt and black leather boots. His heart pounded a little firmer as his mind replayed the previous day's events. Casemiro tamed the thoughts and avoided any further ill-advised mental images. The wizard turned his attention to Harley Sweet and the announcement of the first bout's combatants.

Sweet belted out the first introduction. "Ladies and Gentlemen! Our first combatant for the evening weighs in at twenty stone and hails from the Tyrian Peaks. This behemoth boasts the largest arms in the world. The man crushes rocks and bends steel with his bare hands. I introduce the Buckland Brawler! Ottoooooo Schwaaaarrrtzzz!"

The Brawler stepped into the ring, yelling threats at the audience, intent on creating a reaction. Offended by the lukewarm response, the man antagonized the ringside fans. One man in the front row booed, and the Brawler leaned over the top rope and pointed at the villager. "I'll crush you like a grape after I finish this fool, brother." Those words drew a greater number of negative retorts from the people near the platform.

In the front row, a man held up a sign saying, "My name is Ben, better than being a has been." Casemiro wondered if that might be *the* Ben which Heenan mentioned. At this point, the wizard pondered how much the audience drank before the event to openly mock men twice their size. A glance at the refreshments table revealed a lengthy line, with each person walking away carrying at least one flagon of a drink.

Harley introduced the next wrestler, Nikos Antaeus, as he did the previous day, and the audience roared to life. The actions of the Brawler triggered the audience, and the crowd adopted Nikos as the immediate favorite. A referee, one of Sweet's associates, stepped into the ring, and Harley rang a bell to begin the match.

The crowd hushed, waiting for the action to begin. The grapplers met in the middle and grabbed each other's shoulders. With the obvious advantage in height and girth, the Brawler pushed Nikos towards the corner, and the smaller man flew backward into the ropes.

The Brawler charged to the corner to pummel his foe, connecting on a clothesline maneuver, and a groan emerged from the audience. The Brawler grabbed Nikos by the arm and whipped the smaller man across the ring to the opposite corner, resulting in another loud impact with the man's body meeting the cushioned ring anchors.

The Brawler charged into the corner again, Nikos sidestepped and wrapped his arms around the Brawler's shoulders. Nikos took down the Brawler by sweeping his legs and pulling back on his opponent. The crowd roared to life and cheered the move by Nikos. Nikos performed a series of quick holds, which took a toll on the opponent, but Schwartz recovered. Over the next fifteen minutes, the momentum of the bout shifted between the two opponents. Eventually, Nikos won by using a maneuver to roll up the larger man and cradle him for the three-count. The crowd erupted as much to support Nikos as to disparage the Brawler.

The contestants cleared the ring, and Harley Sweet rang the bell to signal everyone to find their seats for the next bout. Seated by the ring, Nikos Antaeus mingled amongst the crowd as Sweet introduced the next combatants. Sweet lowered his voice and allowed the words to spill from his mouth. "Ladies and gentlemen, let me present our next match." Harley paused and waited for the drum to sound. As the first beat boomed, he began. "Coming to the ring and hailing from the Far East while weighing fifteen stone. Welcome the master of the martial arts and the ruler of the Poison Clan. I present the silent assassin and the destroyer of dreams; the Ninja Serpent!"

A kimono-wearing man with a mask hiding all but his eyes entered the ring. The man pulled off the mask to reveal a white painted face marred by red and green symbols beneath his eyes. The crowd jerked away with revulsion as the stranger grabbed the top rope and hissed at the people, revealing a green tongue. A dragon tattoo covered the wrestler's arm, the same one Casemiro admired the previous day, to provide a further element of mystery. Casemiro admired the performance and wondered how a man's persona turned to heinously evil in twenty-four hours.

Sweet introduced the other combatant, The Priest Pontifex, and exited the ring. During the first half of the match, The Priest controlled the early stages of the bout after performing a powerful maneuver on the Serpent called the Crucifix Slam. He picked up his opponent to perform the move once more, but the Serpent flipped his feet over his head to escape the hold and landed in a standing position. The Serpent then placed a violent kick into the mid-section of his foe and performed an aerial roundhouse kick to the head. The Priest fell to the mat, and the Serpent covered his victim for the pinfall.

After a quick celebration by the Serpent, Nikos Antaeus climbed between the ropes. In a show of sportsmanship, Nikos extended his hand to congratulate his next opponent on the victory. The Serpent slapped the hand away and, without warning, spewed green mist into the face of Nikos and delivered a roundhouse kick to the man's head. The Serpent fled and left Nikos lying in the middle of the ring screaming in agony. The crowd hissed and booed as the Serpent escaped from the hall. Sweet and another wrestler helped Antaeus to the backstage area. One of Sweet's aides dismissed the audience, but not before reminding the crowd the next session began in two hours.

Casemiro waited for the people to disperse but showed considerable concern over the condition of Nikos Antaeus. The wizard caught himself and recognized the skillful showmanship of Sweet and his men.

To his surprise, Laural walked by and acknowledged Casemiro. "Wizard."

The old man replied in kind. "Princess." Laural left the area and walked toward the exit of the keep.

The Prince laughed. "You impressed me with how quickly you got on Laural's bad side."

"Thank you, Prince." Casemiro cursed at himself inwardly.

"I never expected Laural to be upset with you. She considered you faultless for years; even when you never responded to her pleas for aid. I assumed you were a fictional character fabricated by her imagination. Picture my shock the day Heenan found you."

Casemiro turned toward the Prince. "Pardon, but did you say Heenan found me?"

"Yes, Heenan found you and determined the best way to lure you here to become a vital component of the Extravaganza. We yearned for Casemiro to grace us once more and commemorate the events from twenty years ago. Does this upset you?"

The wizard sneered as he now understood Heenan had a motive for bringing the wizard to the village. The wizard wondered what it might be. He also realized the Prince lied to him. "Did Heenan leave already?"

"Yes, Heenan left this morning to conduct his business in Cassenwary. He slated his return for tomorrow evening to coincide with the epic conclusion to the Extravaganza. Does this affect your involvement?"

"Your Highness, I will live up to my end of the bargain. But Heenan owes me an explanation upon his return." Casemiro understood how contract law worked in Gaeleos. Even hurt pride fell beneath a hanging from the gallows, the punishment for not fulfilling a legal obligation to the royal family.

"Well, that session was fulfilling. Did you plan for a meal between sessions?"

Casemiro walked past the Prince. "Sorry, Arenton, but I dine alone when I'm angry." The wizard's excitement over his involvement in the festivities plummeted and his mood soured.

Much like the first session, Casemiro descended the stairs for the second session two hours later. This event attracted a larger audience than the first, and a sizeable crowd formed at the merchandise table. The line of people extended through the wooden doors to the garden of Veritas Keep. The scents of fresh ale and stale sweat filled the cavernous room.

The wizard spotted the two losing wrestlers from the first session mingling amongst the crowd. These men understood promotion and reaching the audience. The word from Harley Sweet rang in his ears. Showmanship.

The next group of matches began as the drum pounded through the hall. Casemiro spoke and the staff sparked red. Upon performing his duty, the wizard found his seat next to Arenton's empty throne. The wizard needed a brief break to recover. It appeared that Laural skipped the evening event, and the Prince's post remained vacated. Their absence left the wizard in charge of the festivities for this session. Casemiro welcomed the loneliness to process the various thoughts running through his mind.

The wizard focused on the investigation, but his mind inevitably drifted to Heenan luring him to Lillenhold. Then cloudiness crept into the wizard's head as a vision involving various images of the Princess and Chantal overlapped and caused emotional upheaval. Casemiro cleared his thoughts, but the vision continued with an image of Mount Siven's peak rising as the wizard's magical abilities failed. His unresolved emotions and guilt drained the power from his body. Casemiro drowned in the imagery of Arenton, Forrest, Chantal, Laural, and a dragon staring at him as his mind fell into a black abyss.

Casemiro's body almost fell from his seat when the wizard's ears latched onto the voice of Harley Sweet. The wizard caught himself before drawing the attention of the crowd. He glanced around, hoping no one witnessed his struggle. In the ring, the promoter performed the next introduction for a wrestler named Paul Perriman, as Casemiro regained his faculties. The wizard glanced around, hoping no one witnessed his struggle.

Following the prepared words, a man sported flowing blond hair yelled at the crowd from the middle of the ring. He wore a blue robe adorned by fake diamonds and fur to conceal his physique and convincingly presented himself as a pompous ass.

The wrestler interjected above the noise of the crowd. "Cut the music! I want you overweight Lillenhold losers to shut up while I take off my robe and show the ladies what they are missing. I am Paul Perriman, The Natural Wonder. This body is beyond the imagination of these pathetic excuses for women. Hit the music!"

The drum played throughout Veritas Keep and the man dropped the robe to reveal an exposed upper body covered in sculpted muscles. Form-fitting leggings concealed the lower half of a well-muscled frame and a woman in the front row swooned at the sight. A snicker of indignation at the woman's emotions escaped Casemiro's lips.

Perriman's opponent drew Casemiro's attention. Horace Ferryman stood in the ring with wet hair, leather pants, and a stained, torn undershirt. Casemiro took on a rooting interest for the bout and sat forward in his seat, supporting The Natural Wonder. To the wizard's delight, Perriman implemented a variety of holds until Horace submitted to a vicious attack on his knee. To celebrate, Perriman pulled a woman from the crowd and kissed her in front of everyone. The woman fell to her knees, begging for more affection.

Sweet waited for The Natural Wonder to clear the ring to introduce the next wrestler. "Ladies and Gentlemen, coming to the ring and hailing from Parts Unknown. Weighing in at nineteen stone, welcome the Master of Disaster. The man whose fists contain the fury of flames and the force of earthquakes. We know him as the world's toughest man. He is the Elemental Hammer!"

The man received a lukewarm reception from the crowd. With a snarky smile, The Hammer stopped and savored the lack of appreciation. He proceeded to the platform and waited for his opponent; a small man named the Flying Ghost. The Hammer shouted a question to the crowd. "Should I beat him to a pulp?" He acted surprised at the crowd's roar of approval. The Hammer nodded with glee and turned to the smaller opponent, then cracked his knuckles and rolled his shoulders to loosen his joints before beginning the bout.

After a brief session of chasing the smaller man around the ring, the Hammer caught his foe and began a devastating assault of ring-shaking slams and suplexes. A brutal clothesline maneuver nearly decapitated the Flying Ghost, and the Hammer stood in the middle of the ring as the crowd drowned him in applause and screams of appreciation for the brutal demonstration. To conclude the match, the Hammer held the Ghost upside down for 30 seconds, all of which the audience counted, before driving his foe to the mat on his back. The pinfall became an afterthought.

Unbeknownst to anyone else, the Natural Wonder snuck back into the ring. Perriman stood on the edge of the platform and yelled at the audience. "Come back tomorrow folks! Tomorrow, I break the Hammer's leg." He shifted his gaze to the Hammer. "Yeah, the guys in the back talk about how you're the toughest son of a gun walking, Hammer. But tomorrow you face the man who owns you. I promise you won't be walking out of here." Perriman turned back to the audience. "In the meantime, you farmers need to go home and lock up your wives before they get a load of the Natural Wonder and I make a real woman out of them. Yooooo!"

The Hammer grabbed Perriman by the arm and smacked the petulant ass across the face. The two threw punches, and a melee erupted within the ring, which required several wrestlers to pull the combatants apart and the fight drifted behind the curtains. A raucous crowd cheered the brawl and, once the scuffle finished, applauded for ten minutes before leaving the building. The matches satiated the crowd's hunger for red meat on the evening.

Seconds after the ruckus cleared up, a stealthy Harley Sweet tapped Casemiro on the shoulder. "Showmanship, I tell ya."

"Successful first day, Harley?" Casemiro asked as the crowd left the building.

Sweet smiled back at the wizard. "Yes, and I appreciate the variety of your spell-casting at the start."

The wizard did not respond, knowing his power dwindled with each usage. "Have you chosen the tournament winner?"

Sweet drew closer, as if he would reveal a secret to only Casemiro. "Not yet, but a couple of ideas pique my curiosity. Each of these wrestlers elicited sizable reactions from the crowd."

The wizard chuckled. "Based on my observations, a full house of people will provide adequate response to whomever you choose."

"Perhaps, sleep well."

"Have a good night."

Sweet shuffled off and Casemiro walked up to his quarters. Halfway up the stairs, Laural descended towards the wizard. He slid to the side to allow her to pass, but the Princess stopped.

"Do I need to explain myself, Casemiro?"

"I moved past the incident."

"Oh, we're referring to it as the incident, are we? My heart warms that I left such a positive impression." She attempted to avoid the wizard, but Casemiro shifted his position to stand in her path.

Casemiro tried to contain his emotions and not cause a scene that might embarrass Laural. "I chose the wrong words before, and then incorrectly directed my anger towards you. A significant part of me suffers as if I betrayed the oath to my wife, Chantal. Even after five years, that emotion drives my reactions and mindset. Even if what occurred comforted me in that moment, the guilt eats away at my soul. I thought you should know the reason for my reaction." Casemiro sidestepped Laural and walked by the Princess.

"Thank you for telling me." She glanced over her shoulder with the beginning of a grin on her lips. "I comforted you?"

Casemiro turned away, trying to hide the flush of red across his face. "I don't want to discuss the incident again." The wizard proceeded up the stairs in silence, knowing Laural scrutinized him leaving the scene with a smile on her face.

13

A CHAMPION CROWNED

After a night of rest and a morning of solitude, Casemiro entered the cavernous hall of Veritas Keep, ready to perform his duty one more time. The magical gold threading shimmered across the blue cloak as the wizard descended the stairs. The drum pounded the same writhing rhythm as the wizard entered the ring. This time, Casemiro produced a blast surpassing the one from the practice session. Sparks of green, red, and gold shot to the top of the hall and thrilled the crowd. The wizard left the ring and joined Harley Sweet on the floor.

Casemiro stood beside Sweet, scanning the audience that grew inexplicably larger than the preceding day. The villagers remained enthusiastic despite the haypiece admittance fee. Again, the Prince showed his knowledge of Lillenhold's people and how to entertain the masses. As they filled the auditorium, one prominent element overwhelmed the wizard's senses, the stench of sweat and the odor of the unwashed.

The wizard glanced over his shoulder to find Arenton smiling from ear to ear at the festivities. Next to him, Princess Laural shifted her gaze from the wizard to somewhere else once she realized the old man peered in her direction. Laural wore a vermillion-colored dress, but dark pants covered her legs instead of a skirt. Casemiro scanned the remainder of the hall and found Oleander back at the merchandise table and Forrest working ring security. Oleander's indigo dress stood out as uncommon for a struggling flower shop owner.

Casemiro turned his attention back to the ring and asked Sweet for an update. "How is Nikos?"

The man laughed. "He is fine. Remember, the wrestlers present a show. How the audience interprets it is on them. The Serpent spat a mixture of water and green dye. Nothing serious. Did you enjoy the matches yesterday?"

"I loved the Natural Wonder mopping the floor with his opponent. I hold a personal grudge against Horace Freeway."

Sweet rumbled and produced a howling laugh. "And here I expected the renowned Casemiro to be above this pettiness."

Casemiro shrugged his shoulders, resigning himself to the fact he enjoyed the event. "I need to find my assigned seat now." The wizard left ringside, hoping Harley did not take offense, but the scent became indomitable.

Casemiro claimed his seat next to the throne for the final three matches of the tournament. The wizard attempted to avoid Laural's glare, but he succumbed to the temptation and turned in her direction. "Princess, delighted you made it this evening."

Laural shook her head and walked over in disgust. "Listen, I grow tired of this being weird between us. Let's move on. After the final match, Forrest, Oleander, and I agreed to visit the Skullery for food and drinks. Join us for an evening of fellowship. Let's consider it a going away celebration since, I presume, you depart on the first boat tomorrow."

The wizard wondered how the Princess reached that conclusion, as he showed no intention of leaving. Despite an uneasiness regarding Laural and the emotions between the two, Casemiro's intuition encouraged him to accept the invitation. "Not sure what gave you that impression, but I will join you at the dining hall. If that makes you happy?"

"Yes." Laural smiled at the wizard with relief spreading across both their faces. The Princess walked back to her seat.

The Prince leaned over to the wizard. "Glad to see you two talking again."

"Yes, my lord. And congratulations on creating this wonderful spectacle."

"Based on the proceeds from last night's second session, and what I estimate is coming in today, we shall clear our expenses and begin replenishing the royal reserves and satisfy my sister." Arenton flashed a sly grin toward the Princess as he reminded Laural of her lack of enthusiasm over the plan. "Now, let's begin the night's festivities." The Prince pointed toward Harley Sweet as the signal to begin.

Sweet climbed through the ropes and welcomed the crowd with his energetic introductions for the Natural Wonder and the Elemental Hammer. Neither grappler wasted their breath, or strength, on pre-match histrionics. The Wonder left his spectacular robe backstage and stood ready in the ring like a lion preparing to pounce on its next meal. The fan's choice sprinted to the ring accompanied by a loud ovation spurring him on, slid beneath the bottom rope, and popped up to grapple with his foe.

Both contestants pummeled each other with suplexes, slams, and clotheslines for twenty minutes. The first indication of the eventual outcome occurred when the Natural Wonder performed an explosive drop on the Hammer's knee from a turnbuckle. The move weakened the Hammer enough that he eventually fell victim to a destructive leg lock, the culmination of a series of attacks aimed at the specific body part.

The Hammer groaned in pain as the Wonder refused to release the hold and applied the move until a stark scream and nasty crack quieted the crowd. The referee ended the match and Perriman released the hold to walk around the ring, smiling as he raised his arms aloft in victory.

Perriman exited the battle zone but stopped at the apron to yell at the audience. "I told you I would break his leg and you better prepare for another one tonight. Yoooo!"

Sweet and Forrest picked up the Hammer and carried him to the backstage area. The victim endured the hold without giving in to the pain. As he left the ring, the Hammer pointed to Perriman and threatened the man. "When I return, you're dead, Perriman." The wrestlers vanished behind the curtain.

The remaining security team members cleared the ring to prepare for the next match. People shuffled in their seats, uncomfortable at witnessing the carnage in the prior match. Any uneasiness became a stray thought when Sweet returned to ringside. Harley flashed a sign to Casemiro and mouthed the word showmanship, and then re-entered the ring to announce the next two fighters.

The Prince tapped the wizard on the shoulder. "What does Sweet mean by that signal to you? And did the wrestler suffer a broken leg?"

"I doubt the leg really broke, your Highness. Perhaps they planned this as part of the show." The wizard and the Princess exchanged a smile, keeping the secret from Arenton.

The second match filled the role of the feature event for this round of the tournament. Based on the prior evening, the crowd rooted for Nikos Antaeus to recover from the attack of green mist to his face. The fan favorite entered the ring with a reddish, irritated countenance, a clear after effect of the attack.

Sweet introduced the Ninja Serpent, who emerged for the match with black face-paint broken by white streaks from forehead to chin. Upon the Ninja Serpent entering the ring, the grapplers applied holds and counters in a flurry of activity. The match's speed thrilled the crowd, who cheered or booed for each move based on the wrestler gaining the advantage.

After the initial energy of the combatants ebbed, the crowd sensed the momentum of the match shift to the Serpent. The Serpent used a series of martial art chops and kicks to weaken his foe. A flurry of punishing moves alluded to the approaching end of the match. The Serpent began the sequence of moves to finish his opponent, just as the Easterner performed the prior day. The aggressor performed a thrust kick to the abdomen of Nikos. But instead of using his finishing maneuver, the Ninja Serpent opted to spray green mist once more.

Nikos dodged the liquid and hit his opponent in the gut. He then locked his arms around the waist of the Serpent and lifted him into the air to execute a suplex. Nikos shifted the Serpent's body to land on his back and the audience cheered. Nikos picked up the man and swung him toward the ropes. As the Serpent rebounded, Nikos flipped the man into a dynamic slam. The people yelled in appreciation, and the volume grew with each count toward the pinfall. At three, Veritas Keep vibrated from the cheers of the crowd.

Nikos defeated his rival and jumped in jubilation and the referee lifted his arm in victory. Nikos stood next to the Dragon Serpent, waiting for his foe to rise. Once the Serpent rose, he and Nikos shook hands and parted ways in opposite directions from the ring.

Following the brief celebration, the crowd quieted in anticipation of the feature event. Sweet announced a thirty-minute intermission to allow for logistical elements of the show. The Prince left the throne to prepare for the final performance and to retrieve the championship belt.

As the crowd waited for the final match of the tournament, Laural left and returned carrying a snack. "You want a bite? They fry the dough and cover it with sugar and an odd spice called cinnamon. Marvelous." She tore off a piece and gave the snack to Casemiro.

Casemiro put the confection in his mouth and the doughy substance melted on the wizard's tongue. "Wow. Excellent."

The Princess smiled at the wizard after taking another bite. "This festival appeals to my basest instincts: food, drink, and violence. I hope Nikos scores a victory after the adversity of battling a larger wrestler and the savage spraying him in the face."

Casemiro nodded. "Yes, it all creates a fantastic story." The wizard once more fell for the narrative spun by Harley Sweet. Casemiro predicted a twist due to his belief that Sweet's showmanship always won out. "I wager Perriman becomes the champion because Sweet always delivers what you least expect."

The wizard scanned the crowd and spotted Heenan, the man he waited an entire day to confront. The Counselor stood near Oleander and talked to the point his face turned red.

Casemiro asked the Princess, "Why does Heenan bother Oleander?"

"The same reason he chatted with me earlier. He is a pig trying to find a place to stay warm at night."

The wizard chased the man, driven by personal motivations rather than concern for Oleander or Laural's dignity. Casemiro pushed through the crowd, sometimes even tapping people with the butt of his staff to move them. Upon reaching Heenan, the wizard pulled the counselor to the wall and pressed him against it, spilling the drink in Heenan's hand.

"Hello Casemiro, is there a problem?" Heenan stood straight and smiled at the wizard as he revealed his true height. Though not the size of Forrest, the counselor towered over the wizard.

"Yes, the Prince shared a bit of how you found me. Why did you search for me?"

The counselor rolled his eyes. "My curiosity wondered about the rumors of a washed-up wizard. A man who lost his power over time, an old fool named Casemiro. And, yes, I arranged the message to draw your attention and lead you to Lillenhold."

Casemiro let go of Heenan. "For what purpose?"

"To expose a wizard's worthlessness to the world. Or at least one unworthy of the admiration paid to you by the royal family. I found proof of your fraudulence."

The wizard held the staff in front of him. Though unwilling to use his power in these cramped quarters, he hoped the counselor failed to understand the self-imposed limitation. "Who are you, Heenan? What did I ever do to you?" Casemiro speculated about what information Heenan owned. Failures cluttered Casemiro's life and finding the specific one Heenan alluded to might be difficult. The wizard slumped his shoulders from the weight of guilt and doubt.

A laugh from Heenan wilted Casemiro's ego and filled the hall. "You do not deserve that knowledge. Not until I embarrass you in front of everyone, and these people witness your true nature." The counselor grabbed Casemiro, spun him to switch positions, and pressed the wizard against the wall. "Now, have we finished? I wish to enjoy the wrestling match."

Unseen by both combatants, Laural appeared behind Heenan, brandishing a hidden knife at his side. "I suggest you let go of my friend, counselor. Before I ruin your evening and everyone else's in Veritas Keep. You wouldn't want to do that, would you?" The Princess shoved the point enough into the man's side to show Heenan her intention.

Heenan let go of the wizard, straightening the man's cloak as he backed away. Then the counselor spilled the rest of his drink on the wizard's outfit. "Appears you cannot control your drink, Casemiro."

Laural threatened the weasel as she brandished her blade. "Next time, I won't warn you."

"If you owned only a fraction of her spirit, wizard." Heenan glared at the Princess. "Perhaps we will experience how you respond if I turn the tables, pretty girl." The counselor walked away.

Casemiro leaned against the wall and dropped towards the floor, struggling for a breath; his body weighed down by the fear, doubt, and guilt. The wizard pictured himself gutted and laid open for everyone in the keep to examine his failings.

Laural propped the wizard against the wall, helping Casemiro rise to his full height. "Ignore Heenan. After I speak to Arenton, my brother will end his service in this kingdom." The Princess glanced around the crowd to follow Heenan and ensure he left their vicinity.

After a moment, the wizard regained color to his face, and the threat passed.

Laural asked, "Want to discuss what happened?"

The wizard refused to acknowledge the event in front of this audience. "Help me back to my seat first." Casemiro leaned against Laural for a moment, peering over her shoulder and finding Heenan across the keep with a smile smeared across his face. The wizard regained his composure as the Princess walked him back to his seat.

Once the two sat, Laural gave the wizard a questioning stare, and Casemiro waved in a dismissing manner. "Forget it. Let us focus on the match and enjoy ourselves."

Laural pounded the arms of her chair in frustration and left her seat. "Insufferable!"

Casemiro ignored the Princess and turned towards the ring. *She possesses no clue of what I am dealing with.*

After the longest thirty minutes in Casemiro's awful week, the audience went silent. Prince Arenton appeared in the ring holding the Golden Dragon Championship belt above his head. The two participants soon entered the ring and the Lord of Veritas Keep spoke. "After the match, the belt goes to one of these two men tonight and I declare the winner the first Golden Dragon Champion of Lillenhold. I wish both men good luck and a safe fight."

Arenton held the belt in the ring as Harley Sweet provided the final introductions of the tournament. Once the pre-match festivities finished, the Prince and Sweet left the ring. When Arenton returned to his throne holding the golden strap across his lap, the bell rang, and the bout began.

Nikos stood shorter than Perriman and weighed less than his opponent. Perriman returned to his normal ring entrance from the prior evening and reminded the women of the sculptures of gods and heroes found in castles and museums. The smaller man received cheers from the crowd, but the Natural Wonder engrossed a group of vocal female supporters gathered near the ring with more than a little flesh showing.

The match started with neither man gaining an advantage until Perriman trapped Nikos in a side-head lock. Nikos wiggled free and whipped Perriman to the ropes. Nikos received a shoulder to the chest from Perriman, knocking the hero to the mat. The Wonder shifted his attack's focus to the shoulder joint of his opponent. The Natural Wonder yelled to the audience, "I don't care how many holds you mastered, you can't do any of them if your arm doesn't work."

As Nikos laid on the mat, an onslaught of knees to the shoulder joint appeared agonizing from the impact and the resounding groans from the victim. The Wonder pulled Nikos to his feet and performed a crushing suplex and ensured his foe landed on the same shoulder. The Wonder kept the attack going and reached down to pull Nikos from the mat. Nikos used his healthy arm to cradle the head of his foe and pulled Perriman to the ground and attempted a pin. A two-count woke up the crowd as the fans sensed a momentum change to the match.

Nikos rolled out of the hold and pulled the Wonder into a whipping move and sent him to the ropes. Nikos used his functioning arm to do a deep arm drag to flip Perriman into the mat with significant force. Nikos repeated the move two more times. He attempted the move once more, but the Wonder reversed the move and threw Nikos to the opposite ropes.

Nikos used the momentum to bounce off the ropes and deliver a flying forearm smash to his foe's head, but Perriman, though stunned, remained standing. Nikos stomped on the foot of the Natural Wonder. Perriman leaned forward in agony, and Nikos placed him in a front-face lock. He glanced toward the wizard and winked at Casemiro before performing the deathdrop trap and put his foe's face into the mat. Nikos paused long enough to catch his breath before covering his foe. The audience roared to life, expecting a winner. His delay cost Nikos as the Natural Wonder kicked out at the two-count. The audience fell back into their seats in exasperation.

Nikos hit the mat with his hand in frustration and stood. His agitation became apparent, and Nikos rushed to grab his opponent for the next move. The younger man's carelessness allowed Perriman to grab his foe's bad arm and pulled Nikos to the mat. The Natural Wonder placed Nikos in a cradle hold and pinned his shoulders to the mat for the three-count and a victory in the tournament.

Paul Perriman, the Natural Wonder, won the belt by creating an abrupt change in the match's momentum. The audience seemed confused and wondered if the match concluded because the ending happened so fast. Inside the ring, the men exhibited opposite reactions; one jumped for joy while the other held his head in his hands. In his continued effort at solid sportsmanship, Nikos rose and approached Perriman with his hand extended. Perriman glared at his foe and walked by him without another glance. Nikos Antaeus retreated to a corner, defeated and rejected.

Watching the events unfold, Casemiro sympathized with the young man and assumed a connection existed between them. At that moment, the wizard believed only one person in Veritas Keep related to his emotions and situation. The wizard glimpsed Sweet climbing into the ring and realized he fell under the man's spell one more time.

Once Sweet announced the official decision to the crowd, the Prince advanced to the ring to begin the post-match ceremony. Arenton awarded the Golden Dragon Championship belt to Paul Perriman, who received a respectful amount of applause and a squeal of glee from his feminine followers. Nikos Antaeus received a silver medal for his runner-up position, and the audience gave a resounding cheer. The audience responded with a deafening roar when the Prince asked if they enjoyed the Extravaganza. Sweet closed the ceremony by thanking the crowd and dismissed them for the evening.

A quarter-hour passed as the people cleared the hall of Veritas Keep, the doors shut, and the wrestlers emerged from their hidden area to meet the Prince. The Prince smiled as he peered around the room. "Thank you to everyone for taking part and producing the outstanding performances. Now, I wish to award this gold medal to the champion as they return the championship belt. You can wear the strap whenever you attend an event at Veritas Keep, but it stays here." The Prince gave the gold medal to Perriman and grabbed the belt. He turned to the remainder of the wrestlers and their crew. "Gentlemen, I provided Harley Sweet your portion of the gate and the agreed upon flat fee, so receive your cut from him. Thank you again, and I hope to conduct another event soon."

The Prince turned to Casemiro, Forrest, and Oleander. "I didn't forget my volunteers. A little bonus." He gave each a small satchel filled with money. "Don't spend it in one spot." Arenton left the central chamber of the keep and walked up the stairs to his residence and to return the belt to its secure location.

The wrestlers and Sweet walked around the room exchanging handshakes and hugging various people, including Casemiro. One wrestler asked the wizard to show him the trick with the explosion sometime. Nikos came over and asked the wizard's opinion on the move he performed in his honor.

"I wish you won, but I loved the move." The two men then shared a laugh.

Once Nikos left, Sweet approached the wizard. "Though the event is complete, something tells me we are bound to cross paths once again. Good luck, Casemiro. And remember, showmanship always triumphs."

The two exchanged handshakes and then everyone left to address their post-match duties. The wrestlers bounced to their job of tearing down their equipment, and the castle guards to securing Veritas Keep.

Casemiro found Laural, Forrest, and Oleander all walking toward the exit. The group of four drew towards each other like magnets. Once the wizard reached them, he asked, "My friends, who else needs a drink and a bite of food?"

As they exited the building, Forrest stopped. "Oleander do you not wish for a ride this evening?"

She smiled back to the troll-man. "I believe the walk will do us all some good."

The foursome headed to the village and they discussed their personal highlights of the event. Each found the action more thrilling than they expected. Once clear of the keep's grounds, the wind whipped at a stronger velocity than normal, and the group coalesced into a tighter circle to minimize the impact of the icy breeze.

The wind's sound intensified, triggering a memory in Casemiro's mind. The breeze pulsed through the air, a rhythm matching a heartbeat. The wizard recognized the source of the extraordinary breeze too late to act. The next gust blew the four of them to the ground. Oleander fell away from the others and rose to her knees. Her dress torn along one side from the fall. Before Oleander responded, a clawed talon reached out and plucked her from the ground.

The others rose and witnessed the colossal beast, a dragon, flying away with Oleander in its clutches. The monster turned in mid-air and flew back towards them. They feared the beast might finish them with a gory display of its power, but capturing the damsel satiated its thirst. The beast glared at Casemiro before racing over their heads towards Mount Siven in the distance, flapping its immense leathery wings and creating a miniature windstorm in its wake.

Forrest pointed and yelled into the sky. "No!" The troll-man's emotional pain echoed through the night.

Laural yelled a question to anyone who might answer. "What happened?"

Casemiro fell to his knees, aware of the answer to the question. The wizard's demons rose once more, and the regret filled his soul for not finishing the job twenty years before. "A dragon. And it took Oleander." The wizard failed to stop the monster from escaping with the woman of Forrest's dreams. Finally, the unspoken truths of Casemiro came back to haunt him and the wizard fell to the ground, gutted and in tears.

14

THE SEARCH BEGINS

The night winds died, and the distant surf swooshed against the rock walls of the port. Almost no one walked in the area between the village and the keep to disturb the near silence. If one ignored the dragon's attack, the setting approached serene. Then the whispers began. Those few that witnessed the event told others. But all of them ignored the three people still lying on the ground in the aftermath. Villagers emerged and investigated the distant sky and the surrounding terrain, unsure of what evil they searched for.

The attack occurred with such rapidity, the trio of Forrest, Laural, and Casemiro were offered no chance to respond. The three friends sat in stunned silence as the beast rode the winds into the nighttime air and beyond their sight.

Laural screamed, "Help!"

Forrest roared at the beast with a mighty yell.

Casemiro rumbled to Laural. "Did the dragon hurt you?"

Laural fell to her knees, crying. "No, but why did it attack?"

The wizard turned to Forrest for an answer. Upon being touched, Forrest lifted the old man and roared into his face.

Casemiro slapped the troll-man and brought his focus back. Forrest realized he held Casemiro and dropped the wizard to the ground.

Casemiro asked the troll-man, "Are you hurt, Forrest?"

Forrest shook his head and showed no injuries from the attack, but returned his eyes to the night sky.

Only when a bystander asked Casemiro about his own condition did the wizard realize someone should report the incident. The wizard began walking back up the hill to Veritas Keep, pushing the guilt from twenty years away. "I need to inform the Prince and then chase down the dragon."

The wizard ignored the world around him, including Laural and Forrest following at some distance in his wake. No words escaped the wizard's lips until he entered Veritas Keep, where his anger swelled to incredible heights. Casemiro ignored the swell of magical energy at his command. Once he reached the hall of the keep, the wizard yelled for someone's attention. "Arenton! Heenan! Anyone! The dragon attacked the village!"

Casemiro yelled and paced in the hall for several minutes. During his rampage, Laural and Forrest entered the hall and joined him. The rage within the wizard roared with a massive blast of energy in the room. It was then the bells of the keep rang to warn of an attack.

Much too late to help Oleander.

The Prince, Heenan, and the Captain of the Guard arrived flanked by a group of soldiers. The group attempted to understand the situation by talking over each other. The chaos grew louder and louder. Crowding out the wizard, Princess, and Forrest as they attempted to deliver the news of Oleander's distress.

As the chaos surrounded the wizard, Casemiro withdrew from the noise and vacillated between guilt and dread for his inaction two decades earlier. Part of his psyche prompted the wizard to jump on the first ship leaving Lillenhold, as Laural intimated earlier in the evening. The other part contemplated saving Oleander from the dragon and chasing honor, a reminder of his old life. The wizard's heart echoed a calling that pushed Casemiro to break free from his guilt, no matter the cost. Enough people paid for his failures over the years, and tonight he declared Oleander as the last.

Casemiro replayed the attack in his mind, running the confrontation backwards and forwards multiple times. Each viewing revealed the building fear that Casemiro recognized this dragon. The warnings the wizard pushed off over the last few days foretold this occurring. Casemiro believed his lack of action allowed this to happen. He could have warned the Prince, Gerard, Heenan, or anyone else to prevent this from taking place.

The wizard needed to understand why the dragon struck. His experience taught him that dragons attacked their greatest threat first, without fail. Forrest, or Casemiro, presented the greatest threats. Instead, the dragon targeted Oleander, the lowest threat to the beast, and grabbed her at the first available chance. The bystanders became inconsequential to the monstrosity, which meant only one reason: the dragon targeted her. Casemiro believed the dragon cared nothing about him, but he wondered what made Oleander an attractive victim to the monster.

Amongst the commotion, Forrest and Laural appealed to the Prince to send a search party to comb the hills for Oleander. Heenan supported Laural's and Forrest's requests, but declined to support their effort with his own physical endangerment. Other voices raised objections ranging from calling a rescue stupid to declaring the task a suicide mission.

With a coherent plan in mind, Casemiro yelled over the noise. "ENOUGH!" The wizard pounded his staff on the floor and the echoes rebounded throughout Veritas Keep and sparks flew into the sky. Everyone became silent and allowed the wizard to speak again.

"Oleander needs our help. Prince Arenton, what are you going to do about it?"

The Prince, wearing a purple robe over his white nightclothes, proclaimed his official stance. "Lady Oleander's predicament sounds tragic, and I share your fondness for her, but my mind provides three obvious options. Option one: do nothing and leave the maiden's fate to the dragon. The second, send a company of soldiers to the dragon's lair, attack the beast, and attempt to save the lady. Or third, send a small group of sturdy-hearted warriors to wrest Oleander from the clutches of this beast. I value the insight and guidance of everyone present on this matter and request each of you voice your opinion."

The Captain of the Guard spoke first. "My Lord, I prefer launching a sizable contingent and remove this beast forever. The gossip about a dragon circulated for months before this attack, but now that confirmation exists. We must kill the creature."

Heenan answered next. "My Lord, I believe the lady Oleander is already dead. We must avoid angering the beast and bringing its wrath on Lillenhold. I recommend we do nothing."

Casemiro recognized Heenan's fear for what it truly was. His willingness to allow the woman he pursued a few short hours ago to die on the mountain rather than risk his own life. The wizard smirked at the predictable response from the worm and glanced at Laural. *She obviously didn't speak to Arenton yet about Heenan. Or did Arenton refuse her request?*

Forrest charged the counselor and hoisted him to eye level. "Heenan, your words come from a place of pure cowardice, and you tempt me to remove your foul body from this royal court. In pieces."

The Captain's soldiers approached and drew their swords to warn Forrest to release the man. The troll-man dropped Heenan to the floor on his backside, growled at him, and walked to Casemiro's side.

Laural provided her vote. "I doubt the effectiveness of a full force attack on the beast but agree something must be done. What does the one person experienced in slaying dragons say before I cast my lot?"

Casemiro's attention drifted to his past interactions with the dragons on Mount Siven. He refocused on the conversation as the Prince approached him for advice.

"Casemiro, what say you? What sage words can you provide at a time like this?"

The wizard pointed around the room. "You fools believe brute force can win the day. This dragon destroys mightier forces than you dare to muster. The dragon's wings create hurricanes, the fires from his throat roast legions of pigs in one breath, his talons exceed the length of your swords, and the beast's hide is nigh impenetrable. Add to this the difficulty of reaching its lair and your failure to account for the beast's greatest strength, a cunning mind, and we face an insurmountable task. Any hope of regaining Oleander rests with a small group. Even though a fool's errand, we possess a single option if we wish to rescue our friend."

Gerard responded. "Does anyone wish to volunteer for this doomed party?"

Many people grumbled with words beneath their breath in reply, but none stepped forward until Casemiro responded.

"I will go."

Arenton smiled at the wizard in a manner indicating a hidden joy for the Prince.

Casemiro sneered at Arenton, but accepted his fate. "Count me in, contract or not, to prevent my guilt from breaking me further. I will go alone, if necessary, but I wonder if anyone else wishes to travel with me."

The Captain of the Guard answered, pushing out his metal-lined chest to project a stance of strength. "Protecting the Prince and the kingdom's welfare remain my top priorities, so I stay."

Casemiro questioned the Captain's heart for the first time. A man of his stature not volunteering for this quest worried the wizard. Though concerned, he pushed away the urge to ask questions over the Captain's courage until after the quest because it did no good in the moment.

Laural stepped forward and stood beside Casemiro. "I plan to take part in this quest on behalf of the royal family. I possess few skills that might defeat a dragon, but wish to bring Oleander back to Lillenhold."

The wizard affirmed her choice with a silent nod of reassurance and then asked a question with a cynical sneer on his lips. "Isn't the Golden Dragon Champion supposed to be involved in these types of affairs?"

The Prince perked up at the comment, having forgotten the other contractual obligation to take part in this act. "Yes, I forgot our newest champion of Lillenhold. Heenan, retrieve Paul Perriman and remind him of his obligation for a quest such as this."

The counselor fled the hall to retrieve the man and avoid the possibility of selection.

In the meantime, Forrest volunteered for the quest. "I must do this to help save Oleander."

Everyone present comprehended the troll-man's true feelings for the lady. Laural grabbed his hand for emotional support and to show camaraderie, silently vowing to bring him along.

The Prince replied to the troll-man with a tone of dismissal. "No, we send three people: the wizard, Princess Laural, and the Golden Dragon Champion. If we send more, we might as well send our armored forces, an act I do not condone."

As the words faded into the air, Heenan dragged the winner of the golden belt into the hall.

The barely dressed wrestler, inebriated by several flagons of ale, glanced around the vast room. "You pulled me from the arms of an amply bosomed woman to discuss a quest?" He spun in a circle and fell to the floor, his eyes red and his breath pungent.

The Prince replied and drew the wrestler's attention to the discussion. "Mr. Perriman, as the champion, you must fulfill the requirements of the title. This quest involves rescuing lady Oleander from a dragon and not doing so leads to a hanging." The Prince paused and looked to his Captain of the Guard. "We need to rethink why hangings became the default punishment around here. Regardless, you join the wizard Casemiro and Princess Laural on this mission."

Perriman raised his hands in protest. "You can put me in jail, if you wish, but I am not fighting a dragon and committing suicide."

Heenan commented, "But your contract states—"

"So, if I'm not the champion, no obligation, correct?"

"Correct, but you can only lose the title if we strip the belt from you, or another defeats you. You cannot vacate the title on your own while living."

Perriman scanned the room to assess his options, and a smile crossed his lips, revealing to everyone he solved the problem. "Does anyone wish to volunteer for this quest?"

Forrest walked over to the wrestler. "I volunteer."

Perriman peered into the troll-man's eyes, well above his own, and whispered an instruction, "Push me down."

"What?" Forrest peered at the man incredulously.

"If you want to go, push me, *trollen*." Perriman received the expected response to the emphasized slur.

Forrest's eyes grew to twice their normal size, and he slammed his hands into the man's chest. The troll-man hurled Perriman across the room and followed to stand above the wrestler, unsure of his next move.

Perriman groaned as he peered at his new opponent. "You used excessive, but effective, force. If you wish to save Oleander, lay on top of me."

Forrest glanced around the room, perplexed as to what Perriman requested of him.

"You idiot, lay across me and the wizard knows what to do."

Forrest dropped to the ground and laid atop Perriman. Casemiro rushed to the scene, kneeled on the stone floor, and counted to three, signifying the troll-man's victory over Paul Perriman. In the dark of the night, the second Golden Dragon Champion's reign began.

"I now welcome your addition to our crew, my friend. I wish such a victory occurred at a more joyous time."

Forrest offered his hand and helped Perriman to his feet as a sign of goodwill. Perriman took the meaty palm and rotated his shoulder to assess it for a separation, but found everything intact.

The Natural Wonder looked at the troll-man with a smile. "If you enter the ring, you might prove unstoppable. Sorry for the insult, but you struck me as the type to not hit unless I pissed you off." The Natural Wonder wandered off to find his buxom maiden and resume his previously interrupted activities.

Forrest walked back over to the assembly and stood beside Laural and Casemiro, their group now complete.

The Prince laughed at the display, finding some humor in the darkest of moments. "Well, we mustered a team. It's important you three rest before departing. Besides, we need the time for Heenan and Captain Gerard to gather supplies and horses for your trip. We'll meet in the garden at dawn."

Gerard asked, "Wait, where are they traveling?"

Casemiro answered the question. "We travel to the peak of Mount Siven and the dragon's lair."

The room filled with fear as Gerard followed up with the question all wished to ask. "How do you know this?"

"From my twenty years of experience, and I witnessed the dragon on the mountain the last few days."

Laural shot a glare of disdain at the wizard. "Another of your unspoken truths? You failed to warn us." The Princess flung a clenched fist at Casemiro, and the group separated them.

"I have witnessed the signs since arriving in Lillenhold. Upon my arrival, the dragon appeared on Mount Siven and I observed it every day since. I prayed my imagination ran wild, but my mind did not play tricks and as a result, the lady Oleander lies in the beast's clutches. Nothing you say can make me feel worse as I carry the guilt for this lapse in judgment to not bring this to the attention of the authorities. But from what Gerard said, others have known of the dragon's existence for quite some time and did nothing about it."

Arenton realized the eyes shifted to him. "Enough! This does nothing to help Oleander. Sleep as much as possible before we reconvene at dawn in the garden."

The Captain of the Guard stopped Casemiro. "Wizard, I thank you for the information you provided regarding the cooper. It aided the investigation, but I fear your choice in this matter. Do you wish to go on the quest with a primary suspect?"

Casemiro eyed Forrest from across the hall. "I want no one else. His feelings for Oleander compel him to take part in this rescue. And between us, I do not think Forrest attempted to kill the Prince."

"Very well, I'll continue the investigation in your stead, and hope your journey proves successful."

Before the wizard replied, the noise of a slap rifled through the hall; followed by a yell from the Princess. "How dare you! I do not care about my reputation. You shall treat me as a lady and as a member of the royal family, Heenan! I suggest you stay out of my sight until I leave the village at dawn, you sacrilegious swine." She turned to her brother. "You need to dismiss this man as quickly as possible or he will be your ruin, brother."

The wizard turned to Gerard as they allowed Heenan to walk away sheepishly. "I believe the Princess, in her present mood, shall provide more fight than anyone expected."

Casemiro left the hall and wondered if comfortable sleep waited for him, or if the nightmares waited to return. Either way, the challenge ahead might end in their deaths. After a brief bout of restlessness, the wizard's sleep held many dreams. All variations featured a visage of his beloved Chantal delivering one message. "Save the girl."

Casemiro woke from his restless slumber early and washed his face and hands before the trip. He shaved off the week's growth of a beard. The wizard doubted a bath existed in the immediate future and wished to tackle this task with clean skin. After dressing in his gray cloak and packing his knitting needles, the wizard waited for Roman outside Veritas Keep, the same routine as every morning this week.

Roman walked up the hill and stopped in front of the wizard. "I heard about the dragon. You plan to kill it?"

The wizard smirked at the boy's innocence. "I will most likely do something stupid and terrible for my health. Beyond that, I can only speculate. Any news?"

The boy shook his head. "Nothing since the Extravaganza. Richard won a wager, but I have no information on how the good fortune impacted his status with the Prince."

Casemiro crouched and established eye contact with the boy. "Listen, the coin still works if I am alive. While gone, I need you to monitor the Captain of the Guard and that weaselly counselor, Heenan, for me. Something between them raises my internal alarms. Inform me if you discover anything about them." The wizard flipped another coin in the air.

The boy caught the gold piece and his eyes lit up. "You sure? You paid more than we agreed."

"You did excellent work, Roman, and consider this an advance payment if I don't return. Your family can use the money. When I return, you get more. Unfortunately, I am the only one who understands what awaits us up there, and it isn't pleasant."

"Casemiro, I hope you return because Lillenhold needs more people like you." The boy hugged the wizard and pocketed the coin before running into the keep to begin his shift in the kitchen.

Casemiro reflected on the boy's words. "I'm not the person you believe I am, Roman; just a powerless wizard." He left the wall and joined the group waiting in the garden.

The sun peaked above the horizon and the sea roared in the background as a salty breeze whipped through the grounds. A guard held the reins of two horses equipped with saddles and full bags. Forrest stood as tall as the animals, and Casemiro contemplated the possibility of him riding any of the standard stallions. Then another, much larger Ardennais emerged and stopped alongside the other two horses. Even the troll-man couldn't break this mount's strong back.

Laural emerged from the keep with the Prince on her heels. The Princess caught sight of the wizard and approached to offer an apology. "About last evening..."

Casemiro beat her to the punch. "I apologize to everyone, especially Oleander. I intend to deliver that apology in person."

The Prince ignored the side discussions and called everyone to attention. "It delights me that you three remained true to your word. I hated the idea of putting out a warrant for your arrest and hanging you for defection and cowardice. Regardless, the Captain of the Guard will brief you on what we provided and may God bless your journey."

Gerard stepped in front of the horses and unrolled a list from which he read. "We supplied a bedroll and blankets to keep you warm at night. Your packs contain a firestarter kit you must keep dry, if possible. Each of you carries a healthy supply of dried meat, herbs, and bread. Be wary of what plants you eat from your path. Many of the indigenous weeds can kill or sicken you. We packed two water sacks. Best to refill your sacks when you cross the rushing stream. Casemiro, we packed the yarn, as per your request. And Forrest, you carry all the cooking gear."

The wizard nodded and patted his breast pocket to ensure he remembered the knitting needles. "Appreciated, Captain." He held his staff in the other hand and his saber grazed his thigh.

The Captain continued his speech in a formal tone. "Following the road to the mountain requires five days to reach the base. The horses cannot scale the steep rise of Mount Siven. Releasing them creates no issues as we trained them to return to Veritas Keep. If you stake their leads for an eventual return, you better pray you come back, or I will extract the debts from your dead body. These beasts are worth more than any of you, including the Princess. No offense, my lady."

Laural smiled at the comment and nodded her head to show she took no offense. The morning light peaked over the walls of Veritas Keep and revealed the splendor of the outfit worn by the Princess. A leather jerkin covered a red coarse top. Black boots accented her black riding pants. Laural carried a scabbard for a short sword at her side and the Princess exuded the appearance of an adventurer.

Arenton walked over to the Princess. "My sister, I wish you the best of luck and Godspeed. I hope you return in one piece, and I already miss you."

The siblings embraced, and everyone paused because of the unexpected showing of affection. The Princess pecked Arenton on the cheek and turned to the group as she pulled her dark, curly hair back into a bun. "Are we riding or not?"

The three travelers boarded their steeds and rode the horses out of the keep. Once they passed through the main gate, the trio headed towards the forest road leading to the base of the summit. Casemiro spotted no movement on the peak this morning as he peered above them, knowing the beast rested after its night of action.

Forrest asked, "Do you think Oleander will last five days?"

"No, but let's not ponder that possibility. On day two, we'll find the stream and then follow a path I remember to the mountain's base. On the way, determine your pack's capacity as we'll be walking and the horses cannot traverse the terrain near the mountain. By traveling at night, we can cut the trip by a day or more." Casemiro turned to the other two riders. "Are we agreed?"

Laural and Forrest nodded.

"Then let's free Oleander, or if we arrive too late, kill the beast responsible." Mentally and emotionally unprepared for the trip, Casemiro feared he led the others to their doom. The troop rode their steeds into the early morning light and disappeared from the view of Veritas Keep as they rounded the first bend in the road and entered a new world.

15

TEA AND TRUTHS

The road zigged from one direction to another, following the fall line of the terrain in a continual climb toward the mountain. Hooves and wheels pounded the well-traveled road into a smooth path ten feet in width over the years. The party rode along one side in single file to hide their numbers if anyone chased the trio and to quickly escape from any travelers coming toward them. The group rode around another bend and a gap in the trees allowed them to view Lillenhold in the valley below, revealing how high they climbed in the five hours.

From the village, the forest contained pine and cedar trees, but once in the woodland's heart, many other arboreal varieties became clear. Wych elms, hornbeam, black poplar, and yew trees dotted the edges of the trail as new blooms and year-round leaves on the overflowing branches provided cover from the blazing sunlight.

The scents from the conifers created an earthy and piney scent the riders welcomed. The searching bramble and vines throughout the forest floor also protected those on the path, as no surprise attackers snuck through the trees or bush undetected. Their lone vulnerability lay along the path and any horses chasing or charging from either direction provided ample advanced warning. This sense of safety helped the group relax and ride at a comfortable pace on their steeds.

The solitary sounds reaching the group consisted of the calming twitters of robins, caws of the crows, and warbles from doves. Peace filled the travelers as they rode on and ate a quick lunch of bread slathered in butter and a piece of dried meat. The water in their pouches remained chilled and fresh.

After stopping to eat, Princess Laural rode alongside Casemiro. "Will you share any unspoken truths before we go up the mountain? Or just spring the surprise of your inability to defeat a dragon on us prior to facing the beast?"

Casemiro whirled toward Laural and pulled his horse to a stop. "I suggest the Princess mind her own business."

Forrest and his Ardennais caught up. "You justify Laural's concern with your hesitance. Can you defeat the dragon, or do we require another plan? Upon reaching the dragon's cave, we limit our options to what we bring into the beast's lair."

"Neither of you understands how delicate the use of magic can be. I will be ready when we reach the dragon's home. Just pray we reach the lair in time to save Oleander."

Laural asked, "Have you at least developed the beginnings of a plan?"

"Yes, determine Oleander's status, and if she lives, extract her. My guess, the dragon killed Oleander. Sorry, Forrest. If the dragon did not kill her, the predicament raises other questions over why the beast abducted Oleander." If this scenario proved true, it created an unsolvable mystery in Casemiro's mind.

Forrest encouraged his horse to trot past the wizard. "Then enlighten us along the way to the issues concerning your abilities."

Laural's horse continued forward as the Princess commented over her shoulder. "Forrest and I agree, if we understand the problems, we might help resolve them."

Casemiro loosened the reins on his horse and allowed the steed to trot ahead to catch the others. "As if your talents might help a wizard."

The Princess smiled back at Casemiro, and the wizard's heart pounded a little harder when her green eyes glimmered for a brief second in the midday sunlight.

The wizard whispered beneath his breath, "You aren't helping, Princess." Casemiro barged ahead of the other two. "Fine, I will tell the story, but bear with me if I become emotional, as this may prove difficult. I rarely share these tales."

Laural and her horse sidled up to Casemiro and his steed. "Take your time. You are among friends who experience occasional frustration with one another."

Casemiro glanced over his shoulder toward Forrest, and the troll-man agreed. Casemiro cleared his throat and sat a little higher in the saddle, firm in his belief that holding onto his hidden truths created no significant issues. The wizard sighed a breath of resignation and began the tale.

"I entered our little house in the tiny village of Foxshire, where we lived. I remember every detail from that day vividly. Flowers sat on the table, wilted. A pot of Bergamot bubbled on the stove and two cups of steaming tea still sat on the table next to her favorite chair. The light filtered through the window before sunset in sheets of orange and purple. Wooden floors covered by a hint of dust allowed your shoes to leave their tracks. And the house stood quiet as a tomb.

"My wife bore no children, as per my wish, and I carried the guilt of withholding that desire from my beloved. My love for magic and adoration from the public left no time for children. I believed bringing children into a life centered on magic to be wrong. But self-indulgence proved my greatest failing, followed closely by vanity and pride."

Casemiro almost revealed an even greater secret, the wizard's greatest unspoken truth, which held him captive to this day. His chance to allow the secret to escape existed at this moment and Casemiro almost spoke the words. Chantal's death offered him a brief exultation and freed the wizard to live the life he desired. But Casemiro would cling to that secret as long as possible.

The wizard continued his story. "Chantal desired nothing more than having a family. I grew to enjoy my wife's family, all except for a lone sister I never met. We hosted Chantal's young nieces, nephews, and cousins many times over the years, but she never gave birth to her own children. An emptiness filled Chantal's heart for the love of a child of her own. An emptiness my wife held over me, and I carried that burden every day."

"As penance for my shortcomings, Chantal threatened to reveal certain truths to the world. Her bitterness and my pride created a divide between us, and, though we loved one another, this divide split our marriage. Chantal committed suicide by puncturing her heart with a knitting needle due to years of unfulfilled desires. A needle identical to those I carry as a constant reminder of my ineptitude."

Casemiro paused as the image of a dead Chantal raced into his memory. Once again, the wizard feared revealing his secret and glanced at the faces of his fellow travelers, wondering if Laural or Forrest might accept his incomplete tale. Casemiro stopped talking and waited for them to reply.

Laural turned to him. "You alright to continue?" The Princess wiped the corner of her eye. "Such a sad tale."

Forrest added a further comment. "Yes, my condolences for your loss."

"Thank you, but allow me to finish. I returned home from my latest exhibition to find Chantal dead in our home. I wept for hours; comfort only arrived when a neighbor passed and heard my wails of emotional pain from the street. As the days wore on and I said my last farewells, I reflected on what created the split between me and the woman I loved. The grief and resentment over the missed memories overwhelmed me. I completed my commitments in the village and left our home in Foxshire, selling the house for a pittance of its true value.

"Not until I attempted to use magic after Chantal's death did I realize the depth of the damage to me. The guilt over imposing my will over her life and creating a situation where Chantal believed it necessary to impale her heart took a toll. I became an unwhole person carrying a shattered spirit, and the magic abandoned me.

"That day, I committed to wandering the world to repair my heart and restore my magic; hoping to rid myself of the guilt for my treatment of Chantal. But the guilt only increased over time, and with each step forward, the magic remained hidden from me." Casemiro let the emotions flow and released most of his secrets.

"The person who defeated the greatest beasts no longer wielded the power to start basic fires. My magical abilities significantly declined after five years of searching for an answer. It took me that long to admit my greatest sin."

Casemiro examined Laural and Forrest with a fire in his eyes and realized his story transfixed them. "Want to know what happened?" The wizard did not wait for their answer. "A part of me experienced relief when Chantal died." The fact Casemiro said the words aloud stopped the wizard. He held back a whimper, but tears rolled from his eyes.

Astonishment covered the faces of his cohorts.

Casemiro refused to stop, as if continuing with the words might cauterize the wound to his soul. "Yes, I said the words. Relief swept over a part of me, but only a small part. I rejoiced in Chantal's death, even in the slightest degree, despite knowing the blame fell on my shoulders. That dreadful thought dissipated swiftly, while my ongoing attempts to rectify my greatest wrongdoing proved fruitless. I contented myself with wallowing in the pain and agony, aware I chose such a lot for my existence. Hope, that most precious gift, became absent from my life."

The wizard took a deep breath and sobbed for a moment, but Casemiro forced himself to finish his confession.

"Over the last five years, I bounced from village to village, finding menial jobs and hoping to hide from the shame and guilt. At times, I performed minuscule feats of magic, but the feelings of blame and culpability claimed my power once more. A lack of hope, love, and companionship for five years made me a bitter, lonely old man living as Casemiro, the woebegone wizard. An old man desiring one more chance to prove his greatness, one chance to not carry the guilt, and one last chance to be loved. All the while, knowing true contentment can never find me, or I it."

The wizard clamored toward the finish of the story. "Two weeks ago, I boarded a ship bound for Lillenhold wearing a gray cloak and carrying two knitting needles, a coin purse, yarn, and an advertisement for a wizard. Along with those few items, I bore a saber on my hip and held a gnarled wooden staff in my hand. I wished for enough magic to fool whoever posted the advertisement into thinking Casemiro might prove a wizard of some worth. I needed money but refused to hold on to hope. Such thoughts became a poison to my soul, even though I needed the income more than anything else at this point."

Casemiro stopped and glanced toward Laural and Forrest, wondering how they might react to his full story and the wizard revealing one of his greatest secrets.

Laural remained quiet and Forrest sat in silence atop his mount, both stone-faced and expressionless.

The wizard pleaded for them to show any type of reaction. "No response? Laural? Forrest?"

Forrest shook his head. "Perhaps I misjudged that Casemiro, thinking he left Lillenhold all those years ago and felt nothing towards my family or me. Though correct, I never imagined your shallowness created a greater scar on your life through failing your own loved one. I hold no more contempt in my heart because you inflicted the greatest damage on yourself."

"You speak the truth." A smidgeon of liberation hit Casemiro's soul from his testimony. The wizard flicked his fingers and a spark of flame emerged. Magic still existed in him, but extraordinarily little.

Laural's horse trotted a few steps to catch up to the wizard. "Thank you for sharing your story. For what it's worth, my brother searching for a wizard and bringing you to Lillenhold made me happy. I hope you find what you seek soon. You paid the penance for your errors."

Casemiro chuckled at Laural's comment. "If only my coming to Lillenhold had been pure chance. I just found out that Heenan intentionally lured me to the village. But for what purpose I do not know."

Laural replied, "We will find that out when we return. For now, we have another job."

Casemiro looked to the sky with appreciation for his two friends and glimpsed Mount Siven. The shroud of guilt returned in the form of a dragon and the wizard comprehended he must reveal his other unspoken truth before reaching the dragon's lair. Casemiro's fear centered not on saving Oleander or attempting the rescue, but further exposure impacting those riding alongside him if he waited too long to unveil the truth.

Laural came beside the wizard and put her hand on his arm. "May I ask one question, Casemiro? Why two cups of tea?"

The wizard's brain relived the memory one more time to ensure he understood the details correctly. Casemiro recalled the image clearly and the second cup still sat on the table, steaming. How did he miss the logical conclusion? The tea's temperature indicated the presence of another person in the house when Chantal died. The shock of the idea overwhelmed him. The wizard fell from his horse. As he crashed to the ground and blacked out, Casemiro's thoughts centered on a lone question. One that might haunt him forever. Did someone kill Chantal?

16

CAMPFIRE STORIES

Casemiro suffered a bump on his head, but recovered from the fall, demanding they continue their journey. The wizard set aside thoughts about his latest discovery due to limited options and asked the others to do the same for the time being. It provided another reason for them to succeed with their current quest.

After a tiring first day's travel, the riders stopped before sunset. The trio rode their horses for thirty miles and all of them needed nourishment, followed by rest. Casemiro dismounted his horse and directed the group to the side of the trail. The wizard pulled the steed through the brush, bramble, and low-lying shrubbery as Forrest and Laural guided their horses in the wizard's tracks. Casemiro found a copse of pines hiding in a small clearing from the road. The wizard dropped his gear to the ground, including the saddle from the horse.

Believing the trio found a hidden campsite, Forrest left to gather herbs and edibles for dinner. Laural scrounged for timber and kindling for the fire and Casemiro prepared himself to light the flame. Laural returned and piled the wood in an area marked by the wizard.

Laural glanced at her riding partner. "You need more?"

Casemiro kneeled by the pile of wood. "Remain quiet and let me concentrate." The wizard closed his eyes and rubbed his hands together, fixing his mind on the happy memories of Chantal as sadness filled Casemiro's heart. The old man reminisced and attempted to expel any negative images battling to enter his thoughts. Smiles of days spent walking through the market and fixing meals in their home morphed into arguments and rash decisions to leave the house to hide in a tavern until Chantal slept and allowed the wizard the chance to return without a quarrel.

Casemiro whispered the words of his enchantment. "Tân Gwesyll."

The wizard opened his eyes to find no flame, and a curse escaped his lips under his breath. Closing his eyes anew, the wizard sought the happiest thoughts from the last few days. The image of Laural smiling at him flashed into Casemiro's mind and the magical energy within him spiked. He said the words again. "Tân Gwesyll."

The old man's eyes opened to a flame taking hold of the kindling. Relief swept over Casemiro as Laural's voice chimed in his ear.

"Hey, the spell worked." The Princess smiled with a modest imperfection pushing her mouth askew in the corner. Her curly hair draped over Laural's face, and her green eyes reflected the flame's ever-changing shape.

The wizard desired to leap into the fire and escape the unwanted emotions. Instead, Casemiro pushed in another log to keep the blaze going, trying not to stare at the Princess. The wizard provided a sardonic reply. "Yes, imagine that. Now, we must get some water boiling."

Forrest emerged from the woods carrying more than timber in his full arms. "I found the herbs and caught a couple of pieces of protein." He dropped a pair of pheasants on the ground. "I assume you want those de-feathered before you eat. One of you better start."

Laural pulled a knife from a hidden pocket in her jerkin. "I'll handle it." The Princess grabbed one pheasant by the throat and used a knife to pick up the other. The Princess went into the trees to prevent blood and feathers from spoiling their campsite.

Forrest and Casemiro stared at each other in dismay and the wizard inquired if Forrest had ever witnessed Laural's expertise. Forrest shook his head in reply and the two went back to getting the pot filled and fixing it above the flame.

The stew of meat and seasoned broth cooked for an hour, and the trio relaxed as the cool night air rolled through the campsite. The group ate the soup and relished in the surprising richness of the food. The night grew silent except for satisfied moans of full, content stomachs.

Laural broke the silence when she stood to stretch her arms and legs. An extended time of sitting tightened her muscles after the long day of riding. "How late do we let the fire burn? We do not want to attract any bears, wolves, cougars, or—"

The Princess left the sentence unfinished, not mentioning the obvious threat, a dragon. Casemiro and Forrest shot her a glare, aware mentioning the animal as the sky grew dark might attract the beast.

"I caught myself. Did you think me foolish?" A frown covered Laural's face as she turned, and both her cohorts believed the Princess almost allowed the careless comment to escape her lips.

Casemiro regretted second-guessing the Princess. "We should suffocate the fire with dirt after the last log burns out to become invisible from the trail or above. Who wants the first watch?"

Laural answered, "I will take it. Forrest cooked and you can barely stand, let alone stay awake."

Forrest grunted his approval of sleeping first. "The middle of the night suits my troll abilities better. When the moon may hide, and darkness overwhelms us."

Casemiro leaned forward and poked the fire again, hoping to coax extra heat. "Forrest, what did Perriman call you to provoke such an action at the keep? I have not seen you that angry since I walked into Lillenhold."

Forrest grumbled as Laural sat on the other side of the fire to view her traveling partners' faces. "Perriman called me *trollen*, an objectionable slur." The troll-man expressed his disgust by spitting to the side.

The Princess turned her attention back to the troll-man and sighed. "Though familiar with the term, I don't grasp its true meaning."

"The word implies I am less than a troll, and a beast subject to man's dominion." Forrest clenched his fists and his olive-colored knuckles turned white in the flickering light of the campfire.

Laural pulled her knees up and wrapped her arms around her legs for additional warmth. "Do you prefer a specific term?"

Casemiro interrupted the conversation. "In magical texts, the scholars classify Forrest as a troll-man or a man-troll. If I recall, both of your parents were half-troll. Correct?"

"Yes, but I prefer none of those terms, and Forrest suits me." He shuffled around to collect the tools for fixing the meal. The others took Forrest's actions as their cue to end the conversation.

The trio finished the chores, and Laural, indicative of her improved mood, hummed a tune. The Princess smiled and turned to Forrest. "When we find Oleander and bring her back, what do you intend towards her?"

Casemiro and Forrest shot a glare at Laural, amazed at her bluntness. They both comprehended the laws prohibiting marriage between a man or woman and anyone carrying troll blood. Either her question blossomed from naivete or ignorance.

Sensing she committed a breach of decorum, Laural backed away. "I'm staying positive. We'll find Oleander and bring her home. Just curious what happens after we do that between the two of you."

The wizard leaned against his bedroll and the saddle for his horse, preparing to fall asleep. "Don't count your chickens, Princess."

"And why do you believe I harbor intentions towards Oleander?" asked Forrest.

Laural grinned at her friend and the firelight glimmered off her eyes.

Casemiro laughed at Forrest's comments. "You leer at her when Oleander stands in your presence and jump to protect her without pause. Arenton, and everyone else, interprets your actions as an attraction to her. The Prince also holds feelings for the woman and has abundant reasons for keeping you away from

Oleander. I say bully for you, Forrest, and I hope you get Oleander, if you desire that."

Forrest held up a hand to signal for his friends to calm themselves. "To prevent being the only one embarrassed, what about you two? You impersonate an old married couple when near each other, and everyone grasps the blossoming relationship between you."

The wizard shot up and exchanged glances with the Princess and both provided incoherent responses.

Forrest chortled, accomplishing his goal of evading the spotlight. "Your relationship does not bother me, but other people pay attention."

The Princess stood up. "I entertain no intentions toward Casemiro and continue to refrain from relationships because of my history."

Casemiro turned the conversation to the Princess. "Since you broached the topic, I want to understand what happened. I divulged my issues around my wife, and we dragged Forrest's love life through the hedge. Your turn to share, Princess. Or are you above such things?"

Laural sat between her colleagues and grabbed the stick Casemiro used to poke the flame. She prodded the fire and stirred up sparks as harmless ash flew into the air. The Princess took a deep breath and began her story.

"Fair enough. My father arranged for me to marry a prince from the continent of Austeria; a baron or duke or something. Stephan, a handsome man seven or eight years older than me, sat next in line for the crown of whatever nation his father ruled. The alliance provided access to a key shipping lane and strategic defense advantages over a couple of Gaeleos's chief rivals, a positive marriage for the crown."

Forrest interrupted. "So, you prefer older men? This explains much."

Laural glared at the troll-man. "Shut up. Stephen, from what our research gathered, kept many suitors a healthy distance away. Though quite handsome and in high demand across the royal matchmaking sect, he came to Gaeleos and lived at the palace for three months with the goal of establishing familiarity between us. At the end of the courting and engagement period, and before my scheduled travel to his home, an argument ensued. Stephan threatened to leave and call off the entire arrangement. I became apoplectic and the entire event angered my father. After a couple of days of discussions, Stephen and I patched up the problem and determined to fix the issue. The entire argument seemed petty in retrospect, but being young, stupid, and naïve I failed to understand. I wished to prove how deeply I loved him and slept with the man. After the act, I believed our love stronger until Stephan went to my father and called off the entire arrangement, declaring he would never marry an impure woman."

Laural stopped talking, and the Princess shook for a moment as a soft whine departed her body.

Forrest, afraid to talk, peeked at Casemiro. The wizard glared back, asking without words how to proceed. An inclination of compassion wormed itself into the wizard's mind. Casemiro slid to her side and touched Laural's shoulder in a caring manner. The wizard nestled close enough to comfort the Princess, but not close enough to appear inappropriate. "I'm sorry."

The Princess wiped a tear away with her hand. "The worst part, Stephen got away without consequence. The King, my father, called for an end to the alliance. My father attempted to squelch the rumors and supported his idiot daughter, but word soon spilled out to the public. Perhaps a servant in the palace reported the incident to a person outside the castle walls. Or, and I would not put it past the lecherous scum, Stephan leaked the news. If you wonder what fuels the rumor mill; gossip over a princess and her besmirched purity does the trick. Other potential suitors withdrew any interest. After the incident, I owned up to my grave error, and if those other asses cannot handle it, they must deal with it."

Forrest reached out and touched Laural's knee. "A healthy way to manage your problems. You are too fine for them, my lady."

Laural blushed. "Just call me Laural. Formality flew out the window the moment we agreed to this little crusade."

Casemiro asked, "If your father openly supports you, why do you continue to wear red? Am I unaware of a certain law?"

Laural glared straight at the fire. "As the reigning monarch of Lillenhold, my brother can demand anyone in my condition wear red in his domain. Arenton does it to reinforce the idea of no one being above the law, even a member of his own family. Arenton loves me, but the Prince is not above using a family member to score petty political points. The point is to remind me and everyone else, Arenton stands next in line for the throne, and I am beneath him."

The wizard reached out and grabbed Laural's left hand. "His actions sound nothing like brotherly love. I empathize with the shame you endure. My words carry little weight, but no one carries a greater heart for this kingdom other than your father. An obvious fact since the day we met twenty years ago. When we return, I will address this issue with Arenton. It won't alter the awareness of the truth in the village, but the way he taunts you every day cannot continue."

Laural squeezed the wizard's hand. "Thank you." The Princess leered at Casemiro with the same sweet smile that flashed through the wizard's mind to help conjure the spell earlier in the evening.

Casemiro smiled back at the Princess as the wizard melted inside. Casemiro swiftly shook off the moment and doled out tasks to the others. "Let us break down this fire so we can attempt to sleep. Due to the north wind, choose another direction to relieve yourself. Princess, you take west, away from the road. I take the south and Forrest you take the east. We'll bury the fire when we return."

Forrest stopped the trio before the others broke away. "Quiet!" He stuck his nose in the air and took a deep breath. "Someone approaches on the road from the north. Less than a mile from here and will reach us soon. We need to hide and extinguish the fire immediately."

The trio kicked at the dirt to cover the fire with a wisp of smoke escaping. This provided the threesome and their horses ample time to move a short distance further into the woods and find an undisturbed view toward the road and their campsite. Then each prayed the steeds remained quiet, and the approaching fools did not attract a dragon.

17

VANDALS

The three adventurers pulled their horses from the campsite and hid in the shadows. In the limited moonlight, their senses sharpened, and every movement caught their eye's attention. Men walking through the brush amplified the sounds of cracking vines, sticks, and rustling leaves in relative stillness. The scent and lingering flavor of the campfire's smoke clung to their tongues and noses.

Casemiro tapped into his magic and attuned his senses to the area, but recognized the magical energy lacking. The wizard's team blended into the darkness, but Casemiro detected Forrest's faint outline. Laural covered her exposed flesh by donning leather gloves and an oversized hood. The old man mimicked the action with his gray cloak. Casemiro feared the men approaching might see the group. The wizard's fingers tingled with anticipation.

The horses behind the travelers sensed the tension and shuffled in the dirt. The wizard stroked the faces of the animals to calm them. Casemiro recalled a spell, "Tawelwch." The equines went still, barely staying on their feet as they relaxed.

Movement occurred beyond their hidden oasis, and Casemiro shifted his focus back to the campsite. The wizard whispered another incantation, "Celu," and the light around the travelers disappeared, creating an impenetrable black mass to any other eyes. Even those within the cloud only detected what existed outside their bubble of blackness.

The first bandit entered the clearing and communicated his findings to the others still hidden in the trees. "They left this site in the last quarter hour. The fire still smolders beneath the dirt." His masked-covered face became visible in the moonlight and any hope for respectable intentions faded as soon as the man drew a sword.

The man continued evaluating the site. "They walked around to gather wood and find food and they scattered their tracks all around the area. Here's the pot they brought with them."

Casemiro raised an eyebrow at the realization these men were from Veritas Keep. A theory formed in the wizard's mind on these men's identities.

Another vandal emerged holding a bunch of pheasant feathers from the trees. "They caught something and ate it. I found a dead bird's remains over here and some fresh blood." The moonlight illuminated a blade in the vandal's hand and confirmed Casemiro's assumption of the bandits' readiness to fight.

A third member of their crew entered the campsite from the other direction. "The *trollen* sniffed us coming. What are the chances of tracking them in the dark?" This bandit stood in the middle of the clearing, next to where the fire burned, and towered above the others. From a distance, the man stood nearly as tall as Forrest, and the familiarity of his frame struck a chord in Casemiro's memory.

The first vandal answered, "No, the night is too dark to track them if they traveled in the woods."

The third man, the apparent leader, inspected the fire and gazed skyward. "The moonlight will not become brighter tonight, making tracking even more difficult. Let's return to the trail and beat them to the stream."

The second one asked, "When we find them, how do we deal with the trollen?"

The leader replied with a laugh. "My chief concern involves the wizard. Even if the boss said Casemiro lost his touch, always be cautious with wizards. As for the trollen, that half-breed cannot handle my massive arms, brother."

Casemiro recognized the man's voice, bringing to mind the Buckland Brawler. Otto Schwartz led these men, and he worked for Harley Sweet. Casemiro remembered every moment with the promoter, but never expected Sweet and his crew to be nothing more than mere criminals; their act in Veritas Keep just another example of showmanship.

A fourth man walked into the frame from the trail. "So, are we catching these fools tonight?"

"Perriman, I told you to stay with the horses. Anyway, they went into the woods. The troll probably smelled us coming on the wind or something. We won't find them in the dark. Either way, they have to cross the stream. We'll set a trap for them there."

After another round of inspecting the fire, the men traversed back to the road. The sounds of horses whinnying and hooves pounding into a trot signaled the departure of the interlopers. Casemiro held the perimeter of darkness for several more minutes, ensuring the vandals departed the scene. Once assured of safety, Casemiro lowered the cloak; revealing a night as bright as noon compared to the previous cloud. The wizard fell to the ground from exhaustion.

Laural fell to the wizard's side. "Are you hurt?"

Casemiro waved his hand to signify his safety. "Just tired."

The Princess remained at his side and asked the obvious question. "What's our plan now that the bandits moved ahead of us on the trail? Must we go through them to reach the mountain?"

Forrest walked toward the still smoking fire. "Who are they working for?"

Casemiro attempted to stand, but faltered, and Laural helped the wizard to his feet. He answered the troll-man's question. "These men work for Harley Sweet and Otto Schwartz led the crew with Paul Perriman at his side. I don't understand what they gain by coming after us. We offer them no value."

Forrest bumped the wizard's arm and pointed toward the Princess. "A precious commodity stands in front of you."

The wizard grimaced as he understood Forrest's implied meaning and wanted to kick himself for not realizing the implications before. In growing accustomed to her presence, the wizard faltered at remembering Laural's true place in the kingdom.

"What do you mean, Forrest?" asked Laural.

"He alludes to ransom. If they capture you, King Skaranon will pay a high price for your safety."

Laural's anger at the notion and the volume of her response both rose. "Well, we aren't stopping our mission, so what do we do going forward?"

Casemiro placed a finger over his mouth as a sign to quiet Laural's tone. "No, but we cannot go traipsing through the woods or on the trail tonight. Nor can we go about yelling like madmen. The immediate trouble moved on and we need rest. We keep to the plan, take turns sleeping, and carry on at daybreak, and we do it without a fire for warmth. Laural, you still have the first watch."

Forrest agreed with the wizard. "If they travel far enough ahead, we can stay away from them tomorrow. If they backtrack, we face the problem at that point."

The wizard remembered his special coin in his breast pocket. "Right, Forrest. But we can gain our own information as well." Casemiro reached into his cloak and pulled out the enchanted coin to facilitate communication with Roman.

The wizard held the coin to his mouth and whispered, "Roman, answer me." Casemiro understood Roman's coin grew hotter with each attempt, and Casemiro repeated himself after a minute with no response. Eventually, the coin would burn the boy, but on the third attempt, a sleepy voice answered.

"What do you want, Casemiro? It's the middle of the night."

Leaning in, Forrest listened to the conversation from the amazing coin.

Laural mumbled, "A talking coin?"

The wizard shot a glare at the Princess, warning Laural to remain quiet. "I appreciate the timing. Listen, we avoided an incident involving people from Veritas Keep. What occurred in Lillenhold today?"

A verifiable yawn came through the coin. "I meant to reach out in the morning, like we agreed."

Casemiro lacked patience and cursed, "Relay the information now."

"You have the patience of my gran. A group left the village and traveled toward the mountain today. They left three hours behind you. Did they catch up to you?"

Casemiro rubbed his hands together to warm them, while avoiding the question. "Anything else?"

"I paid attention to the folks you ordered me to keep tabs on and the guy running the wrestling show talked with the Prince's counselor today. Various men walked around the keep in hushed conversations all day. Also, the Captain of the Guard joined them at one point."

Laural added her commentary on the situation. "They might be planning the next Extravaganza. Arenton wishes to conduct another event after the success of the first."

A pause from the wizard conveyed his contemplation, and Laural's explanation seemed logical. But the evidence from this evening suggested Sweet now stood as their enemy. Casemiro turned his focus on the coin. "Anything else, Roman?"

"Well, on my shift today, Richard gloated about having enough to pay the debt owed to the Prince and leaving town soon."

"The suspects in Geoffrey's murder can't leave town. Roman, can you write?"

The boy chuckled through the coin. "Do you think I'm an illiterate?"

A sneer covered the wizard's face. "Write something for me and sign my name to it. Then first thing tomorrow, give the message to the Gerard. Do you understand?"

Despite their current quest, the mystery within Veritas Keep still occupied a substantial portion of Casemiro's mind and the wizard refused to lose sight of that problem. Casemiro tried to link Geoffrey's death and the assassination attempt on the Prince to these men, but found no connection. They had not arrived at

Lillenhold in time for that to be a consideration. The wizard pushed aside the random thought.

"What's the message?"

Casemiro found the proper words and relayed them through the coin. "Captain, do not let any suspects leave the village until I return, or you obtain proof of my death. You will become a barnacle clinging to my backside for the rest of my life if you don't heed my words."

"That's disgusting. And can you do that?" The intrigue from the boy seeped through the coin.

Casemiro chuckled at the boy's backhanded compliment. "Pass the message along to Captain Gerard at first light and tell him I left the note, but you forgot to deliver it. Thank you for your help, Roman. I'll reach out soon, but use the coin if necessary. Understand?"

A second passed before Roman replied. "Please come back. Lillenhold needs you here."

Casemiro tucked the coin back into his purse, touching the knitting needles for comfort before the wizard turned to his friends. "Well, I bring bad news."

Laural answered, "We heard. Same plan? Or do we start moving?"

Casemiro sat on the ground and patted the dirt on both sides of him, a sign for his friends to join him. "Same plan, because we need the rest. If anyone else arrives, we'll handle it. At least we know somebody tracks us."

"I agree with the wizard. We will defend you, Princess."

Laural laughed at the demonstration of machismo. "A pacifist half-troll and a wizard limping through limited powers defending me." The Princess changed the tone of her voice to a sarcastic drawl. "How will I survive without such powerful men to protect me?" The tone of the Princess shifted back to normal. "I am an expert swordsperson, can fight with daggers, and learned several forms of self-defense. A wise woman develops her skills when she does not concern herself with a wanna-be king and birthing babies."

Casemiro and Forrest smirked as the wizard answered the woman. "Laural, you better be able to hold your own because you may receive a chance to show us tomorrow. Sit and keep watch while I sleep."

Laural and her companions formed a circle, leaning back-to-back. Casemiro fell asleep minutes later and Forrest soon followed. Both snored like hibernating bears.

Too quick for his liking, the wizard noted a buzzing voice in his ear. Casemiro guessed his sleep only totaled a few minutes instead of the three hours he achieved.

"Wizard, wake up." Forrest shook Casemiro until the wizard rose.

"Did I snore too loud?"

Forrest pointed out toward the trail as Laural saddled the horses and prepared for their flight from the coming danger.

Casemiro understood why the troll-man woke him. The wizard's anger rose at the new annoyance, and the spark of his magical power elevated in kind. Once again, Casemiro's emotions triggered his magical abilities, a trick the wizard wished to play with after this threat passed.

Another person arrived near their location, this time carrying a torch to search for their quarry. The torch allowed Casemiro and his friends to spot the person coming from a respectful distance. The person slowed on the trail until they drew parallel to the campsite. Casemiro hoped they continued moving, but the person stopped their horse.

A simple command from the rider changed the course of the wizard's night. A woman's voice ordered the horse. "Stay here. They went this way." The woman dismounted and continued towards the campsite on foot and leaving the mount behind on the trail.

Hoping to avoid detection and a fight, Casemiro's cohorts hid in the trees as before. Casemiro cast his spell of darkness one more time, expecting the enchantment to only last moments as the wizard still suffered from the earlier use of magic. The slim chance of having a conflict-free night disappeared when the person entered their campsite with a blue flame floating above their hand.

That is not a natural fire. It's magic!

The woman wore a shroud that made her body as dark as the wizard's bubble. If not for the mystical flame, she would have been unseen. The woman stopped next to the long-dead campfire. "Oh, the fools are nearby. I smell the filthy trollen." She elevated her head toward where they stood, and the magical fire lit up the woman's face enough to reveal a smile. Her glowing blue eyes then fixed on their location. "And they thought they could hide from me."

Casemiro flashed a glance to his left, realizing his power waned, and the darkness diffused. Not that it mattered at this point. The wizard closed his eyes and called forward all the magical power within him. The wizard yelled the spell, "TARIAN!" and the trio leaped from the darkness and charged the woman on their three horses.

A blast of wind pushed forward from the black bubble as the trio revealed themselves to their enemy. The woman braced herself against the blast of air.

Casemiro charged and swung his wooden staff at the witch. The metal end missed, but their horses appeared to run over the woman as they escaped the campsite. The trio continued until they reached the road, where Casemiro launched a small firework into the air accompanied by a loud explosion to scare the witch's horse. The mount ran back along the trail from where it came. The wizard glimpsed back to the campsite and spotted the woman rising with the flame in her hand. A cackling laugh reached their ears and proved to be their signal to ride as fast as they could manage away from the campsite.

18

THE STREAM

Casemiro spurred the horses on to create additional distance between them and the danger left behind. Once the group traveled far enough to prevent another attack, the crew slowed.

Casemiro climbed back aboard his horse. "At sunrise, we will stop and address any issues. For now, we ride through our fatigue. By continuing on, the horses keep us ahead of whatever that woman was. My trepidation now lies with the whereabouts of our other enemies, both ahead and behind. We must keep our ears and eyes attuned to our surroundings. Stay alert."

Laural maneuvered her steed to one side of Casemiro, and Forrest to the other, to protect their fatigued friend. The Princess whispered to the wizard, "I found an unseen benefit to this chaos. Your magic is returning." Laural squeaked a smile across her face and reflected a glint in the moonlight before she turned her focus to the trail ahead.

Once the trio continued the ride, Casemiro contemplated Laural's words regarding the return of his magic, knowing it to be a short-time reprieve. The wizard noted the power grew as his emotions piqued in the fight, but then wavered as he calmed, and the emptiness returned. Casemiro lost his magic again, but regained focus when a nagging voice spoke to him.

Allow your emotions to help you, Casemiro.

The trio rode their horses in silence for an hour until the first light of dawn appeared through the trees. The morning sky appeared to be on fire as the clouds scattered light, creating rolling orange imagery. The view stopped the riders, and the group stared at the heavens in amazement. Since the trio halted, Laural pulled food and water from their saddlebags.

The group ate in silence and wished to sleep, but the daylight created too many opportunities to be spotted. They kept riding.

Casemiro rode to the front of the group to provide directions. "We hold this course until we reach the stream. At that point, we venture into the woods towards the mountain for a shortcut. Oh, and hope our tormentors do not turn up." The wizard gazed up to the mountain, which grew in size and placed an additional weight on his shoulders.

Laural glared at the wizard. "You're still neglecting to tell us something. Aren't you, Casemiro?"

The wizard shot a glance to the mountain and fixed his thoughts on his last secret, one that might fracture this group. The wizard acknowledged the need to confess the rest of his story before Laural or Forrest discovered the problem. "When the right moment arrives, I will divulge that unspoken truth. I promise to do so before we face the dragon."

Tell the truth, Casemiro.

The trio rode for three more hours in relative silence until they found a single horse tied to a tree. Casemiro recognized the potential for a trap and Forrest's senses forewarned them to be cautious. The group knew more horses should be nearby based on last night's events. The trio stopped to evaluate the situation further before riding into the obvious deception.

Forrest took another deep breath, using his enhanced troll senses to gather more information. "An attacker approaches us from behind on the trail and one awaits ahead in the woods. I do not sense the other two."

The wizard scrutinized the situation. "This group separated to pin us in; but their plan contains a weakness. We can attack these men individually instead of as a group, but we need to be the aggressors. Waiting here only falls into their trap. We must ride."

United on a strategy, the other two followed Casemiro, who pushed his horse into a gallop. They approached the unattended stallion, and the first of their enemies leaped from a tree branch above the trail toward the Princess with a sword in hand. Laural dodged to avoid the body of her attacker. But he found contact with his sword. The Princess screeched from the strike to her shoulder.

The villain fell to the ground, directly in front of Casemiro's horse and fell victim to a justified trampling. The wizard turned the horse and struck the writhing man's head with his staff for the final blow. The attacker laid on the road motionless and the trio continued riding to escape their enemy's first attempt to capture them.

After several minutes, the trio pulled back on their horses to reach a walking pace and Forrest recognized a problem. "Princess, your shoulder is bleeding."

Laural glanced at the wound. "Only a shallow slice through the skin." The Princess ripped a piece of cloth and Forrest helped her wrap the fabric around the wound and tied it off. "I will clean it once we reach the stream. Thanks for help." She winked at the troll-man, who smiled in return.

"We are two hours out from the stream at a full gallop." Casemiro turned to Laural. "Can you handle a hard ride for that long?" asked the wizard.

"You better believe it. How is your fatigue?"

"I will survive."

Laural's horse leaped ahead of her fellow riders in a show of pride, and the Princess beckoned them to follow her. Casemiro and Forrest loosened their reins and allowed their steeds to run.

The group rode for another hour and stopped for a quick meal of dried jerky and hardtack. Their horses also took the chance to eat some grass and drink some water in a standing puddle. At the stop, Casemiro inspected Laural's wound to administer a quick cleaning and apply a bandage from their limited medical supplies. Though the wound appeared clean, Casemiro wished to investigate the injury again at the stream and use the pure mountain water to clear away any infection.

As the group finished the meal, the clopping of hooves on the hardened trail gave away another rider's approach. The three stood by their mounts, readying themselves for an attack, when a man without a mask approached from the trail's bend. Casemiro recognized the younger man.

"Nikos Antaeus!"

The man smiled back at the wizard. "Casemiro!"

With staff and saber in hand, Casemiro approached the young man but stopped well short of arm's length from Nikos. "Don't tell me you fell in with the group trying to stop us."

Nikos stared at the ground in disappointment. "I am sorry, wizard."

"Why are you doing this?"

Nikos continued toward Casemiro. "Business, nothing personal."

The wizard backed away and positioned himself between Nikos and Laural. "I give you one chance to escape without harm on the promise you not to follow us beyond this point. You may return to Veritas Keep with your soul and body intact."

Nikos dismounted from his horse. "I cannot, wizard." He tied the reins of his horse around the pommel of his saddle and turned his attention to Casemiro.

The wizard attempted to project a spell, but the younger man dodged and moved to Casemiro's side before he could react. Nikos swept the old man's legs and knocked the wizard to the ground, taking his breath away. The staff and saber flew from Casemiro's hands to leave him defenseless. With the wizard compromised, Nikos moved towards the next highest danger in his mind, Forrest. Nikos leaped over a charging Laural while running towards the troll-man but fell to the ground mid-jump.

Laural grabbed one of the wrestler's ankles as he cleared her and twisted. The Princess yanked the man's foot and Nikos crashed to his knees. Before Nikos reacted, the Princess produced one of her sheathed knives and laid it against the man's neck.

"You did not expect a woman to stop you, did you? Now, you can either give up and walk away, or I will inflict permanent damage."

Casemiro assumed the Princess lacked the steel to injure the man, but played along. "Young man, we offer you a chance to rethink your stance. Don't let pride get the better of you. No one expects you to best a half-troll and a wizard. Only we will know who defeated you."

Laural rolled her eyes at the insinuation that losing to her besmirched the man's reputation. "Consider this your free pass, but do not let us catch you again." The Princess withdrew her blade and then kicked Nikos in the head, letting the man fall to the ground in an unconscious state.

Laural approached the wizard. "You able to stand? Wouldn't want your reputation to take a hit because a girl helped you to your feet." The Princess extended her hand and aided Casemiro up from the ground with a grin on her face.

The old man found his feet and coughed until catching his breath. The wizard answered the Princess. "Yes, I will be fine. What did you do to Nikos?"

"I told you I could fight. Do not worry, I only dazed the man. We should start moving before he wakes up."

The two of them jumped into their saddles and joined Forrest, who cast a stare of wary awe towards the Princess.

Laural caught the glare and retorted. "Oh, please. I'm capable of handling most of these men in a fight if they underestimate me. And if either of you took down Nikos, you would be proud as peacocks. Now, we need to reach the stream, where I'm sure their leaders wait for us."

After the chastisement, Laural led as Casemiro and Forrest fell in behind the Princess. The group proceeded on the road for another hour. Upon cresting a hill, the long-awaited stream ran through the shallow valley ahead. Mid-day sunlight flooded the open downhill stretch as only a few trees provided any semblance of shade across the first open meadow visible since leaving the garden at Veritas Keep.

At the base of the valley, a wooden bridge built to manage the widest of wagons and hitched stallions spanned the stream. The stream at the hill's base carried water from Mount Siven's spring snowmelt and flowed quickly. The water roared loud enough to drown out all but the loudest of voices as the flow smashed against rocks which buffeted the water and formed white rapids. Between the threesome and the bridge stood Otto Schwartz alongside Paul Perriman. Both men featured enhanced musculature, flowing hair, and stood well over six feet in height with Schwartz approaching seven.

Upon seeing the three riders emerge, the monstrous men stood from a makeshift campsite and walked toward the trio with no fear in their strides. The three riders rode toward the Buckland Brawler and the Natural Wonder at a trot. Schwartz stopped as the riders approached and lifted a massive tree branch armed with a pointed end. The vandal threw the hand-crafted spear at the Ardennais carrying Forrest. Perriman followed the spear as he made a line towards Forrest and his horse.

The horse attempted to avoid the branch, but the wooden weapon barreled into the horse's legs and knocked the steed to the ground like a child's toy. Forrest tumbled off his saddle and sprinted towards the wrestlers as a roar escaped his lungs.

The wrestlers charged Forrest with Perriman dodging the larger troll-man. Forrest lost focus and ran straight into a clothesline from Schwartz. The man's appendage resembled a sinewy metal pole and sent the troll-man to the ground. Before Forrest stood, the Brawler jumped into the air with an extended leg, dropping the leg across the neck of Forrest and attacking his throat. Forrest struggled to breathe in the attack's aftermath.

This opened the door for Perriman to jump into the fray. Paul Perriman grabbed his enemy's arm and applied a vicious wrestling hold. Perriman grunted from the exertion that preceded a snap from Forrest's arm. Forrest's scream of pain drew the attention of the wizard and the Princess. Schwartz then took his turn and began working on Forrest to finish their foe.

Perriman stood up and faced the other two, but reacted too late. Casemiro swung his staff and Laural attacked. The wizard hit Perriman's head with the base of his staff while the Princess sliced through the man's arm with her sword, leaving a nasty cut. Perriman fell to the ground, another victim of blunt force trauma. That left Casemiro and Laural to fight with the Brawler.

Laural ran to help Forrest and hit the Brawler with a forceful kick. The attack did little more than gain Schwartz's attention. Laural yelled a threat at the more sizable man while displaying her blades. "Why don't you try me, asshole!" She knew Forrest had suffered significant harm and attempted to draw away Schwartz.

The wrestler moved quicker than the Princess expected and reached Laural in a blink. Schwartz knocked the knives from her hands with powerful chops to her wrists. Out of instinct, Laural clutched her wrists because of the pain, and opened herself up for a debilitating move.

Schwartz grabbed both wrists with one of his enormous hands and lifted the Princess into the air. With a firm grip, the Brawler slammed Laural to the ground. The booming noise of her hitting the ground and the breath escaping Laural's lungs scared Casemiro, who prayed the move only knocked the wind from the Princess. The wizard's emotions raced, and the magical energy returned as Casemiro's anger welled within him.

Casemiro pulled out his saber and clutched his staff, advancing toward the Brawler with the urge to protect Laural.

The Brawler turned his attention to Casemiro.

The wizard maintained some distance, as the wrestler proved himself faster and stronger. Casemiro mocked his opponent with the hope Schwartz might misstep. "You finished the lightweights."

The wrestler laughed. "You lack an understanding of whom you deal with. I lost in the tournament only because Sweet ordered it, but I'm the strongest and meanest there is. Even

Perriman is no match for me. Your half-troll and the Princess mean nothing to me. Only you are a genuine challenge to me, wizard. Show me what you can do, brother."

Casemiro steeled his body for the coming battle. "Fighting you serves no purpose and only delays our quest. I want to go after the dragon with my friends. You let us pass, and if we survive, the dragon's treasures are yours. We want to save our friend, nothing more. Help us defeat the dragon if you want."

The Brawler laughed. "Sweet said you might attempt some sort of trickery to convince me to help you. I only desire the opportunity to challenge a wizard, not the treasures or the Princess. When I defeat you, I'm taking the Princess to Sweet."

"What if I choose not to fight?" Casemiro slid the saber back into the scabbard at his side to hide his intent. The wizard marshaled his magical energy, knowing a powerful spell created his only chance to defeat the physical specimen.

"I break you in half either way. If you fight, I promise to carry the Princess back and deliver her intact. If you refuse, I take the girl and leave her with Sweet after I have my way with her. Besides, it looks like your time is up. My friend is getting up and yours are both down for the count."

Casemiro glanced to the side and saw Perriman stand, as he nursed the cut to his arm. The wizard gritted his teeth and glanced to find a motionless Laural. The wizard tapped into the emotions and the power inside him spiked from anger, as he feared the worst. The wizard wielded the power of the wind, a long-neglected element in his arsenal. "You will do no such thing. Chwyth!" He let loose with the anger.

"Whatever —."

The Brawler did not finish his sentence before the force of the wind knocked him and Perriman into the air. The spell sent the men flying towards the stream. The rapidly moving water caught and carried away the wrestlers as their unconscious bodies became destined for the Bay of Scars in the distance.

Casemiro fell to one knee and recaptured his breath. Once capable, the wizard scrambled to Laural's side and found the Princess lying still, her eyes open, and breathing slowly. Casemiro touched Laural's shoulders to gain her attention. "Laural, are you hurt?"

The Princess blinked her eyes and pulled herself up. "I believe I am fine. But did you catch the horse-drawn carriage that ran over me at full speed?" Laural shook her head to clear her thoughts. "How is Forrest?"

Casemiro hobbled over to check Forrest. The troll-man appeared to be in a considerably worse state than the Princess. "Can you hear me, friend?"

Forrest squirmed on the ground, groaning from the pain of the injured arm.

Laural jumped to her friend's side. "Is it broken? Can you move your arm?"

Forrest gasped as the injury throbbed. "It hurts worse than anything I've ever encountered."

Casemiro examined the arm and found the source of the problem, noting a clear bulge in Forrest's skin. "No bones protrude through the skin. I can attempt to numb it if you wish."

Forrest nodded and gritted his teeth through a haggard breath as another wave of pain flowed through the arm.

The wizard waved his hand over the injured joint. "Fferru." Forrest relaxed, but Casemiro knew that would not work for long.

"Perriman used the same maneuver on someone's leg in the wrestling tournament. If Perriman intends to harm you, he can do it excruciatingly. Your hand remains warm, which means adequate blood flow, and I cannot identify any nerve damage. See this?" The wizard glanced at Forrest for confirmation. "Fortunately, the injury is a partial separation. My abilities could not repair a complete separation. To perform this procedure, I must pull on your wrist and lever your elbow joint back into place. Even numb, this hurts like hell, so prepare yourself."

Forrest took a couple of breaths and closed his eyes and faced the wizard. "I'm ready."

Casemiro extended the arm as far as possible, palm up. The wizard placed his knee under the elbow and prepared to push on Forrest's wrist. The wizard realized he needed one more thing and turned to Laural. "Put a stick in Forrest's mouth. Better to bite that instead of his tongue."

Laural returned with a hardy fallen branch from a wych elm. Forrest opened his mouth, and she placed the stick between the troll-man's white teeth.

The wizard smiled and explained the process. "I'll count to three and push your wrist down. Ready?"

Forrest shook his head and bit the stick.

Casemiro began the count. "One!" The wizard pushed on the wrist and pushed his knee up, applying leverage to the elbow and forcing the bone to pop back into place. Forrest's muffled scream resembled a bear roaring in the woods. The wizard wondered how the volume of his friend's reaction might rise without the bit or the numbing spell.

The wizard grabbed Forrest's face to capture his friend's attention. "I finished the job. You can relax."

Forrest fainted and fell against his makeshift healer, knocking Casemiro to the ground, and landing on top of the wizard.

"Laural, help me out from under him."

The Princess helped the wizard escape from beneath the unconscious body. "Did you repair the damage?"

Casemiro stood. "I reset the joint, but the injury may cause discomfort and swelling. Forrest needs further treatment, but the worst is over. It's apparent to me now why he's a pacifist. Forrest fights like a child and handles pain about the same." A smile crept across the wizard's face.

Laural hugged the wizard and then stepped back to lock onto Casemiro's eyes. "You did excellent work."

The wizard lost his thought and leaned towards the Princess as Laural leaned towards him.

"Awwwrrrggghh!" The scream of pain from Forrest drew both to him and away from their ill-timed thoughts. Forrest groaned and sat up on his knees. "You said three."

The wizard smiled at the friendly deception. "I wagered you might pull away at three. Your arm needs rest, but we must keep moving. I'll apply another numbing spell."

The wizard did as he said and then realized a sling might be in order for Forrest to travel. Casemiro extracted his saber and sliced at the bottom of his cloak and ripped off a strip of material, and used the remnant to manufacture a sling for Forrest's arm. The wizard folded the fabric over the troll-man's shoulder and tied it behind the arm. The sling, along with the earlier spell, eased the pain to an acceptable level.

Immediate relief appeared on Forrest's face and his breathing became more controlled, as the rest of his body relaxed. "Thank you, much better."

Casemiro shook his head and turned his attention towards Forrest. "Can you handle the ride, Forrest?"

"Yes, but I need some aid to get on my horse." Laural and Casemiro helped the troll-man get into his saddle. A more difficult task than either imagined.

The Princess then raided the saddlebags for both of their enemies before shooing away their mounts. She found some medical supplies, and some alcohol, to add to their own provisions.

Laural walked to her horse and prepared to mount it when Forrest leaned in and whispered into Casemiro's ear. "I caught what you and the Princess almost did." The troll-man grinned and chuckled at his friend's expense.

Casemiro climbed into the saddle of his mount. Before the group launched, Laural gave everyone a small snack to eat as they rode.

The three traveled for two more hours into the woods on their horses. The trio settled on a site near the stream and the wizard addressed Laural's injury to the best of his abilities. After a quick meal and refilling their water sacs, the trio fell asleep to the noises of the rumbling water. Too tired to stay awake, the group placed their hope in a higher power that they might wake without having to face an immediate challenge.

19

TWINE AND ROPE

The rest provided a peaceful break and some needed sleep for the travelers. Unfortunately, the trio woke to Laural developing a fever and soreness in her injured shoulder. They had slept until nearly dawn, exhausted from the prior day's events. The beginning of their day focused on addressing Laural's health issues and preparing for the next stage of their trek.

Casemiro sat on the stream's bank, dipping a cloth into the running waters. The wizard wrung the excess water from the piece of fabric and then placed the cold cloth on Laural's bare shoulder, wiping away at the wound.

Laural winced; not a good sign, and the yellow ooze escaped the wound, indicating more unwelcomed news.

"Sorry, Laural, the wound became infected overnight. The water helps, but alcohol would disinfect the wound better."

Forrest grabbed the saddlebags from the Brawler's horse. "I found distilled whiskey. Can this help?"

The Princess answered, "If not, at least I can drink it."

Casemiro grabbed the bottle and poured some on the cloth.

Laural sucked in a quick breath through clenched teeth and recoiled from the harsh burn, but returned to the disinfecting cloth for her benefit.

Casemiro extracted puss, some globs of blood and a couple darker tinged spots. "I think it's clean now, but the wound needs cauterized or stitched shut."

"Both sound painful. Which is the best option?"

"Cauterization prevents anything else from getting in the wound but leaves a nasty scar and you will probably faint from the pain. Stitches leave a much smaller scar, but you will hate sitting through the process."

Laural turned to Forrest. "What do you think?"

"For my money, stitches are less damaging to your beauty."

Laural chuckled as her cheeks flashed a bit of pink. "As if I care about that, but thank you."

The wizard added another nugget. "Another item to consider; we don't want to close the wound in case any infection remains. Upon returning to Lillenhold, a talented healer may apply an antiseptic salve to the wound and kill any potential infection. Cleaning the wound daily with water and a bit of whiskey might help fight off a dangerous infection."

The Princess provided a resolute nod for Casemiro. "I trust you to do the stitches."

Casemiro gave the bottle of whiskey to the Princess. "Take a drink and then use a bit to sterilize the needle." The wizard wished to caress Laural's other shoulder, wanting to comfort her, but Casemiro caught the thought and pushed it from his mind.

Laural sloshed the bottle and took a gulp, making a face at the bitter kick. "Whoa, this stuff almost killed me going down. No way any type of infection can survive a dose of that."

After thirty minutes of effort, the wizard sutured the wound and applied a bandage. Casemiro then inspected Forrest's arm to ensure the man-troll incurred no further damage in the night. With the medical needs now addressed, the group refilled their water pouches from the stream and mounted their horses to begin the next stage of their trip.

Casemiro took the lead towards an alternative path, attempting to remember the shortcut twenty years removed from his last experience on Mount Siven. "Horses may work for a while, but the will woods become too dense. Per the direction from Captain Gerard, we must trust the steeds to return to the village on their own."

Casemiro led the two compatriots along the banks of the stream and toward Mount Siven in the distance. Aware of no pursuers, the tone of the group became more jovial and uplifting as the group shared inside jokes and sarcastic barbs. The roar of the stream covered the noises of the surrounding forest.

At that point, Casemiro contacted Roman. The wizard held the coin close, called the boy's name, and waited for the boy to answer.

"Yes, Casemiro?"

"Did you deliver my message to the Captain of the Guard?"

"Gerard didn't like the message but agreed."

Casemiro paused before asking his next question. "Did any wrestlers come back to the village? Did anything else occur that we should know?"

"Nothing on the wrestlers. And I haven't seen the Prince's counselor or the leader of the wrestlers today. It's like they disappeared."

Casemiro pondered this information for a moment. "Keep me posted if you see Heenan or Harley Sweet again. I will reach out tomorrow evening if our situation allows."

Casemiro pocketed the coin and faced the Princess. "What makes Heenan and Sweet such close friends?"

Laural shook her head to indicate her cluelessness.

The trio returned to silent mode until stopping for lunch. As the greenery of the forest thickened, the walking paths narrowed and created a struggle for the horses to find safe footing amongst the brush and exposed tree roots. The group dismissed the horses to return to Veritas Keep and dispersed the weight of their travel gear between the three of them for the remaining trek.

The increased amount of foliage and trees diminished the roar of the rolling stream. This allowed the sounds of squirrels and chipmunks rummaging through the leaves to become commonplace. To accompany the new noises, fresh pine scents permeated the air. Streaks of daylight filtered through the canopy and provided illusions of rainbows by combining the sunbeams with the airborne moisture and humidity. The travelers' clothing became heavier from the accumulated layers of dew rubbing onto their outfits from the low-lying plant life.

After some time, silence and boredom seeped into the walk and Casemiro's thoughts drifted to the village and the mystery of Arenton's attempted murder. The nagging question over the apple seeds came to the wizard's mind, and thinking he might gain some needed information for the murder investigation, the wizard started a new conversation.

"Forrest, Oleander mentioned you make hard cider."

Forrest stopped and gave a quick grunt as a reply. "Instead of random comments, wizard, speak your point."

The wizard glanced towards Laural for reassurance, hoping the Princess might lend additional support to the intended direction of his implied query.

Laural shrugged her shoulders and winced. "Stop trying to skirt the issue and tell him. Besides, Forrest killed no one."

Casemiro let out a deep breath, knowing his illusion failed. "We investigated who purchased barrels from the cooper. Barrels like the one containing the poisoned ale in Veritas Keep. Your name appeared on the customer list we received, and I am following up on the leads and clues."

Forrest, irritated at the implied question of his innocence, walked ahead. "Yes, I use barrels for my cidery. Your conjecture probably led you to believe my motive pertains to the Prince also seeking the hand of Oleander. Correct?"

Casemiro and Laural fell in line behind the troll-man and the wizard answered. "Yes, but I found something else, which I held back from everyone else."

Forrest stopped. "Apple seeds. You found apple seeds, which led you to me because of my cidery."

Casemiro shuffled from foot to foot, attempting to hide his embarrassment.

Laural asked, "How do apple seeds relate to the attempt on Arenton's life?"

Forrest kept his admonishing glare on the wizard as he answered the question from the Princess. "Apple seeds contain cyanide if eaten in massive quantities. The wizard wonders if I attempted to poison your brother with apple seeds."

Forrest held onto the silence for a moment, but then released a deep, calming breath. "Being a pacifist, I refuse to harm the Prince, despite the theory's validity. Plus, I give Oleander all the cores to dispose of. She uses them to grow saplings to replace any dead trees in the orchard."

Casemiro lowered his head in shame for even contemplating his friend's guilt. "I'm sorry, Forrest."

"No, I understand you are protecting the life of Prince Arenton and must consider every possibility. If I answered your questions sufficiently, can we move on?"

Casemiro smirked. "From my perspective, being a pacifist isn't your strong suit, and to be fair, killing someone in the name of love occurs more often than you might expect. But I understand your point."

A laugh erupted from Forrest. "I suppose your assertion on my passivity stands correct. But Oleander isn't mine to own. If I cannot win her hand fairly, then I hold no grudge against Arenton."

Laural jumped into the conversation. "So, you are trying to win her hand?"

Forrest stopped and glowered at the Princess before turning to Casemiro. "Walk alongside me, wizard, and I can divulge all my knowledge about a cidery. Let's begin by discussing the variety of flavors I produce, of which ten different batches currently ferment within my vats. It may surprise you how easily one can shift from the traditional apple to another, and more obscure, flavor. Have you ever tried a mint cider?"

The troll-man's conversation lasted an hour before Casemiro and Laural begged him to stop. They all agreed a period of silence might be to their benefit. After two more hours of walking, the group migrated to the stream for their last meal of the day. Casemiro determined the proper spot to camp for the night and the stream's noise drowned out the forest sounds as the wizard approached the fresh water.

The trio closed the gap to the mountain by a significant distance after the day's travel. Another day's walk stood between them and the mountain, followed by a day's climb up to the dragon's lair. Casemiro contemplated the same approach he used twenty years before, only to realize he still needed to divulge to his fellow travelers that tale.

The wizard turned to find Laural glaring at him. "What did I do wrong, Princess?"

"You are deciding when to tell us the secret you hold onto. Blurt out the tale and end your misery."

Forrest stood next to the wizard and took off his sling, flexing the injured arm and wincing at the movement. "We have been through enough together to prove our trustworthiness to you. Whatever the secret, we shall remain true to each other and complete the quest together."

Casemiro glanced at his two companions and concluded to inform them. The wizard dropped his pack, sword, and staff on the ground. "Let's start a fire first, then I'll open up my soul. I stake my claim on finding the wood. Forrest, do you think you can catch some fish from the stream?"

"I will try."

As her compatriots walked away, Laural bent over to inspect something on the ground. "Guys, what is this?"

Casemiro and Forrest walked over to where the Princess squatted amongst a blanket of dried leaves.

"Why is a rope hidden under these leaves?"

The realization hit Casemiro. "Don't touch that!"

Laural turned as she yanked on the rope. "Why not?"

In the next instant, a massive net rose from beneath them and enveloped the three travelers. They were now stuck in an animal trap and lacked the wizard's weapons to help them escape.

The wizard let out a deep sigh. "Because it is a trap."

The net confined the threesome into a tight space and Forrest's weight smashed the other two toward the bottom of the net to create an uncomfortable situation.

Casemiro yelled to vent his frustration. "Everyone stop moving! Squirming like a bunch of worms makes the situation worse. We need to work together to escape before Forrest smothers us. Forrest, can you climb up the netting to create some space for us to move?"

Forrest grunted and groaned as he used his healthy arm to pull his body a couple of rungs up the netting. "I created some leverage. Does this help?"

Laural squirmed to emerge from underneath the larger man. "Can you bend your leg to give me a chance to move out from under you?"

"If I push with that leg, I squeeze the wizard more."

The wizard prompted the troll-man to oblige, no matter if it hurt him.

Forrest moved his leg, and the Princess shimmied through the gap, pulling herself up the netting. "It worked, and I see the next step from this angle. Forrest, turn your body to the right a tad. Then Casemiro can escape from under you."

Forrest shifted his body and grunted. "I can only hold on for a few seconds with my bad arm."

Casemiro climbed out from under their larger comrade and allowed Forrest to relax and rest in the bottom of the trap like a hammock. The wizard and the Princess clung to the sides, taking on the appearance of spiders overlooking their prey. Casemiro surveyed the remaining netting to develop a solution.

The wizard gestured to the trap's highest point where the net hung from a wide tree branch. "The owner hooked the net onto the tree. Laural, can you climb and unhook the net, or cut it with your knives?"

As the Princess started climbing the net, a warning sounded from the trees.

"I would stay still because if you break my trap, I will kill you." A crossbow-wielding older woman stepped out of the trees, pointing the weapon at Casemiro. "Sorry you got stuck, but you trespassed onto my property. So, I suggest you cooperate, or I put a crossbow bolt through each of you. Am I clear?"

Casemiro grinned at the strange woman through the netting. "Absolutely, ma'am. We do not want any trouble."

"It's too late for that. Isn't it, stranger?"

20

A SPOT OF TEA

The elderly woman brandished a crossbow while threatening Casemiro and the wizard's two companions. Other than the weapon, the woman's physical stature of six feet in height and a sturdy frame presented an imposing image. The woman's features sagged and wrinkled due to time more than anything else. The brown outfit she wore, though laundered, still gave the impression of significant wear and tear owing to the lifestyle of one living in the wilderness.

In a hushed tone, Casemiro gave one instruction to his comrades. "Do not tell this woman who we are."

Forrest and Laural nodded their agreement.

With the crossbow still pointed upwards, the woman stood under the netted trap. "What did you tell them?"

"I only checked on my friend's injuries; both suffered harm as we hiked along the trail. My friend hurt his elbow, and the lady cut her shoulder. My concern lay in the fear of the roped netting burning them and agitating their wounds. If you release us, we can continue our journey and chalk this event up to an innocent misunderstanding."

The woman glared up from under the netting. "Why are an old man, an ugly troll, and a young lady traveling together in the woods? How can you guarantee you won't attack an old woman after I free you from my trap?"

Forrest grumbled at the pejorative description. Casemiro gave a soft kick to his friend's shoulder to remind the troll-man an outburst only harmed them at this point.

Laural spoke up. "On my honor, our quest pertains to searching for a friend. We believe some misfortune befell her."

The woman lowered the crossbow, still appearing unconvinced. After a momentary pause, she relented. "Fair enough. I will release you, but I will keep the crossbow at the ready. If you wish to avoid a hard landing, grab the middle of the netting."

The three captives took the woman's advice and grabbed the middle section of the netted apparatus. The woman disappeared, and from a respectful distance, the distinct clicking and clacking sounds of a gear turning coincided with the net loosening. Once the net completed the descent, the trio dropped to the ground below.

Seconds later, the woman returned and pointed the crossbow toward the trio once more. "Now, I want names."

Laural took the initiative and provided pseudonyms for the group. "I am Raspa Cork, and my uncle Harold Cork, and this is Glack, a half-troll. We live near Lillenhold and are searching for Glack's mate. We believe she wandered into the woods a day or so ago and we have not seen her since."

The woman gazed at Laural. "It's safe enough for anything with troll blood out here unless they come across the dragon. In that case, she is a goner. No troll walked across my land; I guarantee that. You can continue and follow the stream towards the mountain. The bend tracking back west marks the end of my land. I do not care what you do beyond my border, but you best start walking."

Laural turned to Casemiro to determine if moving on presented the best option.

The wizard halted Laural at the sight of her wound bleeding once again. "Do you mind if I inspect my friend's wound to ensure she didn't tear her stitches?"

"Don't take me for a fool, old man, and try nothing stupid. But I see the wound is bleeding." The old woman dropped the crossbow. "Blast, I'm such a fool. Instead of cleaning it out here, follow me. I need to go back before my tea boils over. I can examine the wound and determine if this lady needs further attention, or medicine. In the past, I worked as a healer."

Casemiro, shocked at the fortune, speculated about leveraging this to his advantage. "Can we also get some tea? I have a piece of silver to pay for it." The wizard sought knowledge of the dragon from the woman, if she held any.

The woman's eyes lit up. "If you're buying, I'll bring biscuits too. C'mon, you lot."

Casemiro and Forrest grabbed their equipment from near the stream.

The woman inquired about the authenticity of the wizard's staff. "Is that tip steel or iron?"

Casemiro glared at the woman with a discerning eye; believing the woman more knowledgeable than she let on. "Iron. I fashioned it myself years ago. Since you live out here, what can you tell us about the dragon? We witnessed the beast in the sky a few days ago."

"Other than it's a dark red color, eats everything it can catch, and breathes fire hot enough to scorch the ground, not much. Best avoid the beast if you can. As for your staff, a beauty. I'm sure the day you forged it created a fond memory."

The wizard reminisced about the distant day and remembered standing next to Quinto as they dipped their staffs into the forge and let the metal mold around the aged and magical wood. The smiles they shared symbolized one of the happiest days of his young wizarding career. Casemiro scrutinized the old woman walking up the hill, and she gave the wizard a sideways glare.

The group followed the old woman through severe terrain. Once they reached the peak of the hill, the old woman purposefully crossed the hardscrabble to a ramshackle home. Two sheep, three pigs, and a pair of goats roamed in a small pen next to the house while chickens ran around the property. As the group approached, the woman pointed to an elm tree providing shade to the pen.

"Take a seat by the elm. Your trollen friend will not fit through my door." The woman sneered over her shoulder and Casemiro took the words for their true meaning. "I'll bring out the tea and biscuits and fetch my old healing kit to examine your wound, missy."

The trio sat under the elm tree as the leaves swayed in the breeze. The trio enjoyed a few moments of relaxation and waited for the crone to return.

Casemiro turned to Forrest. "This is better than I expected. How is your elbow?"

"Sore, but better. Do not jinx it, friend," Forrest grunted as he plopped to the dirt.

Laural checked her wound. "I think I broke a stitch or two. We needed to check the injury, regardless."

The old woman emerged from the house carrying a satchel and dropped the bag beside Laural. "The tea takes a few moments. The first batch burned, so I started a new one. Let me check those stitches."

The woman pointed at the wound and began tending to it. "Your stitching needs improvement; it's too loose and spaced out. I'll apply some healing salve, and a little homemade 'shine, to kill the infection. I can always give you a jar of my homemade spirits for the road if you wish to tie on a hangover."

To Laural's chagrin, her nurse removed the stitches and put in some new twine without asking and with little effort. The process took under five minutes, and the woman finished by tugging on the twine to tighten the new stitches, causing Laural to squeal in pain. The old woman finished by tying and cutting the line.

Casemiro examined the work and agreed the stitching far surpassed his measly skills.

The woman moved over to Forrest. "Let me check out what happened to you."

After the quick exam, the old woman rubbed a blue liniment on Forrest's arm. "That concoction helps ease the ache and keeps the swelling down. Your friend did a better job on your arm than the young lady's shoulder. But not bad overall. I need to fetch the tea." The woman packed her equipment back into the satchel and walked back into the house.

The woman came out of the house and poured the tea. The scent hit Casemiro and images of Chantal filled his mind. Aromas of Bergamot triggered the memories of his wife and the enjoyment of their early years of marriage. Along with those joyful images came the last somber memories, as well. Once more, Casemiro walked into their house to find his wife still dead. Still stabbed by a knitting needle through the heart. Still two cups of tea steaming.

Casemiro refused the cup as the offer came to him, and the wizard pulled away into solitude. Everyone else went quiet as they enjoyed the bitter drink featuring a bite of spice, ginger, and the richness of Bergamot; a blend originating from Austeria, the continent across the Sea of Storms from Gaeleos. The biscuits complimented the spice of the tea and provided their own buttery flavor.

Laural approved of the drink. "Such a unique blend to find in the woods."

The old woman smiled and revealed her pride. "Glad you approve. My children, who are triplets, love it, but I rarely spend time with them. Oh, and you can call me Mira since we took tea together." She gave the Princess an expectant gaze.

The wizard pulled himself from the malaise and continued the polite conversation by filling the pause. "I'm sorry to hear of your children not visiting you."

"My children are precious to me. All of them blonde, like me in my younger years. I looked more dashing back then. No offense, missy, but much prettier than you. Unfortunately, the authorities exiled me twenty years ago, and I hid in the wilderness. Those conditions take a toll on a woman's body and appearance."

The Princess glared at Casemiro. Laural's face lost much of its color as a concern became apparent.

The glare puzzled the wizard, and Casemiro couldn't ask why with Mira in their presence. Instead, the wizard offered to attend to the tea and dishes. "Mind if I take the cups, plates, and tea back inside?"

"Be careful, or I might swoon with your gentlemanly ways. Place the remains on the table near the door, and refrain from spying."

The wizard walked up to the house and realized he formed incorrect impressions from a distance. This home, shabby looking from the outside, stood in excellent condition. Thick boards and timber supported the walls, windows in select locations to let in the best light of the day, and a sloped roof provided complete protection for those within. The wizard speculated if, like the house, the woman hosting them portrayed a different character than her true self.

Casemiro placed the dishes on the table inside the door and inspected the room to learn about his mystery host. A wooden rocking chair filled one corner of the room, and an incomplete knitting project with familiar looking needles laid on the seat. Casemiro admired the apparent skill from afar. A memory chest covered by keepsakes filled another wall of the room when two items caught the wizard's eye.

A charcoal drawing of a younger Mira look-alike grabbed Casemiro's attention. The woman's estimation of her beauty appeared justified, and the wizard understood how she might attract any man. Casemiro spotted another drawing featuring Mira in her current state, and a man the wizard recognized. Adding a smidgeon of imagination to change the charcoal image to account for blonde hair, the man became the picture of Harley Sweet. Casemiro now understood the ramifications of stumbling upon this house, and leaving this home became his priority.

The wizard replaced the picture and found another image, a charcoal drawing of Chantal, his dead wife. How did Mira come to possess an image of her? Casemiro turned back to the knitting needles, exact replicas of the ones Chantal used and those he owned. A litany of questions filled his mind, and the wizard grabbed the image to carry it with him to confront Mira. The wizard stormed from the house; his anger swelled as he approached their host.

Mira spied the wizard. "Well, since we drank our tea and I checked out your injuries, you should probably leave. I don't enjoy strangers overstaying their welcome, and you should find a campsite before nightfall."

Casemiro ignored the suggestion and went straight to his questions. "Before we go, from where did you acquire that tea?"

Mira nodded and gave a knowing wink to the wizard. "Would I be correct in guessing someone snooped too much? For your information, I receive a single shipment of tea each year from a relative operating my family's old farm, Sucre Sol. The title translates to sweet ground, a play on our family name."

Casemiro walked closer to the woman, clutching his staff. "Interesting. My wife's surname was Sucre, and she also loved Bergamot tea. In fact, I found two cups of Bergamot, still hot, when I discovered her dead from a knitting needle in her chest."

The old woman crossed her arms and stared at the wizard. "I don't appreciate the insinuation and believe your moving on would prove best for you all before a situation you cannot handle occurs." Mira stood in front of the wizard, unflinching.

"Not until I hear why you own a drawing of my wife." Casemiro held out the paper.

Mira noted the image and turned her attention to Laural, still ignoring the anger of the wizard. "I extended my hospitality and receive such awful treatment. First, the fair Princess Laural lies to me concerning her identity and took me for a fool. You can tell Skaranon to piss in his royal wine. Then you, the wizard, level accusations of murder against me. I suggest you leave my land and make sure these two follow you."

Casemiro stepped in front of Mira once more. "Not until I receive some answers."

Mira waved an arm in front of her body, and the pressure in the air rose. Casemiro's ears popped, and he buckled as a blast of wind knocked the wizard and his friends away from the old woman. Casemiro tried to roll over, but the wind pinned his body to the ground. He spied the crone walking towards him.

Mira leaned over and spoke softly to the wizard. "Chantal was my sister. She married you and you denied her the right to bear children. Though unhappy, she refused to leave. I took matters into my own hands and killed her. Such a waste for her to live a lie with you without breeding anymore of our family. Yes, I'm insane and stabbing Chantal probably proved the wrong choice. But my heart warmed as the guilt destroy you, and I watched from a distance. Believing all this time you caused all her suffering and drove her to the point of suicide. You always made everything about yourself. Well, your suffering ends with me telling you the truth; at least about the part where you believe she killed herself."

Mira walked around the wizard, her eyes glowing blue. "I'm half tempted to kill you three now, but you have a job to perform. And you will find out why we dragged your worthless soul here, Casemiro." Mira smiled at the wizard. "Until next time. If there is a next time." The woman snapped her fingers and Casemiro's world went dark.

21

THE SHADOW OF MOUNT SIVEN

The scene played out in front of Casemiro as he stood in the room's corner. As the wizard entered the house, a woman vanished. With an evil smile and a haunting laugh, the woman taunted Casemiro for his failure. The wizard screamed in disgust, fear, and agony as the specter of Mira Sweet tormented his mind. Now he saw the witch in the room and could not unsee it. The scene repeated until a voice interrupted the wizard's thoughts.

Casemiro! Snap out of it! Save the girl!

Casemiro's eyes flashed open to find Laural and Forrest standing above him and screaming his name. The wizard's eyes registered his companions, and he shoved them away, needing a moment to re-engage his senses. Casemiro's mind ached from everything he learned about the death of Chantal and who killed her. Casemiro feared his mind might fall into madness until a slap by Laural woke him from his daze.

The wizard came back to reality, hoping none of what occurred was true. "What happened? Tell me I dreamed the entire thing."

The Princess, tears streaming down her face, appeared frantic. Forrest walked around, alert to any attack from the trees. The trio needed Casemiro's aid, but the wizard provided no help to them now.

Casemiro pushed Laural away as the emotions within him raged out of control. The guilt and grief hindering him before left. Fear and anger controlled the wizard, and his emotions allowed unfettered access to the magical energy denied from him before. Casemiro's insides flamed like a volcano waiting to erupt and needed a release. The wizard lifted his staff and fired a blast that rattled the ground beneath them and lit the sky above on fire. Casemiro sensed the energy flee his body and the torrent of emotions escaped and allowed the wizard to focus on his surroundings.

Laural and Forrest turned towards him with wonder and cowered in fear.

The wizard's frantic eyes darted around the area to find nothing that stood there a short time before. "Where did Mira Sweet go?" Casemiro's breathing slowed and became deeper as his body calmed and the wizard came back from the edge of his emotions.

Laural answered. "Mira fled. Everything's gone. The house, the animals, everything. She might as well not have been here. What happened?"

Casemiro looked to the Princess as his senses calmed and his emotions leveled to somewhere beneath desperation. "Mira confessed to killing my wife. If I ever find the witch again, I shall avenge Chantal's death."

Laural fell into his chest to provide some comfort, and Casemiro hugged the Princess to reciprocate. But he needed her embrace much more in the moment. The energy expended calmed his rage, and the grief returned as the magical connection faded again.

"Casemiro, I'm so sorry."

Forrest asked, "What do we do now?"

Casemiro found Chantal's image on the ground. The wizard picked the drawing up and slid the paper into his breast pocket. "The only thing we can do, Forrest. We save Oleander." Casemiro began walking towards the mountain.

Two more hours passed before the trio stopped for the evening as the sun set in the western sky. They lost more time with Mira than they realized. Regardless, the gap to Mount Siven decreased as the travelers stood near the base of the mountain and in the peak's shadow. The group remained quiet as the daylight slipped from them.

The forest thinned as pines became the prominent specimen while the other trees diminished. The undergrowth of the forest died away and left a course, rocky soil; more difficult for walking and less comfortable for sleeping.

Casemiro selected a spot to stop midway between the forest and the stream, which allowed easy access to the woods for protection from any potential dragon attacks. He also wished to avoid the mountain until dawn of the next day. The group divided the chores, with the wizard fetching wood for the fire while Laural and Forrest caught fish in the stream for dinner. After thirty minutes, each came back carrying their collected bounty.

The wizard placed the wood in a specific pattern and used magic to light the fire without much effort, an unthinkable event a couple of days prior. Using one of Laural's knives, Forrest filleted the fish and tossed the meat and herbs into the pot. Laural raced back to the stream to refill their water sacs. The trio expected to fill their bellies and hoped for a restful night before ascending Mount Siven the next morning.

As the fish cooked, Laural sat by the wizard. "Is the magic returning? You appear stronger."

A wry smile crossed the wizard's face. "My emotions became unchecked briefly and pushed away the guilt and grief from Chantal's death. Those two demons hinder my magic for some reason, and the actions of Mira Sweet removed those filters for a brief time. Also, as we approach the mountain, the magic pulses with greater intensity for some unknown reason. For the moment, I am stronger."

Laural put her hand on the wizard's knee. "Did Mira tell the truth? Did she kill your wife? No one should find out in that way. I cannot imagine dealing with..." The Princess left the sentence unfinished but surveyed Casemiro's eyes with sympathetic pity.

Casemiro covered her hand but held back the emotion and inclination to reach out and embrace the Princess. In his mind, an image of Chantal arose, accompanied by guilt. The wizard's heart diminished inside him, and he pulled away. The familiar pangs of grief persisted with the knowledge of who took Chantal's life. Avenging that death now became his primary goal in life, but that goal must wait.

Casemiro switched the topic of the conversation, hoping Laural did not take offense. "We must discuss what happened with Mira, but let's make camp first." The wizard pulled his hands away from Laural.

Laural walked away and stopped at Forrest's side to avoid the wizard. "Do you need any help to prepare the food?"

"No, this river trout is finicky and burns quickly."

Laural stood over the saddlebags, still trying to find a distraction from Casemiro. "Mira gave us a bottle of spirits for medicinal purposes. We can all enjoy a potent drink tonight."

Forrest pulled the skillet from the fire. "Let the fish cool and then we can dig into the meal."

The trio took their seats around the campfire and passed around the fish, water, and spirits. After a few minutes of silent eating, Casemiro prompted Laural to begin her explanation. "You recognized that woman as well. Tell your tale involving Mira Sweet."

The Princess relented. "After my mother died, a young lady struck my father's fancy. That lady was Mira Sweet. King Skaranon broke off the fast-paced courtship and rumors circulated why he ended the whole affair. My father never explained why he exiled the woman."

The wizard pondered this as he chewed a bite of his fish. "What were those rumors, Laural?"

"The primary rumor involved the woman becoming pregnant out of wedlock with my father's children. My father mentioned nothing to indicate the speculation as being true or false."

Forrest nodded while eating his fish. "If true, the story explains why King Skaranon showed compassion toward your predicament. Perhaps he went through a similar trial."

The group went quiet for a minute. The aroma of the trout filled the air, and the smoke kept the mosquitos at bay. Despite a stiff wind, the fire kept the night chill away. The crackle of the kindling gave a loud pop, and Laural jumped in surprise. The Princess released a slight giggle and returned to the conversation.

"When Mira mentioned exile, everything returned to my mind. I envisioned the same woman my father courted, despite Mira's rough exterior. Everyone in my father's orbit believed she returned to her homeland. None would guess Mira Sweet lived in the wilderness near Lillenhold or that she was a witch. Regardless, her claim of three children concerns me the most."

"Yes, triplets." Casemiro spit out a bone from his fish. "By the way, the food tastes exceptional, Forrest. Anyway, I entered Mira's house and found drawings of her and a child. A charcoal sketch of them sat on a memory chest, and the unmistakable image of Harley Sweet stared at me through blackened eyes."

Forrest asked, "Then who are the other two children?"

The Princess passed along a potential theory. "Do the other two work for Sweet in his wrestling troop?"

Casemiro went silent and drew Laural's attention. The wizard continued thinking aloud. "I should have deduced Mira's identity when she mentioned the family farm in her homeland, Sucre Sol. Chantal received her tea from that farm every year in the fall. I never met Mira, but remember everything my wife shared. My wife called her Miriam, though. I never imagined Mira, her sister, being involved in the death of Chantal."

Laural asked, "What are the odds of Mira being tied to both of us?"

The connections fell into place for Casemiro in an instant. "You're missing the bigger point." The wizard's vision pieced together a plan that surpassed their imagination.

"Explain it to me, then."

"All these events connect to each other, Laural. The death of Chantal, the timing of the Extravaganza, the arrival of the dragon, my returning to Lillenhold, the attempt on your brother's life. Think for a second. If Mira's triplets are your father's children, then one of them may be next in line for the throne and that child could supplant Arenton."

The Princess gasped, and a hand covered her mouth, dropping her plate, as the concept cemented itself in Laural's mind.

The wizard attempted to calm the Princess. "Before we take any action, we must identify the other two children."

The Princess focused her attention on who they might be and offered a suggestion. "You should check in with Roman and find out what happened in Lillenhold today."

Forrest grunted in agreement as he cleaned up the meal.

The wizard withdrew the coin from his purse and called to Roman and the boy answered.

"I planned to reach out after dark, sir. Something weird occurred today, but the job prevented me from getting away."

"What happened, Roman?"

"I talked with Captain Gerard, and he mentioned now taking orders from Heenan. Does that make sense?"

Casemiro avoided answering the question. "Well done, Roman. Any other issues to report?"

"No, sir. Pretty quiet here otherwise."

"Upon my return, you get an extra gold piece. Inform me if anything else changes." The wizard put the coin in his purse and patted the knitting needles as part of his superstitious routine. The piece of parchment holding the image of his wife also grazed his hand.

Forrest asked, "How does this information help us?"

Casemiro rubbed the scruff growing across his chin. "I suspect Heenan, your brother's trusted counselor, fills a spot as one of the triplets. But who might be the third?"

Forrest exclaimed, "Gerard." The troll-man provided further explanation. "He looks the same age and carries blonde hair like the other two. Also, he arrived in Lillenhold a year ago, and received the promotion to Captain of the Guard soon after, even though nobody heard of him before. Coincidentally, his promotion occurred around the same time as the counselor's arrival."

Laural laughed at the ludicrous nature of the events. "I remember this discussion with my father after the fact. Arenton granted a promotion based on Heenan's recommendation and the previous Captain of the Guard's retirement. These knaves played off my brother's naivete, and the Prince fell into their hands."

The wizard patted Laural's shoulder as a sign of his consolation. "Do not be too hard on Arenton. It's possible this plan required years to formulate. He is not equipped to deal with these people on his own. He needs help. But we are out here."

Laural gained a resolute stare. "They are making a play for the throne, aren't they? But which one?"

Forrest questioned the quick jump in logic. "I'm sorry Princess, please explain how they might achieve such an ambitious scheme."

"The crown passes to one monarch by a series of connections to the prior monarch." Laural ran through the rules as if teachers drilled the guidelines into her head during her youth. "First comes age. They prefer the oldest child, if possible. Second comes blood. The heir must be a blood relative of the prior king. Marriage comes into play if legitimacy remains in question." The Princess smiled at her friends, like a schoolchild, waiting for a declaration of her brilliance.

Casemiro added to the explanation. "You forgot the true first consideration. Arenton's position ahead of you in the line of succession relies on the prioritization of men over women. Sweet and his siblings might move ahead of Arenton in the line, if the children are your father's progeny and can prove their parentage. Or it's possible they are just attempting an old-fashioned coup."

Laural grew frustrated with the discussion and removed herself from the campfire. The Princess wandered toward the water and fell to her knees on the bank, crying into the stream.

Forrest coughed to gain the wizard's attention and nodded his head to indicate an obligation on Casemiro to follow Laural.

The wizard understood and rushed over to sit next to the Princess. Casemiro did not hurry to bring Laural back to the campsite, despite her being in the open. The wizard feared a dragon attack, and the moment reinforced the group's need for nighttime protection, but he waited for the Princess to stop crying.

"Do you wish to talk?" asked Casemiro.

"Not really. I do not understand. Arenton is not a bad person. Why hurt him?"

"The crown can bring out the worst in even the best individuals. I doubt it pertains to Arenton on a personal level, as your brother seems to be a nice young man. But I must ask, does your anger stem from the belief that if you wore the crown, this trouble might disappear?"

Laural turned and spat out a response. "No..." The Princess paused. "Yes. I do not understand why I cannot wear the crown. Queens fill the royal lineage. My not being considered because I'm a woman strikes me as absurd."

"I don't disagree, Laural."

The Princess leaned her head on Casemiro's shoulder and relaxed. "I can't change any of this, can I?"

"Not from out here in the woods. If we find Oleander and return to Lillenhold, we can act. The rest sits outside our control for now."

Laural sighed as a sign of her reluctance to accept her lack of influence. "Forrest is tired of cleaning those dishes by himself. Let's return to the campfire and help him."

The pair stood, and Laural grabbed the wizard's hand, staring at the man. "Thank you." Casemiro did not release her hand, holding on as the duo turned towards the campfire.

Laural captivated the wizard. Her charming green eyes drew Casemiro in. Her smile revealed a joyful soul and buoyed the wizard's spirit with a voice capable of charming a lion into giving up a meal.

In that instant, the wizard identified his obstacle. For years, he disallowed himself the chance to live a life because of inner demons and the death of Chantal. Casemiro accepted the blame for his wife's death to spite himself and to deny himself any chance of a happy life. Even after knowing Mira killed Chantal, the wizard clutched onto the self-inflicted wound. The wizard still believed he denied Chantal from living a full life and considered himself unworthy of pursuing such a life as the sentence for his crime. Casemiro's guilt instinctively held fast, and he leaned away from the Princess, attempting to escape the potential of joy.

Laural squeezed his hand before drawing closer and putting her other hand on the wizard's chest. "What's wrong Casemiro?"

"Nothing." The guilt within Casemiro formed a barrier around his heart and prevented this newfound emotion from overcoming his shame.

No. I want this!

The wizard's heart pounded on the wall, and the wall cracked. A smile crawled across Casemiro's face. His heart pounded even harder against the barrier, and the feelings broke loose. The bonds of guilt broke inside the wizard's body as the energy flowed through his arteries and his heartbeat even faster. Casemiro wanted a chance at joy and hope.

The wizard pulled Laural closer and kissed the Princess. Her soft lips met his and then she pulled him nearer, refusing to let go of the embrace. Casemiro held onto the kiss until he needed a breath. The pair separated and caught each other's eyes and stopped, frozen in the moment.

Laural lowered her head and leaned in, her forehead against the wizard's chin. The Princess laughed. "I guess I do have a type."

Casemiro let out a deep breath. "We need to help Forrest."

Laural squeezed his hand as they returned to the campfire.

Forrest grinned at the two of them. "About time you two accepted your fate."

Like embarrassed school children, the wizard and Princess blushed while cleaning up the remains of the food, fish bones, and skin. Forrest covered the fire with dirt to smother the flame. The trio readied themselves for a night's rest in the woods and walked toward the cover of the forest's canopy.

As the duo walked, a pang of guilt came over the wizard, but not related to his dead wife. Casemiro stopped in his tracks. "I must explain why we search for Oleander. As with everything else, the reason comes back to me."

Forrest chuckled at the comment. "Did you strike a deal with the dragon to take Oleander? If not, then I cannot imagine how everything revolves around your ego, wizard."

The last rays of the sun vanished as Casemiro gazed upward. The sunlight painted the day's end in pinks, purples, and blues, and left him in awe. Then the wizard discerned the silhouette of Mount Siven and the focus returned to his mind.

"The king hired me to kill the..." Casemiro withheld the word dragon due to nightfall falling over them. "When I found their lair, the sire approached death because of the injuries sustained in the battle with the King's armies. The mother appeared injured, but she protected a hatchling. My heart refused to cast a death sentence on an innocent life, even one such as that. Instead of killing them, the mother and I made a pact, and she fled with the hatchling. I ended the suffering of the sire, but kept quiet about letting the other dragons free."

"Do you think this one is...?" Laural asked. The Princess hoped the wind did not carry the wizard's word away to other ears.

"This beast closely resembles the father. I will take the image of the sire's armored body to my grave."

The Princess grabbed the wizard's hand. "You can change nothing now."

Forrest appeared more agitated. "Perhaps you can make amends for your failure, and right all your wrongs by freeing Oleander and killing this beast."

"Agreed, my friend. When we rise in the morning, we travel up the mountain to kill the beast or die trying."

The wizard and his two companions reached the periphery of the deep woods and the wind shifted from east to west and picked up speed. The air buffeted the trio in a familiar rhythm, like the beating of a heart, or wings.

Casemiro recognized the pattern, and his nose filled with the scent of dragon, brimstone and death. The wizard realized what word he said in his carelessness and cursed himself.

"Run!" The wizard darted towards the woods with his friends behind him.

From above, a blast of fiery breath fell to the ground and engulfed the trees in their wake. The trio charged beneath the canopy, hoping the dragon might lose track of his prey. The dragon destroyed another section of the woods with its fiery breath as the trio sprinted from tree to tree toward the mountain. The group understood dragons pursued their prey until capture without fail and hopelessness fell across Casemiro amid the pursuit.

The trio ran towards the mountain and found the forest's edge, where the trio stopped before an empty rocky plain which led to their destination. Running into the open area equaled a death sentence, but the firestorm raging through the woods moved toward them at a terrifying speed and eliminated all other options for escape.

The dragon flew overhead and rose into the nighttime sky, blocking out the rising moon and putting the trio into more shadow. Sparing a glance at the mountain, Casemiro remembered the path he took to the dragon's lair twenty years ago. The wizard pointed to a black hole at the base of Mount Siven, their one chance to avoid death.

"That opening presents our only refuge. If we reach it before the dragon attacks again, we may find safety within the mountain. The beast cannot pursue us once we enter."

Forrest asked, "How do you know this?"

"I found an ancient path to the dragon's lair twenty years ago. Our only hope depends on the cave remaining intact."

The wizard bolted forward as the dragon flew away, but remained on the hunt. Casemiro sprinted towards the hole in the mountain's base, knowing their goal was now nearly impossible. Every other second, he scanned the sky to locate the dragon, tracking the monster's progress for another dive at his potential prey. The wizard calculated the distances between the dragon, the cave, and his party. The math told Casemiro the trio stood no chance of reaching safety before the beast returned and they required another solution.

Casemiro developed a plan, but the trio must reach the crack in the mountain's side alive. The wizard believed if they reached the opening, the dragon's claws and teeth were no longer a threat. The monster's fiery breath constituted another matter. But one problem at a time.

Casemiro ran alongside his comrades and glanced to his side to spot Laural. A flash of emotion flooded him as the wizard desired nothing more than to protect her. Within him, the magical energy rose, and he used the power. As the dragon prepared to launch another attack, the wizard lifted his staff and yelled. "TARIAN!" Casemiro unleashed a surge of energy, knowing more power waited if required.

The beast completed the turn and dove toward them with its mouth opened and claws extended as the moon floated in the night sky behind the monster. The glow of a forthcoming blast formed in the dragon's throat as a gleam in its red eyes indicated the beast believed the chase neared completion.

A shimmer of light appeared above the three companions, sparkling until the dragon's flames pounded into the magical shield. As the flames died, the shield crumbled into black soot and drifted on whatever breeze the beast generated. Casemiro secured another scant few seconds of life for the group as the dragon flew past and prepared for another bombing run before the trio might reach safety.

The three continued running and nearly completed the sprint when Casemiro glanced over his shoulder. The wizard spied the dragon, lowering itself to the ground for its ultimate attack. He fell in line behind his friends, dashing towards the opening in the stone wall of Mount Siven. From behind, the winds rose as the dragon flapped his mighty wings and the breeze picked up the three runners, tossing them forward.

The beast unknowingly aided their cause as Laural and Forrest landed near the opening and squeezed into the mountain's side. Casemiro knew true safety ensured the dragon did not breathe fire into the hole. The wizard peeked up to the snow on the mountain, poised to fall from the face over the coming weeks of spring, and the glimmer of an idea hit him.

Another blast of air picked Casemiro up and tossed him the remaining distance to the opening. The wizard stood as the dragon closed the gap. Casemiro held his staff aloft and yelled the most formidable incantation from his lips in twenty years. "Eirlithriad!" Above him, a boom echoed across the mountain and the wizard witnessed the first movement in the snow. A crack appeared in the pristine white sheet hanging on the edge of the mountain. The wizard prayed he timed everything precisely and crawled through the opening with his enemy closing.

His friends pulled Casemiro further into the cave, dragging the wizard as they ran from the entrance. The trio witnessed the dragon approach the alcove through the gap in the stone and froze in awe of the beast and their approaching doom. The glow of fire grew in the dragon's throat. The beast closed the remaining distance and launched a fiery breath as the three of them prepared for death in mere seconds.

Laural screamed as darkness covered them. Any daylight within the chasm disappeared, and the avalanche's sound echoed through the stone alcove. The pressure from the blast of air and snow shook the group and buckled their knees while tossing them to the rear of the cave. The pounding noise from the snow overpowered the screams of Laural and Casemiro and the rolling thunder of the collapse left their ears ringing.

An eternity passed as Casemiro believed death won the day. The wizard took a breath of the chilled damp air and flecks of snow landed on his face. Casemiro sensed the snow enveloping his body up to his waist and understood he survived the avalanche and the dragon. The crisp scent of pure snow and the rush of a chill dominated the black, empty space of the darkened cave. After taking a moment to regain his composure, the wizard remembered his friends.

"Forrest? Laural? Can you hear me?"

A muffled response resembling Forrest's voice from somewhere around him lightened Casemiro's heart, and a smile covered his face. A squeal of a response from Laural followed suit and tears formed in the wizard's eyes. Casemiro's hopes rebounded at the sound of his friend's voices. He stumbled around him, searching for his staff. The wizard's hands found the gnarled wood, grabbed the stick, and held the staff aloft.

"Hold on. Let me provide a light. Tortsh."

The metal end of Casemiro's staff took on an orange glow and expanded the light to cover the entire cave. The depth of the hole in the mountain amazed the wizard. The blast of air and snow threw them thirty feet. Alive, Laural and Forrest lay across the floor in the less snowy part of the hollow.

Casemiro escaped the drift and reached a crying Laural, and a discombobulated Forrest. He laid the staff on the ground and hugged Laural with one arm and grabbed Forrest by the shoulder with the other.

Laural asked, "The dragon?"

"Not a concern right now. We are alive."

Laural shook as she sobbed from the shock of the event and Casemiro held the Princess while she regained control. Forrest sat in silence.

After the Princess regained her sanity, Forrest asked the wizard for the next steps.

Casemiro replied with their lone option. "Ascend the mountain from the inside and then confront the dragon. Follow me to the dragon's lair and Oleander." Part of Casemiro recognized his friends stood here because of his careless act twenty years ago and desired to tackle this part of the journey alone, but the wizard needed their help to accomplish this task.

Forrest held back. "Why should I trust you now?"

"As much as I hate to admit this, you have no choice. Either go with me or wait here for my return." Casemiro wrapped his free arm around Laural's shoulders and helped the Princess advance into the cave. A few paces later, the light from the staff found a set of hewn stairs leading up from their location.

The wizard turned to Forrest, wishing to hide his shame from the troll-man. "We must climb the Cleave of Siven until we reach the lair. I know you are both tired, but we must climb before we rest, to escape the dampness and the cold brought forth by the avalanche. Follow me."

The wizard's last two words contained both a question and a statement. Casemiro invited Forrest with pleading eyes. "I cannot do this without you, Forrest. I..."

"Say no more. Today showed me people must make challenging decisions at times that impact the rest of their lives. You did what you believed best, and I cannot say I would have chosen a different option. For now, we must save Oleander. Lead on, wizard."

22

THE CLEAVE OF SIVEN

Casemiro fought to remain awake, aware one of them needed to remain aware of their surroundings. Laural and Forrest required rest to recover from their injuries. Casemiro drained his magical energy by calling down the avalanche and only remained upright because of adrenaline. He understood their current state opened the group to defeat by any attacker, let alone a dragon. The wizard leaned against the rock wall and found a corner to support his body and nestled into a somewhat comfortable position.

The familiar moist air and damp stairs brought back memories of a visit twenty years ago. Casemiro chuckled at the idea he, Forrest, and the Princess planned a rescue by traveling from the ass end of the mountain to save Oleander from the jaws of death, the dragon's lair. The mountain served as a metaphor for a dragon, and this humored the wizard. Casemiro smiled as he breathed in the heavy air of the stairwell, and his somnolent mind gave in as his eyes closed. Fatigue defeated the wizard's resolve, causing him to sleep on the steps.

In his state of slumber, Casemiro's dreams became vivid, seeing everything through the eyes of a young wizard scaling the steps. He created no noise to warn the dragons in the cavern above of his imminent arrival. Casemiro climbed all day and discovered a naval in the cavern's belly. The young wizard became amused at the scarcity of items in the lair he entered. Stories of massive dragon hoards and limitless wealth pervaded history, but the young wizard found this lair sparse compared to his unchecked imagination.

The dark hall featured charred walls of an endless black color; the matte stone texture revealed nothing to the young wizard. Casemiro rummaged through the cave and entered the foremost portion of the cavern to find a gigantic male dragon staring out the mouth of Mount Siven. From this perspective, one overlooked the entire valley and plains that led to the village of Lillenhold in the distance, and the sunset sparkled any remaining light across the Bay of Scars. Though the young wizard believed himself clever, his appearance did not surprise the beast.

A second dragon, unseen by Casemiro, lifted a viperous head and prepared to strike if the wizard came closer. The body slid across the floor of the cave towards a nest on the opposite wall. The flickering tongue of the beast served as a warning to the wizard. After a hatchling's screech, Casemiro realized this dragon filled the role of mother and her chief priority equated to protecting the child. The young wizard stumbled into a dragon's nest. Killing a dragon became much less important than escaping with his life.

The much larger, and unmoving, male dragon lay on the floor of the cave as smoke flittered from the beast's nostrils and out the edges of a gaping mouth. Several sword-sized teeth revealed their danger to the man. Out of instinct, Casemiro drew his saber and held his staff to defend himself, but kept a safe distance between himself and the beasts.

The female dragon slithered into a defensive position between the wizard and the hatchling. She broke the silence. "Hello, man of Lillenhold. Your fellow citizens did enough damage to my mate to ensure his approaching demise. Are you happy?"

Casemiro discerned the chest of the larger dragon moving as the plated armor shifted with each breath. The dragon's shallow breaths implied the short amount of remaining life for the beast.

The young wizard thought a pithy response was in order. "No happiness comes from the loss of life. I apologize for the coming death of your mate."

The female dragon rose to her full height in the cave and darted to stand between Casemiro and her mate. "Liar! I am aware of who you are and why you come to our home. The King of Gaeleos deemed us a nuisance because my mate became arrogant and greedy. Also, only fools attack a dragon's home."

"I carry no malice toward you, great dragon." Casemiro bowed but retained eye contact with the female.

"You lie once again, human. Why else sneak about like a thief instead of an honored guest? Why else attempt to find us unaware by using a secret entrance to this cave instead of climbing through the open front door? Why else do you bear weapons of death instead of gifts of thankfulness for my hospitality? Lie once more, human, and I shall rip your skull from your body and use your corpse to feed my child."

Casemiro slid the saber into its sheath and lowered the

staff. "Fair enough, your greatness. The King of Gaeleos hired me to remove a dragon from the skies. Now that your mate is injured, his death will become public knowledge soon. But if the men of Lillenhold learn of another dragon, and a hatchling, these men will become emboldened and will come to kill you and your child. May I suggest another option, one where your child lives beyond today? I entertain no desire to kill an innocent creature, let alone a magnificent beast such as yourself."

The dragon lowered her head to the height of Casemiro's and stared into his eyes from a foot away. The wizard held his breath to prevent choking on the noxious brimstone fumes escaping the beast. The female dragon took a deep breath as a small stream of flame shot from her nose. "I do not sense deception, and what you say strikes true regarding the villagers of Lillenhold. They will come for us because their nature is to destroy what they deem dangerous."

"Exalted dragon, forgive my impropriety, but may I call you by your name?"

"The way you attune yourself to my lair reeks of your callous arrogance, human. Or do I dare call you a wizard? The foul stench of unchecked magic rolls off your body. You tamper with powers and abilities you can never master."

The wizard smiled at the dragon, not taking his eyes off her. "You are correct, but I desire to know your name."

"You can refer to me as Marwolaeth, the name I feel closest to in this moment." The dragon slinked back and forth, flicking her tongue, unsure if Casemiro might attack if she turned away.

Casemiro nodded as he translated the name from the magical language in his mind. "Ah, death. We might be more open to accepting death if it took your beauteous form."

The dragon hissed and dark smoke billowed from her nostrils. "Calm your silvery tongue, deceiver. You would sooner cut my throat as invite me into your home for dinner."

"I couldn't fit you in my home, noble Marwolaeth."

"But you might fill half of my gullet." The dragon let the beginnings of a grin edge across her face, but stopped. "How do we proceed, wizard? I grow tired of this pointless exchange as the daylight wanes, and my child will soon wake from hunger. If we reach no resolution by then, you become his next meal."

Casemiro stood and glanced around the female dragon to the hatchling stirring in the corner. "Your mate lost, but you still stand to lose much more. If not by my hand, then by those from Lillenhold in the coming days."

"Is that your proposal, wizard?" She slithered inches closer, her patience fading as the sunlight diminished and Casemiro's hopes of escaping ebbed closer to death with each second.

"My client ordered me to kill every dragon I found for your mate's actions against the village. Your mate raided the farms and livestock of many citizens and attacked multiple families, including a trollen clutch without provocation. Of those attacked, one trollen child and its mother survived. Those families deserve justice."

The female dragon glanced toward her child and slithered away from the unwanted guest. Casemiro sensed the tension in her mind and understood the dragon would compromise if offered a fitting deal. The wizard took her reluctant groan as a sign of her willingness to talk.

"Air your proposal but know that no human hands will touch my child."

"Your hatchling remains innocent, and I will not harm it. My proposal for you and your hatchling allows you to escape on this night from the mountain unseen with the help of the new moon and cloud cover. But your mate must remain, and I will slay him to ease his pain. The King of Gaeleos then gains the remaining treasures within this cavern and the body of a dragon as trophies."

Marwolaeth rose in height and snarled at the wizard. "And why do this, instead of destroying you before your heart beats once more?"

"The people of Lillenhold believe a single dragon caused all this strife. Under this proposal, they fulfill their lust for justice and the two of you leave without harm. You must find a new home, a fair price to pay for the crimes your mate committed." Casemiro regretted the words he used as they placed the blame on the dragon.

A roar, the female's vocalization of displeasure at the proposal, filled the cavern and spilled into the open air. Casemiro recognized the sign as her acceptance of the offer in her mind, but her heart remained uncertain and grieved the loss of her mate even more.

The dragon approached the wizard as she talked. "Crimes per your supposed laws, but we did not upset the balance of nature, as you pretend. Dragons are natural creatures and lived long before your puny species. We need not validate our right to roam and take what we need. Instead, we must accommodate minute migratory pests and not offend their sensitivities for fear of retribution. Maybe roasting everyone in the village presents a better option. Right after I kill and eat you." She stopped six inches short of Casemiro's face.

Casemiro steeled himself to prevent flinching at her rumbling presence, knowing that meant his death. "Then more humans will hunt you, and they won't offer you a choice. The King will hire someone to kill you and your hatchling." Casemiro held his staff aloft and a subtle glow emanated from the iron cap, a sign of his readiness for battle. "You will find me a resolute enemy to defeat, and an even tougher one to chew."

Marwolaeth sneered. "You dare to challenge me?"

"I have no child to worry about, Marwolaeth. This is not necessary. You said it yourself; your mate is doomed. I offer you a chance to escape and restart wherever you wish. A chance to do so with no harm coming to your hatchling."

The dragon backed away, a sign of her acceptance. The female lowered her head and nestled it next to the still-breathing male dragon. She closed her eyes and laid beside the larger dragon's body for a moment for a last farewell.

"Tell me his name."

"YrAwyr, the force of the sky. But you may not say his name unless you earn the right." The female dragon rose to her full height, prepared to finish the exchange. "I accept your terms, but you may never hunt us again, wizard. In return, we shall live out our lives away from this place and Lillenhold. Not abiding by these terms means being bound to serve each other indefinitely or until released. Are we agreed.... What is your name?"

"Casemiro."

The dragon nodded. "Are we agreed, Casemiro?"

"We are, noble Marwolaeth." The wizard bowed to show the respect he held for the beast but kept his eyes on the dragon. Casemiro pounded his staff on the ground and a burst of energy filled the cave. "And that seals our agreement."

"Then I need a moment to say goodbye to my mate of many years. What I must do, no human may witness. If you wait in the back of the cave, the wind will tell you when I escape and signal the time to do what you must."

Casemiro backtracked through the cave, slid down the wall to take a seat, and waited for the rush of wind to signal the departure of the female dragon and her hatchling. The brisk breeze of a hurricane and the sound of a dragon's roar reached him moments later. The wizard ran to the front of the cave and tracked the female dragon as she flew into the night sky with her hatchling.

"Goodbye and good fortune, Marwolaeth."

The wizard turned to see YrAwyr open his eyes.

"You showed her respect. Thank you."

Casemiro bowed to the dragon.

"Proceed, wizard, and put me out of my misery."

Casemiro unsheathed his saber and found the faint heartbeat of the beast through the dragon's chest. The wizard wedged his saber beneath the plate of dragon armor and pushed the blade as deep as his strength allowed. The blade pierced the heart of the beast and received a response of a violent shiver. Casemiro removed the blade and stood back to allow the beast the dignity of a clean death instead of an agonizing one from the various injuries.

The young wizard stepped away to behold the remainder of the sunset over the distant horizon, allowing the beast to die outside of human eyes. Once the beast passed, the wizard sliced and hewed the hide and muscle until the blade reached the dragon's massive heart. Casemiro removed the source of the monster's magic and the organ transformed into a vermillion-colored dragon heartstone, a rare crystalline jewel, once the muscle reached the open air. Casemiro wrapped the gem in cloth and moved away from the body to rest. When he woke, he descended the mountain and returned to the village to receive his reward and acclaim.

The startled wizard woke as someone shook him. Casemiro opened his eyes to the smiling face of Laural and reached for his staff before regaining his senses.

"You alright, Casemiro? You mumbled words regarding dragons, and you screamed in your sleep."

Forrest drew close enough to be seen in the dim light. "Yes, the dream must have been some nightmare."

"How long did we sleep?"

Laural answered, "Not long enough to feel refreshed."

Casemiro dipped his head and pinched the bridge of his nose. The time for complete transparency arrived, as Forrest and Laural deserved the truth about what lay ahead and why the group needed to face it now. The wizard glanced at his friends, expecting disappointment to soon follow. "I need to tell you something."

The Princess shook her head. "Another untruth, Casemiro?"

The wizard recounted the events from twenty years ago. Upon finishing the story, Casemiro scanned the dark alcove, the only light coming from the glowing metal at the end of his staff. The silent rebuke from Forrest and Laural arrived with sunken shoulders from their disappointment.

Forrest stood. "Enough of your lies, wizard. Let's save Oleander and finish the job you did not complete. Then, if you are lucky, you might live."

The wizard glanced in Laural's direction, but the Princess turned away from him.

The Princess shored up her leather jerkin. "I've nothing to say to you."

Casemiro accepted his fate and found no fault with his friends' reaction. The wizard stood and cinched the chain belt around his waist. The wizard led the group up the stairs to the Dragon's home, with the staff lighting the way. Despite having two companions, the wizard now walked up the steps as a lonely man.

23

GLIMMERS

Casemiro caught his breath from trekking up the steps after two hours, a task that he remembered as much less taxing two decades before. The wizard scanned the stairway beneath him to find Laural standing several steps below, and Forrest even further down and barely in the glow. Without words, the group agreed to rest in the soft, glowing light provided by Casemiro's staff. The trio nestled into the corners of the stone walls for a rest as Casemiro dimmed the light and fell asleep.

Within his dreams, Casemiro walked beside his brother, Quinto, on a road bound for an unknown destination. Casemiro's staff beat against the ground in rhythm with each step. The world around the brothers appeared as a forest full of various trees, not unlike the woods outside of Lillenhold.

CHRISTOPHER CLOUSER

Quinto came to a sudden stop, fixated on a question. "Do you comprehend our true purpose here, brother?"

Casemiro looked at his sibling with a perplexed stare. "Oppose evil and uproot the source if possible."

Quinto shook his head. "Are we not beyond that now? What if I decide to search for a new purpose?"

"Brother, you would dare to question our master?"

Quinto pounded his staff into the ground. "Why must we become avatars who consistently weigh in and determine how humanity lives? Perhaps these people required our help to deal with evil versions of us who wished to dominate their lives. But we must move on because humans do not need us, or anyone, standing above them, guiding their leaders, or fighting their battles. Can't we allow humanity to wage their own wars? People face greater difficulties in their daily lives than evil wizards. Do you not grasp this?"

"We discussed this before. Our reason for being here exists beyond our understanding and we are bound to uphold this mission, brother."

"What if I wish to live as one of these people? What if I choose to forsake this power and this destiny? Should we not choose for ourselves? Perhaps we can pursue our own path alongside this role of aiding humanity?"

Casemiro scanned the skies in frustration, looking for a sign from their heavenly father. Quinto asked these questions often, but more so since defeating the last evil wizard. No other problems of this magnitude existed in Gaeleos, Austeria, or anywhere else in the world. Reports of a dragon uprising in Gaeleos drew their focus for the moment, but such a problem fell beneath their combined skill. Even Casemiro occasionally, and privately, questioned if such tasks fell within their mandate.

"Selfish desire has taken hold of you, Quinto."

"Perhaps, but what if mankind does not require our intervention any longer? Don't we owe people the courtesy of stepping away and allowing them to direct their own lives?"

Quinto would not cease his curiosity this time. Casemiro grew tired and pressed his brother. "What do you propose, then? Walk into the next village we run across, drop our wizard's robes, and take on the life of a regular person? Work on a farm or another laborious life? Turn away from our created intentions?"

"Why not? Not change our form, or fundamental nature, but step into another role. I wish to acquire a ship and sail across the sea, perhaps transporting cargo to cover my expenses. Maybe fall in love with a woman or do something else with her." He smiled at Casemiro and winked. "I wish to conquer new challenges and live a life I choose, not one designed for me."

Casemiro stood aghast at the audacity of his brother. "Does this not go against our creator's desires for us?"

"Casemiro, look into my eyes and tell me our destiny from this point forward. Our purpose. We possess the potential for greater experiences beyond shields, swords, and spells. I made my decision, and you cannot change my mind."

"Brother, what if evil returns? Should we not stand vigilant?"

"I'll support you if the need arises again. Until then, I must pursue other passions. Now, you must address other matters and wake from your slumber."

A snore from Forrest reminiscent of a wild beast's roar woke the wizard. Casemiro spotted a stream of light beaming into the Cleave of Siven from above their position. The beacon's glow summoned the wizard to come closer and rediscover the outside world.

Casemiro tapped Laural on the shoulder to wake the Princess. The Princess rubbed her eyes and smiled at the wizard, but her expression turned to a frown as memories of their prior exchange resurfaced. At the sound of movement from the others, Forrest grumbled and woke from his rest. The trio readied themselves for the remainder of the climb inside the mountain.

Laural released a deep breath and nearly gagged. "What is that stench?"

Casemiro answered, "This mountain houses millions of bats. Millions of bats which fed last night and returned home."

Forrest moaned as the repugnance spread across his countenance. "He means guano."

"Bat shit? Disgusting." The Princess shook at the idea.

"Welcome to the wilderness, Laural. There appears to be an opening above to provide the new morning's light to dispel a portion of the darkness of this stairwell. Once we reach the opening, we stop for fresh air, a brief meal, and then complete our hike. Then, we need to be silent for the last climb, or the dragon will hear us." Casemiro began ascending.

The trio climbed another two hours until they drew level to the gap in the mountain's wall. The fissure split the stone wall, revealing a gap as wide as a person's head and as long as their arm, and exposed them to the outside world. The opening allowed daylight and fresh air to flood the cleave. Yearning for the elements, each person squeezed towards the gap.

Sunlight streamed across the wizard's face. Casemiro discontinued the enchantment powering the soft glow from his staff for the time being. The trio sat on a ledge, eating hardtack and jerky, grateful for their remaining provisions after having lost the bulk of their supplies during their escape from the dragon the night before.

Casemiro held up two fingers and pointed up the stairwell, communicating another two hours of climbing to reach the dragon's lair. The information received nods of determination in reply. A quick drink of water preceded the group packing up their bags and resuming their journey. Though silent, the group settled their disagreements for the time being and proceeded with a single task: finding Oleander.

As the companions moved from the ledge, a shadow flashed over the opening. Casemiro leaped to glance through the gap in the stone, taking a last deep breath of the morning air before turning to the others. "The dragon leaves to feed. If lucky, we can reach the lair prior to the dragon returning."

Forrest spoke in a hushed tone. "And save Oleander."

The trio began the last leg of the journey to the dragon's lair, energized by their potential good fortune. As they ascended the stairs, aided by the light of the new day, warmth emanated from the breast pocket of Casemiro's cloak. The wizard reached in and removed the coin. Without the threat of the dragon, he answered.

"What news do you deliver, Roman?"

"Something happened at Veritas Keep. The guards sealed the keep and established checkpoints at the edge of the city, preventing anyone from entering, or leaving, the village. Lillenhold's port remains the sole entry and exit point, where all departing ships undergo inspection."

Casemiro peered at Laural, who shrugged her shoulders in confusion.

"Did the Prince order this by decree?"

"No idea. The guards denied everyone entry into the keep for their jobs today. A fear grows that something unpleasant is happening. What do you suggest?"

Casemiro rubbed his forehead. "Follow their orders and stay safe for now. Do not reach out to us again unless something of extreme importance occurs. Besides, I may not be able to talk to you over the next few hours."

The boy replied after a pause. "I understand. May God bless your efforts, Casemiro."

"And yours as well, Roman."

Casemiro returned the coin to his pocket, grazing his hands along the knitting needles and the parchment. A quick flash of Chantal raced through his mind and left just as quickly. The wizard glimpsed Laural and contemplated her unsaid concerns. The need to speak and energize his friends came over the wizard.

"We cannot do anything about what occurs in Lillenhold. We must complete our mission here and charge up these stairs and free Oleander. Let's attempt to reach her before the dragon returns."

Casemiro grabbed Forrest's attention. "When we reach the top, I may have to battle the dragon. If I signal to you, grab Oleander and take her to safety." The wizard turned to Laural. "You do the same."

The Princess asked, "What about you?"

"I will fend for myself, but our job involves saving Oleander and killing the dragon, if possible."

The trio resumed their ascent to the top of Mount Siven and dread filled Casemiro's heart, but not because of the dragon.

After another two hours of climbing, Laural tugged on Casemiro's cloak as a signal to stop and sit. Her face, covered in sweat and grime, beckoned the wizard for a break. Casemiro realized the ambitious nature of their pace. The idea of a break resonated with him as well. But reaching the dragon drained of energy meant almost assured defeat. No, they would need their full strength to master this challenge.

Casemiro nodded his acceptance of the idea, and the group withdrew their water sacks with no noise. The trio climbed a significant portion of the mountain's height. The air grew cooler and thinner, indicating they reached the top of the mountain. The stairwell narrowed enough that the wizard reached across to touch both sides of the inclining passage. Casemiro reignited his staff to supply additional light because the illumination from the gap below had weakened.

Before resuming their march, warmth filled the wizard's breast pocket. Casemiro anticipated the importance of Roman's message and pulled out the coin, but grazed the edge of his gray cloak as he withdrew his hand. The wizard's fingers, slippery from the drink and perspiration, lost control of the coin.

The wizard dropped the trinket, reaching in desperation to catch the coin as the metal disk fell down the stairwell and into the darkness below. A ringing noise continued for countless seconds and disappeared into nothingness, echoing up to their location every few seconds.

Casemiro imagined the sound of the coin clinking down the stairs as a squeak. Then a second instance of the distinctive noise echoed through the enclosed stairwell. Then a third. Soon, a cacophony of squeaks rose from the interior of the stone monolith towards them.

Fear filled the wizard, and he directed the others. "Climb! Climb as if your lives depended on it!"

The trio ascended the stairs at a faster pace but failed to outrun whatever chased them. The noises became louder as squeaks and muffled gusts of wind grew in intensity until a scratching of claws and a rustling noise reminding one of raking leaves in the fall filled the stairwell.

As the companions climbed, Forrest recognized the noise first. "The bats woke up."

The three hastened up the stairs. Laural tripped, but a quick hand from Forrest pushed the Princess up. The trio strived to move swifter as the noise grew in intensity. The thunderous rumble of an untold number of bats flapping their wings filled the stairwell as they raced higher in the glow of Casemiro's staff.

To their delight, a hole appeared and beckoned for the travelers to continue their ascent to freedom. Casemiro recognized the gap as the same breach he used twenty years before. Right as they reached freedom, the first bat overtook the trio, flying over and around. The animals reached the opening and escaped whatever prompted their exodus and pulsed through the narrow hole.

Laural screamed and wilted beneath the swarm. The Princess latched onto the bottom of Casemiro's cloak and followed as the wizard pulled her along with his burning muscles and his never-ceasing determination. Forrest, the wizard assumed, lagged behind Laural on the stairs. Casemiro lost sight of the troll-man at the onset of the massive wave of winged mammals.

The flood of bats filled every empty space and allowed the trio no freedom. The swirling onslaught of flying animals that circled around and over them consumed them. But this flood refused to pull the wizard or his companions through the gap above them. They must climb through the blitzkrieg.

A wing scratched Casemiro's face while another bat latched onto the sleeve of his cloak. The wizard yelled an inaudible magic word and fired a blast from his staff, which did nothing to discourage the bats. He smashed his forearm against the stone wall to remove the mammal clinging to his cloak. The wizard crawled through the hole at the top of the stairs. Casemiro reached out and found some purchase and then scurried to reach safety. Before losing his courage, Casemiro reached into the opening with an extended a hand. The torrent of bats flew through the hole and kept Casemiro from grabbing the Princess.

Laural's face emerged from the gap, and the Princess reached out, flapping her right hand as an urgent plea for aid and hoping anyone might pull her to safety. The wizard grabbed hold and pulled her free of the massive swarm. With a swift motion, Forrest cleared the opening and sprang away from the hole, much like a clog being dislodged from a culvert.

The trio moved away, allowing the bats to flow through the hole without hindrance. The winged mammals inundated the cavern as the trio covered their heads for protection, hoping the animals ignored them in the madness of their escape. For several seconds, the bats continued through the cavern until they flew off, leaving the travelers behind in the back of a vast cave.

Once the wizard's eyes accustomed themselves to the dimness, Casemiro perceived a vast amount of animal bones littering the surrounding area. In the distance, he registered the movement of a person approaching him.

The beauty and blondness of Oleander exclaimed a greeting. "You survived?" Oleander smiled and drew closer to Casemiro. "You came to save me?"

Forrest and Laural appeared from the darkness with the troll-man answering the question. "We all did."

Oleander turned her attention to the others. "Princess Laural? Forrest? Why did you come?"

"You're our friend." Laural reached out to embrace Oleander, receiving a curt hug in response.

Oleander turned to the cave's opening in the distance as if she expected someone, or something, to materialize. She glared at the wizard. "What did you plan once you arrived?"

Casemiro brushed his cloak free of as much dirt and guano as possible. "Without the dragon here, we should make a hasty escape via the stairs."

Oleander whirled with an incredulous leer. "You found the stairs?"

"This isn't my first time storming this particular dragon's lair. On the way back to Lillenhold, we can share the lengthy tale. Let's leave before the dragon returns."

When Casemiro grabbed Oleander's hand to pull the woman to the opening, a roar rose from outside the cave. A burst of wind pushed the travelers to the ground and across the floor, a familiar sensation each of them remembered from their earlier encounters with the beast. The blast of air pushed the foursome to the far wall, and away from the hole leading to the stairs. They took too long to flee, and an angry dragon entered the cave.

The massive beast collapsed its wings while entering the gaping shelter. Another roar shook the cavern, but Casemiro stood in defiance of the creature. The wizard examined the beast and found this dragon twinned its sire in almost every way. The dragon stood forty feet in full height with wings over twice that in length. From snout to tail, the armored beast measured over one hundred feet. If possible, the son might even exceed the father in majesty.

Casemiro held fast to the magical energy growing within him as the dragon advanced. His confidence grew and his self-doubt diminished with each passing second. The wizard feared only for those behind him. He recognized the need to confront the dragon and remove his friends from harm's way.

The monster roared and shot flames along the edges of the massive cave, lighting torches, and filling the cave with a flickering red light. The illumination provided the illusion of blood flowing throughout the lair. The dragon stepped forward and eclipsed the rest of the cave from his potential prey and blocked the hole leading to the stairway and their escape. Two options existed: surrender or fight.

Forrest stood in front of Oleander to defend the woman. Casemiro stood to the right of the troll-man, raising his staff and saber. Brandishing a knife in each hand, Laural joined them and stood by Casemiro's side. The trio prepared to fight the dragon, believing the battle to be hopeless.

The dragon took two steps and leaned towards the companions as a puff of smoke flew through the beast's pulsating nostrils. The dragon reared back and opened its maw, and prepared to launch another fiery blast. Then the beast stopped itself and spoke.

"We need to talk before I kill you and your friends, wizard. Situate yourself, as you'll be here for quite some time. I suggest you make peace with the idea of not leaving my lair alive."

24

STANDOFF

Casemiro second-guessed his strategy when coming face to face with the massive dragon. In the wizard's mind, the monster before him feared nothing, even though his magic simmered beneath the surface and beckoned for him to call the power forth. Then the dread, grief, and guilt welled up inside Casemiro and, once again, he doubted whether he might save those with him. He believed his limited skills coming into the cave offered no legitimate threat. The wizard hoped to provide enough of a distraction to allow his friends to escape because only the fate of Laural, Oleander, and Forrest mattered.

Casemiro gritted his teeth and prepared to launch a surprise attack on the beast, trusting that route offered their lone path to salvation. The wizard readied himself to be a sacrifice for the safety of the others. At least, if they lived, his death by the fiery breath of a dragon seemed noble and worthwhile.

The wizard challenged the beast. "I would rather die a hundred deaths in battle than sit idly as you slowly kill us with your cunning words."

The eyes of the dragon glowed. "Very well, I've waited a long time to devour you, Casemiro."

Before the wizard began his attack, Oleander stepped forward and positioned herself between her rescuers and the wyrm, delaying any hopes of a glorious death for the wizard. The woman held her hands out towards both, acting as if she separated them through her own inclination, and shouted a command. "Stop, now."

The dragon raised its head in surprise, forced a smirk across its lips, and met the woman eye to eye. "Are you sure you wish to interfere, little one?"

"At least pursue a peaceful resolution before destroying these brave souls. Perhaps you can gain valuable information from a diplomatic discussion."

The dragon veered its colossal head around Oleander and snarled at the three trespassers, casting an especially intimidating glare at the wizard. The noxious stench of brimstone choked the newcomers at this close distance. "I tried that but the wizard —"

"You should talk." After a confident nod from Oleander, Casemiro lowered his saber, but kept the blade at his side, and Laural sheathed her knives. The trio of newcomers became curious about how this woman could influence the dragon. Forrest's renewed his focus on Oleander.

The dragon seethed at the troll-man. "You dwell on the woman as if you never viewed one before? Perhaps focus on the monster wishing to roast you like a pig with a single breath, trollen."

Casemiro stepped forward, taking the leadership role for the team. *If this is the route we must take to get the others out of here alive, so be it.*

The wizard positioned Laural behind him to provide a semblance of protection for the Princess. "If you insist on a discussion, perhaps introductions are in order. How should we refer to your greatness?"

The dragon extended its head to its full height. "Call me Ofani'r."

Casemiro examined the beast in detail for the first time. Ofani'r featured red, black, and gold streaks running from front to back along the maroon torso, thick dragon plating covered its chest and abdomen, and red leathery wings spanned the cave. The long tail slithered back and forth while spikes protruded from various points to provide additional defensive and attacking capabilities.

The wizard felt the rush of energy as the beast approached. The familiar, but long-lost buzz of unthrottled magic flowed through him. His grief and guilt no longer mattered. This magic would not be deterred by simple human emotions. Casemiro remembered how it felt to hold this much power. He also recalled the simple spell to defeat the dragon if it came down to destroying the beast to save the others.

Prepare to lose this battle, dragon.

Casemiro bowed. "Great Ofani'r, we three travelers came to rescue the lady Oleander, believing you endangered her. Perhaps we overreacted, and you present her no real danger."

The dragon glared at the wizard as Oleander came to the side of the beast. Growling, Ofani'r sneered at the old man. "I know you, wizard, and the name of Casemiro carries great meaning in my family. Who stands with you?"

Laural stepped up. "Princess Laural, the daughter of King Skaranon of Gaeleos."

Oleander provided additional commentary. "Laural adores her people, or she wouldn't be here."

"I judge the quality of those coming before me, little one." The beast's eyes shifted back to Laural. "Your father and I own differing views on the value of dragon's lives." The dragon turned to Forrest. "Who leers at Oleander?"

Forrest brought his attention back to the dragon. "I am Forrest, a villager from Lillenhold." He paused with the sudden urge to throw in the new qualification and blurted out his newly won title. "And the recognized champion of Veritas Keep."

Upon hearing the mention of being a champion, the dragon raised a brow and let out a brief chuckle.

Oleander turned to the troll-man with a shocking grin across her lips. "Forrest, when did you receive the title?"

The dragon placed a taloned paw in front of Oleander as if marking the woman as his property. The movement registered the beast's intent with everyone in the cave, especially Forrest, as if they were in competition for the woman's affection.

Forrest scowled at the action. "I won the title to save you."

The dragon interjected. "Ah, now the obsession becomes revealed. This trollen loves Lady Oleander. How quaint." A low rumble of laughter followed the words.

With a pointed a finger to emphasize his point, Forrest responded. "We will return Oleander to Lillenhold."

The dragon raised its body and stiffened its joints to prepare for a fight. The beast moved Oleander to the side with the subtle action of its front leg.

Casemiro pounded the iron end of his staff on the floor of the cave to gain everyone's attention and calm their nerves. "Enough! Before things escalate, you wished to discuss a few matters. I hope to avoid your greatness dominating our puny skills in an unfulfilling battle."

The dragon glared at the wizard, then glanced back at Forrest. "Yes, Casemiro. We must address the events that brought us to this point. Which includes revealing your many failures to those closest to you and allowing them to pass judgment on whether you live or die."

Casemiro snickered at the comment and seated himself beyond the reach of the dragon. The wizard laid his staff across his lap and pulled the hood of his cloak from his head. "We can oblige, but first shall we discuss the safety of Oleander? I hope this doesn't deteriorate into chaos from a misunderstanding."

The dragon swerved its body to conceal Oleander. Ofani'r's eyes narrowed as the beast studied the wizard. "I believe you understand much more than you let on, Casemiro."

"Great Ofani'r, answer this lone question. Did you intentionally capture Oleander? Or was this woman merely an unlucky damsel put into distress?"

The dragon bellowed a deep laugh and shook the cave. "Oleander did not represent a random waif I scraped off the landscape. Because of your predictable response, I intended to snatch her with the hopes of you scaling Mount Siven and returning to this lair."

"Then, with me in your clutches, Oleander and the others may leave. Could we strike a bargain?"

"Perhaps, but not yet. I want you to sweat during this discourse. You must understand your previous actions jeopardize the lives of those who followed you here."

Laural's impatience won out, and the Princess stood while pointing her knife at the dragon. "Why are we talking? If this concerns stroking your ego, I've no more patience. Bats shit on me, my shoulder carries an infected wound, Casemiro gave me stitches, a woman I believed long-dead popped up in the forest, a group of wrestlers may have taken over my brother's village, and, frankly, I am tired and need a long bath. So, move this along."

Casemiro reached out to touch Laural's good shoulder, but the Princess backed away from the comforting hand before returning her focus to the dragon. "And I want the complete truth, no more lies of omission. After everything we went through, I deserve this, regardless of where it leads." She glared at the wizard and the dragon as she wiped a tear away. Laural directed her last comments at Casemiro more than Ofani'r.

The wizard lowered his head as a sign of submission and walked toward Ofani'r. "Before you do whatever you plan, allow me to ask of your mother."

An old sensation burrowed back into the wizard's soul. He recognized and accepted the new piece of this puzzle, knowing he needed to complete the problem before using his magic. Casemiro's compassion for Marwolaeth opened the door for the missing element, absolution. Absolution from the sins of his past and a new beginning free of guilt. The wizard grabbed the freedom and held onto it dearly.

The dragon pulled back its head to reveal a surprised expression. "Why do you care, wizard?"

"Your mother cared enough to strike a bargain and take a vow. She did this for one reason, to save your life, Ofani'r. You are the hatchling I let live twenty years ago. And my friends know this already because I relayed the story to them. Your mother sacrificed her home to protect you, an admirable act on her part."

Two tears fell from Ofani'r's eyes and turned to steam upon hitting the cave floor. "My mother passed from disease three seasons ago. She lived many years in the warm mountains of the continent south of here. I wish to do her memory justice and exact revenge on the people who killed my father."

"And she told you of Lillenhold at some point, I assume. According to the farmers, you have stayed here for at least a year." Casemiro glimpsed Laural's direction to convey his knowledge of the rumors Arenton ignored.

The Princess returned the glance, and something flickered inside the wizard. Casemiro recognized the pang of magic returning to him. The magic within him rose to life, and a door opened to allow the trapped energy to rush out and stampede over what held it at bay. With significant effort, Casemiro pulled his attention back to the dragon in front of him. For the first time in years, Casemiro struggled to control the magic within him. The wizard's sly smile revealed his advantage over the unsuspecting dragon.

Ofani'r nodded its head, acknowledging the wizard's last comment. "You speak the truth."

Casemiro rose to his full height. "I am sorry for Marwolaeth's passing." The wizard's eyes took on a fiery glow as he raised his head. "You started plotting when you came up here, didn't you?"

The dragon still ignored the change to the wizard while it became engrossed in explaining its actions. "To a degree, wizard. In the forest, while looking for food, I encountered a woman and one of her children. She offered me a whole hog to spare their lives and listen to a proposition. The woman recognized me as the son of YrAwyr. She remembered the events of the affair as if she lived through it, despite it happening twenty years ago."

Casemiro smiled at the dragon. "Would I be correct in guessing you met the enchantress Mira Sweet?"

The dragon smiled at the wizard, revealing all of its saber-like teeth as drool dripped from one on the left side of the monster's mouth.

"I would also speculate that this woman learned those stories from her sister, my deceased wife. Whom Mira killed; I might add." The wizard flashed a glance towards Forrest and winked at his friend.

Casemiro allowed the magical power to imbue him and charge his body with the energy. The power rose and pulsed through his body. There was no way to hide this from the dragon. Casemiro tasted the magic on his tongue, and it rang in his ears. It filled his nostrils with the scent of juniper as his body tingled. His eyes glowed as the time to battle approached.

The dragon sensed a change in the cave's atmosphere, not knowing what magic the wizard held back. His animal instincts of preservation came to the forefront, and the beast took on a defensive stance while he slung an accusation at the wizard. "This involves you and that woman's father..." Ofani'r pointed a claw at Laural, "...killing my sire."

Forrest joined in the distraction, pulling the dragon's attention in another direction. "And it does nothing to account for the fact your father killed most of my family as part of his onslaught against this countryside."

Ofani'r turned a sharp glare toward Forrest. "The King baited my father into a trap and used your family and other trolls as bait. Did Casemiro mention this?"

Forrest glared at the wizard.

Casemiro turned towards the troll-man. "I recall nothing of such an event, even if true." The wizard turned back to the dragon. "But nothing changes regarding your being here, on this hallowed ground, wyrm."

The dragon laughed and slithered toward the wizard, pushing Oleander further to the side. "You destroyed your friendships with your lies, wizard. These two do not trust you. But you surprised me with your bravery in confronting me."

"And you surprise me by your ignorance and the erroneous memories of your family, Ofani'r. Your father strafed over this village for years, stealing and eating as he wished, showing no honor until his death. Only then did he display a shred of dignity and accepted justice for his actions when I killed him with the saber I carry today. He might have recovered from those wounds, but sacrificed his life to save you. Laural's father did not kill your sire because I did the deed with my own hands."

Casemiro growled and his staff glowed as he concentrated on his emotions. Unsure what allowed him to regain his magic, the wizard decided to use the opportunity and allow others to reach safety while preventing the dragon from harming them. Then the puzzle solved itself in his mind as a piece from a memory long ago fell into place. A slice of wisdom from his many lessons at the hand of his master.

"Oh, you dare attempt to frighten me, wizard?" The dragon stood at its full height in the cavern.

"No, just proving you lack honor, Ofani'r. Your mother promised something twenty years ago, a dragon's vow. A vow that, if broken by the dragon swearing it, or their offspring, condemns the dragon to certain conditions. Your mother vowed neither she, nor you, would ever return to Lillenhold. Because of your actions, you broke the vow and played into my hands. You cannot harm me."

"Does it appear as if a vow my mother offered twenty years ago concerns me?" The dragon reared back its head and opened its mouth to launch a blast of fiery breath, but nothing emerged from the beast's throat.

Casemiro smiled, confident his strategy won the day. "All creatures of magic must live under the old laws. Even you, Ofani'r. Magical oaths still contain great power." The wizard pounded his staff on the floor of the cave and held his arms aloft. "Corwynt!" Casemiro unleashed a powerful gust of wind with the force of a cyclone and knocked the dragon out of the lair and into the sun-filled sky beyond, but he knew the beast would return.

Forrest recognized the signal and threw Oleander over his shoulder and made his way to the stairwell. Forrest reached the opening first and dropped Oleander into the gap and jumped through behind her.

The wizard grabbed Laural and led the Princess to the hole leading back into the cleave. Casemiro knew they must execute their escape now if his friends hoped to avoid death. Outside the cave, the cyclone faded, and the dragon's roar signaled its imminent return to the lair.

Casemiro whipped Laural in front of him. "We are out of time. Get them to safety. I wish this ended differently." The wizard kissed the Princess and pushed her into the hole.

Casemiro tapped his staff on the stone. "Cau!" The wizard dragged the end of his staff around the hole and turned the edges of the gap into a magma that obeyed his command. The melted stone closed the gap with a clear crystalline substance.

Laural and Casemiro shared one last glance through the window. Laural beheld the wizard one more time with tears in her eyes. Her hand covered her lips as the Princess mouthed a reply to Casemiro. The wizard blew her another kiss as the clear crystal blackened and became the same igneous substance as the surrounding cave. Now, the wizard stood alone with only one choice before him: fight the dragon.

Casemiro breathed as the wind stopped and Ofani'r marched through the cave towards him, shaking the stone floor with each step. The cavern seemed much bigger with just the two of them. The dragon blasted fire throughout the cave, but Casemiro stood his ground as the flames flickered around him, neither touching nor harming the wizard. A magical bubble of protection surrounded him, and the sweat on his brow did not dampen his smile or his magical energy.

When the flame dispersed, the wizard glared at the dragon. Casemiro glowed with his magical powers at their peak as a flame rose from the end of his staff and the energy of a lightning bolt raced across the blade of his saber. "Now, only you and I remain, Ofani'r. And I must finish what started twenty years ago." The wizard charged at the dragon with a yell from his lungs.

The dragon roared and returned the gesture as saber and staff clashed with claw and tooth.

25

DESCENDING THE CLEAVE

The glow from the dragon's flames disappeared as the cavity closed. Casemiro's magic shut the escapees off from the danger above. Laural screamed for Casemiro to open the hole and let them fight at the wizard's side. The Princess banged her fists against the freshly formed stone for several minutes as noise and vibrations from the battle rippled through the rock like a thunderstorm. The reaction by the Princess left little doubt about her true feelings for the wizard and how the separation between them now nearly killed Laural's spirit.

Because of the darkened Cleave of Siven, Forrest only heard the reaction. He grabbed the Princess and held her close, absorbing the shudders from Laural's sobs as he attempted to comfort her. The Princess scratched at the stone, trying to dig through to Casemiro and her tears became so numerous they created a saltiness in the surrounding air. Eventually, the crying from the Princess ceased. Forrest held the Princess to his shoulder until the rumbles of violence from above stopped. With the quieting of the noises, Laural also fell silent, as if the worst had occurred.

Fearing Laural may become inconsolable, the troll-man called for her propriety to step forward. "Laural, we need you to lead us. You need to become the Princess of Gaeleos again."

The Princess pulled back a sob and squeezed Forrest's shoulder and whispered her gratitude. Laural leaned against Forrest as they settled on the top step of the stairwell, which cut through the heart of the mountain.

After several moments in the darkness, Oleander bloomed forward and broke the silence. "What do we do now?"

Laural sucked in a last sob and almost glowed from the energy expended to overcome her grief. Forrest believed he registered her outline through the blackness. "We deliver you to the Prince. Casemiro focused on finishing the job. He ensured we received a chance for that to happen, so we honor the wizard's sacrifice, and complete our escape."

"How can we succeed in the darkness? If we attempt to walk down the steps, we will fall and kill ourselves."

Laural remarked coldly, "Sit on your butt and scoot down or crawl feet-first on your stomach. Once we reach the bottom, we locate water and maybe find some food. Hopefully, we accomplish the task before the bats return."

Oleander shrieked, "The bats!"

The hand of the Princess grazed Forrest's shoulder. "Big guy, you go first. Oleander goes next, and I follow her to protect us from anything coming down the stairs." Laural checked her waistband to ensure her knives remained sheathed and found both blades.

"Are you ready, Laural? We can wait a little longer." Forrest asked out of concern for the Princess, now knowing the depth of Laural's feelings for the wizard.

The Princess reached out and grabbed Forrest's head and leaned her forehead to his. "Thank you for the comfort, my friend. But this task needs done before I lose myself here." Laural kissed the troll-man on the forehead.

Forrest blushed, unseen by the others, and crawled on his stomach to the next step and then the next. "I cleared a few steps. Oleander, you can begin your descent. If you warn me, I can catch you if you lose your balance."

Someone scrabbled above Forrest and then the scratching of feet finding their hold on the stone-hewn steps filled the air. The next scratch told the same story as another foot found its place and then the next.

"This may not be that bad. How many steps are we talking about?" Oleander's voice carried a sense of wonder and enthusiasm about the task ahead of the trio, and her ignorance became admirable for a moment.

Laural answered and returned their new companion to reality. "Enough to make stairs haunt you for the remainder of your lifetime. Let's check on each other every ten steps or so. If you need to stop, speak up. But our task requires what haste we can muster."

With that last direction, the silence deepened in the darkness. Noises arose from the shuffling and scratching of hands, knees, and feet. Periodic checks occurred at sporadic intervals, but the silence lasted for lengthy periods. The trio lost track of the time of day but believed they crawled for hours before reaching the fissure with a soft glow coming from the outside world.

The gap in the mountainside allowed a lone beam of moonlight to filter into the cleave and captured their gaze like the noon-day sun. The glimmer of the moon drew them to the fissure as moths to a flame. In exhausted silence, the group settled alongside the gap to rest and to ensure their eyes still worked. Forrest questioned whether continuing the journey seemed wise. The descent presented only their first obstacle of the many waiting for them below.

Laural broke the silence with a welcomed question. Their voices gained life in the light and took on a tone of cheerfulness in the black of the Cleave. "Forrest, how are you doing?"

Forrest ignored the soreness in his joints and the scars building up on his knees. "Reaching the bottom would resolve my issues." The soreness gave way to fatigue, and his body required rest. "But stopping for a spell makes sense." In the minimal light, Forrest found a corner to rest his back against, relieving the weight off his knees and feet. Forrest caught sight of the blonde hair of Oleander and became curious about how the woman fared. "Oleander, how about you?"

Oleander squeezed into a corner opposite Forrest as the light silhouetted her head and allowed the woman a clear view of Forrest in the full glow of the moon. "My body screams as if someone wrings it like a wet cloth. My knees are numb, and the tips of my fingers scabbed over." Oleander took a deep breath and leaned against the wall of stone. "But I will not quit."

Laural peered out the crack in the mountain once more, as if she ignored her two companions. The Princess crawled down to a step below the others and found a corner to nestle into.

Each sat in silence and their blank stares spoke to their emotionless and exhausted states. Oleander broke the silence with a question, unwilling to give into the need for sleep. "Why did you come to save me?"

Forrest replied without hesitation. "Not knowing if you lived or died, I couldn't stay in Lillenhold. My thoughts turned towards bringing you home or avenging you." In the pale light, the troll-man smiled, and his teeth glowed with the happiness of achieving his primary goal, saving the woman he loved. The troll-man wished to offer himself to her at that moment, but he hesitated, unsure of what reaction would come from the woman across from him.

Oleander leaned forward, her blonde hair gnarled, and black grime smeared across her face and mane. "Forrest, you flatter me." Then the woman dismissed the troll-man and turned her head toward Laural's heavy breathing. "Princess, did Prince Arenton commission the quest out of his devotion to me?"

Laural paused for a moment and Forrest perceived the Princess visibly pull her mind back from the edge of sleep. "Arenton seemed concerned when he found out and appeared intent on saving you. However, the Prince made us wait until daylight before beginning the quest."

Oleander replied with the giggle of a schoolgirl. "I understand the Prince favors me, and I fancy him as well. If we escape this predicament, I have many questions about Arenton for you. I wish to become more acquainted with the Prince on our return."

Forrest's heart sank, and a worthlessness filled the hole as Oleander reinforced the troll-man's perpetual unworthiness of any woman's attention. His desire turned to getting away from Oleander as soon as possible. Mustering the courage to keep going and hide his emotions, Forrest focused on the mission. "Time to continue the descent. What about you two?"

An exasperated moan came from Oleander. "If we must."

The request received a hearty reply from the Princess. "Staying here leads to sleep and too much lost time. Regardless, descending is much easier than the climb. Lead the way, Forrest."

Laural focused on the night air and a view of the mountain surroundings through the fissure. This provided enough refreshment for the moment and adjusted her attitude about their remaining task. The Princess needed a break from her companions and the stench of their sweat. But Laural kept her thoughts focused on her companions to avoid thinking about Casemiro's fate.

Laural's attention hovered on the periphery of their conversation until Oleander answered Forrest's unasked plea for her to reciprocate his devotion to the woman. As the words left Oleander's mouth, Laural witnessed Forrest's heart breaking in the moonlight. All his unspoken love for Oleander fell to pieces with a few words from her lips. Laural desired to console her friend, but Forrest masked his defeat by turning to the task before the trio and descended the stairs into the darkness.

The Princess glared at Oleander, knowing the woman possessed no knowledge of the damage she inflicted. "After you." Laural envisioned smashing her boot into the perfect features of the florist all the way down the stone steps. "We should keep going."

Oleander gave a polite grin that glowed in the last gleam of moonlight and began her descent.

Laural took an inventory of her injuries as she crawled over the steps once more. Her fingertips were still wet from bleeding and her shoulder, tender from infection, did nothing to stop her from continuing. The Princess hesitated, and her anger took hold; she spit below her in the direction of Oleander.

Oleander screamed a second later. "What did that?"

Laural grinned at finding her target. "Bats."

Oleander screamed again, and the shriek echoed through the stairwell.

Laural laughed and began the descent on her stomach. "Thankfully, most of the bats hunt during the night or your scream would have woken them up."

The group left the comfort of the stray moonlight and reached blackness once more. As the light left the trio, so did the conversation, and silence joined the darkness. Laural concentrated on her repeated motions of scrambling to find a step with her foot and backing her body down to the next step. The Princess conjured ways in her mind to make Oleander regret her treatment of Forrest and failed to pay attention to her surroundings.

Forrest asked, "What made that noise?"

The Princess wanted to kick herself when the first squeak hit her ears. The second arrived and Laural yelled to the others, understanding they created their own problem. "I spoke too soon. We stirred up some bats that stayed in for the night. Cover your head and face and don't lose your balance."

Within seconds, the tumult of the bats swept over the group. Screams from Oleander met scratches and flapping wings. The rustling noise of their fluttering wings and squeaking calls went away, but Oleander continued screaming. "I have one in my hair! Get it out!"

Laural crawled to Oleander through the tumult and searched for the beast in the blonde mane. The Princess pulled the bat away and flung the animal into the air. "Did it bite you?"

The florist wept for a moment. "I don't think so."

Laural took pity on the woman and patted Oleander's shoulder. "We need to keep going." Even she did not wish Oleander to be bitten by a disease carrying animal. Not seeing

Oleander's reaction in the dark, the woman lowered herself to the next step to encourage the florist.

Thankfully, no more incidents with bats or other creatures occurred during their descent. But the silence overwhelmed everything around them as the group settled into their familiar routine of scratching along the steps with occasional checks to make sure none of them fell to the dark below. The quiet and darkness became oppressive.

After a while, a shriek from Oleander shattered the silence and startled Laural and Forrest, causing them to scream in response.

Laural took a second to capture her breath before asking what caused the reaction. "Did you hurt yourself?"

Oleander scrambled around. "Something on the step burned me."

"Keep going down while I determine what caused that to happen." Laural descended another level and scoured the surface of the step to find the offending object, a round metal disk. The heat emanating from the item shocked the Princess, but the device did not burn. Laural held the metal disk close to her face, searching for something besides the cold humidity of the Cleave. In her hand, the Princess caressed the round shape and then remembered Casemiro dropping the coin at the top of the steps.

"Forrest, I found the coin. It remains warm from Roman trying to contact Casemiro."

"Finally, a beneficial turn. Try the coin."

Laural held the coin to her lips, hoping it worked for her. "Are you there, Roman?"

The Princess tried again after receiving no response. A brief delay passed before a reply came through the coin. "Who is this?"

Laural pumped her fist in excitement. "This is Laural."

"The Princess? Oh, my lady. I attempted to reach the wizard."

Laural glanced above her, imagining the sight of Casemiro staring at her from the top of the stairway. The Princess shook her head and answered. "We got separated. Listen, Forrest and I rescued Oleander and need help to return to the village."

"If I tell Gerard, he will understand what to do."

"Roman, listen carefully. We need help to escape from Mount Siven. We traveled inside the mountain and snow covered an opening on the southern side. Someone needs to clear that for our escape. We also need food, water, and medical attention."

"I understand. What about Casemiro?"

Laural sucked back a sob. "Roman, this may be difficult..."

"Princess, the coin works, so Casemiro must still be alive."

Tears rolled from her eyes as Laural forgot the magic continued if Casemiro lived. The Princess took a deep breath and shook from the realization the wizard must be alive. "Roman, I needed those words. Can you send help?"

"Will do Princess. Be—"

In the darkness, no one witnessed the shock cross Laural's face. The color left her countenance as the Princess experienced the grief of losing Casemiro once more. She screamed and yelled at the coin, hoping to receive another response from Roman. Anything to signal the magic still worked and that Casemiro still lived. "Roman! Answer me! NO!"

Thick arms grabbed Laural and held her close while the Princess released her emotions once again, but this time the feelings hurt much more. Laural did not understand how attached she grew to the wizard. The brief belief that Casemiro remained alive lifted her and created a greater crash when Laural believed he died soon after. A chasm split her heart and the agony filled the Cleave of Siven. The Princess clutched the coin with enough strength to split the skin in her hand.

Forrest held Laural for several minutes and whispered consolations into her ear. When her sobbing ceased, Forrest said something that brought the Princess back to their mission. "We reached the bottom. I stepped into a puddle before you found the coin."

The Princess nodded her head to accept the reality and pulled herself together, knowing the time to grieve would come soon enough. Forrest and Oleander needed Laural's strength in this moment, and Laural once more donned the mantle of Princess of Gaeleos. "Then we wait. But the silence nearly killed me before." Laural found the wall of the cleave and leaned against the cold stone.

Oleander snickered from below. "Then I can start asking you questions about your brother."

Forrest replied in a bitter tone. "Does this seem like a time for frivolity, Oleander?"

The florist answered the troll-man's question with one of her own. "Forrest, why do you always use such proper language and present yourself with such propriety?"

"Simply, to portray something other than the monster people might see at first glance."

A laugh from Oleander followed the comment.

"What is so funny?" asked Forrest.

"You should know everyone still only sees the monster."

A hush filled the surrounding space. Laural stared in the direction of Oleander's voice in disbelief at her rudeness to Forrest. She quickly second-guessed their reasons for rescuing her. The Princess wondered what it was about this cruel woman that attracted her brother's attention. Then she remembered the beauty of Oleander. Perhaps Arenton was as vacuous as others believed.

Laural searched for a distraction from the quiet. The Princess retraced her steps over the last several days, trying to find the error in their ways. A random memory came back to her, Oleander's name on the cooper's customer list. Laural asked her own question to kill time and distract their minds.

"Oleander, how often do you go through barrels in your flower shop?"

A pause filled the darkness as Oleander shuffled to find secure footing. "Odd question, considering our predicament. I suppose I require a new barrel every three months, perhaps sooner in the summer. Which reminds me, I need to purchase a new one once we return to the village."

Forrest followed up on Laural's inquiry. "The other evening, you mentioned someone took the full barrel from your shop instead of me removing the barrel as I usually do. Who moved the barrel?"

The Princess asked her question to avoid any queries into the peculiarities of Arenton. Laural waited for the reply through another moment of silence.

"Prince Arenton sent over a robust man with a muscular physique. I don't recall the man's name, or even if he mentioned it, but he looked like one of the wrestlers."

Laural's eyes opened wide with the realization Forrest referred to the night Geoffrey died from poison. To her knowledge, the wrestlers arrived the next day. Oleander either lied about who moved the barrel, or the wrestlers were in Lillenhold before the day they were scheduled to arrive. But what purpose did that serve?

Oleander added a point to her answer after a pause. "I told Casemiro this same information. Did the wizard not tell you?"

Laural did not remember the wizard disclosing that information, but the way Oleander phrased the reply bothered the Princess. "No, Casemiro never mentioned it." She hoped the florist lacked knowledge of her suspicions.

Oleander asked, "Can we discuss your brother now?"

The Princess hated the idea of fielding questions about her brother and knew how much the questions would irritate Forrest. She remembered the cruelty Oleander exhibited towards the troll-man. "No, I'd rather not. We have a wait in front of us until help arrives and I'm tired."

26

SHOWDOWN

Casemiro and Ofani'r battled for hours with neither gaining an edge. The power of the broken curse buoyed Casemiro's resilience, while another source of magical energy, unidentified by the wizard, added to his power. Ofani'r's endurance, as expected, extended to unnatural lengths due to pure rage at the wizard refusing to die from any previous attacks. Both realized a resolution must arrive soon.

Ofani'r sneered at Casemiro as the dragon swayed back and forth, trying to determine a weakness in the wizard's defenses. The monster billowed smoke and snorted flames into the air, an intimidation tactic which never failed until today. The dragon's intent to disorient the enemy and create a much easier evisceration flopped in this case. A slight grin grew across the dragon's face as a claw the size of a shortsword slashed at the target of his fury.

The wizard stood his ground and blocked the strike with his staff, which responded to Casemiro's thoughts as if connected to his mind. The fact the wooden weapon did not snap surprised both combatants. Casemiro countered by swiping the saber at the dragon's paw and drew blood. The small droplets sizzled upon hitting the floor of the cave, leaving tiny rivulets of molten liquid that cooled into black puddles of gelatinous goo.

The walls of the cave reflected a glorious scene of shadow and light as the battle flowed across the stone canvas. Magical sparks from the mystical shield around Casemiro flew through the thick air. Flames rippled through the room, providing deep reds and oranges to the display, while dancing blacks and grays might enchant any bystander. The fluidity of the participant's movements reminded one of shadow plays that entertained children in a small village.

Why are you continuing this struggle? An unfamiliar voice posed the question in the wizard's mind. *You have the power to end this now.*

The dragon charged; its mouth opened wide enough to take in the wizard with one bite. Casemiro dodged to the left and avoided the razor-sharp teeth. As retaliation, the wizard swung the staff and smacked the dragon in the jaw, a move intended to irritate Ofani'r.

Casemiro dodged a swiping wing and the razor-sharp claws at the apex of the leathery appendage. The wizard ran alongside the belly of the beast, aware nothing but a direct strike might penetrate the armored hide.

How long have you been doing this? Casemiro recognized the voice as Quinto's, but wondered how his brother reached into his head.

The monster's long tail swept across the floor and Casemiro leaped to avoid the slithering appendage and pushed aside the distracting voice. The tail's slothfulness provided the wizard an opportunity. Casemiro jumped aboard and used the saber to ensure he stayed in place by driving the blade deep into the exposed flesh of his enemy.

The pain from the wound forced the dragon to roar loud enough the cave shook from the noise. The monster responded by breathing fire hot enough to turn every living thing into jelly except for a wizard protected by the ancient magic related to a dragon's broken vow.

I need to finish this and help the others. Casemiro hesitated, ensuring his own voice made that internal comment.

Still enjoying the effects of magical endurance and strength, the wizard climbed the back of the dragon and ran up the beast's spine. Casemiro used the saber to secure a grip at the neck of the beast, eliciting another massive roar. Having found an advantage, the wizard wondered how to end the battle.

The dragon sensed the pause in Casemiro's actions and attempted to wrest control of the clash. The beast turned to run from the cave and take flight. "I may not kill you, wizard, but a drop from the top of the mountain would."

The exhilaration of a potential flight aboard the beast tapped into an unknown desire for the wizard. But Casemiro gripped the saber tighter to prevent falling from the beast, fearing the result. Out of panic, he yelled a command. "Stop!"

To the wizard's amazement, the beast halted mid-step with wings spread and head lowered, prepared to launch from the lair. The wizard tumbled forward from the force of his own momentum and flew over the beast's snout, landing in the gravel and stone near the cave's entrance. His sword came free of the beast and it clattered to the side with the wizard's staff. Casemiro's inertia did not stop, and he slid towards the gaping mouth of the cave with no hope of stopping.

The wizard yelled, "Help!"

A claw reached out and snatched the wizard from sure doom and pulled Casemiro back to safety. The claw dropped the wizard in front of the dragon. Casemiro waited for one second, expecting the dragon to devour him.

With no further movement from Ofani'r, Casemiro laid on his back for several seconds and allowed his heart to recover from the experience of nearly falling to a spectacular death. The wizard's mind stuck on one realization; the dragon followed his commands. The wizard wished to use this to his advantage and help his friends who needed aid. With a pause in the action, Casemiro calmed himself as he registered the aches and nicks of battle announcing themselves.

A voice came to him. *The magic connects you.* The wizard understood; Casemiro and the dragon shared a bond because of the broken vow. Through the bond, the wizard tapped into the beast's magical energy.

Casemiro pulled himself upright and walked in front of the dragon, aware the longer the wizard controlled the dragon, the angrier his foe became. Disgust glowed in the dragon's yellow sclera, searching for a way to destroy the wizard. The toothsome sneer on the dragon's maw and a drop of saliva slipped off a jagged shard of bone, detailed to the wizard how much the wyrm wished to devour him.

Casemiro assessed how to best break this stalemate. The wizard sat in front of the cave opening, keeping the beast contained. The wizard gathered his weapons and sheathed the saber while laying the staff on the ground beside him. Casemiro drank what water remained in his pouch after a substantial portion evaporated because of the heat in the cave. The wizard also snagged a piece of jerky from his dwindling supply.

Casemiro coughed and then swished the liquid in his mouth, clearing away the bitterness of soot and smoke. The jerky's saltiness awoke his nasal passages and elicited saliva as the wizard chewed the durable meat. The movement within his mouth became a release of tension from the constant gritting of his jaws. Once Casemiro downed the drink and food, the wizard smiled at the waiting dragon.

"To be honest, I relished the power flowing through my limbs once more. But we are better than this, Ofani'r. We have fought for hours and could continue for days. You cannot defeat me because of your curse, and killing you requires significant fortune on my part. Either way, we accomplish nothing and waste considerable time. You promised a discussion when I entered your cave and I now desire this conversation, but I need a promise of cooperation. What say you?"

The dragon growled in a low tone and agreed to the wizard's demands with a nod.

"I release you."

The dragon regained control of its body and backed away from the wizard. "How did you do that?"

"When you study the old magic, you learn a few tricks. But the old texts never indicated how to resolve a broken vow."

Ofani'r paced in a circle through the cave, like a massive dog, and dropped to the floor with his full attention on Casemiro. "Let's discuss whatever you wish and end this."

"What does Harley Sweet want from Veritas Keep?"

The dragon laughed. "I do not concern myself with the man's petty squabbles and I care nothing about the man's motivations. The human promised the chance to avenge my father's death and devised a plan to lure the great Casemiro to my lair. I agreed to the terms of the proposal and waited for the designated moment to capture the damsel."

Casemiro replayed in his mind multiple times the night the dragon flew into Lillenhold and captured Oleander, splicing the scene into as many manageable vignettes as possible. The wizard sensed a missing clue in the sequence.

The dragon lost patience. "If you grow contemplative, why not smoke a pipe? Isn't that typical for wizards nowadays?"

"Smoking ruins your lungs and, one day, someone might prove me right on that point. But questions remain. What assured you of my arrival?"

The dragon smirked. "Sweet assumed your conscience, and an incessant need to fulfill your debts would force you to meet a contractual obligation. I left the means in his hands. His plan worked, but I did not expect the others who accompanied you. The dragon rose onto its rear haunches, preparing to pounce. "Where do we stand? Do we continue the fight? Or do you wish to prolong our discussion?"

Casemiro grabbed the staff and saber, showing he understood the dragon's intent. "I think you need to relax, my friend." The wizard's mind turned back to the dragon and commanded the beast to heel.

The dragon dropped back to the floor and realized the uselessness of any attempt to wrest control from the wizard. Ofani'r surrendered to the old magic and laid down.

Casemiro relaxed and exhaled. "Now, let me talk through where we stand and then you can help me decide how to proceed. At my whim sits a dragon bound to me through a broken vow. My friends, stuck in the stairwell leading to the base of this mountain, cannot escape because of the avalanche blocking the exit and they require aid."

"An avalanche of your making, mind you." A smile crossed the lips of the dragon, revealing several massive gleaming teeth.

Casemiro nodded his head and avoided staring at the mouth of the dragon. "Point to you. I created that problem."

"The spell proved impressive, and I believed for a moment the avalanche might capture me."

"You want to talk impressive; your fiery breath is the most destructive... Your sire would have been proud."

Casemiro remembered once more the day he slid the saber under the plated armor and recalled the muscle resisting the blade until the point found its target. Casemiro realized that moment didn't bring out the best in him, despite justice prevailing. Power does not rise from taking down your enemies.

The dragon glanced away from the wizard. "Can we stop the pillory and puffery, and return to your feeble attempt at decision making?"

Casemiro walked in circles in front of the dragon as he chatted aloud. "Right, my presence here exposes the Prince to an assassin, which I believe to be Harley Sweet and his brothers, J. J. Heenan, and the Captain of the Guard, Gerard. The same evidence, from what Laural said, suggests these villains may be heirs to the throne. What do you think of this?"

The dragon yawned to show his lack of interest. A cloud of smoke flew through his nostrils and covered the wizard, who walked out of the floating mass, hacking and wheezing.

The wizard regained his breath and stood in front of the dragon. "What about Oleander? You appeared to protect the woman earlier. Not what I expected for a beast intent on luring me into his cave."

"The woman proved incidental to my part of the plot, and I promised to not harm her and return her to the village when my business with you concluded."

Casemiro pondered this answer for a moment. "The real problem lies with me, and my friends stuck in this mountain, and the situation I need to resolve sits in Veritas Keep." The conclusion came to the wizard's mind. "You turned into a distraction. So, I need to aid my friends and return to Veritas Keep as quickly as possible. And I have an idea." Casemiro smiled at the dragon.

The dragon frowned. "I will not take part in this idea."

"I promise to release you from the curse when we complete the job." Casemiro understood the monster wished to resist and understood the deepest desires of his foe. Negotiating a peaceful settlement with the cunning dragon required caution on the wizard's part.

The dragon stood, raising its head to full height in surprise. "You can do this without either of us dying?"

"Remember, I studied old magic. I could release you on the condition you will not destroy me and my friends. You must leave Lillenhold and uphold the original vow your mother struck with me."

The dragon cast a glare toward Casemiro. "How can I trust you to release me?"

"If I do not, then you control me because the power of a broken magical vow works both ways." The wizard waited for a response but continued when none came. "I will not break my vow, and you cannot lie. Another one of those laws I learned while studying—"

"The old magic." Ofani'r understood, bowing his head to the cave floor, locking eyes with the wizard. The dragon peered at his enemy to determine the strength of the wizard's character. Ofani'r replied, presumably satisfied with the results of the query. "What do you require of me, wizard?"

"My plan starts with me riding on your back to the base of Mount Siven. We figure out the rest at the bottom."

The dragon chuckled at the idea of letting the wizard ride him. "Be prepared, this won't be like riding a horse. No saddles fit dragons." Ofani'r lowered its body, and the wizard climbed aboard and found a place to ride and established a tight grip. The dragon asked, "Want to shout a pithy command?"

"Fly to the base of the mountain. Away!"

The dragon barreled forward from the cave and launched itself into the air.

Casemiro's stomach almost exited through his gaping mouth as the wizard screamed with the loss of gravity. The plunge from the cave toward the ground scared the wizard. Casemiro's yells missed his ears because the dragon flew so fast. Only the whipping and buffeting of the air as Ofani'r plunged straight to the ground below registered in the wizard's ears.

The ripple of the dragon's muscles as it flapped enormous wings shook the wizard. The breeze flew through Casemiro's hair and pulled on his cloak. Holding fast took the wizard's full strength and concentration. In a matter of seconds, the ride drained years from the wizard's life. A couple of wobbles from turbulence and drifting to avoid the tops of the tallest of trees preceded the quick deceleration and thump of a landing.

The dragon fell flat to the ground and shrugged its left shoulder. The resulting wave of muscle nudged the wizard enough to bump him from his perch and he tumbled down the side of the beast. The dragon's voice boomed without the wind whipping around them. "We arrived. Now what?"

Casemiro grinned from ear to ear after the experience of flying atop a dragon, a dream come true. "I need to do that again. Incredible!" The wizard pointed at the avalanche-blocked stairwell entrance and directed the dragon. "Create an opening at the base of the mountain so Oleander, Laural, and Forrest can escape the stairwell."

The dragon rolled his eyes. "You mean for me to clean up your mess?" Ofani'r walked over and waved one of his mighty paws at the snow and swiped away half of the unmelted drift. The dragon let loose a blast of flame to melt any remaining snow in front of the entrance.

Once the steam cleared, Casemiro ran to the opening, slopping his way through the mud and puddles. The water trapped within the alcove rolled through the entrance. The wizard entered the mountain's base to search for his friends. Sounds of people descending the stairs encouraged the wizard and he hurried to meet them. "Laural? Forrest? Are you safe?"

A second later, a reply greeted the wizard with the troll-man's deep voice. "Casemiro? You are alive? How did you reach the bottom of the mountain?"

From above, Laural plowed into the wizard, knocking Casemiro to the floor of the alcove in an embrace. Mud splashed across his back as the wizard's head landed in a puddle. The Princess cried into his shoulder and refused to let go until she kissed Casemiro. Laural's embrace prevented the wizard from coming up for air. Then the weight of her body left the wizard. Casemiro gasped for a breath as he rose above the surface of the puddle.

Forrest extended a helping hand to the wizard. The troll-man held Laural aloft in his other hand as a smile defined her entire countenance. "I'm relieved to behold you once more, wizard. Let's leave, if you don't mind."

The wizard smiled at his friends. "A surprise awaits you outside."

As the group emerged from the cave into the sunlight Laural, Forrest, and Oleander covered their faces until their eyes adjusted to the daytime. Forrest asked the obvious question: "Why is the dragon here?"

Laural clung to the wizard, frozen by fear. Casemiro held her close as he replied to the troll-man. "My friend. We have a great deal to discuss."

27

THE GLORIOUS RETURN

Oleander and Forrest, with Laural over his shoulder, emerged from the cave at the bottom of Mount Siven with Casemiro in tow. Oleander continued as Forrest stopped upon exiting the cave and placed Laural on the ground. Casemiro held Laural as he welcomed the group from the darkness and into the daylight. Forrest and Laural appeared confused by the dragon in front of them.

Laural collected herself and pushed herself away from Casemiro. "I remain upset with you, but we can deal with that later." The Princess extended her hand and held out the coin. "I found this on the stairs and spoke to Roman. Something disturbing occurred in Lillenhold."

Casemiro's elation at seeing Laural evaporated in an instant, crushing the wizard's spirit, and reminding the wizard of his shortcomings. The act of rejection released his guilt, and it crushed his soul, but only dampening the wizard's connection to the magic. Casemiro weakened but continued portraying the image of strength for the others. "We need to return to Lillenhold, regardless."

The Princess and Forrest's gaze fixated on the dragon.

"What is that doing here?" asked the Princess.

The wizard released a timid laugh as Casemiro caught sight of Oleander petting the dragon on the cheek. "For now, the dragon is bound to me and obeys my commands. We reached an accord and Ofani'r agreed to fly us back to Lillenhold."

Forrest and Laural appeared less enthusiastic than the wizard expected, but Oleander jumped at the chance.

The lady beamed. "A splendid idea."

Ofani'r responded by dropping his shoulder to accommodate the women climbing aboard for the trip. "Ladies, find someplace comfortable and hold on tight." The dragon allowed Oleander and Laural to scale its hide, though the Princess showed visible hesitation. "The wizard and his friend must travel in my clutches." The dragon provided an eerie smile towards Casemiro and Forrest. "The trip only lasts a few minutes because I can cover the distance quickly." The words reassured Casemiro more than his travel companions.

Forrest obliged but stated his reservations. "This expedites Oleander's return to the village. Otherwise, I would not allow this dragon to touch me."

Casemiro gripped his staff as the dragon lifted the wizard and the troll-man into the air. Ofani'r flew at a lower height, less than a meter above the treetops, to avoid disorienting the passengers more than necessary.

Once aloft, the flight remained steady as the dragon avoided turns and other potential opportunities for the weight of the women to shift. Ofani'r only changed elevation to avoid any trees poking above the canopy of the forest. The women rested their heads on the beast's back, avoiding wind and turbulence during the flight. Forrest and Casemiro proved not as fortunate as the beast exposed them to the full force of the elements but avoided scraping their feet on the treetops below. The wind buffeted them all, but the men benefited from seeing the surrounding landscape from an incredible height.

The dragon progressed toward the village of Lillenhold, and Veritas Keep soon came into view. Ofani'r arrived after only a few minutes in the air and landed in the clearing between the village and the keep. Even though some citizens hid in nearby buildings, the dragon attracted the attention of the people in the area. None grasped the nature of the beast's visit and prepared for the worst based on the recent news of Oleander's capture. Anyone within sight sought cover from any potential attack.

The dragon dropped the wizard and Forrest to the ground and then lowered itself to allow the women a chance to dismount. Oleander leaned against the beast and whispered something, drawing a meek smile from Ofani'r.

Casemiro, curious about the woman's connection to Ofani'r, walked in front of the beast.

The dragon stood to its full height. "Wizard, does this eliminate my debt to you?"

"If you avoid returning to Mount Siven, you may leave freely. At this stage of my life, I harbor no petty grievances, but if you break your promise again, I won't be as lenient."

"You wish me no harm?"

"No, I never intended to harm you. We fought in the cave because you wished to kill me. I doubt you'll ever perceive me as anything other than your father's killer. I stayed my hand instead of killing you and your mother because ending your lives served no purpose then or now. We can part as enemies, friends, or neither. Your choice, Ofani'r."

"If this proves our final meeting, then we are no longer enemies, but we shall never be friends."

The dragon flapped its massive wings and spread dust and dirt across the area as the beast launched into the air. Oleander and Laural ducked, shielding their faces from the flying debris while Casemiro and Forrest tracked the dragon rising into the sky, racing over Lillenhold and out over the sea. The foursome traced the dragon's flight until it disappeared into the distance and then they exchanged glances, unsure of what to do next. The quartet realized everyone in the village gathered around, staring in disbelief.

Laural took charge while casting a wicked glare at Casemiro. "We need to announce our victory in returning with Oleander to my brother. But you and I need to talk, wizard, after we complete that chore."

Oleander and Laural marched ahead of Casemiro and Forrest.

Forrest looked at the wizard. "I'm still upset over your lies."

"Unspoken truths."

The troll-man sneered at the wizard. "The same thing."

Casemiro nodded his head. "I understand that now."

"I am not sure about our future, but I shall bury the hatchet since you offered to sacrifice your life to ensure we escaped. I recognize the gesture for its worth. For now, let us follow the women and witness the Prince's reaction to our return."

Casemiro extended his hand. "Thank you, my friend. Now, if Laural were as accommodating as you."

Forrest grabbed Casemiro's hand. "I never understood this custom. If people were honest, these empty gestures become unnecessary. As for the Princess..." He gave a questioning glance.

"Ask away, my friend."

"What issues exist between you and Laural now?"

"I wish I knew, Forrest. I wish I knew."

Casemiro and Forrest caught up to the women and, within minutes, the group entered Veritas Keep. The guards recognized the troop under a week's worth of dirt and grime and brought them before Arenton in the vast chamber of the keep. The Prince hurried onto his throne to receive them and smiled as the party approached. Casemiro's attention turned to the haggard and harried Prince, an unusual presentation for the Highness. The wizard wondered if the stress of the search for Oleander, along with suspecting a killer in his presence, created an unforgiving environment for the Prince.

The Prince exclaimed an exuberant welcome to the group. "The rescue party returns and you brought the lady Oleander back as well. Your success demands a glorious celebration. Tonight, I waive the existing curfew on Lillenhold and commemorate the return of the fair maiden." The Prince beamed at Oleander.

Forrest shifted his weight and turned away from the exhibition of affection. This reaction intrigued the wizard, and Casemiro surmised something unpleasant occurred within the Cleave of Siven. Casemiro scrutinized the woman, oblivious to her admirer even after Forrest helped save her from the dragon, and then focused her attention on the Prince. The answer was obvious; she rebuffed Forrest.

Wishing to welcome the others, Arenton stepped away from the throne and embraced Laural. The Prince regarded the injury to her shoulder and the blood on her frock. "Our best healer must tend to your wound." Arenton's eyes scanned the room, shifting from spot to spot, as the Prince drew her closer to whisper a final sentence that Casemiro overheard. "We must talk."

Laural pulled away with an inquisitive stare. "Casemiro tended my wound, but I appreciate another set of eyes from an experienced healer." The Princess patted Arenton on the shoulder. "Let's talk once I clean up."

Casemiro noted that she failed to mention Mira Sweet.

"Of course, my dear sister. You require a nice bath and a change of clothes after your time in the wilderness. Guards escort the lady Oleander and Princess Laural to the bathing chamber while I attend to Forrest and Casemiro."

Laural shot a glance towards the wizard before parting ways. The Princess attempted to communicate something to the wizard, but Casemiro failed to understand anything from the simple gesture.

As the Princess left the room, Casemiro realized he once again lost the connection to the magic. The wizard reached inside to find the energy, and the power flickered in comparison to the raging blast furnace he encountered on the mountain. With his emotions in upheaval, the wizard now understood the increased energy required a connection to the dragon. With the source of the power eliminated, the insane amount of magical energy disappeared.

Casemiro questioned how he missed the need for a connection between him and the beast. Nonetheless, the wizard wanted to put an end to the problem and move to the next stage of his life, whether that life included Laural, magic, or neither. He accepted his fate.

The Prince approached the wizard and troll-man. "So, the two heroes required to take part in the quest returned. How impressive that you returned with everyone alive and intact. But you did not kill the dragon. Why?"

Forrest chuckled at the simplistic idea of killing a dragon. "My lord, we lacked the numbers and weapons necessary for such a task. With luck, we escaped and owe our lives to Casemiro's gift of diplomacy. If not for Casemiro, the outcome..." The troll-man paused, realizing the immense debt he owed the wizard.

The Prince turned to Casemiro. "Is this true?"

"It does not matter. I am fortunate the dragon failed to harm me, which required more luck than skill. I must discuss something else of great importance, Prince. The matter concerns the person trying to kill you."

"You can broach that subject in due time. First, Forrest, at the event tonight, we will honor you with an immense reward for your bravery as the champion of Veritas Keep. My guards will escort you to the royal bathhouse, where you may use my personal space in the facility."

A guard fell in line behind Forrest as the troll-man left the room. Casemiro sensed the possibility of this being their final meeting as the troll-man glanced at the wizard and left the hall.

"Wizard, continue."

"Yes, my Prince, Harley Sweet deceived us and implemented an elaborate plan to harm you. Sweet devised a scheme to remove you from the line of ascension. The man also conspired with the dragon to take Oleander up to the mountain, knowing my obligation to retrieve her and, therefore, leaving you vulnerable in Lillenhold. This allowed the dragon to exact its revenge for the death of its father by my hand twenty years ago. Also, Heenan—"

The Prince held up his hand to stop the wizard. "Casemiro, let me assure you, I realized their orchestrations and addressed these criminal activities in your absence. I became much more cautious since unraveling this scheme, hence my disheveled appearance. Your friend, the boy named Roman, who works in the kitchen, provided information that helped us apprehend those men. We addressed the situation, so you need not be concerned about my safety anymore."

"Explain yourself further, please."

Arenton walked over and sat on his throne. "We found out the wrestlers acted out of fear of Sweet, and we chased him off. His men remain in Lillenhold and wait to find new jobs. Sweet's concealed brother, Heenan, sits in a cell beneath Veritas Keep, awaiting a trial in two days. Because their crimes involved treason, my father must be in attendance for the trial. We await my father's arrival before we execute my former counselor. Finally, a crime fitting of hanging from the gallows."

"And Captain Gerard? I fear his involvement as well." Casemiro hoped his guess about Gerard being the third brother proved correct and the Prince's actions ended the entire operation.

"Gerard left Lillenhold after I relieved him of the position. Though innocent and unrelated to Mr. Sweet, Gerard revealed himself as a gullible fool. Does this address your concerns?"

Casemiro rubbed his chin, thinking through the information relayed by Arenton. "I believe so, but the identity of the third Sweet child remains a concern."

"Third child?"

Casemiro realized some danger still existed, but the wizard needed time and rest to organize his thoughts. "Sorry, perhaps I can share a long story at the ceremony if you allow me a few minutes? I do not believe it to be an immediate concern. Especially with Heenan in custody and Sweet out of the village."

Another untruth, Casemiro. The familiar voice returned to the wizard's mind.

"Sounds lovely, wizard. Go to the bath awaiting you. My heart warms that you were successful. The crown appreciates your efforts and will reward you handsomely."

Casemiro bowed and removed himself from the sight of the Prince. The wizard went upstairs to his room on the second floor of the keep. As mentioned by Arenton, the warm bath waited, and Casemiro fell into the water after removing his clothing and gear. From the door to the tub, a trail of cloak, saber, and staff lay across the floor.

The water turned dark from the dirt accumulated during a week of travel and the fight with Ofani'r. Casemiro drew a second bath and soaked long enough to relax his muscles while removing any remaining grime. The old man used oils to wash his hair free of whatever nested within the mane and shaved the scruff from his face. The wizard emerged and donned a new blue cloak provided by the Prince. Though clean and beautiful, the material lacked the magical golden thread of Casemiro's own robe, which took on a state of disrepair.

Casemiro pulled the last pieces of jerky from his travel bag and ate the dried meat, knowing he needed a meal. The wizard tossed the hardtack to the side, not willing to eat the stale bread-like substance. The wizard needed a drink and decided to leave Veritas Keep. He grabbed his coin purse and remembered he owed a generous sum to Roman, and the Prince owed him even more. The time to collect his prize and settle his debts arrived.

The wizard opened his door and, after descending the stairs, walked through the empty hall of the keep. Casemiro continued walking through the building until stumbling into the kitchen where the Princess stood with hair still damp from her bath, eating a leg of pheasant.

Laural shot a glare at the wizard. "Looking for something to eat?" The Princess shoved a plate of the remaining bird in his direction and took a second glance at Casemiro. "You shaved."

"I'd prefer a drink, and whoever can pay me the coin I earned. I owe Roman some money and wish to settle that debt. How is the shoulder?"

"Cleaned and infection free. Thanks for your help with it."

Casemiro examined the garments the Princess wore. "You're not in red."

Laural tipped her head back and drained the flagon in her hand, ignoring the comment. "Let's get your coin. You earned the money."

With the Princess leading the way, Laural asked over her shoulder while heading towards another throughway. "Are you leaving soon?"

The wizard winced as he lied. "I only hope for a night's rest to clear my mind before I decide tomorrow on my future."

Laural continued leading the wizard through the maze until the duo reached an unknown room to Casemiro. The Princess knocked, and a voice beckoned her to enter. Laural attempted to wipe away tears, but the tracks remained visible to the wizard as she turned, and the wizard regretted his unspoken truths once more.

The desk hid a smiling middle-aged man who stood half the height of the wizard. "Princess, to what do I owe the privilege?"

Casemiro recognized the man as the villager from the Extravaganza who sat in the front row with the sign and smiled at the gentleman he believed to be Ben.

The man sprung up from behind the desk. "I am a massive fan. You provided a wonderful performance at the Extravaganza. I hope you participate in the next event. My name's Benjamin." He shook the wizard's hand without asking and returned to his seat.

Laural motioned toward the wizard. "Anyway, Benjamin, we owe Casemiro money for his duties regarding the Extravaganza and the rescue of Lady Oleander." The Princess turned to the wizard. "How much?"

Casemiro calculated his wages. "Three days of work for the Extravaganza. The round trip to the mountain took about six or seven days. I lost track of time once I began fighting the dragon."

Benjamin's eyes went round with wonder. "You fought a dragon?"

Casemiro blushed, but nodded. "Yes, it's less glamourous than you might think."

Laural turned to the man, hoping to accomplish the job in quick order. "Don't encourage him. Just give the man fifteen gold coins. More than enough to cover his contract and give him a little extra to spend when he leaves Lillenhold."

Benjamin counted out fifteen gold coins from a box. One fell and Benjamin chased the coin, disappearing under the desk before emerging like a turtle popping out of water. In his hand, he held the gold piece and flashed a smile at Laural and the wizard. "Got it!"

Laural lost patience, grabbed the entire pile, and gave the coins to Casemiro. "Thank you, Benjamin. Apply any extra against my tab for the month." Pushing the wizard out, the Princess promptly closed the door.

Casemiro yelled back to the man, "Thank you, Benjamin."

With the door shut, Casemiro turned to Laural. "You said you had to discuss something with me."

"Yes, I fear we may have saved Oleander believing she is someone else. After saving her, it became apparent with the way she treats Forrest that she is not who I expected. She is quite cruel."

"So, you believe her to be a wolf in sheep's clothing?"

"Perhaps, but I do not know to what end." Laural stood in the hall, arms crossed. "Anything else?"

"Why didn't you mention Mira Sweet to Arenton?"

"Probably the same reason you didn't. I don't think he would believe me."

Casemiro wanted to discuss what happened on their journey and discover what changed Laural's opinion of him and their relationship. The wizard understood how untrustworthy he appeared, but Casemiro never intended to deceive the Princess. Casemiro never believed withholding his unspoken truths created a problem until the proof materialized. The wizard learned, but his sins demanded a sacrifice and he agreed to give up any happiness if required. Casemiro decided to ask what happened in the Cleave that changed Laural.

Before he spoke, Laural grabbed the wizard's arm. "I need to tell you something. Something happened after we got separated on the mountain."

Casemiro's heart leaped, and he wondered if this became the chance for Laural to express her true feelings? Would the Princess confess her love? "I need to say something else as well. But you go first."

"Casemiro, when you closed the opening, I lost control of myself. I never thought I would see you again. I questioned how to manage the sudden dread filling my heart. All my body ached from the despair, but we continued and climbed down the Cleave. Then we found the coin, and I talked to Roman. I realized if the coin worked, that meant you still lived. Then, the coin stopped working and the same emotions flooded my soul again. I believed we lost you. I'd lost you again." Laural wiped her eyes.

"Laural..."

She held up a hand to stop him. "But once you appeared in the cave, relief swept over me. Then I remembered your lies once we emerged into the daylight."

Casemiro's chin dropped to his chest and the wizard leaned on the staff for physical and moral support. "I apologize. If I—"

"I only wanted to tell you the coin stopped working. Leave and disregard the rest of what I said."

Casemiro tossed out a lure to attract her back to him. "Care for a drink in town?"

Laural scanned the ceiling and shook her head. "No. I want you to share with me what you held onto since we arrived at the mountain. Will you do that?"

Casemiro stared at the floor and confronted his feelings for the Princess, as much as he hated such introspection. Salvage a relationship with Laural or explore other options. Part of the wizard still wanted to rediscover his magic and live a normal life. Casemiro weighed the question of the Princess presenting a better future for him and Laural.

The image of his dead wife appeared in the wizard's mind as he glanced at the Princess. Guilt avalanched over his heart, and Casemiro viewed himself as a worthless wizard and wilted in front of Laural. Casemiro's guilt deemed him unworthy of her, unworthy of Chantal, and unworthy of the power he once held. The wizard succumbed to the negative emotions again.

"I can't."

Casemiro turned and walked down the hallway with his staff, putting the coins in the satchel and tucking the coin purse into his breast pocket. The wizard patted twice, remembering the knitting needles remained in the other cloak. The knitting needles must wait, as well as the saber. He needed to escape from Laural before good fortune somehow found Casemiro.

Laural yelled from behind the wizard. "Then I guess you leave tomorrow." The Princess sucked in a sob and the noise echoed down the hallway. "Goodbye, Casemiro."

28

BROTHERS BY BLOOD

The glorious meal celebrating the return of Oleander began in less than an hour. Casemiro found the idea of sitting in a crowd repulsive. Plus, returning for the meal meant a worse fate, being in the same room as Laural. No, the wizard needed to leave Veritas Keep for the evening, and Casemiro craved a stiff drink at the Skullery more than anything else, and perhaps a good meal.

Casemiro exited the compound holding the heavy coin purse in one hand and his staff in the other. The wizard pulled the magical coin from his satchel and rubbed it with a finger to re-initiate the magic. He spoke to the coin. "Roman?" He hoped reigniting the magic resolved the issue with the coin's performance, even though the device served its purpose. Casemiro believed the amount of power exhibited by him and the dragon overwhelmed any other magic in the vicinity of their battle.

A voice replied from the disk after a brief pause and confirmed the wizard's belief. "You are alive! I worried when the coin stopped working."

"Yes, the coin suffered a malfunction. Superb news, I possess the payment due to you, and will be at the Skullery this evening. If you join me, you get your money, and I may tell you about the dragon and the quest. Fair warning, you better arrive before I drink the coins away." The wizard grinned at the comment, and his heart welcomed the levity after the fallout with Laural.

"I am happy you returned and will check in after I finish working this evening's shift, sir. Now, do not drink my money away."

"Just glad someone cares, Roman." Casemiro dropped the coin in the purse and patted the pocket out of habit, remembering the knitting needles stayed in his room at the keep. The wizard also left the saber behind, believing the weapon unnecessary for the evening. His sore muscles and bones demanded the staff.

Upon leaving the keep, Casemiro made his way to the Skullery in the village for a greasy meal and drink. The village seemed quieter, and the faces appeared glummer as evening approached. Though an overcast day, the wizard expected the excitement of the dragon and Oleander's return to brighten the spirits of Lillenhold. Casemiro's demons preoccupied him, and the wizard ignored the people he passed, thinking only of his last interaction with Laural.

The image of Laural nonchalantly waving him away decimated the wizard. Did their relationship deteriorate to where their connection meant almost nothing to her? Could the Princess throw that connection away because of his withholding truths that created unexpected impacts? Guilt flamed through Casemiro's spirit and pushed him deeper into the depression.

Casemiro wondered how much lower this hole went and if filling it with drink might help. The jingle of his coin purse reminded the wizard of his newfound money and prompted him to reach the Skullery at a quicker pace.

Casemiro proceeded into the dining hall, expecting Roman to appear once his shift at the keep finished. The wizard almost knocked a man to the ground and apologized before realizing he bumped into his brother, Quinto.

Quinto's face filled with a smile. "Casemiro! Imagine the chance of us meeting here. Word reached me that you returned in one piece." Quinto embraced Casemiro in a vigorous hug.

"Yes, it's a long story, and I lost track of the days. I thought you departed with your next payload."

"We launch tomorrow at dawn. Will you join us on our next voyage?"

Casemiro paused, uncertain of what to say, and his thoughts returned to Laural. The sight of his brother pulled the wizard from his malaise and back to a version of normal. "Save me a spot, but If I do not arrive in time, launch without me."

"Did a problem arise on this job? Rumors around town say you did something stupid."

"Nothing I can't manage. And what about these rumors?"

"Something about a dragon and the Princess." Quinto examined what Casemiro wore, a change from the usual gray scraggly blanket. "Why the new cloak? Not that I complain because the other one stunk of ship swill."

"Mine got ruined during the trip." Recalling the dragon prompted Casemiro to think of Laural and caused his expression to darken.

Quinto angled his head and grabbed the wizard's arm. "The ship requires me, but you need to talk. Let's eat something together."

The wizard patted his brother on the shoulder to signal his acceptance of the offer. "Maybe a meal with my brother might ease the burden I carry."

Casemiro scouted the room and found an open table along the far wall. The same seat where Casemiro ate his first meal with Forrest and Laural in Lillenhold. The location proved fitting if his last meal took place in the same spot. The wizard pulled his brother along as the duo walked through the crowd. The people proved less difficult to navigate than the scent of burned fish and stale drink.

Casemiro waved down a waitress. The woman featured an olive complexion and dark hair while standing over six feet in height and sporting a scar down her right cheek. "Is any of Forrest's cider on tap? And I do not remember you working here."

"New to the job, sir. My name's Raquel and I will check on the cider. What do you want if we're out?"

Casemiro glanced at Quinto, who shrugged his shoulders in reply. "If no cider, then one ale each. And two bowls of the soup, please." The wizard pulled out a gold coin. "Does this cover the bill?"

Raquel smiled. "On it, sir." She took the coin, knowing a portion would find its way into her pocket.

Quinto asked, "So, you want to give me the dirt on your little expedition? The rumors and a dragon both flew through the port earlier today."

Casemiro relayed to his brother the details of the quest and what happened involving the dragon and Laural. While going through the highs and lows, the food and drink arrived. After finishing the story, Casemiro sought advice from Quinto on a specific topic. "Why can't I regain the power?"

Quinto gave a sly grin to Casemiro; aware of how desperate the wizard must be to ask him. "It doesn't require a healer to diagnose your guilt as the problem."

"But the magic returned when I fought the dragon."

"I do not pretend to understand magic; let alone the raw power we wielded at one time. At some point, the magic proved unmanageable and felt foreign to me. I relinquished the power, and a completeness overtook me. The illusion of trying to hold a gallon of mead in a tiny cup stopped. I may wish for a maelstrom at sea, but the meager magic I can still wield remains adequate. Happiness and fulfillment, or an evening with a pretty barmaid, allow me to access the power if needed. Perhaps the dragon helped you bypass the emotional connection and opened a larger vat of power. Those beasts are high-powered creatures of magic. You need to ask yourself what happened when you battled the dragon. What emotions did you encounter?"

Quinto took a drink of his cider as he waited for a response from Casemiro. Nothing escaped his brother's mouth, and the ship captain filled the empty air. "This cider is rather refreshing. Tell your friend he does excellent work."

Casemiro acknowledged the compliment towards Forrest and refocused on the conversation. "I cannot clear this hurdle since Chantal died. And then I regained my true power for a fleeting time, only to lose that power again. Why must this be so frustrating?"

"Did you think of Chantal when you dealt with the dragon? Did you experience any shame or guilt, then?"

Casemiro raised his eyes. "Quite the opposite, because I said goodbye to Laural, assuming I would never view her face again. Pride and conviction dominated my emotions because I saved her and the others. I broke free from the pain for the first time since I found Chantal dead in our home."

The ship captain took another swig. "Why you continue to pursue this power confuses me. The curse permeates your life, and you still chase dragons, evil wizards, and villains. For the last five years, you pursued magic as if you were a bloodhound. Doesn't the chase tire you?"

"Unlike you, I cannot fill that emptiness." Casemiro swallowed a spoonful of soup. The brine of the food cut through the sweet aftertaste of the cider.

Quinto took a slurp of his meal. "I do not imagine it does. What kept the hole filled while you wielded the power? I doubt your love for Chantal helped."

The wizard pushed the bowl away from him. A tear filled Casemiro's eye as guilt seeped its way back into the emotional hole, believing he should never find happiness after the life he lived with Chantal. "Brother, be honest. Was I a good husband?"

The ship captain took a drink before answering. "You tried hard and, hell, you showed promise in those early years. But you always chased something else, whether it be fame or appreciation. Your desire for affirmation tainted your role as a husband."

Casemiro gazed at the cup in his hands. "You speak the truth, and I fear this prevents me from ever being happy again. I chase contentment, whether it be magic, a woman, or something else, to only deny myself that happiness forever."

Quinto reached across the table and grabbed his brother's hand. "None of us achieves perfection and Chantal was not the paragon of wifely virtues, either. Based on my observations and others' accounts, the woman became cold and vindictive. You need to understand this about your deceased wife. She killed herself because she wanted you to suffer as she did throughout your marriage."

Casemiro glared at his brother in a fit of agitation. The tip of the staff glowed as his emotions roiled as he got to the part of the story he glossed over earlier in their meeting. "You don't know the entire story, and neither did I until a few days ago. We stumbled upon a witch named Mira Sweet in the wilderness. I had never met her before, and she claimed to be Chantal's sister. And murderer."

Quinto pulled away as his mouth opened wide, and the color left his cheeks. "Oh, what horrible news to hear! And in that situation. Did she tell you the truth?"

Casemiro nodded. "I believe it in my heart. She answered all the questions I carried inside me since that day. She did it. And she seemed delighted by it."

Quinto moved closer to his brother and held his shoulder for a moment. "Does this not absolve you from at least a portion of your guilt?"

"Perhaps, but her actions don't change the way I behaved."

Quinto kept one eye on the orange hue of the iron as he continued talking. "Cas, Chantal went into your marriage expecting children and a family. You denied her a dream while you still received what you wanted. Based on the last five years, I think you used your allotment of self-pity to penalize yourself. You made some mistakes, but every single person does. It does not eliminate you from ever finding joy, hope, and happiness again." Quinto took a drink of his cider.

Casemiro leaned against the wall, the glow dissipating from the staff. "Yes, the last five years were difficult, and I did not realize how much I missed our marriage until she passed away. Then guilt and grief flooded over me. Do I just ignore those feelings now?"

"For God's sake, no. But you need to overcome them. If not, the consequences become undesirable. Learn from this incident and figure out the right direction. Is it staying here? Is it going on my ship tomorrow? Or something else? Release the guilt and move forward. Perhaps you regain the use of your magic, or perhaps not. But does having magic become that important to you?"

Casemiro shot a sideways glare at his brother. "If I start over, I stand alone."

"Bullshit." Quinto laughed loud enough to draw the other patrons' attention. "Brother, you are never alone. Do you sometimes imagine another person's voice in your mind? As if someone watches over your shoulder? Do you ever envision things happening somewhere else without knowing why?"

Casemiro gave Quinto a confused glare. "Often, especially in the last few days. When I fought the dragon, I swore your voice entered my head."

Quinto nodded. "Your voice reaches my ears from time to time because our brotherhood links us, and it does not matter how much magic we control. We can always contact each other. Not a complete conversation, but a stray idea can go between us. I experienced your fight with the dragon, and how much power you possessed. You held the power to destroy the beast with just one word, but didn't use it. You let this other stuff cloud your vision and keep you from seeing the obvious things of this world in front of you, like a woman's love."

"How did I not comprehend this?"

"You have always been too self-centered. You pay little attention to your surroundings. That made you into a great wizard. By far better than me." Quinto took a drink. "No matter how much you imagine that loneliness, you won't be alone. Hold on to the Princess for now; she might need a reason to trust you once more."

Casemiro drank. "I wish my life proved as easy as you portray it."

"Do not give up hope, brother. Even without fighting dragons, I impact other people's lives. Leading a normal life can be just as noble as embarking on fantastical quests and engaging in magical battles. Your next chance to influence other people may appear from nowhere, and magic makes no difference in your success."

The bell by the door rang and an enormous figure, recognizable in the darkest nights to Casemiro, walked into the Skullery, catching the wizard's attention.

Quinto glanced towards the door and turned back to Casemiro. "Your first chance presents itself. I think another person can use you right now." The ship captain stood and took his last sip. "Do not forget, the ship leaves at dawn. Show up, or the Fierce Siren departs without you."

Casemiro lifted his flagon and turned to the new person.

The ship captain slapped Forrest on the shoulder as the troll-man walked by. "He's all yours."

Forrest stepped up to the table. "Room for another, wizard?"

Casemiro smiled at Forrest. "Always room for a friend."

29

BROTHERS BY TRIAL

Casemiro pointed to the chair opposite him, and Forrest sat. The wizard ordered two more ciders from the waitress named Raquel and the troll-man ordered a plate of hash. The friends said nothing until the drinks arrived.

"Isn't a dinner being held at the keep in our honor, wizard?"

"You are also a guest of honor. If you skipped, then my decision seems even more reasonable." Casemiro's eyes peered over the edge of the flagon of hard cider. "I left because of the welcoming atmosphere of the Skullery. Why didn't you attend?"

Forrest nodded with a shared understanding. "Woman trouble, what more can I say?

Casemiro gave a chuckle and pointed to his cup. "I enjoy your brew. My brother passes along his approval as well."

Forrest replied to the first comment. "I used apples, strawberries, and pears to create one of my finer concoctions. Then remove the cores, pass them to Oleander to grow saplings from the seeds, mash the remainder, add yeast, and wait two weeks."

Casemiro took another sip. "Well, whatever you did created a sweet and tasty product. A delight one must be careful drinking, or they will suffer through a rough night. Excellent job, Forrest."

Forrest nodded, accepting the compliment. "The other man was your brother?"

"Yes, a shipowner I occasionally book passage with. His ship leaves tomorrow at dawn."

"And the real reason you sit here?" Forrest asked, even though the truth appeared obvious.

"I got paid, and Laural turned against me. I escaped the keep for a while." Casemiro ate some of the hash from Forrest's plate and finished the flagon of cider. "So, woman trouble."

Forrest finished the tankard and pushed it aside to signal to the waitress the desire for another. "What happened between you and the dragon? Your appearance at the bottom of the mountain shocked us all, and you never divulged what transpired in the cave on Mount Siven."

Casemiro contemplated keeping the information to himself but decided revealing the details to Forrest harmed no one. "I controlled the dragon, and the reason doesn't matter. Neither of us realized the situation existed while we fought in the cave. Once the notion occurred to me, the fight ended, and we conducted a brief discussion." The wizard picked up another forkful of the food from Forrest's plate. "You could say we hashed out our differences." The wizard shoved the food into his mouth and took another swig.

After swallowing the food, the wizard continued the story. "We worked together to overcome our mutual problem, and the dragon promised to not harm me if I released the bond. Once we agreed on terms, the dragon flew me to the base of the mountain and cleared the opening for your escape. You witnessed the rest. Pretty simple."

"Well, you missed a little from our escape."

A grin flashed across Casemiro's face. "You opened up to Oleander and discussed a future in Lillenhold?"

Forrest waved for the waitress and ordered two more plates of hash, including one for the wizard. He nodded thanks to Raquel for the quick response. With one gulp, the troll-man finished another flagon and let out a table-rattling belch.

"I can't imagine why Oleander isn't interested." Casemiro smirked at his friend's uncouth response.

Forrest grimaced at the wizard. "Oleander wished to discuss Prince Arenton during our descent. To Laural's credit, the Princess attempted to redirect the questions towards me, but Oleander holds no interest in me. Though polite about the matter, Prince Arenton infatuates the woman."

"Laural indicated Oleander was less than delicate."

Forrest just replied with a slight nod, enough of a message to tell the wizard to drop the topic.

The waitress brought two plates of hash, and Casemiro requested more cider. Raquel smiled at the troll-man, and Forrest remained oblivious. The wizard lost his concentration when the scent of sage-filled hash hit his nostrils.

The waitress interrupted the wizard's contemplations on sausage and potatoes. "The barkeep asked me to ensure you gents can pay before we serve anymore. Too many people stiffed him this week."

Casemiro grinned at the woman with raven-colored hair, which draped over her face and hid the scar on the right side. Raquel's eyes bounced off her olive skin and her white teeth illuminated an enormous smile. The waitress in the Skullery failed to capture the men's attention due to her abnormalities. But the wizard realized Raquel hovered around their table, attempting to attract Forrest's attention. The wizard noted to make a point of the peculiarity to Forrest.

The wizard then addressed the current irritation. Casemiro cast a glance over Raquel's shoulder and sneered at the barkeep. The wizard reached into his coin purse and pulled out several gold pieces to show the man. "Does this appear as if we can pay?"

The barkeep nodded and went back to his business.

The waitress smiled shyly. "Sorry, only doing my job, sir."

"Not your fault, Raquel, and you are doing an excellent job. Isn't she Forrest?"

The troll-man nodded as he shoveled in another forkful of hash.

"Thank you." Raquel left the table and returned with more cider and another smile for Forrest.

Forrest, still clueless, dug into the food and between bites answered. "Yeah, impressive job. So, what problem exists between you and Laural?"

Casemiro huffed at the comment. "First, are you always this clueless? Raquel has hovered around our table since you arrived. It's unlikely due to undying dedication to her job. She paid much less attention when my brother joined me."

Forrest shrugged his shoulders as a reply and continued eating the hash.

"As for Laural, I wish I understood. It does not matter now. I leave tomorrow for wherever my brother's ship can take me. Life's too short to suffer such headaches."

"You sure the proper response involves running from another problem?"

"Laural cannot accept that I didn't lie. I only withheld the truth until it became necessary to share some of my history. A man can hold on to secrets if he believes they do not affect others. For example, were you aware that I knit?"

Forrest chuckled at the idea of the wizard using needles and yarn. "No, I did not. Why do you knit?"

"Not so funny story." Casemiro took another drink from the cider. "My wife always knitted. I hoped to extend the duration of the happy memories by taking up the hobby. But the hobby only added to the guilt, like everything else in my life."

"How does the Princess affect that?"

"My guilt increases when I think of Laural."

Forrest smiled with his bright teeth. "I think we both grasp why that would add to the guilt. You believe you are disrespecting your marriage and the vows you shared with your wife. An easy thing to understand, wizard."

Casemiro nodded in agreement with Forrest. "Is it fair for me to be happy after my first wife passed away? When joyful thoughts and emotions fill my mind, guilt arrives. My wife died. Why would I ever rejoice again?"

"Before I answer, do you contemplate this question a lot?" Forrest finished the plate of hash and waved for the waitress once more and pointed to the empty flagon.

"Always."

"At first, I understood why you might feel that way. But Mira killed your wife. Why not let the guilt go now?"

"Our marriage suffered at the end. We suffered, her more than me. We held onto that commitment because not doing so seemed wrong."

Forrest leaned back and kept quiet, waiting for his next drink, and refusing to talk.

Casemiro finished his flagon of cider and continued chatting. "Why are you so quiet?"

"I find no satisfactory way to react to your friend discussing his late wife." Forrest interjected some levity into the discussion. "Also, I don't want to pay for your food and drink, so I'm waiting for your guilt to consume you before we leave the Skullery."

The wizard laughed and his mood lightened. "So, you believe I'm allowing this guilt to impede with living my life?"

Forrest received the next flagon and took a drink, monitoring the wizard.

In the silence, Casemiro continued talking. "You think me an idiot for letting this guilt impede with having a life after the wife of my death? I mean the death of my wife. And from having a wife with Laural. Uh, a life with Laural." The wizard paused. "How much alcohol does this cider contain?"

"After a few drinks, the 8% alcohol content noticeably impacts someone of your stature."

Casemiro took another drink as the frustration returned. "You seem judgmental for someone who can't..." The wizard paused, realizing the insensitivity of his impending comment, and taking out his annoyance on his friend. "Sorry."

Forrest waved his hand as if the words did not affect him and leaned toward the table. "Wizard, you wish to convince yourself that guilt explains everything wrong in their life. I believe you folks refer to this as a pity party. I, nor anyone else in the Skullery, judges you negatively for attempting to live a life after your wife's death. If you want advice, tell Laural everything you just told me, except for the bit about the cider, and wait for her response."

Casemiro reached into his coin purse to grab some money and slid five pieces of gold across the table. The wizard smiled at Forrest as the words settled and comforted his soul. "You're a smarter man than most, Forrest. This covers the food and drink. I must return to Veritas Keep and talk to Laural. Oh, pay attention to the waitress and listen to your own advice."

Stepping away from the table, the wizard recognized a familiar face standing near the bar. Casemiro walked over and tapped the man on the shoulder.

Holding a flagon of mead, the wide-eyed man turned around. "Casemiro! You are alive!"

"Well, if it isn't Niiiikos Antaaaaaeus!" The wizard, still registering the impact of the cider, almost fell as he embellished the yell of the name, but the wrestler steadied him. "Thank you, lad. What brings you back here?"

"I switched sides after our incident on the road. I made a mistake and desire to meet your friends to apologize in person to them as well."

Casemiro pointed back to the table where Forrest sat. "Luckily, one of them sits at that table. The Princess sits in Veritas Keep, but allow me to pass along your apology to her. Now, I need to run off." The wizard gave Nikos a quick embrace and walked out of the Skullery.

The wizard escaped the entrance and found Roman standing outside the establishment, watching the flow of human traffic. Casemiro tapped the boy on the shoulder to gain his attention. "It's been over an hour since I came inside, young man. Why didn't you enter?"

Roman ducked his head in embarrassment. "The Skullery only allows adults to enter, sir."

"My misunderstanding then, lad." Casemiro fished for his coin purse once more and reached into the fabric to withdraw one gold coin at a time. The wizard gave five of the pieces to the boy, and each coin prompted the boy's eyes to grow larger. "Oh, and take the magic silver piece."

Using a hand gesture, Roman refused the old man. "Sir, you promised much less." Roman shook the five gold pieces. "Besides, keep the silver piece for luck. You never can predict when you might require a spy in Lillenhold."

Casemiro put the silver back in his coin purse. "Anything unusual in the village since we last talked?"

Roman leaned close to the wizard. "Contrary to what anyone believes, Mister Sweet oversees the keep."

Casemiro stood upright. "But the Prince said Sweet disappeared."

Roman shook his head. "Sweet remains hidden in the forest, but he stationed his men in Lillenhold. Others carrying the Marquis of Cassen's flag blockade the other edge of town. The situation does not look promising, Casemiro, sir."

The wizard pieced together the clues and concluded Harley's hiding spot: Mira Sweet's home. Casemiro girded the chain belt a little tighter. "No, it does not. Perhaps the Prince and I need to discuss what events occurred during my absence once more. Thank you for the information, Roman. Worth everything I paid you. Spend the money wisely."

In a surprise move, Roman hugged the wizard before running down the street. The wizard turned to Veritas Keep as the gray skies foretold something awful arriving on the breeze. The wizard now discerned a darker disturbance existed within the stone walls of the keep. Deceit and betrayal triumphed over the goodness of Arenton in Casemiro's absence and the Prince fell captive to their hold. Casemiro needed to break Arenton free of this prison if someone imprisoned Arenton against the Prince's will. The wizard reached down to tap into the little magic energy within him and he found nothing. Casemiro spent his magic similar to the way a sailor runs through their wages on shore leave.

The wizard reflected on his guilt, which faded and left a hole for the wizard to fill. Casemiro's mind now understood magic did not determine his strength and worth, but his heart required catching up. With or without magic, Casemiro understood the extensive work needed to restore order in Lillenhold.

Before Casemiro walked ten paces down the road, the wizard lost his balance as a side effect of the cider. The fall did not dissuade the wizard, and he laughed at his own expense while leaning on the staff for support. Casemiro stared towards Veritas Keep, aware of the danger before him. The time arrived to eliminate the evil in Lillenhold and defeat Harley Sweet and J. J. Heenan. Casemiro stood and wiped off the dirt and dust as he marched to meet these oppressors.

Anger swelled in Casemiro, and his magical energy spiked. The wizard tapped into the energy and, as he walked towards Veritas Keep, he said a quiet word. "Sobr." Within a second, the alcohol in the wizard's blood dissipated, and he stood as stout as a man his age may. The magic grew in Casemiro with each step, though it did not fill the gap in his soul. The magic sat at the gap's edge, wishing to replace the grief. Casemiro needed something else to fill his life. If not magic, then what?

"It does not matter what I need at the moment. It's not about me, it's about doing the right thing."

3✦0

KIDS IN THE KEEP

The walk from the village became one of perseverance for the wizard. Upon leaving the Skullery, a monsoon struck Lillenhold and cleared the streets of any stragglers, creating a lonely and wet walk to Veritas Keep. Casemiro slipped at least once and fell into the mud, besmirching the new cloak to the point the entrance guards didn't recognize him. Before granting entrance to the keep, the guards thoroughly inspected the wizard to ensure he was not a wandering vagabond seeking shelter.

A muddy Casemiro entered the hall with his eyes attuned to the surroundings and scanning for suspicious activity. The guards appeared familiar, but their helmets hid their faces, and the armor concealed any potential clues to their identity. A portion of Casemiro's psyche doubted any infiltration occurred, but Roman's warning forced him to expect the worst.

The noises of clinking glasses, clanging utensils, and chortling partygoers floated from the central hall. A fire blazed in the hearth and warmed the festive atmosphere within the cold keep. The aroma of roasted deer with potatoes, carrots, and other root vegetables pushed through the air. Casemiro's stomach craved the cooked meat, but the hash and soup from the Skullery satisfied him.

Despite the event appearing as a festive gathering, the wizard's caution and the looming threat at the village's edge prevented him from misinterpreting the signs. He wondered why no one raised any alarms for the impending assault.

Casemiro remained in the shadows as Arenton led the festivities at the long table. The Prince acted distracted and unsure of his surroundings while fidgeting and glancing to the corners of the room as if he anticipated something to occur. Did the Prince become paranoid because of recent events? Or did Arenton truly expect a dastardly act to befall him and Veritas Keep? Despite seeming ridiculous in the wizard's mind, Casemiro contemplated the possibility of the lad's involvement.

Then the wizard spotted Laural beside the Prince with an empty seat, possibly for Casemiro, next to her. Seeing the Princess raised his level of attention to their surroundings. He knew he must protect her.

He watched as Oleander mooned over Arenton. The other attendees seemed clueless to anything other than filling their stomachs off the Prince's best offerings. Casemiro stumbled into the light and the Princess caught sight of the wizard. Laural excused herself and walked over at a heightened pace.

"Where did you go? And why are you so muddy?"

Casemiro peered over Laural's shoulder and caught Oleander glaring in their direction. "I fell on my way back from

THE UNSPOKEN TRUTHS OF CASEMIRO

dinner at the Skullery with Forrest. None of which matters right now. I need to speak to Arenton alone. Something is amiss, and I fear for your safety and his."

Laural scrunched up her nose and scoffed at the comment. "Nothing is wrong, and we expect considerable news tonight. It's better if Forrest isn't here since Arenton plans to announce his engagement to Oleander. And from what I gather, she already accepted. Don't spoil this evening, even if it's unwanted news for our friend."

Casemiro replied, "Though I'm happy for them, something appears wrong. Unbeknownst to anyone in here, Sweet hid in the forest with his mother until an invading force arrived, which now sits on the edge of the village. Also, you and I need to talk, but our drama can wait." Casemiro squeezed Laural's hand to communicate his intent and pushed by the Princess to approach the table.

Arenton caught sight of the wizard and welcomed Casemiro to join the party with a permanent smile glazed across the Prince's face. "Ladies and gentlemen, the hero of the day and the master of dragons approaches. Without Casemiro, the lady Oleander and my sister would have perished in the dragon's lair. Please pepper him with your adoration, as the wizard deserves recognition for this wonderful achievement." Arenton examined the cloak of the wizard. "Even in his mud-soaked state. But may I ask where our Golden Dragon Champion is?"

"Forest thought it best to avoid the dinner."

Everyone nodded at the explanation and gave a round of applause for Casemiro. Most stood to convey their appreciation for his effort. The wizard nodded toward the people, attempting to keep focus on his mission without drawing attention to the danger and sending everyone into a panic.

The wizard leaned toward Arenton. "Your Highness, I must discuss something of the utmost importance that may endanger yourself and your guests."

Arenton's eyes widened at the danger proclaimed, and Casemiro contemplated sharing this information with those sitting at the table. "Excuse us for a moment, my fine folks. Enjoy your meal as I discuss something of import with our skilled wizard. When we return, the next course of the meal begins. Oleander, please tell the kitchen staff to bring out the food."

While others chatted, Oleander smirked at the wizard and Prince before departing the hall to convey the message.

The Prince and Casemiro traversed to a distant corner. Arenton asked, "Did the dragon return? Does Forrest wish to challenge me for Oleander's hand? What concerns you so much to drag me from my guests, wizard?"

"Arenton, Harley Sweet attempts to take over Veritas Keep as we speak. While you believe Sweet hid in the forest, his men, the wrestlers, assumed positions inside your troop of guards. They are prepared for an attack by the forces of Cassen, which sit at the edge of the village. Let's focus on getting you and Laural to safety and notifying the rest of Lillenhold."

Arenton surveyed the room, and he noticed the reddened eyes of the Prince. "Show me proof to support this claim because I mitigated the threat of Harley Sweet."

"An informant kept me apprised of the situation in the keep. I remained in contact the entire time I traveled to save Oleander. This contact passed along information concerning what happened beneath your nose. You, your sister, and your guests are in peril this evening."

The Prince narrowed his eyes before erupting in laughter and refusing to take the wizard seriously. "Are you shifting my attention from the table, maybe for an unexpected twist? Quite enjoyable wizard, but now we must return to our guests before they think me rude. Sit and never speak of this again." The Prince's smile transformed into a glare, signaling the wizard to stop talking.

Arenton moved away from the wizard and returned to his spot at the table. "Crisis averted, and Casemiro now joins us for the rest of the evening."

Casemiro, not willing to give up, grabbed the lone empty chair from the far side of the table and moved it between Laural and Arenton. The wizard concluded keeping them close proved the best way to protect them, even if they ignored his warning. As Casemiro took his seat, the next course of the meal arrived, and the wait staff passed bread, cheese, and dried fruit to the attendees.

Arenton searched the room. "Excuse me, did any of you notice where the lady Oleander wandered off to?"

One of the staff answered the Prince. "Yes, my Lord, she said to tell you her imminent return would occur after addressing a private matter."

Arenton's cheeks flushed as the Prince turned to Laural and then turned to the crowd to update them. "When the lady Oleander returns, I wish to share some exciting news regarding the future of Lillenhold."

Casemiro shifted his gaze to the room's perimeter. The number of guards along the hall's edge rose from the time the wizard arrived. Out of the corner of his eye, the wizard spotted an armed guardsman standing at the entrance carrying a somewhat familiar frame. The wizard's curiosity outweighed his hesitation and he moved towards the closest guard. The wizard examined the armor and found Otto Schwartz's grinning countenance upon lifting the face guard.

"Hello again, wizard." The Brawler threw a punch and connected with the older man's stomach to drive Casemiro to the ground and his staff skittered across the floor and out of reach.

Laural leaped from the table to help the wizard, but the armored foe grabbed her arm as she attempted a strike. The Princess proved too weak to break the hold, and she dropped to the hall floor next to the wizard before assistance arrived.

The Brawler stood over the victims. "Everyone, remain calm and no one gets hurt. Or you can fight, and I break your necks. Your choice." The deranged smile and accompanying laughter frightened the guests. Many ran for the exit, screaming.

Another guardsman entered the hall, leaving a trail of rainwater across the floor. Based on the wet armor, Casemiro surmised the man represented the true guard for Veritas Keep.

"My Lord, their forces came from outside the city and broke through our defenses. They overran us!"

Before finishing the warning, a man barreled over the boy and push a sword through his victim's neck, just below the helm. With a quick pull, the blade slid from the body and left a mess on the floor. The holder was Harley Sweet and behind him stood his brother, J. J. Heenan.

The two brothers approached the table, exchanging smiles of satisfaction. Casemiro noted more similarities between the men than just the blonde hair. The duo shared many characteristics: their identical chins, the shape of their eyes, and their torsos took on similar silhouettes.

"You fools killed that man. Why?" asked the Prince.

Arenton attempted to protest as another guard pushed the Prince back into his chair. The man removed his helm and revealed himself to be Paul Perriman. "Such a simple fool." Perriman then slapped the Prince to the ground.

Casemiro attempted to stand, but a warm, feminine hand grabbed him and laid a blade flat against his neck. A voice the wizard recognized from the forest raked through his ears.

"Hello, Casemiro. I bet you hoped to never see me again."

Mira Sweet's voice sent shivers down the wizard's spine, despite not seeing her face. "My sister-in-law's presence would be more enjoyable if she didn't threaten me with a knife."

The voice provided a husky laugh in his ear. "Yes, such details ruin the mood when these family gatherings occur with such short warning. Kindly sit next to the Princess at the table. Such a shame your trollen friend missed out, but we can deal with him later. And forget about regaining your staff. That wooden stick rests in my capable hands."

Arenton yelled, "Guards, take these people down!"

The armored men standing around the hall failed to respond.

Casemiro's questions around the Prince's involvement were now answered. He interjected to explain the events to Arenton. "Save your words, Prince. Those in armor are the wrestlers, not your guards. They replaced the real guards and, for now, we stand at their mercy. My guess: the true guards rotated to positions outside Veritas Keep and now fight against the forces of Cassen who attempt to overthrow your rule. I apologize for not warning you earlier." With his staff in Mira Sweet's hands, Casemiro wondered what purpose he now served.

The Brawler returned to Casemiro's side. "Not so indestructible without your staff, are you, wizard?" Schwartz planted a boot on the wizard's chest and knocked his opponent to the ground once again.

Casemiro snarled at the man.

"You still show some fight, at least. Your actions in the forest earned my respect and I will not underestimate you again. But do not be stupid."

Mira, with the staff, walked over to her two sons. "The proper party begins once a couple more people arrive. Meanwhile, let's remove the unnecessaries. Everyone except the Prince, Princess, and the wizard must leave." As the guards escorted the other people from the keep, Mira examined the wizard's staff and waited for the rest of their expected company.

The screams of horror lasted until the unwanted guests fled. Soon after, the doors of the keep blasted open, and another group of guards piled into Veritas Keep. These forces wore armor lined with red fabric and carried different shields. A man with flowing blond hair, who everyone in the room, including Casemiro, recognized as the Marquis of Cassen, marched towards Prince Arenton.

"Hello, nephew. I must say, I expected a greater struggle to overtake your home. Your defense of Veritas Keep disappoints me. I guess taking the compound from someone who lacks an appreciation for it only makes sense."

Arenton showed a spark by standing to confront the man. "You aren't supposed to be here." Before the Prince did anything stupid, two soldiers pointed their swords at his chest and Arenton backed away to sit in his chair.

Casemiro still thought the Prince's reactions to the incursion seemed odd but chalked it up to youth or shock.

The Marquis leaned toward Arenton. "Sorry, boy, but did you say something?"

Arenton offered no response.

The older man spied Casemiro and pointed to one guard. "Bring the wizard and Princess to me."

Another broad-shouldered wrestler in disguise dragged the wizard and Princess to the Marquis. Once in his presence, the Marquis leaned towards the wizard. "Rumors say you saved lady

Oleander. I appreciate such bravery and give you a hearty well done." The Marquis glanced around the room. "And where is the lady Oleander? I wish to give her my regards."

The puzzle pieces fell into place and the entire chain of events connected in Casemiro's mind. The wizard closed his eyes and cursed his idiocy. "Oleander is the other child."

Not hearing what the wizard blathered about, Arenton barked out a threat. "If you hurt—"

The Marquis slapped the Prince, forcing Arenton to the floor. "Shut your yap, child. The adults are talking."

Oleander's voice came into the keep before she appeared. "They did not hurt me, Prince Arenton. I allowed them free entry. I released J. J. from his cell and opened the back door for Mira's entrance. Without assistance, Harley walked through the front door."

Oleander emerged from behind a pillar and joined Harley Sweet and Heenan. The florist's true identity became obvious to Casemiro because of the blonde hair and facial features. The wizard muttered, "How did I miss the connection?"

Oleander sauntered toward the wizard. "Let me guess. You assumed the third child was another man, correct? You presumed Harley, or perhaps J. J., dreamed up this entire uprising. Well, guess again, Casemiro. My plan, including the dragon, led to this. My plan proceeded as expected, including the food tester dying. Well, almost. I still wonder how you survived the encounter with the dragon."

Oleander stood at her full height and glowered at the wizard with disdain. "But that problem does not matter. A little ol' florist batted her eyelashes and outsmarted a Prince, his sister, a wizard, and everyone else in this forsaken village. The best part: I did nothing out of character, or even lied. All of you assumed I enjoyed the role of the stupid damsel in distress. An oversight which allowed me to be natural in my actions and to fool you all. Not bad for someone everyone assumes is only useful for a good fuck, growing some pretty flowers, and nothing else." Oleander mockingly clicked her teeth to give a false smile to the wizard.

Oleander turned towards the Prince. "And I anticipated your intended proposal. Though flattered, you can keep the engagement ring in your pocket. I do not require your hand to aid my ascension to the throne any longer. Being enchanted by me sufficed to implement my plan."

Laural objected to Oleander's tirade at her brother. "You are not worthy of Arenton. I cannot believe we fell for your act."

Oleander snickered at Laural. "Princess, your brother became my backup plan if things did not work out the way I intended. But I never wanted him. My man surpasses your little brother and the trollen in every aspect." Oleander moved to the side of Paul Perriman, who wrapped his arm around her waist as she kissed him on the cheek.

Laural suggested with her middle finger what Oleander could do.

The Marquis banged on the table. "Enough! Clear out the rest of these people and bring me some hot food. I am hungry! Storming a keep creates an appetite."

Mira pointed toward the wizard and Laural. "Where do we put them?"

The Marquis glared at the prisoners with obvious distaste. "Lock up the wizard in the dungeon cell. Hell, put my niece and nephew with him. They may prove useful when my brother arrives. Until then, they can sit and rot together in the dank darkness of a cell beneath Veritas Keep."

The Brawler reached out and jerked Casemiro to his feet. "Either walk, or I knock you out and drag you down the stairs, old man. Your choice."

Casemiro grabbed Laural's hand as the Brawler led them to their cell. Perriman pushed Arenton across the room to join them. The two wrestlers escorted the trio to the dungeon while assaulting them with insults and verbal barbs. The men pushed the threesome into a cell, slammed the creaking ancient door, and broke the key off in the lock. Perriman and the Brawler laughed, then left the prisoners in the dark to ponder what just happened.

In his head, the wizard mused on the possibility of things getting worse. Rainwater seeping into the dungeon through the wall cracks reminded him of the storm outside. Casemiro fell as far as possible. He landed in a jail cell devoid of magic, with a lovesick idiot and a woman the wizard believed now despised him. Then the rats emerged to make matters even worse. The wizard allowed himself one roar of disdain and self-pity before beginning his search for an answer. Casemiro wasn't sure what he hated more, being in the jail cell or that Forrest was right about him.

31

DARKEST HOUR

The dead rat lay against the wall of the dark cell, where Casemiro kicked the lifeless body after stomping on the animal's neck. The dead vermin served as a warning for the other rodents contemplating entering the wizard's domain during the cold, wet night.

When the ruffians, Perriman and Schwartz, left the threesome in the cold cell earlier, they failed to search the group for any items that might help them escape. Laural produced one of her knives to cut their bindings, but the trio progressed no further towards escaping the dank cell. Casemiro periodically tested his magic and physical strength on the cell door. Arenton remained quiet, not saying a word since being captured, and reeked of warranted embarrassment.

Casemiro grew tired of the Prince's wallowing and attempted to ignite the Prince's anger and elicit a reaction. "I allowed you adequate time to contemplate our woeful situation. Your Highness, shall we discuss our escape plan? Or sit and wait for these ruffians to kill us?"

Arenton mumbled a reply.

Casemiro feigned anger once more. "Sorry, perhaps you need to speak up."

The Prince yelled, "They still find us useful, so we are not in imminent danger. Loud enough, wizard?"

The wizard laughed aloud. "God, you are nothing more than a stupid child, after all." Casemiro stared at the black shape the wizard speculated to be Arenton. A paltry amount of light from the moon snuck in and broke through the blackness. Casemiro second guessed his decision to antagonize the Prince into action. He searched for anything to help the trio escape before their usefulness, and their lives, expired.

Laural rose from the shadows and admonished the wizard. "Arenton remains my brother, and we still owe him our allegiance. Regardless of how stupid the Prince acts."

The Princess walked across the room and sat beside Arenton. She plunged into the role of older sister and protector of her brother.

Casemiro sighed in frustration, expressing his displeasure with the Prince's ego. "Apologies, your Majesty." The wizard sat on the floor and stared at Laural and Arenton's silhouettes. "But we still need to escape. And they will kill us when it suits them."

The Prince and Princess remained silent, knowing the wizard to be correct.

The wizard prodded the siblings when they did not respond. "You never answered my question, Princess."

Laural's head tilted to the side; her green eyes shone as the darkness of the cell shrouded the rest of her features. "What question?"

"You stopped wearing red?"

Casemiro took in her head turning towards to the Prince.

"I held onto what you said in the mountain and decided to not let others determine my value or to allow others to dictate my life. Going forward, I ignore my brother's demands to wear red and erase the constant reminder of my error in judgment. Sorry, Arenton." The Princess squeezed the Prince's shoulder.

The Prince waved his hand to dismiss the comment. "Stupid rule, anyway. It does not matter now."

"Actually, the decree mattered to Laural. She wishes to become her own person instead of being defined by her position as Princess." Casemiro scooted into a position next to the Princess and patted Laural's leg.

The Princess grabbed Casemiro's hand and brushed it away. "Really, wizard? You seem more than content to be defined by your past instead of pursuing a different future. And touching me in an unsolicited manner remains inappropriate because I am the Princess."

Arenton's head rose with piqued interest. "Should I leave the room? Oh wait, I can't."

"You are fine, and Casemiro lies."

Casemiro sighed, and with no other pressing matter, confronted the issue. "Can we discuss this problem and pretend my voice matters, Princess? You declared a stance without asking why I did not share my secrets."

Arenton interjected, "His proposal sounds fair. Allow Casemiro to answer your charges."

"This doesn't concern you, brother." Laural pushed away from the Prince and turned her back to Arenton.

"As your Prince and the one you owe your allegiance to, as you mentioned earlier, I command you to listen to the man."

Laural accepted the order in silence, but her body language screamed of indignance.

The wizard nodded toward the Prince. "Thank you."

Casemiro replayed the discussion with Forrest in his head, but jumped into a more concise explanation. "The complete truth is I did not tell you everything because whenever we discussed our relationship, guilt overwhelmed me. Every time I look at you, I betray my wife and fifteen years of marriage. Despite the struggles, I loved Chantal for fifteen years and still do. The guilt arises from clinging to the past instead of opening up to you."

Casemiro continued rambling while staring at the Princess. "This is my struggle. I thought holding onto those memories and secrets allowed me the best of both worlds, a relationship with you while keeping my promises to Chantal. I thought holding back did not affect you. I apologize for any shortsightedness and now realize I should have told you earlier about the unspoken truths I held onto."

A sniffle came from Laural. "Is this the reason for your silence on these matters? Guilt over the belief you might betray your relationship with Chantal?"

"Pretty much."

"God, now I feel like an ass."

Arenton giggled. "Rightly so. I wondered what occurred between you two. You came back a pair of brooding sods and I assumed something serious happened. You two do not realize how compatible you are. Do not screw this up. Being an idiot doesn't make me blind to things." The Prince shook his head and chuckled at the irony of the comment. "Richard owes me money again because he said you two were not relationship material."

Casemiro laughed at the joke. "I apologize, Arenton. I do not take you for an idiot; just young, immature, and naïve."

Pausing, the Prince shook off the comment and stood, casting an immense presence over the room. "I agree with that assessment. I sure missed the whole thing concerning Oleander and now I need to grow up a bit."

Once again, the wizard speculated about the Prince's role in the scheme. He believed Arenton to only be a pawn, but needed verification. "You want a chance to prove your growth? Tell us what mischievous scheme you wished to enact. Don't keep any secrets like I did. I can tell you planned something."

A sigh from the Prince sent a warning throughout the room that he indeed played a part in their current predicament. "The entire plan centered on Oleander and I being together. She approached me with the idea, and we brought in her siblings, Heenan and then Sweet. I thought she adored me. Then odd things started occurring. The unplanned death of Geoffrey shocked me. Oleander assured me justice would follow for the killer and claimed the event only helped our plan. Then the dragon snatched her."

Casemiro leaned against the wall to relieve his body from the stress of sitting on the stone floor. "You fell in over your head, Your Highness. What happened while we journeyed from the village to save Oleander?"

The Prince shifted his weight and leaned against the wall of the cell. "Heenan and Sweet forcibly took control of the city after you left and kept it from most of the village. Heenan stayed in the dungeon as a canard. Sweet left his men in charge of the grounds and shielded me from outside contact. I lied to you about their influence and location when you returned because I feared they might harm you and Laural.

"Your return surprised all of us. The brothers believed you all would die on the quest. Your return forced their hand and I guess they brought in the Marquis to take over Lillenhold."

The wizard chuckled. "This was their plan all along. What did you think was going to happen?"

"My plan was to figure out a way for Oleander and I to be married and make a life together here at Veritas Keep."

"She played you like a violin, Arenton."

Laural sounded exasperated. "Arenton, why didn't you tell me?"

"Your presence here served as a spy for father. I did not trust you either and, until she betrayed me, I only trusted Oleander."

"Don't be too tough on yourself, Prince. The woman fooled each of us." Casemiro stretched his arms, legs, and back. "I believe I understand everything now. Laural and I ran across Mira Sweet, the triplets' mother, in the wilderness on our way to rescue Oleander."

The Prince turned his head toward the wizard's voice. "Hold on, the old crone father exiled long ago is their mother? I believed her a fairy tale until today."

Laural answered, "Yes, everyone assumed Mira Sweet left Gaeleos. Instead, she lived in the woods near the base of Mount Siven all these years."

The wizard continued the story. "Most people assumed the King exiled her because of intimate relations yielding an unwanted pregnancy. Sweet bore three children: Harley Sweet, J. J. Heenan, and Oleander. I concluded that Harley and Heenan were two of the three children, and incorrectly assumed Gerard the third. I missed not identifying Oleander and, upon reflection, she gave us the clues and did not even bother to hide her lineage from us."

"Hold up. So, who attempted to poison me?"

"Oleander used her access to various poisonous plants, along with the apple cores from Forrest's cidery, to create the poison. She worked with her father to transfer the mead from the Cassenwary distillery into a barrel she purchased from the cooper. She then conveyed the poisoned drink into the keep beneath everyone's noses. That covers the means and opportunity. The motivation becomes obvious at this point."

Laural followed up on the comment. "The wrestlers were in town earlier than we believed. She used them to move the barrels for her. Forrest asked her about it as she typically used him to move them. But what of the dragon?"

Casemiro explained, "Oleander planned that as well. The dragon told us it met Mira and one of her children in the wilderness. I assumed it was Sweet, but more than likely it was Oleander. I guess Oleander befriended the dragon and convinced it to snatch her to draw me out and away from Veritas Keep. I bought into the deception and pursued the lure. All speculation, but the scenario explains why the dragon did not harm her. Part of me believes she deceived the dragon as well."

The Price and Princess took a moment to process the shocking news. To fill the time, Casemiro attempted to break the lock once more, but failed. The wizard turned back to the siblings. "Any other questions at this point?"

Arenton asked a follow-up. "How does this involve my uncle attacking Veritas Keep?"

"I believe the Marquis fathered the triplets, and Mira did not carry an unwanted pregnancy from her relationship with your father. I presume the reason King Skaranon exiled Mira centered around an affair with the Marquis that might besmirch the family's reputation. And now the Marquis attempts to force your father's hand through a coup led by his three children and Mira. The Marquis attacked Veritas Keep because the king's young son rules here and that provided a weak point in King Skaranon's chain of command."

Laural asked, "Why do you jump to the conclusion the Marquis is their father?"

"Genetics. Do either of you recall anyone in your family ever having blonde hair?"

Arenton shook his head. "No, we sport dark brown, or black, hair throughout the family."

"Correct. The Marquis is adopted. If those triplets truly carried your father's blood, fair hair would be unlikely. And I guess your uncle always carried a grudge about Skaranon taking the throne, correct?"

Arenton answered, "Always, and he never approved of me taking this position." Arenton halted, gazing at the wizard in the dark, hoping Casemiro would solve the problem. "But my father arriving tomorrow evening should disrupt their plans."

Laural understood the explanation for the King coming to Lillenhold, even if Arenton did not. "They know his presence is required for a trial when the crown accuses someone of treason. Father is walking into a trap, Arenton."

Casemiro gazed at the cell's door. "So, we must escape and quell this little uprising before the King arrives. Any suggestions for our escape plan?"

Laural walked across the cell and grabbed Casemiro. "I'm sorry." The Princess searched for the wizard's face with her hand and pulled him close enough to kiss.

Casemiro fell into the kiss and enjoyed the connection. A flicker of power in his soul erupted to life. After a moment, the magic diminished.

Arenton coughed to break them apart. "You two need to stop before I become sick. Even in this darkness, I can tell you are displaying affection."

Casemiro smiled toward Arenton. "Very well, Your Highness. The time has arrived to change our luck."

Laural leaned against the wizard. "Without your staff, can you perform any magic?"

"Perhaps, but unnecessary. Good fortune smiled on us when you found my coin at Mount Siven and when those brutes refused to search us." Casemiro pulled out the silver disk which caught a glint of light. "I can arrange a rescue."

Casemiro called for Roman, and he answered. "Roman, we need your help once more."

"Whatever you need. I caught sight of the troops as they made their way to the keep."

"Yes, our captors put us in the dungeon of Veritas Keep. We need help to escape. The Prince and Princess are with me. We need to free them and reach a boat called the Fierce Siren before the ship launches at dawn."

"What do you propose I do, sir?"

"Find Forrest and tell him what happened. And we need an escape plan."

"I'll do what I can, sir."

Arenton stood once the conversation finished. "You entrusted a boy with our fate?"

"Roman proved himself more dependable than you, Your Highness. And I put my faith in Forrest. Since we have no clue when our rescuers might arrive, I encourage you to sleep while you can. Rest up, people."

Casemiro projected a courageous exterior, but inside the wizard's confidence hovered just below lacking.

Forrest and Nikos left the Skullery, and the barkeep locked the door. The troll-man's attention veered up the hill towards Veritas

Keep and picked out an interesting detail. "Why are troops with a yellow flag advancing on the keep?"

Screams from running people shattered the silence of the village. A man wearing armor, carrying a spear, and displaying a shield with a gold eagle followed behind them.

The shield carrier caught sight of Forrest and Nikos and changed direction. He waved the spear at the troll-man. "You, go to your home and clear the streets. We carry orders to arrest any offenders and make an example of them."

Forrest grabbed the spear from the soldier and snapped the weapon in half across his knee and, with a thump to the head, the man dropped to the ground, armor rattling. The victim of the blow lay unconscious in the street.

Forrest turned to Nikos. "What is happening?"

"Those troops attacking the keep hail from Cassenwary and stand loyal to the Marquis."

Forrest stepped away from the Skullery and began the long walk towards Veritas Keep.

Nikos stayed back. "What are you doing?"

"I plan to defend the keep as part of my duty. I am the Golden Dragon Champion."

Nikos laughed. "You believe your imaginary title matters."

Forrest walked back to Nikos and stood to his full height, towering over the man. "It does to me, and it matters to everyone who calls this village home. Including my friends, the ones who supported me in battle. I fight for them and this village. So, the title matters, Nikos."

Nikos nodded his head, accepting the proclamation as fact. "You are right, big man. Let's do what we can."

Forrest viewed the troops attacking Veritas Keep in the distance for a moment. He lacked familiarity with the keep's design and wondered how to gain entry and do the most harm without being caught. The troll-man walked forward without a plan, knowing action often led to beneficial results.

Nikos asked. "The Cassen forces occupy the main gate. How else can we enter the keep?"

Forrest answered over his shoulder. "Brute force, as much as I detest the method."

A flash of a person ran in front of the troll-man. The boy stopped in front of Forrest, out of breath and grabbing his knees as he doubled over. After catching his breath, the boy said his piece. "I might be able to help you enter the keep."

Forrest examined the little one. "Did the wizard send you?"

The boy nodded.

"I'm guessing you're Roman."

The boy nodded again. "Yes, and Casemiro needs saving. The invaders locked him, the Princess, and the Prince in the dungeon."

Forrest smiled. "Typical wizard. Did Casemiro say anything regarding the lady Oleander?"

Roman shook his head.

Nikos jumped into the conversation. "Wait, you mean the lovely blonde lady who runs the floral shop?"

Forrest turned. "What do you know of the damsel we saved from the dragon?"

"I hate to tell you this, but Oleander is no damsel."

Forrest picked Nikos up, ignoring the boy for the moment. "Explain yourself regarding Oleander."

"You mean Sweet's siter. Everyone in the troop knows she is not a delicate flower. She's been Perriman's girl for years now."

Forrest's illusion shattered in a second, knowing the man told the truth. He dropped Nikos and turned to the keep. He quickly wiped away a tear before turning to Roman, concealing the shattering of his heart and the end of Forrest's hopes for a relationship with the woman.

"You work in the keep, correct?"

"Yes, sir."

"Can we enter without those troops seeing us?"

A smile crept across the boy's face. "Of course. Who all do you have?"

Forrest whirled with his arms extended. "It's just us, boy."

"Don't we need a plan?"

Forrest scanned his surroundings and gestured towards the crumpled man in armor, a plan forming in his mind. "He does not require protection anymore. Nikos, put on the armor."

Nikos nodded and began pulling off the various pieces of metal. "I dislike this, but your plan might be the best option. Can you help me put this on?"

Roman checked the man before aiding the wrestler. "You knocked him out, Forrest. I have never seen you be violent."

"If the wizard asks, tell him I am an angry drunk." Forrest smiled with his white teeth at the boy, trying to defuse their anxiety with the appearance of some humor.

32

JAILBREAK

Casemiro leaned against the iron jail cell door. No other rats risked their life that night, and the rain ceased. In a corner without puddles, Laural and Arenton slept.

The wizard spent the time in concentration, attempting to tap into his magic. Which proved to be a perplexing task without his trusted staff, and Casemiro resigned himself to a brief nap after trying in vain to break free. With the first light of dawn cracking through the stone wall, Casemiro woke and recognized the spike of warmth in his breast pocket.

Casemiro withdrew the coin. "Good morning, Roman."

"Casemiro, I lined up several friends ready to enter the keep through the kitchen. Since few people are around at this hour, we might be fortunate and find you without being seen. How do we find you?"

"Our captors put us in the dungeon. The entrance leads off the right side of the hall. Also, watch for my staff. Forrest will recognize it if he spots it."

"Look for us soon."

Pocketing the coin, Casemiro admired the dawn's light filtering through the gaps in the stone. Despite the rainy night, the morning brought hope. In the faint light, the wizard regarded the tattered clothes of Laural, Arenton, and himself. Amidst this predicament, the wizard laughed at caring about clothing.

The laughter disturbed the Princess, and she rolled over to find the wizard standing above her. "Why did you laugh? Do I have a rat on my head?"

"It's nothing. Roman's assembled a crew to help us escape. We should be prepared to leave and ready to run."

"Any ideas on where we escape to if they free us?" Laural jostled her brother to wake the Prince.

"I have an idea, but it needs to happen soon, or we might miss our chance. Wake up your brother, and be ready."

"I'm awake." Arenton took a deep breath as he pulled himself upright, stretching his muscles and eliminating the pops and cracks of bones from having slept on the stone floor overnight. "I thought I only dreamed about being caged. This reality is so dreary."

Casemiro stood by the cell door and monitored the hallway, expecting the crew to arrive quickly after entering the keep. Without warning, a body tumbled down the stairs, sounding like a sack of potatoes hitting the floor. The body notified the prisoners that their rescuers had arrived. Five people rushed into the dungeon, with Forrest in the lead. Behind the man-troll came Roman, Angus the Cooper, Gerard, Ben, and someone dressed as a Cassen soldier. Roman proved himself capable of twisting the arms of many people to aid their cause.

Roman charged to the door. "We arrived, sir. Gerard provided the directions. How do we free you?"

"Move, child." Forrest nudged the boy aside and grabbed the door with his meat hook hands and pulled. The grate broke off the hinges like a child's toy. "Does this work, wizard?"

Arenton viewed the wizard with amusement. "Why didn't you do that?"

Casemiro cast a glare of unseriousness at the Prince before turning to Roman. "My staff?" The wizard longed to hold the wooden device again.

With a downward glance, Roman told the wizard everything. Proceeding without the weapon became the lone choice for the wizard.

"Who's in the armor?" asked Casemiro.

The man raised the visor to reveal the face of Nikos Antaeus. He smiled at the wizard. "Your favorite wrestler."

Gerard stepped up and provided some needed focus and urgency. "Enough chatting. We need to move."

The captives barged through the open grate and followed their rescuers. Nikos took the lead, due to his wearing the Cassen armor, and paused at the top of the stairs to ensure no one blocked their escape through the hall. Once assured of a clear path, Nikos led the group toward the hallway leading back to the kitchen and their escape route from Veritas Keep.

The absence of patrolling guards surprised the wizard, who rarely ventured around the keep at this hour. Their feet created the lone noises within Veritas Keep until the group approached the kitchen.

Nikos guided the party into the kitchen, where the first guard appeared. Seeing a crew escorted through the keep by another Cassen guard gave the man little reason to pause until he caught sight of Forrest. The sight of the unexpected adversary shocked the man. Forrest reacted and blocked the rest of the group from the guard's vision while knocking the man unconscious with a slam of his fist.

Gerard ordered them ahead. "Keep going. The guards begin their rounds at any moment."

Casemiro chuckled inside as the wizard passed the defeated guard. The idea of Forrest turning into a person willing to use his fists humored the wizard.

Not bad for a pacifist. The voice belonged to Quinto. A mental image of the ship in port entered Casemiro's mind.

Casemiro replied with a message he hoped his brother understood. *Hold your ship, Quinto.*

The team continued through the kitchen. Chef Richard stood at the rear door, watching for any danger, and pointed the group to the alcove housing the barrels of wine and ale.

Forrest led the way, peeking out the door to assess the open field behind the keep.

Before the party fled, Roman tugged on Casemiro's cloak. "Sir, I must leave you here. I will cover your tracks from this end. Nikos and Forrest will lead you to safety."

"Thank you, Roman. If this succeeds, the Prince owes you a large reward." The wizard hugged the boy.

As the Prince passed the chef, he acknowledged the aid. "I forgive your debt, Richard."

Chef Richard nodded. "Just come back, my Lord." The chef ironically blocked the exit with an oaken barrel full of a fine vintage from the Cassen brewery.

Gerard chided the group along, maintaining the role of leader for the crew. "Enough talking, folks. Time to go."

"What's the plan?" asked Laural.

Forrest answered, "We plow through the rear gate and run for the village. The Cassen forces fortified the main gate too well for an escape. If we reach the village, several people are prepared to conceal us. Follow Nikos and stay close to him."

The rear gate stood open and unguarded. The team sprinted through the yard of the keep, staying together while exiting through the gate in the stone wall. Forrest covered the rear of the line and Nikos led the way, hoping the charade of the Cassen armor might aid their efforts. Once the team rounded the first corner, their escape was almost derailed as a couple of guards in Cassen armor met the group.

The surprised guards froze when they unknowingly encountered the fugitives and their rescuers. Their hesitation allowed the escapees to split into multiple groups and run past the guards. By the time the guards responded, the escapees reached the open field between Veritas Keep and the village. The guards trailed them and yelled for support from their fellow watchmen at the main gate. The Cassen forces chased the crew down the hill to Lillenhold, not knowing who they pursued.

As part of the plan, the group scattered when the party reached the edge of the village. Bob, Gerard, and Angus darted towards the village's east end to lure a portion of the guards away from the port. Forrest and Nikos led the trio of fugitives into the heart of Lillenhold. Still with a sizable lead, the group of escapees sought cover and hid in an alley between two wooden buildings after taking the first turn into the village. As the group caught their breath, Nikos kept an eye out for chasing guards.

Forrest glanced at the trio still with him. "We freed you from the keep. Any suggestions on a place to take you?"

Casemiro pointed toward the port. "I have connections with a ship we can board if we hurry."

Laural asked, "So you planned on leaving?"

"Can we not do this here?" The wizard looked at the Princess with a perturbed glare but refused to conduct the needed conversation at that moment.

Arenton laughed at the twosome between his deep gasps for breath. "You're acting like a married couple again."

They both turned to the Prince. "Shut up!"

Forrest interrupted the spat to focus the group. "So, to the port then?"

Casemiro nodded, and the group began their mad dash to the sea. Nikos led and weaved the group through alleyways, streaked the fugitives behind buildings, and bustled them through communal areas to avoid any confrontations with the Cassen forces. The group navigated multiple twists and turns until they reached the corner of a wooden hovel, the Portmaster's home and the entrance to the port of Lillenhold.

The group sprinted to the back of the Portmaster's home for their last chance at cover before the final dash. They avoided all obstacles up to that point, but found multiple armed guards stationed at the entrance to the port on high alert. No other path existed to reach their lone opportunity to escape Lillenhold. Once more, it appeared their luck ran its course.

As the group peered around the corner of the Portmaster's hovel, Nikos asked, "Which ship?"

On the far left end of the port, Casemiro spotted the trireme with three grand sails. From this distance, the wizard spied the crew of the Fierce Siren completing the last steps to launch the ship. Their time ran short to escape aboard the vessel.

Nikos determined the plan they needed to follow. "Forrest and I will create a path and a diversion, and you three run to the ship. Do not stop for anything."

Arenton bent over, still gasping from the previous exertion.

The wizard asked, "Can you make it, Your Highness?"

The Prince nodded and waved his agreement, inspiring little confidence he might reach the ship. Arenton glanced back toward Casemiro as a green tinge overtook his face. "What is that stench?"

"The sea." Casemiro turned to Nikos. "I promise to get the Prince on the ship."

Nikos turned to Forrest. "Ready?"

Forrest nodded, and they charged forward with the Cassen armored Nikos at the front. The group moved around the Portmaster's home, but not at a run which might draw unwanted attention. Nikos leading them in the armor proved a sound tactic and allowed the trio of fugitives a few seconds of freedom to approach the port without anyone thinking anything of their movement.

Casemiro and Laural grabbed Arenton and pulled the Prince forward as they maintained their pace to match their protection. The trio all kept their faces turned away from the crowd to prevent anyone from recognizing them. The wizard hoped to avoid too much attention or raising the guard's suspicion as long as possible. Casemiro kept Laural and Arenton a few steps behind their escorts, hoping to avoid the fallout of the impending tussle awaiting them. The wizard relied on Nikos and Forrest to create a distraction, and enabling them to pass by the Cassen forces unnoticed.

As the group approached the port's entrance, the Cassen guards ordered the escapees to stop. Neither Nikos nor Forrest halted their march. The armored officials only realized they were under attack when the duo jumped into the middle of the Cassen forces. Forrest pummeled one soldier to the ground.

The fracas distracted the remaining guards and created an opening along one side of the entrance. This allowed the trio of

Laural, Arenton, and Casemiro to flee from the melee as a crowd of watchers moved in and surrounded the Cassen troops. As the wizard passed, Casemiro spotted Nikos applying a deathdrop trap on one man who crashed through the wood planking of the pier.

Without stopping, Casemiro pushed Laural and Arenton around the crowd drawn to the outburst from the port. The trio wove through the people similar to snakes slithering through a tussle of weeds until they emerged onto the open pier. Casemiro briefly assumed that they reached safety.

A Cassen guard yelled at the trio from behind. "You three, stop!"

"Keep going!" Casemiro pushed the two royal children beyond the rumble. The wizard turned and spotted a troop of armored guards escaping the melee and entering the port's ingress. The ex-prisoners' lead shrank and they lacked the ability to compete with the guards' speed, in their current health.

The wizard needed a diversion but lacked his staff or any other tricks. Casemiro glanced to the side and found a vat of whale oil. Above him hung the still-lit torch used to illuminate the port at night. Casemiro tipped the vat of whale oil, spilling the fatty liquid across the wooden pier and then knocked the torch to the ground. Within seconds, a fiery wall spread across the wooden path and stopped the guards, allowing the wizard and his fellow escapees to flee.

Ahead of Casemiro, the Princess and Prince reached the boat and walked across the gangway with the aid of a crew member. At the end of the pier, the ship loosened its moorings and began floating through the water. Casemiro waved toward the ship and yelled for the Fierce Siren to wait as he closed the distance. The wizard reached the ship and jumped aboard just as the vessel moved beyond the long wooden pier. The wizard landed face first on the boat as the crew retracted the gangway.

Looking back up the pier, Casemiro witnessed Forrest and Nikos evading the guards and retreating into the village. The red-clad guards appeared to focus on putting out the fire instead of chasing the ones who helped the wizard and his friends escape.

Casemiro relaxed, knowing his friends reaching safety created one less worry. The wizard feared what might befall Nikos and Forrest if the guards captured them, assuming the Marquis valued their lives far less than those of his niece and nephew.

A hand landed on the wizard's shoulder and turned him around. The captain of the Fierce Siren greeted the wizard. "You pressed your luck, but I waited as long as possible. Mind telling me what this entails and who boarded my ship?"

A group gathered around the trio of newcomers as Casemiro coughed and captured his breath. "Prince Arenton and Princess Laural, meet my brother, Quinto and the captain of the Fierce Siren."

Quinto huffed and, sensing he needed more of an explanation, dismissed the crew to their assigned stations before the guests relayed any sensitive information. Without asking, Quinto accepted the idea of his ship carrying royalty for some cause his brother believed in.

Once the crew went back to their duties, Quinto turned back to his brother. "Explain to me why the Prince and the Princess of Gaeleos boarded my ship."

Casemiro pulled his brother to the side. "Someone attempted to overthrow the Prince and wished to use them as bait. King Skaranon sails into a trap. We need to find his ship and warn the King."

Quinto's sense of humor disappeared. "Brother, why must you always be involved in these elaborate ordeals? We better leave the port promptly. I appreciate any help you may provide

357

in getting this ship into the bay and open waters. Prince and Princess, if you can row, please jump in and do so."

The wizard grabbed Quinto's shoulder. "I lost my staff in the rush to flee."

Quinto gave Casemiro a disappointed glare. "Wait here." He walked away only to return holding a long wooden staff. "Here, it doesn't feature an iron tip like yours, but I held onto this staff for several years in the event I ever needed it."

Casemiro smiled and hugged his brother to show his appreciation for the staff and the rescue. The wizard's joy prompted the magic to the surface and filled the emptiness of the wizard's soul. With a casual wave, Casemiro used the magical power to generate a breeze to fill the sails. He then cast a spell, forcing the waves to push the boat harder. The jarring shift in the vessel's momentum knocked a gasping Arenton to the deck. With Laural and Casemiro's help, the Prince regained his footing as the ship sailed away from Lillenhold.

Once the crew assured Quinto that the Fierce Siren cleared the port, the captain returned to his trio of stowaways. "You better hope a ship isn't chasing us. Trafficking people, let alone royalty, is not my usual trade."

The Prince answered the comment. "No royal ships sit in port this week. Clear sailing awaits you and your crew."

Quinto pulled his brother to the side. "You're certain this girl is worth it, brother? She appears to be a keeper, but you ask much of me."

Casemiro glared at Quinto. "Not now, please, I beg you."

"Fine, but who will compensate me for saving their blasted hides?"

The wizard smiled as he patted Quinto on the shoulder. "You may ask King Skaranon yourself when we intercept the path of his boat. Once he becomes aware of the problem at Veritas Keep,

I am sure he will reward anyone involved with the rescue of his children."

Quinto smiled at the idea of the ample coin lining his purse. "Fine, but what about you, freeloader?"

Casemiro reached into his pocket, removed a gold coin, and slapped the payment into the palm of his brother's hand.

The captain laughed as he put the coin away. "Who can direct us to the King's vessel?"

The wizard grabbed Arenton. "Prince, do you think you can tell the navigator how to find your father's ship?"

"Most definitely. My father sails through the Bay of Scars along the shores of Gaeleos. He avoids the open waters. They consistently follow the same route, and we can expect to find them by mid-day if their ship stayed on schedule."

Quinto took the Prince to the ship's navigator to plot a course to intercept the King's famous trireme, the Lion's Roar. The man led Arenton to the stern of the ship, where the navigator stood over a map.

Laural stood against the rail, taking in the view, as the port of Lillenhold shrank in the distance. The Princess turned to the wizard as the wind whipped through her dark hair and her green eyes reflected the glistening morning light flashing across the small waves. Her hands slid across the wooden bar until they ran across something odd. "Interesting." Laural's hand rested beside the dedication Casemiro had inscribed into the rail years before.

The wizard smiled at her hesitation. "Funny you should find that. Honestly, I scratched that into the wood right after I got married. But we can talk about it later." Casemiro grabbed the rail to keep his balance as the boat bobbed over the undulating waves. "Forrest and Nikos escaped. The guards became preoccupied with putting out the fire I started."

"I am relieved our friends avoided capture." Laural grabbed the wizard's hands. "Are we safe?"

"Depends on what your father wishes to do, Laural. But I will see this through." In the middle of the night, Casemiro decided he belonged by Laural's side, even if she needed convincing. The wizard's mind remained unchanged now that they escaped from their captors.

Laural nodded, understanding the wizard's intent. "Seems convenient you lined up this ship to leave. Should I be concerned? Or consider us lucky?"

"I ran into Quinto after our argument yesterday. I knew the ship launched at dawn and couldn't come up with any alternative solutions."

Laural crossed her arms. "I have no choice but to believe you." The Princess paused and took on a green cast as her stomach let out a lurching sound.

Casemiro pointed to a set of stairs leading below deck and into the hull of the ship. "You want anything to eat? The crew makes biscuits every morning and carries other concoctions to address seasickness."

"Is it obvious?"

"Yes, you need something to counteract the condition before it starts. Once you know the secrets, seasickness is easy to overcome."

Casemiro extended his hand and headed towards the stairs, but Laural turned her head to lean over the rail. The mal de mer claimed another victim.

33

THE LION'S ROAR

Casemiro overlooked the sea to the west as he stood along the aft rail of the Fierce Siren. Even at a quick clip, the horizon appeared to be never changing. The rhythmic waves and light on the water moved the wizard's soul as he experienced his kinship to the sea. The wizard latched onto an old memory of when he and his brother arrived on this plane and in these very waters.

Next to him stood Laural. The wizard, stunned by how striking the Princess appeared, even with her pale skin from the seasickness, fixed his eyes on her.

"You feeling better?"

Laural nodded, but her pallor reminded him of a ghost. Ginger chews and biscuits settled her stomach and addressed the nausea, for the most part. The Princess maintained her vision on a fixed point in the distance and implemented the other tricks given to her by the crew to combat the affliction.

"Your father's boat approaches. The man in the crow's nest spotted the ship a moment ago." Casemiro glanced skyward to view the duo banners of Gaeleos and an all-white banner, the latter indicating the Fierce Siren undertook a peacekeeping mission.

Keeping her eyes forward, Laural replied to the wizard. "Three months can drastically alter things. It's been that long since I saw my father."

"How long since Arenton saw King Skaranon?"

"My father installed Arenton as the Prince over Lillenhold nine months ago. My brother is so immature, and I wonder about the fragility of his confidence at this stage. I pray this entire affair does not defeat my brother's spirit."

"We can assign blame to multiple parties for this fiasco. I believe only a small portion falls on the Prince's shoulders."

Casemiro turned toward the interior portion of the ship as Arenton and Quinto approached.

Casemiro's brother smiled at the wizard. "Prince Arenton appears to be a sharp lad, but I would not turn my boat over to him. After we meet up with King Skaranon, my ship continues on our route. Will you accompany them or stay aboard, brother?"

Casemiro glanced at Laural before turning his attention back to Quinto.

Quinto laughed. "Say no more. I return to port in three weeks, and hopefully, the Fierce Siren will anchor in Lillenhold."

Arenton extended his hand. "Thank you for your help and if our plans go right, you and your ship are most welcome within the port of Lillenhold. If I return to the throne, your port fees for the next year disappear."

The captain accepted the offer. "Much obliged, Your Highness. My men must prepare to move you to the Lion's Roar once they set anchor. Princess, you enamored me as well."

"Likewise, Captain."

The wizard peered ahead and caught his first glimpse of the Lion's Roar, the flagship of the Gaeleos fleet, and the personal ship of King Skaranon. Dark polished wood reflected the sunlight from the sky and water. The boat hoisted three immense canvas sails on three massive masts, nearly double the height of those on the Fierce Siren. The Lion's Roar, the largest ship Casemiro ever viewed, dwarfed his brother's boat.

Once the Lion's Roar floated alongside the Fierce Siren, the ship dropped anchor to remain stationary on the waves.

A call came from the crow's nest above and signaled the trio to change ships. "Ship to port!"

The Lion's Roar sat alongside the Fierce Siren with ten feet between the two boats. The Captain of the new ship stood at the rail in a tailored uniform. "Why did you hail us?" Several men backed the officer with drawn swords as a threat to anyone contemplating an attempt to hijack the ship.

Quinto responded, "Captain, I carry a couple of things belonging to the great King Skaranon." He pointed to the Prince and Princess.

A man sporting a full black beard and an impressive mane of hair appeared from behind the Captain. King Skaranon stepped to the rail and his eyes opened wide when he spotted the passengers. "Laural and Arenton, what are you doing aboard this ship? Are you hurt?"

Laural smiled at the King, and her father. "No, sir. Quite the opposite. These men provided us safe passage and deserve a handsome reward for their efforts. But if we join you aboard the Lion's Roar, Arenton and I can explain how this came about."

The King glanced behind Laural and stopped his scan of the other ship upon finding a familiar face, one unseen by him in two decades. "By my father's beard, do I see Casemiro the wizard? Even after all this time, I still recognize him instantly."

Casemiro nodded and responded with a courteous reply. "Yes, Your Highness, but perhaps a little less glorified than you remember. I traveled to Lillenhold prior to these ill events unfolding. May I be so honored to join you aboard your ship to discuss the details, and then offer my help?"

Skaranon addressed the ship's crew. "Bring all three aboard, now. And someone prepare a bag of gold for the Fierce Siren's captain." The men got to work and, in a brief time, the trio boarded King Skaranon's personal trireme and waved goodbye to the Fierce Siren, now a heavier ship from the receipt of one hundred gold pieces.

After quick embraces with Laural and Arenton, the King ordered his crew to make their guests at home. "Find them fresh clothes and food. Then I wish to discuss what transpired in Lillenhold. Casemiro, I want you to share every detail with my children adding any other necessary information. What you relay determines my approach for the rest of my trip. Captain, hold position until we understand what awaits the Lion's Roar in Lillenhold."

Once refreshed with clean clothes and warm food, Casemiro relived the long tale to King Skaranon, with occasional clarifications, or additions, by Laural and Arenton. The entire tale shocked the King and at many instances Skaranon exclaimed amazement at the actions of his children and Casemiro and the many others involved in the undertaking.

"Your deductive skills remain top-notch, Casemiro, to figured out all the plans of my adopted brother and Mira Sweet."

"I only figured out their scheme after the fact, hardly anything worth crowing over. But we still lack understanding of what happened between you and Mira Sweet. We believe we pieced it together, but only you know the details."

"Yes, a sorted affair it was. After I rebuffed her advances, he fell under her spell. I endured the criticism to protect my brother from embarrassment when we pushed Mira out of Gaeleos society. But the acts confined my brother to running the keep at Cassenwary. Evidently, the role did not satisfy him. After we rectify this, even though I love my brother dearly, he must pay the price for his deeds."

Casemiro turned his head in thought. "My Lord, how do you rectify this? You sail with one ship while your foe commands an entire garrison and controls Veritas Keep."

Skaranon laughed and shook the desk by pounding it with his hand. "My old friend, I expected a potential problem based on the communication we received. I prepared a show of strength to remind certain people of Arenton serving at my behest in Lillenhold. We filled this ship with two hundred of my best soldiers. The Lion's Roar became a warship in every sense when we left Porthcallis."

The King rose from his chair, extending his hand to warn the others to not leave their seats. Skaranon opened the door to his cabin and yelled for the battalion leader, Captain Weir.

Once Weir arrived, the King gave him his orders. "Develop a battle plan with Arenton. I shall return in a few minutes after passing along the word to the crew to prepare for battle when we reach Lillenhold."

Weir entered the room and began discussing the issues with Arenton. Casemiro and Laural sat beside each other, awkwardly making eye contact, but neither knowing what to do. As the King returned to the conversation, Arenton finished marking a grand piece of paper.

Skaranon asked, "Where did we store a map of Veritas Keep and Lillenhold?"

Weir pointed his thumb at the Prince. "The Prince drew it from memory. The accuracy aligns with my recollection of the village. Apparently, the Prince carries a fine mind for battle mechanics and cartography. You should be proud."

"Always." Skaranon smiled at his son and the Prince blushed.

Laural patted her brother on the back, drawing a smile from Arenton.

The King brought the focus back to the meeting. "So, get on with the plans."

Arenton explained his battle scheme. "Based on what we know of the Cassen forces, we own a two-to-one advantage in soldiers, plus any advantage we gain from citizen additions or enemy dissenters. Two bottlenecks present potential problems for any attack: getting off this ship and entering Veritas Keep through the main gate. So, I propose a different tactic for each."

The Prince directed their attention to a small inlet on the map. "The waters run deep here and allow for anchoring the Lion's Roar close to the shore. The terrain conceals this location from the port, the top turret of Veritas Keep, and anyone else wishing to see our actions. We drop the men from the Lion's Roar and allow the soldiers to approach the keep from the concealed trails in the forest. These trails run up to the rear of the keep's property and provide additional cover. To aid in the ruse, The Lion's Roar enters the port and causes a distraction for the guards at the pier and those watching from Veritas Keep."

King Skaranon nodded. "The plan appears promising if we can drop our soldiers and not raise suspicion. How long is the walk from here to the village?"

Arenton thought about that for a moment. "A two-hour walk at night on the trail, perhaps. It is a little over two miles from the village."

"Do you think we can drop the soldiers quickly to not raise any suspicions?"

"This ship carries four lifeboats. We transport the men to the shore in two trips. The ship won't be visible to the port watchers until we reach this spot." Arenton pointed to a small peninsula extending into the water on the map. Casemiro recognized it as the same spot visible from the Cornelius Inn's dining room.

Casemiro asked, "And what of the main gate of the keep?"

"The delivery entrance for food and other items, including mead from Cassenwary, exists on the keep's rear side, facing the forest trails. The same gate we used for our escape. Even if guarded, with the stealth employed by our advance team, along with it being dark when they reach the point of attack, they should catch our enemy off guard. Plus, the gate is wider and easier to break through than the main gate. Thus, allowing for a quicker entry into the grounds of Veritas Keep."

The King pondered the plan and revisited some details. "When do we arrive at the port?"

"Dusk. Fortunately, very few people work in the keep at this time unless a special event takes place. We do not want to harm any innocents upon our return."

Skaranon glanced at Weir, the battalion leader, for his input. "What do you think?"

"Simple and direct. If things go according to plan, we own the element of surprise. We can rout their forces and win back Veritas Keep."

"Any concerns, son?" asked Skaranon.

"The dragon."

The King and Weir jolted to full awareness. "I thought you said the dragon left Lillenhold, wizard."

Casemiro cut into the conversation. "The dragon should not be an issue. We ended our confrontation on amenable terms. Do not be worried about the creature."

Skaranon scoffed at the words before turning to Arenton. "We must take your word for it, wizard. In fact, if the dragon returns, you take responsibility for the beast." Skaranon walked around the table and embraced the Prince. "Excellent work, son. Now let's make this plan happen, show the kingdom your worth, and send a message that no one should trifle with my family."

Skaranon returned to his seat and dismissed everyone except his family and the wizard. After the others left, the King addressed the wizard. "I wondered where you went, Casemiro. You disappeared after finishing your previous job in my employ."

"Your Highness, a woman and I relocated from Gaeleos to Austeria for a tranquil life. We eventually moved back to Gaeleos, but she passed away five years ago in our modest home in Foxshire. Since then, I wandered from town to town until stumbling upon a request for a wizard in Lillenhold. With my history in the village, I became curious. The position turned into more than your son promised." Casemiro turned his stare toward Arenton.

The Prince blushed and averted his eyes from the wizard.

Skaranon spoke, "My apologies for your beloved, my friend. From personal experience, I understand the difficulty of overcoming such a tragedy. May you find someone else soon."

Laural's head shot up and flashed a glance between Skaranon and Casemiro.

Casemiro took the chance to broach the subject. "Sir, if I may talk in private, I wish to discuss this matter."

Skaranon glanced at Arenton and Laural. Their reactions informed the King of the coming conversation. Skaranon, a wise man, understood what Casemiro wished to say, but still required the wizard to declare his intentions.

The King asked the Prince, "Do you wish to be present?"

"God, no. Please excuse me and call me back to review the battle plan when you're ready."

Skaranon waved him away, and Arenton left the room in a flurry.

The King glared at Laural. "Do you want to tell me, daughter? Or let him?" He pointed to Casemiro. "I noticed the fidgeting between you two and how close you came to touching hands multiple times. It relieves me that you brought this topic before me, and I respect you for doing so and not cavorting behind my back. I frown upon courting a member of the royal family in secret, as such activities often lead to embarrassment for both parties involved. I speak from experience; my own and my children's."

The King smiled at Laural and transitioned into a smirk to indicate his approval of the choice.

Laural sat at full height and smiled back at the King. "Father, at first, I wondered if my interest in Casemiro rested in childhood naivete, but it goes beyond that. The relationship started well, but we must address some misunderstandings. Would you call this a fair summary, Casemiro?"

The wizard nodded at Laural to confirm her assertion and maintained a calm demeanor in front of Skaranon. Even though he experienced something new in his emotions, anxiousness. He wrung his hands, awaiting the blessing from the King.

The Princess continued with a smile across her face. "And father, I recognize the age difference but, if I recall correctly, you are a few years older than your current wife."

Skaranon pushed away from the desk, blinking at the resolve and abruptness of his daughter. Perhaps Laural owned a stronger will than Casemiro realized. From the wizard's perspective, the Princess forced her father, the mighty King of Gaeleos, to relent.

The King turned to Casemiro. "Anything to add?"

Casemiro answered the question. "Once we resolve these other matters, we wish to explore the relationship and then determine our future. Do you agree, Princess?" Casemiro turned to Laural.

"Yes!" she answered without hesitation.

Across the desk, the King stood. "I should warn you, wizard, dissuading my daughter from something she sets her mind to is nigh impossible. So, good luck and I bless you. But I own lofty expectations and hope this remains uncontroversial. Are we agreed, wizard?"

"Yes, great King Skaranon and thank you." Casemiro smiled at Laural, and the Princess grabbed the wizard's hand.

"Wonderful. Now the two of you exit my cabin. I must prepare to win back this annoying little village. I only wish there was a way to establish communication with the people of Lillenhold to arrange some type of cooperation."

Casemiro smiled at the King and pulled a silver coin from his pocket. "Actually, your Majesty, I can help with that request."

34

RETURN TO LILLENHOLD

Casemiro and Laural stood at the rail as Arenton coordinated deploying the forces from the Lion's Roar to the shore. Over a half hour, each lifeboat went on two trips while the Lion's Roar remained anchored. The ship remained out of view from the port of Lillenhold, so their actions remained hidden from anyone in the village. Once the empty lifeboats returned to the ship, the Lion's Roar raised its anchor and the King's personal trireme floated towards their next destination.

Skaranon smiled at the Prince. "You designed the plan well, my son. If only your mother were here instead of at the palace in Porthcallis. Your performance would delight her."

"Thank you. Your compliments warm my heart. I believe you overlook my cleverness. One day, I hope to impress you."

Casemiro studied the Prince's face, hoping the younger man's sneer represented youthful arrogance and not potential treachery. The wizard grappled with the notion of the young man falling under Oleander's manipulative tactics. Then he tossed away the thought as idle speculation with no substantive evidence.

Skaranon and Arenton settled into a comfortable spot on the Lion's Roar to monitor the approach towards the port of Lillenhold. Casemiro remained at the boat's port side, watching until the last soldier disappeared from view. The troops worked their way into the woods to begin their sneak attack on Veritas Keep. Casemiro walked to the side of King Skaranon as the Lion's Roar moved back into the predominant sailing channel.

A new third sail with a crest of Gaeleos; a purple crown sat atop an axe and a drawn bow with a nocked arrow across the yellow canvas rolled up the mast.

If the King wished to draw the village's attention and that of Veritas Keep from the stealthy attack coming from behind, this sail might do the trick.

The King draped his most regal cloak over himself and stood tall at the bow of the ship. Skaranon appeared to be the tallest man on the ship, standing half a foot taller than the wizard. The King's dark hair whipped in the breeze, and he steeled himself for the danger ahead.

With the King stood his dutiful children, Laural and Arenton, while Casemiro stood a step behind. Laural reached out for Casemiro's hand, and the wizard accepted. Arenton held the map of Lillenhold and Veritas Keep, studying the document one more time before the ship floated into the port. The Prince and his father reviewed the plan one last time with the soldiers aboard the ship, who accepted their duty of a decoy.

The King asked the wizard, "Are your friends ready, Casemiro?"

Casemiro withdrew his coin and reached out to Roman.

"We stand ready, Casemiro."

Casemiro held no doubts that Roman, and the others, would achieve the goals put before them by the King.

"We cleared most of the guards from the port. You should have seen Forrest in action."

Casemiro chuckled at the image of the troll-man in a fight. "Excellent. We dock in the next few minutes. Remain hidden until our arrival."

"I don't think remaining hidden is possible."

"What do you mean?"

"That will become apparent in a moment, sir. I think I see a large yellow sail. Welcome back to Lillenhold."

Casemiro tucked away the coin, and the King nodded his approval, having overheard the conversation. Skaranon returned his stare toward the front of the ship, expecting an undesirable greeting from his adopted brother.

"So, you trust these people, wizard?" Skaranon scratched his chin as if a doubt surfaced.

"With my life, your majesty."

Laural answered as well. "They proved themselves, father."

"Very well. Then we put our faith in them once more." The King winced, Skaranon's eyes squinting at the setting sun and the shimmering water. "It appears our arrival received the exact type of response we discussed, but I find no guardsmen awaiting our ship."

"They said they would surprise us, my King."

Skaranon tapped the wizard on the shoulder. "You seem to lack a weapon for close combat." The King extended a scabbard containing a sword to Casemiro. "The men retrieved one from below. Do you remember how to wield one of these?"

"I left my saber in Veritas Keep and miss the blade hanging from my side. I thank you for the use of the weapon and hope it remains only ceremonial. If I must draw a blade, then true disaster looms."

The King commanded the captain of the ship. "Drop anchor when we reach the dock, but hold off on lowering the ramp. I wish to address the people in the port before any confrontation occurs."

The King received a response of "Aye, aye!"

As the ship entered the port, Skaranon went to the bow of the boat and Roman's comment struck home. Waiting on the pier and bleeding into the village gathered a crowd of supporters who roared in response to the King waving his hand. No one ever numbered the inhabitants of the village, but one might wager everyone but the invalid stood in the port of Lillenhold awaiting their ruler.

Skaranon waved at the people and grabbed the rail as the ship drifted to the dock's edge. The King's attention shifted to the crowd as the anchor plunged into the water and the crew secured the boat to the mooring posts. The limited number of Cassen soldiers, clad in red armor, pushed their way to the front of the crowd.

Skaranon smirked at the hopelessly outnumbered four men and began the speech to the crowd. "Loyal villagers of Lillenhold, I address you as your King. I return to find someone attempting to usurp my reign. The scoundrel is my brother, the Marquis of Cassen. He attacked Veritas Keep and forced my son, daughter, and those loyal to them to evacuate. The Marquis' interest lies in ruling your village, not in your well-being. So, before my forces leave this ship, I ask those aligned with the Marquis to rethink your position and join our forces today. I offer no judgment, just a warning that the Marquis misled you through deception regarding the actual situation here. In five minutes, my men walk from this ship to Veritas Keep and will defeat any standing in their way. I implore you to make a decision that leads to less violence."

The King stepped back from the rail while Casemiro remained at the front of the ship to witness the Cassen guardsmen's struggle. The guards appeared flummoxed by the crowd and became belligerent. A brief tussle occurred, and the people pushed the small faction into the water. The men swam to a less crowded pier and emerged from the water with waterlogged armor. The guards departed from the port to inform those in Veritas Keep about the impending attack from the Lion's Roar.

Casemiro informed the King after turning away from the melee. "Bloodshed will not mar our entry into Lillenhold. Your strategy incited the people, causing the few loyal soldiers to Cassen to leave the port."

The King nodded. "I hoped for such an outcome." Skaranon faced the ship's captain. "Let's go ashore. Lower the gangway."

At the sight of the wooden plank landing on the pier, the citizens of the Lillenhold gave an approving roar that filled the air that undoubtedly traveled to Veritas Keep on the breeze. The cheer foretold a coming battle and warned the Marquis to prepare. All remaining soldiers aboard the vessel marched to the shore. The entourage of Skaranon's closest associates, including the Prince, the Princess, and Casemiro, walked onto the pier, and a path cleared for King Skaranon to walk through the village.

Forrest, Roman, and Nikos emerged from the crowd at the end of the pier and hoped to rejoin Casemiro and the Princess in their adventure. A round of handshakes, hugs, and embraces with Casemiro, Laural, and Arenton occurred to show the camaraderie between the group. The King turned his attention to the three newcomers to the central squad.

Skaranon recognized the troll-man first. "Forrest, it has been too long since we talked. After a brief discussion with my children, we need to talk about past events and how this community treated you. I owe you a great debt for the way you protected my children." The King extended his hand as a gesture of goodwill.

Forrest pushed the hand away and hugged the King, and the crowd cheered. "It is I who owe you a lifetime of gratitude. You allowed me to join this community instead of making me an outcast. I experienced challenging times, but Lillenhold became a home." Releasing the King, Forrest kneeled beside the wizard, tears of happiness falling from his eyes onto the wooden surface.

Casemiro eyed Raquel, the waitress, standing behind Forrest with a beaming smile across her face, which told the story as her hand caressed the troll-man's shoulder.

The King thanked Nikos and Roman for their aid and service. The focus then returned to the march toward Veritas Keep. Once their entourage broke through the enormous crowd at the Port, the King and his party advanced towards the stronghold atop the hill.

The march reached the meadow separating Lillenhold from the main gate of Veritas Keep and the King stopped. Skaranon requested an update on the status of the other battalion approaching from the forest in waning daylight. The King sent two scouts around the keep. In the meantime, he consulted with Arenton and his core council on the next steps.

"Do you believe we can secure the exterior of the keep, Arenton?"

"Father, from here it appears no Cassen troops man the main gate. I would be cautious, but I believe we can. If they moved their forces inside the stone walls of the keep, an ambush might await us. We need the scouting reports before we decide."

Skaranon checked with the wizard for his opinion, and Casemiro nodded in agreement.

The nervous energy of the crowd grew as they waited. After thirty minutes, the scouts returned with an excellent report. Troops from the forest entered and secured the keep's exterior. Every entry point into the walls of Veritas Keep appeared secure, and the approach by King Skaranon proceeded.

After the news spread, the crowd of people walked toward the main gate of the keep, with Skaranon leading the village's citizenry. When they reached the stronghold, Commander Weir met King Skaranon with a smile.

"My Lord, we secured the exterior portions of Veritas Keep. During our infiltration, the enemy shut themselves into the primary structure. We estimate under fifty soldiers still align themselves with the Marquis, including a few other men and women. Once we gain access to the structure, we plan to make quick work of them. To be prepared, we took a tree from the property for use as a battering ram. We suffered no injuries or casualties during the expedition."

The King gave Weir a pat on the shoulder. "Well done. Now, we must end this. Let's establish a base camp outside the building and regroup before the direct assault."

Over several minutes, the soldiers and populace filtered toward Veritas Keep's garden. Before the entire crowd attempted to enter the garden, the King addressed the mass of people. "Very commendable that none of you lost any blood. I cannot promise this good fortune will continue once we enter those walls. I hope for a positive outcome, but many may perish. I make no promises on your life if you go into battle. If you wish to avoid fighting, leave for your homes now. I only hold my soldiers to their vow, the rest of you may leave. Now, to Veritas Keep."

The brief speech led to an enormous mass of people leaving and heading home. The King's soldiers remained and stood alongside another fifty individuals joining from the populace. Casemiro noted Gerard, Ben, and Angus amongst the crowd. The group readied to attack the keep with the King leading the charge.

Then the surprise occurred, and the traitors sprang from the doors of Veritas Keep as a unified force and caught the forces of Skaranon unprepared. The attackers totaled forty strong and formed a wedge intended to drive a hole through the King's forces. Weir, Skaranon's battalion leader, shielded the King but suffered a wound in the initial attack.

Casemiro pulled Laural and Arenton away to avoid the assault. Forrest and Nikos ducked the initial charge but re-engaged after the wedge cleared their location. Though a sound strategy by the traitors, the larger numbers of the King's forces proved too difficult to overcome. The skilled soldiers absorbed the sudden attack and responded with a disciplined defense. Once the enemy's wedge lost momentum, the battle splintered into smaller fragments across the grounds, leading to numerous small bouts with one Cassen soldier against two or more of the King's loyal troops.

Amid the battle, the wizard spied a small group trying to flee from the keep: the Marquis and his three children. Mira Sweet's absence struck the wizard as odd, but Casemiro took action to prevent their escape. Casemiro grabbed Laural and Arenton and the trio chased down the quartet of blonde hoodlums racing to exit the grounds. Casemiro avoided bodies along the way to cut off the traitors' escape. Once they reached their foes, Casemiro stood against the opposition, with Laural and Arenton flanking him.

The triplets formed a barrier in front of the Marquis, who quivered in fear behind them. The trio were intent on busting through the wall of their enemies. The two crews exchanged no words and began the fight. Arenton struck first by hitting Heenan on the head with the butt of his sword and rendered the counselor unconscious. "I finally shut you up, Heenan!"

Sweet charged Casemiro. The wizard swung his brother's staff, which Sweet avoided with a duck, but left himself open to another attack. The wizard stomped on top of his enemy's foot with his brother's staff, then put Sweet in a front facelock and dropped him to the ground face first. The wizard whispered in Sweet's ear. "It's not all about showmanship, Harley."

Laural squared up Oleander and assumed a fighting stance. The florist motioned for the Princess to attack and Laural unsheathed her knives and smiled. "It's about time a woman in this town showed she was willing to fight."

Oleander whipped a leg at Laural, which the Princess caught against her side and absorbed the blow. Though the strike knocked the air from the Princess, Laural refused to let go. The Princess adjusted her stance and stabbed the knee with a blade from her left hand. Laural fell to the ground and forced her weight on the opponent's leg, bending the knee at an awkward angle. Oleander screamed in pain after something snapped in her knee. Laural released the injured appendage and stood over her foe. "You deserve more for messing with my brother and my friends, bitch." She kicked the florist in the jaw and knocked Oleander unconscious.

Arenton and Casemiro raced to grab hold of the Marquis and held him in place as they waited for the fighting to stop. Several fights concluded across the field: Forrest stood over a fallen Paul Perriman; Nikos dragged Otto Schwartz to the side of the field,

Ben, Roman, and Angus bested other Cassen guards. In most cases, the forces of King Skaranon prevailed in the small skirmishes across the grounds.

With victory nearly assured, Skaranon and Weir moved across the battlefield to Casemiro's location to confront the King's adopted kin. "I cannot contain my disappointment, brother. What will I do with you?"

The Marquis laughed. "Oh, Skaranon, you will do nothing with me. I will win this day. In fact, my victory arrives as we speak."

Out of nowhere, a roar filled the sky, and the winds picked up. The breeze followed a distinct and familiar rhythm for those who previously experienced the sensation. An orange flame engulfed the field of battle, causing devastation for many combatants as others raced to find protection. The dragon landed in the center of the garden and shook the ground.

The magical energy rose inside Casemiro. It piqued so fast the wizard became dizzy and fell to the ground. The rush of power overwhelmed him, but when Casemiro's senses recalibrated, the wizard understood what the return of his power meant. This was his time to prove himself and fulfill his destiny.

The Marquis yelled. "I think you forgot a key factor in this battle, Skaranon!"

The tide of the battle turned with the monolithic monster's arrival. Defeat now stood in the middle of Veritas Keep in the form of the dragon named Ofani'r.

Casemiro pulled himself to his feet and focused on the dragon. The wizard found the missing Mira Sweet sitting atop the beast, holding Casemiro's staff. The woman cackled loud enough to fill the air. Casemiro's mind reached out to the dragon, attempting to connect with the beast.

The wizard found the soul of the beast, scared and not in control of its actions. Panic and frustration bubbled within the beast as it wished for freedom. Ofani'r's yellow sclera featured streaks of red from busted blood vessels as the dragon glared in confusion at the wizard. The strain overwhelmed the creature's body as the dragon's muscles twitched from the pain in its mind and its body.

Casemiro found Mira manipulating the most potent weapon in all Gaeleos to her will through the use of the wizard's staff. He felt the agony of the dragon through their connection. The wizard feared they lost everything by falling into this trap. Then the dragon turned its full attention to him. An orange glow erupted from the beast's throat and blasted towards Casemiro with no warning.

35

CREATURES OF MAGIC

Casemiro and Quinto arrived from a higher place, a location filled with creatures of magic. Neither of the brothers dwelled on their beginnings on this plane, the magnificent events and miraculous victories, tales to live through time, and lore to be relieved by thousands over flagons of ale. All of their life determined for them by a higher power.

But then their lives varied from the path of a predestined life. The brothers became human in almost every conceivable way, with one last notable exception. The line between magical and human became blurred for Casemiro, and he attempted to claim both, not knowing this prevented him from having either.

This realization became clear the second Ofani'r's flaming breath surrounded the wizard. In that isolated instant, the perspective Casemiro desired had arrived, and he understood where he lost direction so long ago. The wizard aimed for the greatest of both worlds, but his life became a disaster. Casemiro now understood he owned one last chance to choose his path. He now knew a choice had to be made.

Somehow still alive after the impact from the fiery blast, Casemiro found himself in even greater danger, and confronted by a deranged witch and a possessed dragon. Whatever magical abilities the wizard gained from his connection with the dragon saved him. Casemiro opened his eyes and scanned the surrounding area. Laural and Forrest stood nearby with fear etched across their faces. Casemiro understood that loyalty, more than common sense, drove his friend's decision to remain at his side.

Casemiro rose and brushed the dirt and dust from his cloak and turned to those same supporters. "Whatever happens, stay behind me." The wizard approached the dragon and Mira Sweet, knowing he would win the battle.

As the wizard neared the beast, something from within the dragon called to the wizard. Casemiro accepted the primal connection to Ofani'r and opened his spirit to the dragon, an experience unlike anything the wizard lived through before. The dragon's soul searched for a conduit and found a lifeline with the wizard.

The wizard finally and fully accepted his role as a creature of magic. Casemiro opened the gateway and allowed the magical power of the dragon to fill his spirit. The unchecked power swept away the emotions and grief attached to the death of Chantal. Casemiro allowed the weighted blanket of life to be lifted, which freed Casemiro to be the creature of magic his creator always intended. His spirit now enjoyed a blank canvas onto which he could now paint the future of his life, not a pre-destined existence formed by another hand.

In the moment, the wizard's connection to the beast grew. He experienced the dragon's fear of not being in control and reveled in the anger towards the woman who dared to control the magical beast. Casemiro beat against the mystical shield around the dragon's soul, but the barrier held fast.

Casemiro opened his eyes, undeterred, and sneered at Mira, the cause of the dragon's plight. "What did you do to him?"

"Nothing you did not already do, wizard. I found your staff and connected to the power within. I tapped into the magic and discovered the connection to this lovely beast. Your power allowed me to seize control of the dragon. This dragon ensures our plans succeed and our kingdom grows. None can stand in our way, including my beloved's brother. You, and everyone else, shall bow to me and my children." Mira laughed and held the staff above her, calling forth a spell that sent lightning across the battlefield.

Casemiro stepped closer to the dragon. Heat radiated from the beast and the oppression of Ofani'r's brimstone breath almost overwhelmed the wizard's physical form. As the wizard drew closer, the power within grew as the connection between the creatures of magic went to a far deeper and more fundamental level. Casemiro's power grew strong enough that his brother's staff became unnecessary, and he tossed it aside. The magic dripped from him, almost as thick as the sweat rolling off Casemiro's body.

The wizard reached out to the beast, hoping to communicate with Ofani'r's mind. Ofani'r stared at the wizard, pleading for freedom from the torture of this possession, the unfamiliar magic, and a voice of pure evil filling its brain and trapping its soul. The dragon craved liberation from the evil, whether it be freedom or death. Casemiro still held back from relinquishing himself to the complete control of the unbridled magic.

The wizard reached out and touched the tip of the dragon's snout. "I will release you, my friend."

Casemiro launched his mind back into the physical arena and opened his eyes which glowed with the light of a thousand fires.

Mira waited for the wizard and put up another shield and sent her own magical blasts toward Casemiro.

Casemiro waved the blows aside like cobwebs and slipped beneath Mira's defenses, drawing close enough to engulf her magical aura from harming the others on the battlefield.

The witch sensed the dragon slipping from her manipulation but failed to recognize she had already lost. "You dare to wrest control from me? Fool!" Mira spent the remainder of her energy in an effort to eliminate any rivals to her domination. She waved the staff, pointing the weapon at the soldiers across the field. "Burn them! Destroy them!"

Casemiro sensed the dragon succumbing to the demand and glimpsed Laural and Forrest out of the corner of his eyes. The reaction came, and the wizard's emotions erupted to protect those he cared for most and everyone else in Veritas Keep. The wizard pulled on the power from the dragon and his untapped resources, overloading his body with magical energy.

"No!" The wizard yelled an incantation. "Tarian! Tarian! Tarian!"

The dragon launched a fireball the size of a horse at the wizard. The blast stopped in mid-air as golden strands of magic formed a dome above the wizard. The magical structure sustained itself until the fire from the dragon died from a lack of oxygen. He knew the time to end this battle had arrived.

Without a pause, Mira prompted the dragon to fire another bolt at the wizard. Casemiro sensed Mira's desperation as she failed to maintain her control over Ofani'r. Out of instinct,

Casemiro retained the mystical shield. The magical dome held once more, but Casemiro weakened as he reached the limits of what a human body found manageable. The world froze in that second.

Casemiro realized he failed to fully embrace the ramifications of becoming a man with desires, loves, and friends. The wizard's thoughts drifted back to Laural and his new friends in Lillenhold, a human life. Casemiro lost his focus and the dragon's blast shattered the shield and sent the wizard, and those around him, flying across the field.

After such a violent attack, even Mira and the dragon required a moment to regain their bearings. In that moment, Casemiro took in the surrounding scene to find Forrest and Laural laying on the ground beside him. In the distance, Casemiro viewed a screaming Arenton and Skaranon drowned out by the rest of the din of battle. The wizard feared the worst and the wizard's emotions overcame him. Casemiro lost control and exposed himself to the raw power of the magic once more and restored the connection to the dragon. The energy surged through him stronger than before, but he was ready to end this. He allowed the magic to take control.

The energy supercharged his senses. The wizard registered Laural's breathing and the pulse in her neck. He picked up the same vital signs from Forrest's body. Knowing they remained alive, the wizard walked forward with one intention: to protect the people he loved. Even if the result meant his death.

The wizard radiated energy, covering everything around him in golden light as he approached the witch. "I offer you a final warning, Mira!"

The magic raised the wizard's awareness of everything around him and he connected to the dragon's mind.

The dragon's eyes shifted to the wizard once more. *Help me!*

Another thought drifted into Casemiro's mind. *Finish the battle, brother.*

Casemiro stopped everything around him as if the world paused for a heartbeat. The wizard passed a thought through the magical connection to the dragon. *I will end this now.*

Mira ordered the dragon to strike once again. The beast lacked a choice in the matter, but the wizard endured the monster's punishing blast and his magical shield held strong as the power started to consume him.

Casemiro turned his full power towards Mira. "My power exceeds yours, witch."

Mira yelled at the wizard above the din of the battle. "I carry your staff. You cannot resist me. You fool of a wizard are merely a man."

Casemiro's eyes glowed in the darkness as he gave himself over to his true nature, a creature of pure magic. The wizard absorbed the flames and every ounce of surrounding magic, including his shield. His body flashed with a magical light. The wizard extended his arms as the magic rested in the palms of his two hands.

"Not just a man. You lack understanding of my entire being, woman. Let me show you who I truly am."

Casemiro opened his mind to Mira and flooded the witch with the images of his creation, his life, his pure nature, and his destined victories. Within the onslaught, the wizard sensed Mira's feeble attempt to fight him off. Casemiro waved the effort away like a gnat and the witch succumbed as her spirit snapped. He sensed the life leaving her body.

"You are one of the five?" The feeble question escaped the lips of the desperate witch before she relinquished her hold on this life.

Casemiro glared at Mira. "No longer. But a creature of magic that you should fear. Now, this is finished." The wizard closed his eyes and said one more word in a whispered tone. "Chwyth."

Every bit of the energy Casemiro absorbed launched from his hands and attacked the woman, and the blast caught Ofani'r in its wake. The air grew still before a thunderclap echoed through the sky. Pressure from the blast and the resulting wind blew across the field of battle, knocking anyone standing off their feet. When the energy left his body, Casemiro fell to his knees, his hands smoldered, and smoke rose from the wizard's eyes. All his magical energy released with one blow at the woman.

Then, everything turned silent, and the breeze died. Casemiro scrutinized his foes through fog-filled eyes and found his friends in the moonlight shining across the field. Laural remained behind him, clutching his ankle, squeezing it to tell him she lived.

Casemiro collapsed beside the Princess, reaching out to hold Laural. "Are you safe?"

Laural smiled at the wizard. "I am fine. Where did that come from?"

The wizard paused; aware he must reveal every unspoken truth. "Can I tell you later?"

"I think so. But do not do this ever again."

Casemiro laughed and embraced the pain across his body, a beloved sign of his humanity. "I won't."

Laural grabbed the wizard's hand and squeezed, bringing back his focus through the pain of his burns. "I need to tell you something."

"Me too. I love you, Laural."

The tears filled Laural's eyes. "I know."

They laid in silence until a groan of agony snapped them back to reality. Casemiro sat up and found Forrest working to stand. Seeing his friend reminded the wizard of the unfinished job before him. The wizard stood and walked toward Mira Sweet, needing to verify the blast incapacitated the witch.

The crone lay on the ground motionless as the smoke and vapors drifted skyward and cleared the battlefield. The blast broke her body and next to the witch laid the remnants of Casemiro's staff, shattered into multiple pieces and beyond repair. The wizard kneeled and confirmed Mira's death.

Casemiro then turned his attention to the enormous dragon sprawled across the ground. The animal's breathing seemed shallow, and several gashes in the beast's plated armor bled onto the ground below, hissing and bubbling as the fluid destroyed anything it touched until the dirt absorbed the liquid.

Casemiro approached the dragon, still maintaining a connection that drifted ever so slowly away as the dragon's life force faded. The wizard stood by Ofani'r's face, meeting the beast's drifting eyes and cupping the jaw of the dragon.

"Is it finished, wizard?" asked Ofani'r.

"Yes, she cannot control you. I freed you once again."

A smoldering breath escaped, and brimstone filled the air. "Thank you. The blast proved more than even I could absorb." The dragon coughed and smoke billowed from its mouth, but the wizard remained at Ofani'r's side. "I require a favor of you, wizard, before I die."

"Just ask, my friend."

"Use my essence. Absorb my power and use it to right some wrongs in this world."

Casemiro closed his eyes, sensing the dragon's power leaving its soul and searching for a new home. The wizard reached out, touching the drifting and unseen aether. The dragon's power flowed into his body, allowing the wizard to sense countless things. His injuries and burns healed themselves as Casemiro grasped the thoughts of the individuals in the field and Veritas Keep. His mind drifted to the mystical plane, and he viewed his past and understood once again his true personage. Not only an intellectual understanding, but a knowledge permeating Casemiro's existence on every level.

The wizard became a creature of pure magic once more. Casemiro's glowing eyes scanned every plane of existence. He hovered above his brother, Quinto, on the Fierce Siren as the ship bounced over the ocean's waves. Casemiro experienced his entire lifetime with Chantal in one moment. His attempt to balance being a man and a magical creature left his life in tatters. Casemiro experienced the reasons his life turned to ruins once more.

Casemiro glimpsed a potential future where he accepted this fate and became the creature of magic his creator destined him to become. The image provided a gloriousness in which the wizard basked, and his imagination went beyond explanation to a spectacular end. But emptiness still engulfed Casemiro's soul, as if he desired more than this glorious, pre-destined path.

Casemiro's mind hovered above his body, looking at the frontline and the people of Lillenhold, his enemies, and his friends. The wizard picked up stray thoughts from across the battlefield from everyone. Laural, Skaranon, and Arenton projected images, ideas, memories, and feelings. For a second, the wizard focused on Arenton and found something amiss, but was too quick to understand it all. Casemiro turned his attention to Laural, the woman who terrified him. Casemiro sought more than his predestined life, but to accept it meant he must release his fear and grief.

Casemiro now understood the necessary choice for this life, for his life. For too long, he denied living his predetermined destiny and also the life of a normal human. Fate now presented the chance to embrace his destiny and use the power given to him to fulfill his creator's path. Or the opportunity to pursue a different path, embracing something new and equally grand and daunting. Casemiro might reject his own identity and destiny and seek something different and unrelated to his purpose and presence on this plane. A path filled with the chances of failure and fear stood against a path of safety and untold greatness.

Casemiro became fixated on fear, and its partners grief and guilt. They controlled him for years and the chance to avoid them for a lifetime appeared before him. The safe choice resolved those issues. A fearless life called to him and Casemiro welcomed the life offered. Casemiro almost gave in to the craving.

A familiar voice entered his mind. *Don't allow fear to dictate your decision, brother.*

The wizard opened his eyes and peered at the dragon. "I can use your essence, but I cannot accept this gift, my friend. I choose a different path."

"I understand, Casemiro. Goodbye." The dragon's eyes closed one final time and Ofani'r's spirit left the physical plane.

Casemiro allowed the magic to leave his body, and it moved around him to bathe and settle in the grounds of Veritas Keep. The magic returned to its home, the earth. The wizard received a last vision of a future filled with wonderful blessings for the village from the dragon's essence imbuing this sacred ground. A genuine gift from the nearly omniscient power he held momentarily.

Without pause, Casemiro withdrew the sword provided by Skaranon and pressed the blade against the frame of the dragon. He found the perfect spot to cut and stabbed the blade into the beast's hide, piercing the dragon's heart. Casemiro waited for the organ to stop beating and then, for several minutes, sliced and cut his way to Ofani'r's heart. Casemiro withdrew the piece of muscle from the beast and held it aloft with the cold blood draining down his arms. Now exposed to the air, the dragonheart crystalized in his hands to form a globe-shaped red jewel three feet in diameter. Casemiro dropped to his knees under the weight of the gemstone and wept for the dragon and its sacrifice, knowing what the act meant for the future of Lillenhold, and for him.

The remaining people on the battlefield moved away from a motionless Casemiro, creating space around the wizard. Skaranon's men continued with their duties and gathered the remaining rebels. Others mingled back and forth to determine the casualties of the battle. But all, except one, avoided the bodies of the dragon and the wizard.

Laural approached Casemiro and sat next to him. The Princess embraced him for several moments before asking the question. "What happened?"

Casemiro's attention snapped back to this reality. "I chose to keep this life instead of pursuing another." He turned and grabbed the Princess and held her close. Then Casemiro kissed Laural, not caring that the magic left him or that dragon's blood covered him. She didn't mind either.

The wizard then scanned the surrounding area, noting the carnage and the death from the battle. Casemiro cried tears of relief, anger, joy, and sadness all at once. Every emotion escaped from him, cleaning the wizard's spirit of the burdens and fears he brought with him to Lillenhold a week before. With a clean slate, Casemiro began this human, and only human, life.

36

AN END TO BEGIN

Three weeks passed since the battle. It took each of those days to clear the bodies, remove the dragon carcass, conduct the funerals, repair the grounds, and try those guilty of treason. The event took place twenty-one days ago, yet what happened remained fresh in the memories of many. No one in the village emerged unaffected by the events within Veritas Keep. King Skaranon set this day aside to commemorate the sacrifices from three weeks prior and commence the fantastic future destined to come.

With heavy hearts and exhausted bodies, the people of Lillenhold packed into the garden of Veritas Keep searching for a signal of life returning to normal. They expected a burnt wasteland as it appeared three weeks before. Instead, the grounds welcomed everyone with softer grass and the garden crops already sprouting, a renewal of nature and an uplifting of their spirits. The miracles of Lillenhold had begun.

Casemiro stood next to King Skaranon in front of the crowd, with Arenton and Laural on the other side. The wizard monitored the people shuffling around the vast garden, searching for a place to stand. With the King calling a village-wide meeting, the people hoped for some exciting announcements.

The King turned to Casemiro and Arenton. "It appears the people are ready to start. Are you?"

They each responded with subtle, but quick, nods.

The King raised his hands to signal the start of the festivities and the villagers stood at attention, hanging on Skaranon's every word.

"Ladies and gentlemen of Lillenhold, I come before you today to commemorate the events which occurred a mere three weeks ago on this spot. Our brave people, soldiers, and leaders defeated an uprising. We stood arm in arm against an evil threatening each of us. Many acted with swords and fists, others with their soul and spirit. Many fought other men, but some fought unimaginable creatures and menaces."

The King glanced at Casemiro, who stood still to avoid drawing any unwanted attention.

"Those who fought and died showed mettle and bravery to be remembered for generations. Forty-seven of our fellow citizens fell on this ground twenty-one days ago. Each deserves our respect and recognition as they battled the greatest of enemies.

"On this spot where I stand, a witch attempted to destroy us by commanding a dragon. But our own Casemiro defeated her and released the beast from her control. Then, through his mercy, allowed the beast to die free of evil's influence. The dragon's death released the magic which led to the abundant growth of grass and crops in the garden, signifying the blessing bestowed on this ground."

The King stepped aside to reveal a six-foot tall black rock statue. "To commemorate the moment, I commissioned a memorial plinth to honor the fallen and our ongoing blessings. For ornamental reasons, a replica of the dragonstone sits atop. The key aspect of this monument rest on the lower half. The stone bears the names of all those who sacrificed themselves that day. By royal decree, each year on this date, the ruling dignitary of Veritas Keep shall read these names aloud to serve as a permanent reminder of their dedication to this village."

The King then read each name aloud for everyone to acknowledge the heroes. The audience applauded loudly for several moments after he finished the list. Once the applause dwindled, the King held his hands aloft again to request silence.

"This statue represents what we value and celebrate. Today, I have many exciting announcements to celebrate. This morning, Prince Arenton and I appointed a new Captain of the Guard. Forthwith, Nikos Antaeus serves as the captain of my son's soldiers, and I task him to protect the lands of Veritas Keep and Lillenhold. Congratulations on the honor, Nikos."

Another round of cheers rumbled through the audience.

The King continued his speech. "Also, because of its popularity, my son, Prince Arenton, shall continue the practice of the Extravaganza annually to mark the date of this historic battle. To help facilitate the event, the crown will invest in the community by training new wrestlers. The current Golden Dragon Champion, Forrest, and Nikos Antaeus will train those who meet the requirements. If you meet these requirements, you may become part of the Guard and receive a full commission and pay for your regular duties."

The people yelled in exuberance once more.

"Last, I wish to formally announce the intended engagement of my wonderful daughter, Laural, to a hero within our community, Casemiro. A date for the ceremony has not been determined but will be communicated soon. I hope each of you is as happy for them as I am."

The King hugged his daughter and shook Casemiro's hand, and the crowd erupted with a cheer. After a fleeting period of additional pomp and circumstance, the crowd dwindled, leaving Skaranon, his children, and Casemiro alone on the stage.

Skaranon began the process of saying goodbye. "I must return to Porthcallis and leave within the hour. I wish to tell you how proud I am for managing everything over the last few weeks. Arenton, I am confident you will be an excellent Prince for these people. Laural, you are a crown jewel. Casemiro, I cannot thank you for how much your service means to me."

Casemiro brushed aside the emotional moment and diverted the conversation. "Not to dampen the enthusiasm, but you must still deal with the traitors, your Highness."

"Actually, I arranged for something to occur while we conducted this ceremony. I thought it best to not bring up such awful memories for the people. We won't be seeing any of those traitors ever again. But before I go, I wish to propose something to Laural." The King turned to the Princess. "An opening exists in Cassenwary. I expect your response within a week."

Laural responded with a giggle and a nod of her head.

King Skaranon turned to Arenton. "Son, one last thing before I go. A new ally wishes to visit you and to start up trade relations from the continent of Austeria. He is the Duke of Vithur and arrives in a week with his daughter. I understand she is smart and beautiful, and seeks an arrangement. Spend quality time with them to build a connection. Then tell me what you think."

Arenton answered with a curt line. "Yes, sir."

Casemiro desired one more moment with the King. "Your Highness, if I may."

Skaranon and Casemiro shifted their discussion and position away from the Prince and the Princess. "Yes, Casemiro. What concerns you?"

"Lord, I held my tongue for too long and my experience with your daughter suggests disclosing my secrets is preferable to hiding them away. A concern over your son clouds my mind. I felt something when I held the power of the dragon and remain uncertain if Arenton is prepared for the role you desire for him."

The King placed his hand on the wizard's shoulder. "My friend, I share your concern. It worries me that the events here grew into the problem they did without my son addressing them. Or raising them to my attention. He overestimated his abilities and is more clever than I believed, but Arenton can become a fine leader. He still needs someone to watch over him, if for no other reason than to prevent this from happening again. This is why I wish for you and Laural to move to Cassenwary. She will become the Marcioness of Cassen. Am I clear?"

"I understand both your stated and unstated demands, my King." Casemiro stepped away and allowed the King one last moment with his children.

After a quick hug with Laural, Skaranon gathered Arenton, and the two walked away, discussing the future meeting with these new dignitaries. The Prince asked several questions pertaining to the Duke's daughter as they walked away from the remaining pair.

Casemiro and Laural walked in the opposite direction and collided with Forrest. Raquel stood by his side, entwining her hand with the troll-man's, with an egregious smile across her face.

The troll-man asked, "So congratulations are in order?"

Casemiro nodded. "Thank you, Forrest. Listen, we need folks to stand up as attendants for the ceremony. I still need to check with my brother, but do you wish to be part of my crew?"

"The honor is mine, my friend. Sorry to run, but I must return to the cidery for a new batch today. I absorbed the contracts previously filled by the folks in Cassenwary. Plus, Raquel works a shift at the Skullery. We will reach out to you later."

The group exchanged hugs and the larger duo left.

Casemiro grabbed Laural's hand. "Are we finally alone?"

Laural glanced over the wizard's shoulder at someone approaching from behind. "I don't think so."

A tap on Casemiro's back told him someone desired his attention. He turned to find Quinto standing beside him. After three weeks, the brothers hugged tightly, having not seen each other since Casemiro boarded the Lion's Roar.

Quinto broke the embrace to talk. "The news travels fast. Congratulations!" He then reached out to Laural and hugged her.

"Well, I'm glad to be part of the family." Laural kissed Casemiro before leaving the brothers. "I wish to tell my father goodbye once more. Besides, you two need to catch up."

Casemiro stared as Laural walked away and his brother moved to his side. "So, you seem different. What happened?"

"I'll give you the details over drinks at the Skullery, but let's say I made the choice."

Quinto laid his arm across the shoulders of Casemiro. "Wonderful! You will not regret it. I never have."

"The magic still pulls at me, an itch I can't ignore. Does this instinct ever go away?"

"No, making this choice does not mean you cannot do the occasional bit of magic. You do not think I have gotten by on skill and my dashing appearance alone, do you?"

"I assumed you bought off anyone that created a problem."

"That helps too. Off to the Skullery?"

Casemiro smiled at his brother. "Sure. But you are paying, because of your skill and dashing appearance."

"I will buy this time, but only because we celebrate your engagement. You are responsible in the future because you wield the King's purse. I just noticed the new belt. What happened to the old one? I kind of enjoyed the statement the hook and chain conveyed."

"I returned it to the prior owner."

The brothers headed out to escape the confines of Veritas Keep and walked towards Lillenhold.

Casemiro reached into his pocket and pulled out the enchanted silver coin. "Oh wait. I have no further need for this coin. Let's consider releasing it my first step forward." He then flipped the coin to a young boy who appeared to be down on his luck.

EPILOGUE

Arenton took a deep breath as he prepared to enter the stone room of confinement. The confidential room, a secret held by the Prince and this one guard, attached to the Prince's bedroom in Veritas Keep. The guard stood behind him with the key, ready to open the heavy wooden door and allow Arenton to visit the treasonous Oleander.

"You sure you wish to enter by yourself, Your Majesty?"

Arenton asked, "No sound escapes from the other side, correct?"

"No, sir. So, if you yell for assistance, the noise won't leave the room. Signal your need to leave by banging loudly on the door and the shaking of the door will alert me."

Arenton took another deep breath. "I understand. Open it." The Prince shook his head to indicate his preparedness for what awaited him on the other side.

The guard inserted the key, turned it, and opened the door. "You are a braver man than I, sir."

"This will not take long. Give me five minutes."

The Prince stared ahead to view Oleander shackled to a bolted-down chair. The woman's hair appeared snarled in at least

400

two spots. Her clothes filthy and she stunk of sweat and grime. Arenton searched the room for any other notable items, discovering a side table with water and a washcloth, along with one additional chair. With a slam and a click, the door shut behind Arenton as he walked in. A smile covered the Prince's face. "My love. Has my guard treated you well?"

Oleander met his smile with her own. "I told the others of your devotion to me. When will we finish this charade? You can release me anytime and we can get married. Like we discussed so many times in your bedchamber."

Arenton pulled up the other chair to lock eyes with Oleander. "We needed to ensure the others paid an adequate penance for the crimes you and your family committed. Treason is a serious charge and presents many questions to answer. Again, who else took part in the plan? Is there anyone else outside of your family you pulled in to help? Anyone aware of the details besides those two wrestlers who oversaw the others?"

Oleander shook her head. "We covered this. We involved Schwartz and Perriman enough to understand how to direct the other wrestlers. The others followed the orders they received from Harley and Heenan. My parents became involved when we expanded the plan to attacking the keep. Nothing more. Don't you believe me? Didn't I earn your trust?"

Arenton nodded. "I wanted to make sure. I believe you have no reason to lie. But trust... no."

"Please release me. I understand if I must leave Lillenhold and never come back."

Arenton placed the spare chair back to its prior location against the wall. "What do I gain from such a reprieve, my dear Oleander?"

Oleander's smile disappeared. "This plan came from you. Everything about baiting your father into coming to

Lillenhold. Getting my father to attack Veritas Keep. Having my mother bring in the dragon—"

"No!" The Prince's eyes flashed with anger as he stood over the woman. Arenton collected himself and continued his answer. "You proposed using the dragon. You heralded its ability to kill the people we needed to remove, but the price involved luring the wizard into the creature's grasp. I did what you asked, but it backfired. All because I listened to you instead of my intuition. My plan would have worked."

The Prince pounded his fist into the wall. He examined the hand and shook it as if he might discard the pain. After a second, Arenton turned and banished the ache with a deep breath. "You changed the plan, not me. We planned to sit your father on the throne in Lillenhold and bring his bloodline into the royal lineage while I took the crown in Porthcallis and lead all of Gaeleos. But your family grew too bold. They attempted to oust me as well."

Oleander cried. "Can't we return to the original plan?"

Arenton shook his head and reached into a pocket, withdrawing a dagger. "No, we cannot. My father became suspicious before, due to the funds I siphoned from the reserves to cover the costs of your lecherous brothers. Now, he plans to marry me off to a woman from Austeria. A woman who supposedly upholds righteousness. Even her title, Paragon, speaks of her moral standing. She may become my bride, but she will also function as a spy for my father. The King is too smart to fool again. And now the added problem of the wizard looms over me. I must bide my time and play along until another opportunity presents itself where I can eliminate my father and take the throne from him."

Oleander's gaze locked onto the weapon. "What are your intentions for the dagger, my Lord? To cut my bindings?"

Arenton twirled the dagger in his hand. "My purpose in visiting you involved concluding this mess and leaving no loose ends. The ordeal ends today."

Oleander nodded and added a smile. "I did not lie. No one else became involved in the plan. We can move forward."

Arenton walked behind Oleander. "For your information, the others died today for their crimes. We hung them from the gallows. All of them passed to the afterlife. You're the last person to face punishment. My father allowed me one last visit with you because of my heartache." A single tear escaped the Prince's eye, revealing some hidden emotion for the woman. Part of Arenton loved Oleander, but just a small part.

From her seated position, Oleander leaned back to look at her lover's face. "You still fool them as we speak. I know you like no other."

"I keep telling them how clever I am. I must be to appear so inept at times." Arenton leaned over and kissed Oleander's forehead, the tear rolling onto her face.

Oleander concluded Arenton would not free her and tears streaked down her cheeks. "Did you ever love me?" Her destiny now apparent.

"As much as you loved me, sweet Oleander. But alas, you doomed our plan to failure. The silver lining, my bride-to-be, is more ravishing than you. She at least offers an enjoyable way to release my tension."

The woman's face shifted from fear to dismay. "Why utter such a cruel remark to me at this moment?"

The Prince cupped her left breast in his hand and reached around with his right. Arenton plunged the dagger into Oleander's heart. "I wanted your failure to cut a little deeper when I prune you from my life." The Prince slid his left hand up to cover her mouth, on the off chance the woman's screams escaped the door.

The Prince held fast and muffled her squeals. His stronger arms held Oleander tight in the chair as she wriggled to fight free. His right hand held the dagger in her chest, not allowing the pain to pass until the end arrived. The struggle faded and stopped when Oleander passed away. Arenton then cut the woman's bindings to make the scene appear as if she attempted to escape.

The sweat from the exertion dripped down the back of Arenton's neck. The Prince walked to the water basin, washing away the blood from his hands and wiping the sweat from his brow and neck. The Prince, appearing panicked, lathered himself up, banged on the door, and screamed in agony.

Upon opening the door, the guard absorbed the sight of a lifeless woman occupying the chair.

Tearfully, Arenton pleaded with the man. "I was an idiot. Oleander grabbed my dagger and killed herself in front of me." The Prince fell to the floor, wailing in agony, pretending to grieve for the woman. The Prince despised the situation he found himself in but chose to deceive his father and everyone else for a bit longer. However, Arenton took solace in avoiding Oleander's fate and would find more comfort in his soon-to-be bride's embrace.

AUTHOR NOTES

The Unspoken Truths of Casemiro started as a dream. I don't mean one of those long-standing desires to someday complete a specific goal. It literally was a dream that woke me up in the middle of the night. And the next day, I started drafting the story you have in front of you now. Maybe I should back up a little bit to set the context.

In June of 2023, I hit the button to publish *The Gold in Their Eyes*. I planned to take a month or so off from writing before starting the next book. The next book, by the way, was already planned. The book you are reading wasn't even on the radar. For that other story, I still needed to work up some world building and shoring up the outline, but it was going to be the next book project and become either a 2 or 3 book series. It will probably still happen, for those that might be interested.

Then, the night after I hit that button to publish the last of the *Marco Flynn Mysteries*, I woke up with a full story in my head. I went to my office, jotted down the main ideas of what the story was about on the whiteboard, and went back to bed. Usually, I have no problem remembering things that come to me in the middle of the night, and this was no different. But why take a chance?

The next day, when my dedicated writing time began, I jumped into Casemiro's story. That's right, I plotted nothing ahead of time. I did not spend any time figuring out the world. I pantsed it. The first writing session yielded a chapter of around 2,500 words before I closed up shop for the day. And I did that for the first ten or so chapters. Then, my mind told me it was time to solve the puzzle I wrote over that first two weeks of word-spewing and figure out how to reach the ending I envisioned for the story.

Normally, when I begin drafting a story, I have a stretch goal assigned to the project. Maybe it's exploring a new genre. Maybe it's using a different POV, or plotting style, or whatever the goal is. In this project, it was stretching myself by just writing without a net under me. I had nothing to guide me other than that dream. With it came some unique ideas, like using a wrestling troop. Did it work? You can be the judge. From an experience standpoint, it gave me a fresh approach to writing and gave me confidence that I could just write something with a fraction of an idea instead of a well-developed concept.

What exactly inspired this story? I have mentioned this to several people over the last few months in the development process and pre-marketing of the book. I wanted to get back to my roots as a writer and reader and do a classic fantasy story with a wizard and a dragon and many of the standard tropes. That meant going back to the master, Tolkien.

In *The Silmarillion*, Tolkien talks about an order of wizards known as the Istari and five wizards being sent to Middle-Earth. We are all familiar with Gandalf and Saruman. Those that read *The Hobbit*, or endured the three theatrical adaptations, also know of Radaghast. Well, there were two other wizards known only as the Blue Wizards. No one knows what happened with these two.

The premise of this book is that those two wizards left the order and pursued much more human lives. They became Casemiro and his brother, Quinto. I postulated what their lives would become if they left behind the trappings of wizardry and dumped the ambitious roles of avatars for larger scale elements of society. In this story, we are witnessing Casemiro's struggle to reclaim a life that he feels was wasted on grief and guilt. I wanted these two men to come across as people instead of these untouchable tropes and infallible conjurers.

In Tolkien's writings, he uses the wizards as avatars for large-scale thematic structures in the world of Middle-Earth. Gandalf represents the potential of humanity as he shifts from the gray to the white. Saruman is a clear construction of industry and governance that shifts form the ideal (white) to an amalgamation of ideas (many-colored robe). Radaghast is the clear avatar of nature. Even Sauron, a wizard apart from the order, is a representation of tyranny and authoritarianism. I envisioned the blue wizards striving to become regular people and accepting of their limitations and flaws.

The other obvious thing that came from the dream on that fateful night was the setting of Lillenhold. I knew it was going to be a port town with a large keep and an ominous mountain overlooking the scene.

Yes, very much a trope driven story and I employed many of the exceptional story forms. The dragon hiding out in the large cave (overcoming the monster), the damsel in distress (the rescue), the trek through the woods (the quest), etc. I embraced the plot and character tropes and went with it. I wanted this to be a familiar story with all the fantasy elements pushing the external plot, all while the dominant story focused on the journey of Casemiro pursuing his humanity and reclaiming something he had lost. Oh yes, I also threw in a mystery and relationship storyline, as I often do. In many ways, I want to say this might be the quintessential Clouser story.

The one element of truly original storytelling was the incorporation of the wrestling troop. That came out of nowhere as I wrote the early chapters of the story. The issue was my ignorance on the subject matter since I hadn't watched professional wrestling in probably twenty years, if not more. Much to my wife's chagrin, I began streaming older wrestling matches and dove back into the world of Hulk Hogan and Ric Flair, which I attempted to pay homage to in this story. I also added a touch of a couple other characters that I found remarkably interesting in my research. During my viewing, I realized these performers are just putting on a theatrical presentation. It's not Othello or Hamlet, but it is their variation of storytelling. It includes elements of building tension and knowing how to pace the story (a match) and knowing how to lead up to that point of resolution. Is it as complex as a novel? No, but it should not be overlooked as a form of storytelling.

One other thing I experimented with in this story was expanding my prose to a deeper level. That required changing my editing process. Usually, I use a software tool called ProWritingAid to help me. With this project, I also evaluated a product called AutoCrit to see if it could lead to better results. The fifth revision pass (yes, there were over five passes) focused on prose development and editing with these tools. In previous projects, I've attempted to just amp up the prose as I worked through various passes. This was the first time I dedicated a complete pass to this one aspect. As expected, it generated a much better product. This will be a modification to my writing process in the future. I just don't know if I will use just one editing tool or two in the future.

One aspect of the world-building for this story came to me after I completed the first draft. This story refers to a continent far away from the kingdom of Gaeleos. At some point I decided that far away land would be the continent of Austeria, the central setting to my first epic fantasy story, *The Forsaken Protector*. The story of Casemiro takes place much later in the timeline, so there is no overlap other than pointing out that these two novels are part of a shared universe.

Lastly, I want to talk about the ending to this story. In almost all my stories, I go in with a clear idea of whether it will be a stand-alone or a series. And I plan the ending accordingly. I always leave the ending open just enough that I could come back and revisit the characters, especially if a big publisher wants to pay me to do that. But usually, the door requires a solid nudge to open it back up. *The Unspoken Truths of Casemiro* is the exception.

In this instance, I knew pretty much how the ending would work from the start. As I worked through the development of the story and the revision process, something changed. I grew attached to the characters but wasn't sure I wanted to commit to writing a series. As a result, I consciously left a much wider opening at the end of this story. This isn't to say that another trip to Lillenhold is in order anytime soon, but I can clearly see a path that might bring me back by this little village in the future, much like how Casemiro returned after twenty years to find something that he may have left behind.

Acknowledgements

Thanks to Nichole Matthews and Carol Hall for giving me some great feedback on this project. Also, thanks to my wife for her support and allowing me the time to focus on the craft.

Thanks to PX Fuel Wallpapers for the image file that provided great base image for the cover background.

Thanks to Apostrophic Labs for the Endor and Immortal fonts. The main body of this book uses Libre Baskerville 10 as the primary font.

About the Author

Christopher Clouser, by day a finance and accounting professional, lives in the Indianapolis, Indiana area and pursues writing speculative fiction in his free time. His family consists of his wife, two children, and multiple grandchildren. He has written sixteen books, novels, and novellas and one play in the fantasy, science-fiction, mystery, and sports history genres while contributing to several compilations, along with multiple articles in national publications. He also has spoken to many local and national organizations on fixed asset accounting, creative writing, and the career of Perry Maxwell, a noted American golf course architect.

https://clouserwritesbooks.wordpress.com
www.facebook.com/christopherclouser.authorpage
instagram.com/christopherclouserauthor

Milton Keynes UK
Ingram Content Group UK Ltd.
UKHW030947140324
439440UK00001B/81